IN THE SHADOWS OF LAEOLIN

The second book in the series
The Kingdom of the Free

By Matthew R. Bishop

Books by Matthew R. Bishop:

<u>The Kingdom of the Free</u> series:

A Land of Our Own (Summer 2013)

In the Shadows of Laeolin (Summer 2014)

<u>Legends of Elyria</u> series:

A New World Wakes (Christmas 2021)

Of Gods and Men (Christmas 2023)

How can I sing of a bud in the sun,
A flower in the morn,
Or one cut down, burned and buried,
The fault of one man's scorn

For Papa

On his Ninetieth Birthday

With Love and Thanks

From Matthew

PART ONE: HOSTAGE

- Chapter One -

A dark cloud descended upon the city. It covered all the land from the boundary hills of the east and west to the river's mouths in the north and south. A great thunder rolled in the distance, approaching— threatening.

The first night had descended, and there was a solemn silence cast about the entire Tower of Laeolin.

Kamira could see it in their eyes. It was a confusion filled with terror and surrender. It was everything lost— dreams died that had hardly even had a season yet to live. Cries broke the silence. There were few who did not cry.

Kamira refused to. She did not yet believe in the death of all their dreams. As such, she sat by the narrow window slit and observed as the storm gathered around her. There was no speaking, no arguing, no crying. There was just watching and waiting.

Arguments fumed around her. "They will kill us" young women said, "we need to leave! Break out!" The elders would sigh. "Our only chance," they retorted, "is to wait. We stand no chance against soldiers in a hostile city. Protesting will earn us a sudden death, and no sane man could commit such a crime as it would be to kill us in the open purview of all the world!" The young women, with an energy the elderly had long forgotten, would still protest: "Complicity will kill us! If we wait, we die. If we fight, we have at least a chance for escape!"

The cries drowned out all of these arguments. The cries drowned out everything. They became louder and louder, echoing in her ears. Even the smallest whimper was as a wailing sob in Kamira's mind. The arguments faded.

She did not notice when the tears began to fall down her face. Until the taste of salt fouled her lips, she had been fully unaware that she had been crying as one among them. She was not disappointed. It was empowering to experience this weakness, this terror and sadness. *I know now from what terrible depths we must rise*, she reassured herself, *and I know we must rise*.

The prisoners tried to feel comfortable in the tower. They told each other that the king would set them free once they established the borders of a new free country. They would not worry about such things.

Those sorts of discussions were rare, and when they occurred they always ended in fights.

Standing was tiresome. People had resorted to sitting in the laps of— or in some cases on top of— other people, oftentimes stranger upon stranger. The stench was terrible— Gaolnians rarely had the opportunity to bathe, and being cooped up in such a confined area created a miserable, offensive smell. After some number of hours few people still noticed the smell. There were other, darker things to keep their attentions.

The inside of the tower was utter blackness, so black that no eyes could adapt to the complete absence of light. Only on a few occasions did the moonlight shine through the very thin slits on the walls that served to air the tower, and at such times the tower seemed suddenly flooded with light, dark though it remained. Kamira did not need to see through the blackness to know what was happening around her, however. There were noises to tell her of such things.

For one, there was the sound of nails scraping against the walls. These sounds were often accompanied by soft cries. Then there were those who wept openly, uncontrollably, and from them no other sound came. At last there was the screaming, which Kamira took to either mean hysteria or nightmares, or both, she supposed. There was nothing to keep the sounds from stopping. She could cover her ears, but the sounds echoed in her mind. She could not even bear the hope that they might leave. She wept more quietly, and did not waste her time scraping. She examined the thin slits on the walls when the moonlight revealed them, but there was no weakness to be found— even if there were, it was only a sheer drop to the bottom.

That first night passed very slowly inside the Tower of Laeolin.

Kamira was already tired of the discussions by the time the pre-morning light finally penetrated the dark of the tower. But before the sun had rose, the arguments were fuming again.

An old man spoke out against a young boy: "We can't get out of this city alive, what Juron said was true. Our best chance is to wait." An elderly woman agreed. In defense of the boy, Kamira joined the argument.

"Do you really believe that our soldiers in Skaen would give up their freedom? Look at it from their point of view: If they win in Skaen, they only have one objective left, and that is to free us and take us to Skaen. But if they surrender, we will— all of us— be back to where we started, without having accomplished anything. We'll be summarily killed, every last one of us, as soon as we're back in Gaoln."

The elderly woman shook her head slowly. "Life is a gamble, you know. Sometimes you win and sometimes you lose— sometimes, after all of it, you find yourself right back where you started."

"Will you go back there?"

"I would not wish to," the old woman said carefully, "but the only other option appears to be immediate death, and my grandchildren are somewhere around this tower— I would like to see them get out of this alive."

"Why, so they can go back to Gaoln, and then die a slower death?"

"So they can have, someday, another opportunity to be free," answered the woman. "It appears we have failed in this attempt, and we will not be free after all— but I do believe that someday my grandchildren can be, because I believe this opportunity is bound to rise again."

"I think you are mistaken," the elderly man chimed in, turning to the lady. "I do believe we will get out of here. There is no sense in them killing us; it would only upset Gaoln and those who sympathize. And there is no sense in King Centreal surrendering. You've resigned yourself too early, both of you— one thinks of returning to Gaoln, the other of escape— our best chance, really, is to remain here, and the wisest decision that the King of Laen could make— "

"Do not presume that he is wise!" The old woman said, suddenly angry.

Kamira tried to reason: "Think of your grandchildren— what do they want to do? Would they prefer to suffer for years of their lives preceding a slow and painful death, eating the dust in Gaoln, or would they risk their lives now, and take the wildest gamble to be free?"

"The young lady is right, I think," said another woman. Some of those around them nodded in consent.

"We cannot escape this alive," the old man reassured them, "but even if we could, there is nowhere safe in this city to hide. The people are against us, and that is our ultimate dilemma in considering escape."

"They're not, though!" said Kamira. The old man rolled his eyes. "It's just that those who support us cannot show their support. If they did, they would be thrown in Gaoln too, right in this tower with us! I've spoken with people who lived here, truly."

"I have heard the same," another woman vouched for her.

"Well, great," said the old man, "on three, we'll all bust out and kill the guards, then liberate the city from the tyrant and live happily-ever-after."

Kamira lowered her head. "I'd sooner try that, than wait here to be slaughtered and thrown on top of your bodies, to never escape this tower and see the sun again." The man shook his head, but said nothing.

The sun did not break through the clouds until mid-morn. The light shone brightly through the small window slit on the east side of the tower, but the hostages were slow to rise. When the argument had stalled, there seemed to be a stillness that came over them all.

The stillness broke in the evening. It became dim, and then dark abruptly, as an overcast sky enveloped Laeolin and its Black Tower. The rain released as a volley of arrows, out from a sky that had been clear just moments before. Those thin little slits on the sides of the tower proved wide enough for rain blown by the wind to drench those near the sides. People scurried and shuffled about, trying their best to stay dry, but the rain would not relent. At some point, enough prisoners stopped caring so that the crowd could settle again.

A dim thought had come to Kamira's mind. Had they been held here in the cold season, that rain would have killed those near it over the course of the freezing night. As it was, it may be enough to kill some of the prisoners here simply by causing them to become sick. And what would happen if a deadly sickness were to spread in such an awful, crowded place as this tower? *We would die, every one of us*, she knew. *We have to get out.*

But no escape came. Less and less people murmured dissent. Less and less arguments came up. Less nails scratched at night. For all of this, the screaming and the crying never did change much.

It took only days for them to lose track of how long they had been in the tower. There were plenty of people keeping track in their minds, Kamira felt sure, but they would soon disagree with one another and doubt themselves. Time blurred together, into one meaningless mass. It had only one beginning, their captivity— and she became increasingly convinced it had only one end, and that was their death.

Juron sat alone in his room. He held his head in his hand, his elbow propped against the table. On the far side of the table a single candle burned, casting a light that danced across one side of his face. He closed his eyes. He tried to listen to the sounds outside, but all he heard were the screams in his head, the screams which had surrounded him during all the weeks that he had led the campaign to round up the prisoners in Gaoln. He smacked the candle, putting it out, then threw it across his room, hardly feeling the wax. He stood there for just a moment— then he opened the door and left the room.

He sat down in the hallway, his back against the wall. The whole hallway was silent, but still in his head he heard the screams. "Juron?" Juron jumped up quickly and his eyes popped open.

"Oh, what…?"

"I'm sorry, I didn't mean to startle you." It was a captain of his, a small, younger man with short black hair. He looked rather confused at finding his superior officer in such a position. "I wanted to know how things are going with King Seagraul."

"That's not your business. I'll tell you your orders when I receive them myself."

That sounded more like Juron. The captain almost smiled. "Okay then, I wanted to know how you were doing. I heard you screaming— "

"When was I screaming?"

"Just now, in your room— quite loudly."

"Are you sure?"

"Oh," said the captain, "quite sure."

Juron sighed. "Get back to your room."

"Yes, commander."

He sat alone in the hall for quite some time. How long had he been screaming? How often had this happened before? He could hear the screams in his head, waking and dreaming, but he never imagined that he himself would be the one screaming— was *he* making some of those noises? He lost track of time, but at some point he realized that there was a man standing down the hall, toward the entrance. He was not moving, and in the dim light Juron could not see his face, but the silhouette revealed an elderly man of medium build with a very long, ancient-looking beard. At once, the man walked toward Juron, and stopped right before he reached him, extending an arm to help him up.

"Menuld…what are you doing here?"

"I've come to speak with you, Juron. I have heard that you've been troubled lately."

"Was it that captain who told you? I'll clear out his room right now…"

"Who told me is of lesser importance, but no, it was not him. We should move into your room, and speak in confidence."

"Very well… come on then."

The door shut behind them, and there was nothing but the darkness— then Juron lit his candle again, picking it up from the floor. "What is it you wanted to talk about?" he asked Menuld quietly. "My dreams are of no concern to you."

"They should be," Menuld replied kindly. "Juron, how content are you with your position? With your duties, the things that King Seagraul asks you to do for him?"

"I will not discuss this with you. Are you trying to get me to say something bad about him, just so you can go up to him and tell him that I cannot be trusted? I will tell him of your hatred of his recent actions, if you do. Don't think I won't. The king doesn't trust you as much as he used to, he is becoming keener to your deceit."

"Deceit? Deceit, interesting, I do not recall swearing fealty to the King of Laen. It is of no matter— I am not here to talk about King Seagraul. I think you already know why I am here."

Juron sat down behind his desk, and let himself fall back into his chair. He let out a breath, and looked at Menuld apologetically. "Menuld, there is nothing that I can do for the prisoners in Laeolin."

"Well, that's not correct— you could tell the king, as I have, that it is most advisable to reach a more agreeable bargain with King Centreal, and then to set the hostages free."

"He isn't going to kill them."

"For all your time under the king's command, Juron, I fear that you do not know Seagraul like I do— "

"King Seagraul."

"*King* Seagraul," Menuld said with disgust. "Anyway. I wanted to assess how you feel about the present situation."

"It is not my duty to assess the present situation. You should be speaking with the king."

"Our last argument was rather distasteful. I am not so sure that he would be overjoyed to see me, at the moment. Juron, if you stood up to King Seagraul— "

"I would not even consider doing so."

"— it would mean so much— "

"It will not happen."

"Well, commander, when I heard about your night terrors and the screaming— "

"That was not for you to hear about!" Juron shouted.

"Juron, do not mistake me, I am not here to chastise you, I am here to help. Your terrors are not arbitrary— they are the result of something terrible, which we, together, have the power to change."

"I will not discuss it."

There was a pause, which quickly evolved into a silence. "You disappoint me, Juron. I had hoped you would consider thinking of your dreams and your fears as more than something natural, something which you will just accept as one of your many duties. But I suppose I was wrong again."

"You were. You are dismissed, Menuld."

"Am I? Well, I will leave you alone with your terrors, then, and you can get back to screaming— "

"You are dismissed, Menuld!" Juron shouted. Menuld turned and left the room.

- Chapter Two -

Gendorn and Bendoraun walked out into the desolate expanse of Gaoln. The ships drew up the plank to return to Skaen— the Army of Gaoln needed the ship, the sailors insisted, and they would return to take the three of them (Kamira had to be included, the boys assured them) back to Skaen after Gendorn had a chance to rest on dry land. So they watched the ship depart and bid their farewells, with promises of meeting on the shore at war's end and returning to Skaen.

With hopeful hearts the two soldiers turned their backs to the ships, and walked through the dirty brown mist inward toward the heart of Gaoln.

The mist had only begun dissipate shortly into their journey when Bendoraun stopped in his tracks and put his arm out for Gendorn to do the same. Bendoraun's eyes were fixed on something, and his nose recoiled as if he recognized the scent of something…well, something definitely not good, Gendorn could tell. *Death?* Gendorn looked around, as if expecting something, but found nothing. "What, Bendoraun?"

"Something is wrong. Look."

The mist was clearing faster now. The grey sky overhead was growing thinner. Daylight would soon break through the clouds. They could see for a short ways around them, when they focused. Bendoraun seemed to have already caught something— when at last Gendorn noticed, his mouth fell open and his heart sank low.

Bodies.

There was one, and then two, and then three and then four, and then five— as the sunlight broke through, more and more were revealed. Everywhere the mist receded it left bodies in its wake. It was a nightmare— it *had* to be, it looked and felt so horribly unreal. But the mist kept receding, the sky kept clearing. Ten bodies. Fifty. As far as the eye could see in every direction. These were not just the emaciated corpses which were a common sight in Gaoln, but something horribly different. Corpses with rags stained in red, torn to bits and pieces, their hair still matted in thick red clumps.

It couldn't be real. It couldn't be. Could it? Gendorn screened the dustscape, searching for a sign of life. He saw only bodies, strewn between skeletons rotting in the dust. No one's voice. No one's face. Nothing he had known for all of his life was alive. Nothing. The boys fell to their knees and collapsed on the ground, but neither of them noticed. Neither of them could understand. The Gaolnians were all dead. How could that be?

For some immeasurable span of time, a span that seemed odd— a time from a dream, perhaps— the two of them stood there mute. Somehow they ended up down on their knees, but their gazes were still locked. He was crying, and at some point noticed that his empty socket was aching badly, and that worried him enough to control himself.

But it did nothing for the numbness, nothing for the defeat. Nothing for that wretched sunlight that broke through the clouds and revealed to them that their darkest fears were still real, still awake and alive in the open world. They were dead, all of them. Wars did not matter. Victory could not exist beside such defeat. And this was defeat. Absolute defeat.

They did not notice one another. They did not notice the time passing. They noticed nothing. They were as frightened children, senseless but for their sadness and disorientation, weeping into the dirt.

They did not get up for a very long while, until the sun had begun to set. Maybe it would help to not get up, so that they would not be forced to see everything, to know the reality and entirety of their world's destruction. But then they rose. At some point they realized that through their numbness they were making their own choice between life and death.

The two heroes set out for Kamira's pel, but the journey was only more disheartening. They learned the story of what had taken place here simply by looking at the bodies. A naked woman with gash marks across her body and a face no man could describe meant that she had ran from the invaders, and likely been caught, beaten and raped before being left for dead. A row of women, however, with pickaxes and shovels, indicated a group that had decided to stay and fight. Such a sight was rare. Even these bodies were often naked, but the tools were a sure sign that the women had fought the invaders. The most tragic were the young. There was only one occasion where Gendorn and Bendoraun saw a line of young boys, with shovels and axes sprawled around them, their faces literally torn off, their tiny bodies cut into pieces. Looking at them without shedding a tear, Gulaus Gendorn and Gulaus Bendoraun did not feel quite so young anymore.

There was one heartwarming fact in all of this, though it gave little comfort when they looked at the rows of bodies. Gendorn voiced it aloud: "There are too few." Bendoraun gave him a look, not quite understanding. "Too few bodies. There are not enough of them. We've been at it for almost two days and two nights, and how many have we seen? They've all gone somewhere."

Bendoraun disagreed, by the look on his face and the shaking of his head. "I wouldn't dare say such a thing. I think one of these days we will see a huge swath of land where the bodies are piled high atop one another for as far and wide as we can see. There's no escaping from this place. No escaping at all." His voice dropped. "They've all been killed, Gendorn."

Gendorn was silent only a moment. "Let's keep on walking."

Pel after pel proved empty. Some rags would be hanging on the lines, and buckets were cast about outside the huts. The deep grey sky above stood as motionless and dark as it had been the day of their arrival.

On the third day they came upon one of the market blocks in the west of Gaoln. These were walled enclosures with guardhouses where the guards had once lived, with stalls and warehouses surrounding them where the prisoners gathered to receive their rations. The guardhouses had all been torn down in the First Rebellion, of course, and soon afterward the walls had been destroyed. So it was to be expected that they find the place in a state of disrepair.

But long before they approached the walls of the market, their hearts had already sunk the lowest they could go. One could see from half a day away that there was not a soul left, not a voice hanging in the air, not even a footprint. Even from such a distance there was a profound emptiness. Never had this place been so empty. From the moment the two set eyes on the ruins of the walls and tower, saw the poles sticking out where the banners once flew, it struck them that this was a place fully and completely abandoned. Not a living thing stirred. The change meant something that Gendorn, on that day, could only begin to understand.

Inside the market, these suspicions were only confirmed. The bolts of cloth that hung from the walls were dusty and dry. The doors into the storehouses were halfway open, not moving. The stalls themselves were splintering into pieces. There was not a single scrap of food to be had, not a single drop of good water. For a long while they sat in silence in the middle courtyard, as the wind whipped through the buildings and threw dust on their empty faces.

When the wind stilled, there was an absolute silence such as the two had never known in their whole lives— a complete absence of sound. It might have been stunning, had it not indicated to the two boys as much as it did on that day. When at last he spoke, Gendorn's harrowed voice might have been heard a full mile away: "We have to tell them. Gonaka."

Bendoraun nodded, and after letting an eternity pass between them, answered: "I know."

"We should be on our way."

Neither of them moved. They let the silence take them again.

- Chapter Three -

Gonaka's walls, coated in a beautiful red orchalin metal and bright under the light of the high noon sun, simply did not end. They stretched from the Cold Ocean in the north, south along the western border shared with Gaoln all the way to the border with Kale at Gonaka's southern end, then eastward along the Kale-Gonaka border all the way to the Endless Water of the West. It was only at one of the giant gatehouses that connected Gaoln to Gonaka where Gendorn and Bendoraun might find a chance inside those walls. Tired, starved, and one of them bleeding and near death, the two of them together did not quite fit the picture of a company of merchants passing through the penal colony as a short cut from Kale to Gonaka, especially without guards in such times as these. Bendoraun convinced Gendorn that story would be easily picked out as nonsense. And so they were to tell the truth. It was Gendorn, hardly able to keep himself up, who approached the tall, muscular guard— a man who had the benefit of good food, good home, and good health, Gendorn thought. "We have been fighting with the Army of Gaoln, but we were sent home for our injuries. But they are gone," Gendorn said in a near-whisper to the guard, "everyone in the colony is gone, and we haven't any idea where they are."

The man's face seemed caught between doubt and something darker. It was no comfort to the boys. "You come from Gaoln? And you have not heard?"

"No. You know what's happened, then?" Gendorn wondered.

The guard sighed. "Yes, I know what's happened."

"You don't sound happy about that," observed Bendoraun.

"No, well, I'm not. You should come inside and find a place to stay."

"Come inside and— " Gendorn blurted out, "— and, what!?"

"Our policy toward Gaoln has officially changed due to Laen's actions in invading the colony."

"Come inside of Gonaka?" Bendoraun asked, to be sure he had heard right— it was, of course, the dream of every Gaolnian who had ever lived to be able to walk through these shining red gates and into Gonaka.

"Yes, come inside. Where should we put you— there is a village two days hiking to the southwest of here. Can you make it? We'll give you this map, and some instructions on who to ask for in the village, and you shouldn't have any trouble at all." He opened a box tucked behind the corner of the gate and started sifting through some papers.

"Yes..." Gendorn said, "Yes, we can make it...thank you, sir..."

"My pleasure." He handed them a map and gave them a friendly nod. The gates lay open before them. Just like that, Bendoraun and Gendorn walked into Gonaka.

Gonaka was warm. Perhaps it was the heat that swelled up inside them as soon as they crossed through the gate, but it had to be at least in part because of the bright sun shining upon them. There wasn't much along the outskirts of the border, but there was one huge city they could see in the distance— one of Gonaka's famous "gons" which were legendary in strength and beauty and size and population, in culture and arts and industry. They caught only a glimpse of it, however, as they were hiking in the opposite direction. They could make out thick lines in the sky, which they took to be towers of some sort— they were not guard towers, as they were square and wide, and were each large enough for at least one hundred Gaolnian pels.

The further they walked into Gonaka, the more grass grew on the ground, as if some magical spell were lifting and allowing things to grow. At one point Bendoraun looked down and saw a flower— and then, before they knew it, they were hiking through fields and meadows.

They spent their first night at an inn, using some of the little money that they had taken with them from Skaen. It was a small town where they stayed, and the fee was next to nothing. The innkeeper, who knew these two boys must be from Gaoln, provided them with free food and treated them nicely. It dawned on Gendorn that whatever had happened in Gaoln must be common knowledge in Gonaka, and that it must have changed the way the Gash thought about the Gaolnians. Toward the end of their meal Gendorn looked up and asked bluntly: "What happened to Gaoln?"

The innkeeper turned toward them, his expression now grave. "They came," he said in a near whisper. "King Seagraul's men. They took everyone, all of them, back to Laen. I thought you would have known?"

Gendorn's mouth dropped down, and Bendoraun stared dumbfoundedly at this man. "They're in Laen— all of them? Alive!?" Gendorn blurted out.

"Yes, of course they're alive! Can you imagine how the other nations would react if they just got up one day and decided to kill all the women and children they've chained up on their walls?"

"They're chained?" Bendoraun asked.

"That won't be the worst thing that happens to them, I'll say."

"No, it won't..." Gendorn said quietly. "Sir, thank you for telling us this— but what can anyone do about it? Does anyone even care?"

"You underestimate your friends!" The innkeeper said, "Gonaka cares for the Gaolnians, you know, and she is taking every step to make sure that King Seagraul keeps those prisoners alive."

"What can we do?" asked Gendorn.

"We?" The man said curiously, "Well, we cannot do anything but wait."

That was not the answer Gendorn had wanted to hear. The next morning he and Bendoraun set out for the village they had been told to go to, more determined than ever to do something about the hostages in Laen. They marched with a fervor the entire day, and arrived at the village in the mid-evening. They asked around for the man they were told to meet, Deiknahr was his name, and a group of villagers led him to the south of the village and into a blacksmith's workshop.

"Can I help you?" asked a tall and muscular man, who was busy pounding away on an anvil.

"We are looking for Deiknahr," Bendoraun said.

"I am Deiknahr, blacksmith of Uoahnu. You two seem lost," answered the man.

"We were told by the guards at the border of Gaoln to come see you," Gendorn told him.

"Ah, you're from Gaoln— that explains the smell. Yes, terrible thing what happened in Gaoln. I've agreed to take any remaining Gaolnians into my home, that's why they've sent you. You two will stay with me until King Nowhawna has worked out an agreement with King Seagraul on the release of the prisoners, and then you will return to Skaen."

"We can't stay here doing nothing while our families and friends are locked in that tower," Gendorn said plainly.

"Well, unless you plan on marching into Laeolin..."

"We could," Bendoraun said boldly.

"I would advise against it," Deiknahr said with a humorous smile. "I sympathize with you, I really do, but there is just nothing we can do."

"What is the king doing, then?" Asked Gendorn. "What are his plans?"

"I..." Deiknahr sighed in resignation. "Well, you may be able to help me convince the man. Maybe I should bring you to the palace."

Bendoraun was caught between skepticism and open laughter, but Gendorn wasted no time in his response. "When are we going?"

"We will have to wait for Kio. He should be stopping by this village sometime in these next few days...travels by litha, of course...if we can convince him...you two better get together a moving story, if you plan on changing anyone's mind. Especially the king."

Bendoraun's eyes were wide now, his mouth hanging open, stunned into silence. Gendorn carried on as if it were nothing out of the ordinary: "And we can ask him what he's doing?"

"Well," said Deiknahr, "he can tell us whatever he wants to. We're not interrogating him, you know."

Gendorn nodded. "Thank you."

Deiknahr scratched his stubbly chin as he examined them. "Well, I should show you two boys your new home then."

Bendoraun was a bit slow to follow.

Deiknahr's home was a small, one-room building with a bed along one wall and several drawings hung up on another. Gendorn was at once reminded of Behk and Synla's home, although this home was much smaller and meant only for one person. It made Gendorn rather sad to see that this Deiknahr fellow, such a kind man, lived alone. Some fine-made blades rested on a clay end table, with designs on them. Some broken tools lay on a dresser, and there was a tunic on the floor that Deiknahr picked up and threw in a corner. "You'll have to be sleeping on the floor."

"It's better than sleeping in knee-high snow," Bendoraun commented, half of his wits still lost, "believe me about that."

They spent the rest of that day learning some of the very basic tenets of blacksmithing, and of life in Gonaka and its gons, in which Bendoraun and Gendorn had a particular interest. Buildings as tall as towers, walls the size of twenty-story buildings, and towers whose tops simply could not be seen, reaching high into the sky— these features were what made gons unique in the world of Fengorian, Deiknahr explained. Laeolin, with something like one million people, was larger than any city in Gonaka— but it was wide and relied on two surrounding towns connected to rivers for its very life. Gons were condensed versions of Laeolin, Deiknahr explained— Laeolins with half of the population but with buildings three times the size and which did not need to rely on outside towns for survival. There were bridges and tunnels and networks everywhere. At seemingly every point, Deiknahr had to explain the usefulness or necessity of each feature.

As the days passed he taught them about markets and industries, shopkeeping, shipwright, carpentry, agriculture, and foreign nations— and of course all about rocks, ores, metals, and blacksmithing, his favorite topic by far. They sparred often, learning basic maneuvers for the various weapons and the special potentials and abilities allowed by each design. Deiknahr had a lot of creative weapons that the two boys had never seen before, and they were given the chance to try out each one. And so it was that they found themselves sparring on one particularly eventful afternoon.

"Block!" said Deiknahr, tossing a broadsword to Bendoraun. Bendoraun looked at it with a mixture of surprise and fear, struggling to catch the whirling blade. Deiknahr came at him with his own self-made greatsword, and tossed another blade to Gendorn, who caught it without trouble.

"Gendorn! Help!" said Bendoraun with a laugh. Deiknahr was already engaging them both, and pushing them back rapidly.

"You need to learn how to master the sword to survive," Deiknahr said, "What weapons did you use in the army?" He swung furiously around as he backed Gendorn and Bendoraun into the side of a shop next to Deiknahr's own.

"But the war's over!" argued Gendorn, putting up his sword to block as he ducked his head.

"Hah, so it is. No matter, it's still fun," said Deiknahr, staring at Gendorn with a mixture of pity and humor as the boy turned and ran off laughing.

"I surrender! I surrender!" yelled Gendorn, running as fast as he could. Deiknahr and Bendoraun lowered their blades, smiling as they watched Gendorn run away.

"We sparred every night in the army, we've practiced with swords before, even if they're not our strong point. How did you get so good?" asked Bendoraun.

"I spar every now and then at the village barracks, been doing it ever since I got my first wooden sword at the age of five— a gift from my father," explained Deiknahr. "Many boys are raised here in such a way. The Great Wars are not so long in the past, you know."

"I see. Well, I have to go pursue Gendorn. Can't let him get away. Very dangerous enemy," Bendoraun said to Deiknahr. Deiknahr nodded.

"Of course— shall we go together?"

The two men chased Gendorn around the shops, split up, and cornered him next to Deiknahr's house. "Thought you would run away?" asked Bendoraun. Gendorn charged at him, and Deiknahr stepped back to observe. "Good as you are, Gendorn, are you really better than me? Do you really stand a chance?" Bendoraun mocked.

Perhaps it was those precise words, or the confident smile that Bendoraun had on his face, the same smile Gendorn had seen on him as they were charging Port Tekal. In an instant the scene around him changed, and he saw Bendoraun lying dead on the floor. His head was bashed in. Tejk was where Deiknahr had once been— and Gendorn could see him dying as he was nodding and apologizing for being too late, he could see someone coming right up behind him, and stabbing him through his gut, then cutting off his head, his still-talking head. He turned his eyes away and looked down at his own sword, and what he saw troubled him to his very core— there was a being at the end of his sword, a person impaled— at first it was the unmistakable face of the first man he had killed at Port Tekal. It became the face of the second man, also unmistakable, engraved in his mind— and it shifted, then, twice more, to Behk and then to Synla. Their faces were mute in shock and horror— Gendorn had killed them! And he could not tear his eyes away from them, he could not avert their accusing, terrible gaze. He felt a sudden feeling of disgust— what did this man, who made swords and played with them all day long, actually know about war?

Bendoraun must have noticed— he put down his sword and looked at Gendorn with concern. "Are you alright, friend?"

"I'm okay. I'm done— let's go inside. It's late."

When finally they retired to the house, the moon was high and the stars were shining bright in the deep blue sky.

Gendorn stood outside that night, searching for something lost in between those stars. When Bendoraun came out to join him, he found a man there that he had not known a year before. He approached silently and stood beside his friend. Gendorn didn't move. Bendoraun said, only half-jokingly, "Looking for Kamira up there?"

"Something like that."

"We're going to Laeolin, aren't we?"

"With or without the help of kings and their kingdoms, or soldiers and their swords," Gendorn promised.

"That's a dangerous road, and one not likely to end in freedom."

"I'm not free until the rest of our people are free with me. And neither are you."

"King Centreal will know what to do, Gendorn."

"King Centreal didn't know what to do when we landed in Skaen, Bendoraun. He didn't know what to do when he lost an entire division. He didn't know what to do when he let his captains run around burning villages and terrorizing an entire country."

"He knew what he was doing. He was trying to set us free. Necessary evils for necessary goods. Luncas isn't wrong about everything, you know."

"You weren't with me when I stood beside those villagers and helped remove the rubble that was once a home. I wouldn't expect you to understand."

"You're forgetting where you come from. We are Gaolnians, and we are Gaolnians because that is what other people wanted us to be! The Skaelin wanted us to starve, they wanted us to freeze, they wanted us to die without our freedom!"

Bendoraun realized that he had been talking very loudly, and quickly shut up. Gendorn turned to look at him, but kept quiet. He let the warm wind buffet them and steal away any chance for a rebuttal. It was some time before he spoke again. "The people in that village did not want us to die without our freedom. And that is all I know."

"Don't feel guilty for the sins of others. You didn't burn that village."

"I killed two people at Port Tekal who didn't even know what this fight was about. They weren't even the king's soldiers. They were old— they were veterans who just wanted to live in peace and had no home left."

"Gendorn, be a little tougher. These things happen. You can't let them haunt you like you did today. You have to get over it."

"Since when do these things happen? And *why*, by all the constructs of Time and Fate, must they?"

Bendoraun shrugged. "Should I know?"

"I'm just trying to make sense of things."

"Okay. I'm sorry. I'm going with you to Laeolin."

"I know."

"With or without kings and their kingdoms."

Gendorn nodded. "With or without."

- Chapter Four -

Gendorn awoke to a strange man in the house— a tall man, as tall as Deiknahr but not quite as well-built. He had long blond hair and was dressed in long, flowing robes of red and white. He stood alone, motionless in the house, and for a brief moment Gendorn believed he and Bendoraun would be taken to Laeolin— but then he spoke: "Deiknahr, wake up."

Deiknahr turned over in his bed, saw the man, and turned back around. "Do we really have to start this early?"

"The king is impatient."

"Fine— Gendorn! Bendoraun! Get up! We're meeting with the king."

"Meeting with the— " Gendorn stammered, "what, today? Now?"

"In about..." the robed man began, "yes— quite soon, actually."

"Isn't it something like two weeks to the palace?" Bendoraun wondered.

"Oh yes," the man answered, "but it's quite close if you're flying." Gendorn's eye grew wide, and Bendoraun suddenly looked much like a child again.

Sure enough, when the four of them walked outside into the dawning daylight, there in front of them stood an enormous litha, whose green and white body was twice the size of the only litha Gendorn had seen up close before. The wings stretched further than Gendorn could have imagined— they were simply huge. "This little fellow," the man began— the litha grunted, and shook its head— "alright, this large fellow"— the beast nodded— "is Gonaka's oldest litha. Most lithae can only carry one or two people, if that— but this fellow, well, the four of us will all be riding on him. His name is Big Litha," the man smiled affectionately. "This is the largest litha alive, the biggest who has lived for generations. They're usually rather lanky-looking creatures, not like Big Litha. Closest thing you'll find to a dragon, Big Litha is."

"Dragon?" Gendorn wondered.

"Yes, what, you've never heard of dragons? Well, they were essentially much larger lithae, except they couldn't swim— "

"Lithae can swim?" Bendoraun exclaimed.

The strange man looked at Bendoraun as if he were stupid. "Well, there are the sea lithae and the land lithae, that is, the land lithae really should be called the sky lithae. And there was a time when sea lithae could nest on land, so that the two kinds of lithae could meet together, but now they very seldom do— and then there are the legends of the older lithae, who could swim, fly, and live on land! And the lithae used to be much larger, more like the size of dragons, who could never swim, of course— haven't you heard any of this before?"

"No," Gendorn and Bendoraun both said.

"You really don't know much about history. We grow up with stories of the ancient days, it's part of being from Gonaka, you know— lots of mythology in every story that we tell. Gonaka is an ancient place. Good history. Well, we can talk all about it later, we really should be going. My name is Kio— I forgot to introduce myself. You two must be Gendorn and Bendoraun." They both nodded. "Right then— well, let's be off. Gendorn, Bendoraun— just hold on to me and Deiknahr, and you'll be fine. Big Litha won't let you fall."

Gendorn and Bendoraun held tight to Deiknahr's jacket. The sun was out, and it was a rather warm day, considering Trest had just begun, but when the litha got to full speed, the wind seemed chill and vicious. Kio, in the front, absorbed most of the wind— he was wearing some sort of goggles, Gendorn could tell, although he could not see much beyond the large figure of Deiknahr, and he seemed to have on some special jacket. Below, Gendorn and Bendoraun saw the fields of farmers sprawled out beneath them, connecting towns and villages and huge gons all together. Rivers and hills ran beneath him as they ran from the rising sun.

They stopped periodically to warm themselves, as the wind was rather brisk at such a speed, but continued without delay for the whole stretch of the day. The journey had been fascinating at first, but as the sun began to set it had already become tiresome and had lost any appeal it had earlier enjoyed.

From the sky they saw it appear, revealed by a breaking in the clouds before them. The orange-colored clouds gave way to a city of glittering red, and as the clouds still obscured their vision, it seemed as if it were a thing built high up in the sky, its spires reaching far above the sun. Gendorn stared, and the cold air overtook him in a single instant. He knew without asking. *The Glorious City*. A city where legends lived and died, where great stories began, where the rule of law was supreme, where a fair and wise hand governed, whose walls no man could ever think to besiege, whose promises were enough to make all the children of the world smile as one. From the sky it greeted him with open arms. He felt hope, of all things, and such a feeling it was. He had missed that feeling sincerely.

The litha veered down sharply, and Gendorn almost fell right off. He and Bendoraun gripped their companions with renewed strength. When they looked ahead, right beneath them was a great expanse of decorative buildings and a polished white wall and trees planted in perfect synchronization around the enclosures, with small brick paths leading from one building to the next. Gendorn felt disappointment at not seeing the city, but whatever laid before him was stunning in its beauty, every inch of it conceived before construction and laid out perfectly. Before he could even take note of the entire complex, they had touched ground.

King Nowhawna was just as large as Kio and Deiknahr, and dressed in the same robes as Kio, but he had a long blonde beard and his hair reached across his back. For a moment Gendorn wondered if every Gash man was this huge, but then he saw the two guards surrounding the king— not nearly as tall. The four of them approached the king together, and Kio walked up in front of them. The king turned his eyes toward Gendorn and Bendoraun. "Follow me," he told them.

King Nowhawna led the four of them to a room at the very top of the palace and on the side, with windows all along one wall that looked out to the fields between the palace and the gon, and windows on the other wall that looked out to the gon itself, to its towering buildings and its smooth, ancient walls. There were portraits all along the red walls, and in the middle there was a beautiful table of bright red orchalin, with dark wooden chairs placed all around it. King Nowhawna sat in one of the chairs, and beckoned for the other four to do the same.

"Well," the king began, "you must have heard of what happened in Gaoln since your arrival here in Gonaka."

"Is it true?" asked Gendorn, unable to restrain himself.

"Yes. It is true." The king's eyes met Gendorn's own, and Gendorn knew that the king had pity for him. "We are, I assure you both, doing everything we can to reach a settlement and release the prisoners. I brought you here so that I could tell you this personally. It is one of the most important things we are doing at this moment. I mean that truly. The balance of war and peace lies in our own efforts, and the willingness of King Seagraul to cooperate— which is not saying all that much."

"We have to set them free," Gendorn said. Deiknahr and Kio both looked at Gendorn with surprise— did this boy just tell the King of Gonaka what he had to do?

King Nowhawna smiled. "I know. We do." Deiknahr and Kio relaxed. "We are going to be negotiating for some while, it looks like, and in the meantime the safest place for you is either here, with Deiknahr, who would take you on as apprentices, or with the army back in Skaen. Kio has agreed to escort you to either place. I do have some happier news for the both of you." The boys' attention was renewed, though their grim expressions did not change. "Gaoln is free." No reaction. "King Centreal won the day at Seun Bastion, killed King Sendroun, and proclaimed the birth of the Kingdom of the Free. Your war in Skaen is over at last, and your men are free. There is no Gaoln. There is only the Kingdom of the Free. No Gaolnians— now you are all Freemen." The two soldiers relaxed only a small bit. Their minds were still without rest. The king saddened visibly. But when Gendorn spoke next, it was in a softer tone, as if some duty of his had been relieved at long last and he was eager to enjoy the rest he had for too long delayed.

"Thank you for the good news. But isn't there anything else we can do? Can't we be of any service?"

The king raised his eyebrows curiously, and smiled when he looked back at Gendorn. "I think you will make a great leader someday, Gendorn. But no, there is nothing you can do at this moment. We are trying our hardest, and the most you can do is stay out of it."

"We cannot stay out of it," Gendorn argued, "we have to be a part of it— those are our families!"

"The best chance of their survival lies in our negotiations and in the Council of Nations. Your army attacking Laen would only encourage King Seagraul, in all his madness, to execute the hostages. I advise you and your king to remain in Skaen, and I will be flying to King Centreal shortly to tell him this myself. So you have to make your decision— you may stay here with Deiknahr and learn his trade, work for him— or you may return to King Centreal and help him build the Kingdom of the Free."

Bendoraun, who had been silent this whole time, looked unable to think or answer. With one glance, Gendorn discerned this, and answered for the both of them: "We'll go back to Skaen."

The king nodded. "In that case, I think I shall accompany you. I really should speak with King Centreal as soon as possible, and I can think of nothing more important that I must do at the moment. Deiknahr, you had planned to come along?"

"Yes, my king, I would like to make sure that all is well with their return. I may stay for some while and help the Freemen with their work— I think my background as a blacksmith and as your assistant…" Gendorn and Bendoraun looked at Deiknahr, shocked— had the man told them that he had been the king's personal assistant?— "…my input and efforts would be well-received."

"Good." The king turned to Kio. "I will leave Joel in charge of affairs in my absence." Kio nodded.

"I'll be sure to relay the message."

"Good," said King Nowhawna. "Let's be off for Skaen."

- Chapter Five -

They met in the darkness, in the cold of a room that sat in the basement of the academy. There was only one flickering candle in the room, which did not let any light escape to the door— there was to be no one who knew of this meeting, but for the group of eight people inside. "We need to assess our numbers before we consider a rescue mission," Ciso began, "how many do each of us have on hand? I know of fifty people, reliable, who would answer the call."

"Fifty."

"Thirty."

"Forty."

"Forty-five, maybe."

"Twenty, if I have to be sure they won't tell anyone else."

"Ciso," said one of the women, without providing a number— "can we expect a rescue mission to succeed when we have so few numbers, and yet have to trust so many who we would not normally trust? I think we should either keep this mission between ourselves, and try and sneak around the buildings to unlock the prisoners and let them out, or we may as well recruit an army if we are going to trust so many people."

The eight of them were quiet. "You're right," Ciso said abruptly. "I have been thinking about it for a long time now, really. And— well, I can't say who else I have been in contact with. But some very wise and experienced people have told me it is time to raise an army in protest, you know. But if we raise an army of so many people, one of them will go to the king, or to Juron, and tell them what we are planning. It happens all the time. We can't trust that many people. It should be just us— just the eight of us."

"It's too presumptuous to assume that we could find a reliable army," another agreed, "I have a lot of contacts who would be eager to partake in such a mission. But it takes one person— just one person— to ruin it. We risk too much. It should just be the eight of us."

"All we need to do," the girl's voice range out again, "is unlock the doors, and then the Gaolnians can escape and run into the safehouses, which we will display with small markings and try to direct them to in secret. An army of us could not fight the Army of Laen, in any case— letting them out of the towers is the most we could do."

"It will still be extremely dangerous," Ciso warned them, "and we could all die, every one of us."

"We're not stupid," the girl said.

"Well, then, I suppose we should begin. We will have to scout the buildings and the tower almost every night. And we should begin tomorrow. We need to know exactly how they operate, where they walk at exact moments, their precise line of sight— everything."

"I'll go with you, Ciso," said one of the rougher voices from the darker corner, "you and me, tomorrow night— we'll take the first shift."

"Alright," said Ciso, "we'll work out our nights tonight, then meet back here next week, this time, this room."

The next night, Ciso met his friend Radur outside the center of Laeolin. The city had just gone to sleep— the lights were out, and everywhere there was nothing but the darkness and the silence and the towers of stone, black in the shadows of night. The moon overhead could not be seen through the clouds, but when it made its way into the clearer parts of the sky it revealed a city devoid of waking beings, without more than two pairs of feet walking upon its otherwise empty streets.

The scene changed when they entered the plaza of tall square buildings that held all the hostages from Gaoln. Along every wall armed guards stood in a wakeful vigilance. In the center of the plaza stood the Tower of Laeolin, and every stone on the floor of the plaza pointed toward the tower, until just outside the tower itself, where the stones pointed toward one another in a concentric circle, symbolizing, by some old tradition kept by the rulers of Laen, that this tower was the source of all the life and power of Laen, and at once the point where all that power converged. Around the tower itself stood no less than twenty armed guards from the Army of Laen.

"The first obstacle," Ciso whispered, "is to get past the buildings and into the plaza. We can't let the guards see anyone who has been freed until the tower itself is free, because if anyone along the outside rim of buildings escapes first, they will close off the center. The Tower of Laeolin must be free first, and the guards will converge on it— then the surrounding towers can be unlocked and the Gaolnians inside of them can escape, and they will not have to fight as many guards."

"The nearest barracks are— " Radur began, but Ciso cut him off—

"Just around the corner, I know— but we will have the barracks taken care of, you don't need to worry about that."

"Who do you mean by *we*?"

"Don't worry. All we have to concern ourselves with are the towers."

"Okay, so how can we possibly get past these guards— we need to get to the top of this building, Ciso! Otherwise we cannot get a good enough view."

"No!" Ciso whispered quickly, "There are guards up there. And do not use our names here! We have talked about this."

"I'm sorry, I— "

"It's alright— we're going to backtrack, and then find a way to get to the top of that building behind us, which is not guarded— from there we can see the tops of the buildings surrounding the plaza, and then we can decide how to reach them."

"Okay," Radur agreed, "let's go."

When they reached the roof of the building behind them, they could see the tops of all the buildings surrounding the Tower of Laeolin. There were guards on every rooftop and all over the sides of the buildings, and ten guards who marched in a circle around the Tower of Laeolin. "There is no way," Radur told Ciso, "that we can get around all of those guards." Ciso nodded in solemn agreement.

"We'll have to wait," Ciso said.

"For what? The guards to leave?"

Ciso nodded. "Exactly."

"Ciso, they take shifts."

"They won't if they feel sure that nothing could happen to the prisoners."

"And how are we going to convince them of that?"

Ciso smiled cunningly. "Wait and see. And stop using my name!"

In the aftermath of Seun Bastion, teams of the Free Army had been cracking down on the Skaelin Resistance. The last of the strongholds west of the mountains were taken by the end of the week. The resistance, the king concluded, would likely base itself within those mountain strongholds in the east, and could hold up for years, so long as their supply lines and trade routes did not fail them. "We are investigating their routes, I assure you," King Centreal had told Luncas, "but we have to make a settlement with them, one way or another. We have our kingdom now, and we can let them keep theirs. We can't beat them in the mountains."

Alaisio was marching with Commander Luncas and King Centreal when he heard a clamor arise from the rear of the line. Shouts and laughing filled the air, and he turned with the king and commander to see what had happened. A great beast of green and white grazed the clouds, coming straight for them. Alaisio and the commander stood with wide eyes, but the king looked as if he had been expecting to see this, and only smiled. A gust of air marked the litha's landing. One of the four people who climbed down from the beast wore a distinctive eye patch over his left socket, and Alaisio smiled. "Captain," he said, turning around, "I think we've found the rest of our regiment." Commander Luncas came bolting through the crowd.

"Why are you riding on a litha!" Luncas yelled. "I should be riding that! You're just a child!"

"Good to see you too, captain," Bendoraun said, "and you Alaisio. Did Seun Bastion leave a mark on you?" he asked, nodding at Alaisio's missing arm.

"Only a mark," Alaisio said with a smile. "This man has told you how it ended, then?"

"He said something about a very large battle and the establishment of something called the Kingdom of the Free," Gendorn answered.

"That's about it," Alaisio said. As they began their reunion, however, there was another gust of air and the sound of people whispering, and everyone pointed at another litha behind them, a slimmer red and white one that carried King Nowhawna of Gonaka in his flowing royal robes of red and white.

King Central went out to greet King Nowhawna, and met him as he landed. They spoke in confidence for only a moment, then came to speak with Kio and Deiknahr and Luncas, Gendorn, Alaisio, and Bendoraun. Addressing the entire circle of people, King Central spoke: "We need to discuss something which King Nowhawna deems very important, regarding the hostages in Laeolin." Everyone's attention peaked, and they looked at the two kings, waiting to hear more. "We should set up a tent, and speak in confidence. Gendorn and Bendoraun, and you, Deiknahr, may accompany us."

They ignored the murmurs of the army as they pitched the king's own tent. There were whispers, of course, of the King of Gonaka, that legendary moral compass of a man whose sympathy had allowed the Gaolnians to plot their escape and rebel. Few among the soldiers had ever seen him before. But there were even more whispers among them, and more excited by far, of Gulaus Gendorn and Gulaus Bendoraun returning from Gaoln. Two of the greatest heroes from the war, who had hidden themselves in an enemy castle to learn of the evil king's plans, and had returned to the army just in time to save it from destruction. Rumor had it that the two boys were friends of King Central, even advisors to him! Or that they had never really returned to Gaoln, but instead had snuck inside Laeolin to learn about the hostages and spy on Seagraul himself. Such whispers went far. But the furthest and loudest of them all were never claims, but only humble questions: *Does he know anything about our families? What does it look like, Gaoln? Is there anything left? Are my children alive? Can he tell me?*

It pained the two boys greatly that they could say nothing of those left behind which the army did not already know.

Inside the pavilion, the eight of them sat around in a circle on the ground. King Nowhawna began by addressing King Centreal. "Confronting the new Skaelin king, holed up in those mountains, is a waste of time. As long as you gain the favor of your new country you have the support you need. Engage them, rebuild their country— your country. Coupled with garrisons you will deter the Skaelin in the east. It would be much more effective to seek a diplomatic solution than to try and threaten them— we both know, anyway, that you could never defeat them at Cavfurt, and resistance fighters will always attack from behind those walls— and it may be that you can get them to agree to the new borders. Many of your new countrymen look upon the Skaelin in the east as heroes, you must realize. The sooner you gain their support, the sooner you really secure your nation." King Centreal nodded.

"I came to this conclusion on my own accord," Centreal said. "We need to find incentives for peace. Those come to us not as often as we would like."

"And you should begin construction on new cities, new settlements," Deiknahr added, "that are free of any anti-Freemen sentiment. And so that there is ample housing for when the hostages are sent back to their families, now here in Skaen. Otherwise we would need to set up camps."

King Centreal nodded again. "Yes, I certainly agree. I am going to begin a campaign of construction. The ex-soldiers will build 'freetowns' that are intended for Freemen who wish very strongly to remain set apart from the Skaelin. Freetowns will be exclusively for the Freemen. But on to the hostages, of which I am most concerned about...I and my people, we are certain in our decision. We will not surrender our power to the former regime, nor will we return to Gaoln as prisoners again. Never, ever again."

"No," said Kio, "I don't think any of you here would. But we need to convince King Seagraul that what he wants to happen simply isn't possible."

"King Centreal," King Nowhawna said gravely, "what I am asking you to do is to remain here, with your people. Your life would be in grave danger were you to join us at the Council of Nations, when we meet in Laen to discuss the hostages. You are much safer here, and more importantly your people need you— if the Skaelin Resistance know that you are gone, they will seize upon it and renew their attacks. The Skaelin themselves might send their army out from the mountains. We know your position, and how strongly you feel about it— we will not let them win, I promise you."

"I cannot stay here, where half of my people need me, when in Laeolin the other half of my people need me even more," Centreal answered. "They are Gaolnians too, and have suffered more than we have. They must be free. Commander Luncas is perfectly able to see to the Kingdom of the Free in my absence. The Council of Nations must hear what I have to say."

"The new king in the east would use your absence as propaganda, King Centreal, and would convince the country that you have fled in fear, that you've gone to beg the King of Laen to release the hostages. Seagraul only seeks your surrender, and by ignoring his blatant disregard for human dignity, you deny him of that surrender, as odd as that sounds. Victory will come to you, and with it the rest of your country's people, the women and children and elderly held in Laeolin. But you must remain here, where you will be a symbol of strength to us all. We at the Council of Nations will say of you that you felt so strongly of your position that you considered it a dishonor to attend the negotiations— that unless the hostages are returned immediately, The Kingdom of the Free's next target will be Laen— "

"Now wait a minute— "

"And Gonaka will be coming with you."

King Centreal sat in silence. "Very well," he said after some time. "that is the message you will give them, and deliver it with courage and purpose."

King Nowhawna smiled at the King of the Free. "I will."

The morning after the arrival of the king and the two gulaus-heroes, King Centreal woke early. Before the sun had peaked out he went to saddle up the two lithae, and by the time he had them fastened, the red circle was already coming up to shine on the meadows. Fenidaln. What a sweet smell these meadows had, the taste of morning dew on the grass and rain in a distant forest, and every morning came a fog that rested over the whole great stretch of the meadow for hours into the early morning. For the first time in quite a while, the king felt some personal joy— *what a sweet place to call my home.*

When the others awoke, they found him ready to go. Nowhawna and Centreal both took a litha, taking with them Kio, Deiknahr and Commander Luncas. Captain Alaisio had agreed to walk with Gendorn and Bendoraun, though where exactly they were going was a mystery to the two boys. "Freetown," Alaisio insisted, "is the newest great thing in our new country. It is going to be the capital of the nation, the king says, once it starts to grow. Until then the capital is wherever the king goes, but in truth most of our administration and power is held up in the castles. Bellford, Gatsesilli, Seun Bastion, the whole like— but Centreal says he wants to build a fortress in the heart of Freetown such as the world has never seen." Alaisio scoffed in a friendly way. "He can be crazy, sometimes. Does he mean to build something better than Seun Bastion? Better than Gatsesilli? Better than Bellford? We would do better if we tried to integrate those places, and didn't spend so much time daydreaming about great cities in the sky for Freemen only. I don't mean to be so critical. But it's the truth."

Alaisio went on like this for quite some time before the two boys realized they must be hiking toward this Freetown. "It's only a collection of mud huts right now, hardly better than any of the pels in Gaoln, but by the Spirits, that man can dream the greatest city the world has ever seen, even if he can't build it."

"When were you made captain?" Gendorn asked, hoping only to break off this tirade.

"When Luncas was made Commander of the King's Division."

Gendorn and Bendoraun stopped dead in their tracks. Luncas? Their captain? *Commander of the King's Division!?* It paid to be friends with a king, Gendorn concluded.

For a brief instant, Alaisio considered revealing Luncas's secret to the boy. Gendorn would understand, wouldn't he? Bendoraun would cut Luncas's throat while he slept, he knew that for sure, and would never dare to tell him— but Gendorn, could Gendorn understand what the man had gone through? He could understand the change— but could he ever understand why he had been the way he had once been, why he had made the choices that he did? More importantly, even if the boy did understand, was he still willing to forgive? And would he be as angry as Bendoraun? His sigh went unnoticed by the younger soldiers. He would not risk it. He kept his mouth shut, and soon enough they were hiking in silence.

Toward the northeastern edge of Fenidaln Meadows the three of them spotted something growing among the tall grasses. Nestled between the trees that surrounded the meadow's far edge, the collection of a few dozen huts that made up Freetown claimed a plot of flat land where the grass had been cleared. A few crops sprouted from the ground between the huts, and some thin creeks ran between them, drawing water from the river that lay to the north, running from the Thin River Highlands in the east all the way to Kensebach-Tycagra in the west as it looped around in the north. Gendorn and Bendoraun smiled. However small the homes, it was heartwarming— more than that— it overwhelmed them with happiness— to see Freemen living freely, in a land that they could finally call their own. For a precious moment, nothing in the world seemed to matter outside of these meadows.

But the fact that they were all men was not lost on the boys. The soldiers here walked with a slowness in their step, and with something lost in the light of their eyes. Gendorn still remembered the sight of land, the first sight of Skaen through the sea fog, and the shouts and the laughter all around him. He could see men kissing the earth and stretching their hands toward the sky, and it seemed a memory lost in such a place as this. For all the happiness that surged up inside of him, there seemed to be none of it here. These men were not the same.

There were a few smiles and welcome arms. One or two people even shouted welcomes to *Gulaus Gendorn* and *Gulaus Bendoraun*.

The two kings were in conversation at the edge of the forest, where the village ended abruptly. Inside the forest there was only a small furnace and some anvils cast about under a tile roof. Deiknahr was there at an anvil, hammering away at some thing or another. A bell, that's what it was— a great, gleaming red orchalin bell. He took no notice of the boys, and the two knew better than to interrupt the man's work. They approached the two kings straight away.

Central smiled. "It is good to see the both of you in such good health. Gulaus Gendorn, I did not believe I'd see you alive again."

"With good reason, my king," Gendorn answered with a smile. He dropped the smile pointedly, and looked gravely at the king. "My king, what are we meaning to do about the prisoners in Laeolin?"

It was the King of Gonaka who answered. "The nations of the world are arrayed against Seagraul," he told them reassuringly. "There is nothing he can do to harm the prisoners. The Council of Nations is meeting in Laeolin in Tun-Trest, and there'll be nothing to stop us from freeing the prisoners when Seagraul finds himself unaided and alone. They'll join the men soon enough. It is only worry that keeps the men here from smiling."

Central nodded. "Nowhawna is right, on that account. But I do think I should be there."

"An envoy will be enough," Nowhawna insisted. "Your strength is needed here in the Kingdom of the Free."

"I have already given my word to you, Nowhawna. I'm not a man to break it."

"Good, then. You are making the right choice, Centreal. You'd only put in jeopardy what you've already won."

"We've talked long enough about this."

"Then it is time for me to go," the King of Gonaka said to the King of the Free. "Time and Fate be on your side."

"Is that all we can do?" Gendorn asked once the King of Gonaka drew out of sight. "Wait?"

"No," Centreal said slowly, "there must be something else we can do."

"I'd like to go to Laeolin."

A smile crossed the king's lips, and his eyes seemed to shine. "You?"

"Yes. Bendoraun and I. We want to go to Laeolin. It will be easy enough for the two of us to hide."

The king nodded. "I suppose it would, but what you suggest merits more thought than you have given to it. There is no need for haste tonight. We will take the evening and the days coming to work this out, and decide if it is even possible, or practical, for that matter." The two boys nodded. "What did you two see in Gaoln?"

Gendorn waited to decide how to phrase his response, but he could not get through a single thought before Bendoraun blurted out "Bodies." The king's attention was fully on Bendoraun now, and his eyes gave away his sad desire to hear more. "There was a lot of killing when they came. I can't remember how many we saw. There were lines and clusters of people, some with shovels and picks, some with nothing, some without even their rags to cover their bodies." The king's eyes grew a bit wider. "It was no relocation. It was a massacre. An absolute massacre." The last was said with pointed disgust.

Gendorn picked up after Bendoraun fell silent. "I am afraid for the people in Laeolin. If Seagraul's soldiers can kill without regard, if they can chop up small children and get away with it, what's to keep them from murdering the hostages? We need to get to Laeolin. If not with an army, then by ourselves."

The king nodded, but gave no answer other than to look away and let his head hang lower. He did not even look up at them as he spoke, and his voice was soft and somber now, decisive but laced with newfound doubt. "Get to work helping the men build more homes and clearing plots of land. I'll see you at sundown. Thank you for bringing the news."

Work shoved out worries over the prisoners in Laeolin. There were few things that Gendorn or Bendoraun had done in their lives as meaningful to them as clearing farms and building homes in what would one day be the capital city of the Kingdom of the Free. They found it very difficult not to feel at least some small sense of hope with every load of dirt tossed from their shovels, with every plot hoed, with every cabin going up slowly to replace the mud huts. At one point Bendoraun tried to make a joke, and Gendorn even smiled at his effort. On that day alone, six or seven more huts were built, as another team of men arrived. *What will this place be like in one year*, Gendorn wondered— *ten years*? His smile grew, and he almost laughed. Almost.

For the next week he and Bendoraun dug ditches, cleared and leveled fields, cut logs, and sorted out the materials that others gathered. They knew nothing of farming or construction, but there were plenty of simple tasks, and those composed a large part of the work to be done. By the end of the week he and Bendoraun were growing anxious to set out for Laeolin, whether or not their king intended on giving them permission.

They had been in Freetown for eight days when the central component of the town hall was finished. In its current stage, it was only a large, three-story log cabin with an open third floor devoid of any furnishings. On that floor hung the bell Deiknahr had forged for the new kingdom. There were no walls there, so that the sound could echo through all the town, and the bell was displayed ostentatiously. As ostentatiously as anything can look inside of a log cabin, that is. Deiknahr, along with the Freemen apprentices he had claimed, hung it up in a ceremony late in the afternoon. The shining red bell had been engraved with the insignia of the Kingdom of the Free, as chosen by the king himself and agreed upon by the soldiers in a vote. The one lonely tree by the hill stood out against the red, and the slope of the hill was visible against the sea beyond. The king addressed the gathering of people after the bell went up.

"This kingdom", King Centreal proclaimed, "is one fundamentally created upon the idea of freedom, both in the physical sense and in the sense of the human spirit. As long as our kingdom prevails, freedom will reign, and justice, the world over, will be done."

King Centreal was the first man to sound the bell, and its ring brought tears to no small number of the men arrayed before him. He stepped down, and by his invite every man present came up to sound the bell. Gendorn and Bendoraun each rang it; Luncas and Alaisio rang it with heartfelt smiles; Deiknahr rang it, as one among them, a man who had agreed to harbor any surviving Gaolnians. The bell tolled hundreds of times that evening, until the sun set upon it and the red light faded from the metal surface. Suddenly, Gendorn was very glad he had remained. There was something profoundly historic about all of this, he decided. And profoundly wonderful after so many years of bondage and extermination. It was nothing he or any other could express in words. But in the sounding of the bell, time and time again, not a man thought of anything else. The chills that ran up and down his arms and legs and spine lasted well beyond the fading of the daylight.

Around the campfire that night, Gendorn felt as if he were back in the army again. They had not had such a large fire, or such a great gathering, since the celebratory nights after

Gatsesilli, before the ambush that took Gendorn's eye. Gendorn shook his head at his own thought, in the way a father might shake his head at a misbehaved child. *Damn wars. I'll miss that eye.*

The celebration was almost equal to the festivities around the fire after the great victory at Gatsesilli. Most of the men compared it to the fires after the victory at Seun Bastion, which they said lasted well beyond sunrise. There were flutes and drums and dancing, storytelling and laughing to accompany it. Again Gendorn found himself sharing his memories with Luncas, Alaisio, Bendoraun, and the King of the Free himself, and now Deiknahr, besides. It struck him that Nolor was absent, although a man who had known him was present, and together they remembered him well.

There was one thing that disturbed the one-eyed gulaus, and that was the men's joking about the hostages in Laeolin. It was all just a matter of time to them. They believed their families would be returned to them. *Would they?* Gendorn shook his head. *You saw what they did in Gaoln. Don't make the mistake of believing.* Still, he could not help but laugh at one particular man, who went on by himself for near half the night about how his woman would react when they freed her:

"'Shurtau, why weren't you in the tower sooner!? I was being marched through the city all alone, and they were yelling at me and throwing things— why weren't you there!' 'Well, honey, I was fighting a war, and...' 'War!? You think that lets you do anything you want!? You think you can ignore me for war!?' 'Well, see, at the time there was this man trying to kill me, and he had a sword...' 'Do you think I care about swords!'"

Gendorn tuned it out. He stopped listening to the noises of men bragging about what they'd do to the soldiers in Laeolin. He was tired of it all.

It seemed he was not alone in his doubts, for at some point the bragging stopped, and some other men expressed their worries. That killed the conversation. The music continued all the same.

At some point a silence descended suddenly, one of those surprising silences that is the natural result of multiple conversations ending at the same time and which seems to occur at least once in every such gathering of people. One man, in particular, had been waiting for this silence, it seemed to Gendorn, as he rose quite quickly from his seat before conversation could begin again and placed himself by the fire in the middle of the wide circle. There was recognition on a few faces, but the man introduced and explained himself all the same:

"Freemen, my name is Alai-Ku, and in my youth I was a bard on board a pirate vessel. My father, the captain of that same ship, was sent to Gaoln with me when I was a child, but in Gaoln I continued my work for no other end than merriment and the fulfillment of the hopes of the human spirit, which I believe can be found in song.

"This is an important evening for us. It is easy to be lost in the dreams of our future when we are building it every hour of every day. But let us remember where we are from, and who we left behind, in this song. Let us remember the days of our youth when ourselves and our parents and their parents sang this song as they made the hike into the mines while the stars were still unchallenged in the deep night sky. Let us remember that those who we sang with, and those we gave our hearts to, live an ocean away, in the very heart of evil, and that it is we alone among all men who have the heart to save them, because we shared this song, we shared this dream with them, for all of our lives."

The Freemen stood and put their hands over their hearts. One man from the crowd cried out: "For those who shared our dreams and our song." The rest of the men echoed: "For those who shared our dreams."

The bard began in a wavering, deep tone, alone in the silence of the night with the cackling fire:

> "Children,
> Children run,
> Children,

Children run,"

The Freemen joined in soft and slow:

"Oh Children, we pray for thee,
The pain inside you can't yet see,
The hate we hide should never be
Your own,

Oh children can you see?
There is no hope for you and me,
There is no love that's spared for thee,
Run, run!

'Cause it's a dark and dim and dismal place
Without a ray of light to trace,
Without a home or a hiding place,
We are,

You can't help it, can't change it no
And there's no hope, no hope I know,
You fight the darkness,
But it's faster than the light,

Oh children run, be free!
Across the ocean in front of thee
Across the ocean, fly until
You're free!"

The Freemen stopped then, and the bard carried on alone:

"Yeah if it were up to me,
You would not be here groveling,
You would have food at your feet to spare,"

And at this, the music picked up, the flutes and drums and lyres and the voices of all the Freemen:

"But this world is no place for we!
It's not a place for you and me!
Not a place for those who would believe,

That we can find our better days,
That storms always pass into a haze,
Of greater things and greater things to come,

And it's a dark and dim and dismal place,
Without a ray of light to trace!
Without a home or a hiding place,
We are—

Bound to the evil
Like the roots to the earth!
And we are the product
Of what we're worth!
We are the dirt,
The nothingness, do you see?

Oh! But were it up to me!
You would not be here groveling!
You would have food at your feet to spare!

Oh children where have you gone?
You are the only hope for the dawn
Of the day we only dream that we will see,

You will stand and tell them soon,
That we'll not be enslaved and abused,
We'll not be their pawns,

Tell them and tell them loud,

That we have faith and we are proud,
To be the ones, the ones who have to run!

Children,
Children run..."

It grew silent again. All the music stopped. The bard came forward into the firelight, and he sang one last slow and harrowing stanza, alone in the silence of the night with the cackling fire:

"Oh children can you see?
There is no hope for you and me,
There is no love that's spared for thee,
Run, run!"

- Chapter Six -

In the morning, the king called Gendorn and Bendoraun together in the town hall. The insides were as simple as the outside— it was nothing more than a small room, but the wood floors, the arched ceiling, and the glazed wood walls assured them all this would be a more permanent structure than the mud huts. The king took no time for idle talk.

"You are free to do as you wish, here in the kingdom or abroad, in Laeolin or in any other city," he told the boys. With a wink, he added, "just make sure I don't know about it unless I need to, or unless you need help and believe it is worth the risk of communicating. If the latter should ever prove to be the case, know that I would send our entire army if it meant the safe return of our women, children and elders. But do not attempt to communicate unless you feel that goal is within reach, because doing so could jeopardize their safety, should Seagraul ever uncover it." The boys nodded, and the king gave them a friendly smile. "Construction has already begun on the first Freeman port town, Doneaihr. You'll find it in the middle stretch of where we first landed here in Skaen. Commander Luncas will be taking you there, and Alaisio may be going as well. I believe you'll find some ships there that will prove large enough to hold you and some teams of men besides, should you decide the scope of your mission requires it. I do not know what the two of you have planned, precisely, and I do not think anyone should. You've shown good judgment and quick thought, the both of you. Luncas is experienced in these things. He can help. He has the authority to cancel your plans should he judge them reckless, so make sure to be as careful here as you have ever been. If you ever need to be in contact," the king slipped a paper into Gendorn's shirt pocket, "ask for Joel at the Council of Nations, and tell him to get your word to me as fast as he can. He is Gonaka's Chief Ambassador to the Council of Nations, and a loyal ally and sympathizer to our cause. The best of luck to you both." The soldiers bowed their heads and turned to leave.

Eight days on the trail with just the four of them proved to be a decent reunion. Luncas and Alaisio spent more time with the boys than they ever had, and Gendorn was surprised to find that his image of Luncas improved.

Decent as it was, it was the oddest and most unsettling feeling to be travelling through this part of Skaen in the first weeks of Trest, where the sun shined on fields of green just sprouting from the newly warm earth, in a time of peace. *There should be snow, and villages burning*, Gendorn thought. But where they passed they saw the sun shining on farmers who looked up at them, and when they passed merchant trains on the trail, the Skaelin men would bob their heads and smile. *What reason have they to smile? No more reason than I have. Many of them less, to be sure.* He smiled back, the man with the one eye. And on occasion a man would spend a moment longer looking at Gendorn in particular. Something passed between them. Something important.

He saw more traders on the trail to Doneaihr during those eight days than he had seen in all the wilderness throughout the entire course of the war. To see the land flourishing with warm-weather activity, from trading to crafting to clearing new fields and building new villages, it was all very wondrous, and there are not the words to describe the feelings that put a smile on his face day after day. He would pass a familiar hill, and remember battle, and think to himself: *Someone died there. I watched lines of people push back and forth for an hour, I saw piles of bodies on that hill.* But as he looked there was nothing but a group of children playing, or a man surveying his fields. He shook his head and sighed. There were surely such feelings in this world as this, feelings which he would never, ever understand.

Gendorn lost himself in his thoughts, and the silence of his friends proved that their own thoughts were not so far different from his own. In the evening of the eighth day the four of them arrived in Port Doneaihr.

Construction had only just begun on the port, but the place already seemed overwhelmed with residents and workers. For every home there must have been fifty or sixty men still living in huts or tents, working long days to build the town. The first part of the harbor was already completed, and three giant vessels lay in anchor out beyond the docks where the smaller fishing boats were tied up. Gendorn smiled when he saw them. *Those will be going to Laeolin*, he thought.

There was little else that had been completed. A large barracks complex lay by the dock, on one side of a paved stone street. On the other side of that street were cleared lots and some stone foundations, and across the opposite side of the barracks lay only a few large warehouses. Most of the goods in the town were under open-air pavilions, locked up tight in boxes or barrels with painted labels. *What a kingdom this will be*, Gendorn thought to himself proudly. Abruptly Luncas signaled to a group of men and spoke to them as they approached, and Gendorn realized they had trekked in total silence since morning.

"Soldiers, what is going up in those lots across the street from the barracks?"

"Houses, Commander Luncas," Answered the seniormost man.

"Is that one taken?" Luncas pointed to a lot just north of the barracks and on the other side of the street from it, keeping it far enough away from the water so as not to suffer the smell from the fisheries.

"No, commander. It is not."

"Good. Build this house there." The commander took out a piece of paper and handed it to the man, who looked unsure for only a second before nodding his head and agreeing to do as the commander asked. "I drew that up too long ago, and it's time I finally lived in the place." He smiled as he said this, as if there were something more than he had revealed, but he explained no more. "There will have to be someone to watch over the next generation of soldiers as they train, to shout at them when they mess up. It may as well be me. That is all. You are dismissed."

"When did you draw that up? Is that the plan you told me about? From that girl?" asked Alaisio.

"It isn't our plan anymore, just mine," the ex-captain said with a smile that hinted at a pinch of sadness, "But it is still a good house." Alaisio nodded. Gendorn and Bendoraun shrugged at one another, and kept their silence.

The four of them spent their nights in a large pavilion with sixteen other men, and they spent their days in the warehouses or in the fields, with Luncas overseeing construction and Alaisio working alongside the two boys. The days passed quickly in this way, or slowly if the sun beat too hard on their backs, but Gendorn and Bendoraun were preoccupied with their own designs as well.

It started with work gossip. Idle talk in the fields or in the houses, or by the docks when the men broke for dinner at sunset. The two young leaders sowed interest in the mind of a single man, and then another, and one more, and his friends heard about it secondhand. By the end of the week there were five. By the second week, there were thirty. By the close of the month, Gendorn and Bendoraun were turning men away and interviewing them to see who might be the best. All around them Doneaihr grew into a city. And inside of the two heroes something else grew— it was an urge to set sail again, into the very shadows of Laeolin, and it was an urge they could not keep at bay for even one more day.

- Chapter Seven -

It was hot inside the tower. It had been hot for too long. If she pressed her memoires hard enough, she could still remember a time before the tower— but that seemed a different life in another world. Certainly not her life, not in this world. She had known when ten days had passed— she had known, hardly, when twenty had passed. How many had it been now, somewhere beyond thirty, she was sure— beyond forty, close to fifty? Some of the prisoners were saying they had been there for a hundred days. That was surely possible. Some had clearly gone mad, and said they had been there for years or decades. Kamira knew one thing, that for as long as she had been here, every day had grown hotter and hotter, and it was unbearable. They did not have the water to survive the heat inside the tower, and there were too many bodies packed too closely together. It wasn't right, Kamira knew— it wasn't human, and humans could not live like this. *We are going to die.*

She remembered the first time she saw a dead body being dragged from the top of the tower to the bottom by two of the guards. She remembered, most vividly, her desire to kill them, to tell them that this was their fault. Her tongue was swollen, and her body had stopped producing sweat— hardly anyone sweat anymore, even though it was the hottest it had ever been inside the tower. Then there was the day when the guards came back, and dragged two bodies away. Then there was the day when the guards came and dragged three of them away, and then another one, and then another two— and these days, these deaths began to blur into a single moment or a single day, and she forgot them just as she had long ago forgotten the rising and the setting of the sun.

Every time there was a storm, she prayed for lightning to strike the tower down, to set them free, give them a chance. Every time she saw a bird flying past her, however distant, she imagined that she could speak with the creature, and she would say the same thing— *tell the world what is happening here, tell them, and bring them here— bring our salvation, we are helpless*. On one occasion she saw someone riding by the tower on a litha, and she swore the litha turned to look at her— swore they locked eyes, and that the litha nodded at her— did the litha nod? Everyone around her said she was crazy, speaking to animals, losing her mind— she would join the others, they said, the ones who claimed they'd been trapped in the tower for decades. But the birds never brought their salvation, the lithae never came to fight against the Army of Laen, and the lightning never struck the tower. The days grew unbearably hot, and bodies were hauled out of the tower day and night.

The days came when everyone in the tower sat motionless, as if they were already dead, and they would remain there, not moving, not talking, from sunrise to sunset, and then to the sunrise after. They would fall in and out of sleep, realize at times they were eating, or at times someone had gotten up, or at times the light had changed in the thin windows along the sides of the room, or that some corpse was being dragged off somewhere off in the crowd where they couldn't quite see.

The scratching was more subdued now. Many of those who had been scratchers had died of going crazy. It was a real thing to die of, Kamira learned. When a person was consumed by grief so badly that they lost their mind, they might cry for hours and hours, cry for their whole world ending, and the heat would take them. No one survived if they cried too much. The most gruesome tales were more immediate, of course. Crazed women banging their heads against the tower until they split open. People trying to eat parts of themselves, or of someone else, and being killed by the other prisoners. There were no happy tales in these days. Hope was hard to find.

But the threat of sickness remained. As soon as the weather turned colder, the prisoners would need to attempt an escape, or they would be as good as dead as soon as the first person got sick on the first chilly night. Kamira wondered who else had realized this. By the looks she got every now and then, she presumed it must be a good number of them. That was good for what she was planning. It would have to be good enough.

PART TWO: CHASING CLOUDS

- Chapter One -

It was a warm day, and the sun was bright. The meadow was alive with life— there were tall grasses and huge flowers and creatures all around— butterflies and other flying things, small creatures scurrying through the grass— and it seemed very out-of-place for Gendorn, who could not have felt any less at ease, or any more discomforted. He looked around him— it was so calm, and so beautiful, and so simple, this place with the sunshine and the warmth, and the creatures all around him, just behaving, just living, as they did every day. He couldn't comprehend it. It was not the same world in which men had died for their simple and cherished freedom— not the same world in which Kamira was a prisoner in some distant and dangerous city. The scene before him belonged not in the same world where these things were true— it belonged in the world where Gendorn and Bendoraun had just arrived in Skaen, when they stood beneath those tall snow-covered boughs and dreamed of freedom and warm fires and good food and a strong roof over their head. It belonged with the world where Gendorn and Kamira were sitting beneath the last tree in Gaoln, drawing pictures of what their lives would be like on the other side of the Cold Ocean. There was nothing shared between these two worlds, when Gendorn sat there in the meadow, thinking of these things. There was nothing that connected them at all.

It would be dark in Laeolin— he knew it. They would keep the tower shut, and let the heat build up, and someone would die of thirst, and the Lonins would only use that death as a reason to hope that negotiations would go their way. He had seen this in his mind— he saw it every night now, before he went to bed.

He would see the moon, and he would ask the sky every night, and the wind that blew in it, that one day Kamira could see the moon again, that one day she could feel the wind herself.

There were two clouds in the sky. One of them was chasing another, slower cloud— they were thin things, almost transparent. As the one neared the other, closing in, the cloud which was escaping the first one disappeared— it simply vanished— and the cloud which had been chasing it stood still. *It's like a man who chases his dreams*, Gendorn mused, *and when he begins to make his dreams a reality, the reality simply vanishes....it's just gone...* Gendorn began to make shapes out of the remaining cloud, when he heard Bendoraun's voice behind him.

"It's been almost a hundred days since Seun Bastion," he said, and he sat down next to Gendorn. "They want to go to war again, to seize Laeolin, the men in Doneaihr. The king still says it's too risky."

"I'll go there myself, I don't care. I'll find a way. It'll be easier than getting out of Gatsesilli— Gonaka can help me."

"You're not going to Laen, Gendorn," Bendoraun said rather sincerely, "and if you are, I'm going with you. But we were told to wait for word from Centreal before we set sail, after all this news. I am not sure what will become of it, but isn't it better to wait?"

"I just don't understand, Bendoraun. I just don't."

Bendoraun put an arm around his friend. "I know, Gendorn. I don't think any of us do."

Three days later Gendorn and Bendoraun gathered with Alaisio and their old captain inside Luncas's new home. A huge part of the army was in Doneaihr these days, building the town up as if they only had a few weeks to do everything. Ships from Gonaka and Kale came in every week. Still, some had remained in Doneaihr for another purpose— indeed, some had travelled to Doneaihr for that same purpose— because they believed, or wanted to believe, that the invasion of Laen and the rescue of the hostages was not far away.

This great mass of soldiers crowded inside and outside the city, in tents and lean-tos and in the homes going up every day. They arranged themselves in companies, and for those companies that had survived the war intact, they awaited word from the king. It seemed that more than one in three soldiers, entirely without orders, had shown up in Doneaihr ready to set sail. And if they never received word from the king? Commander Luncas sighed, as he turned these thoughts over in his head. *They will set sail either way*, he finally conceded.

"King Centreal has sent only a few regiments to the ports," Luncas told the three of them, "and now everyone thinks they're going to set sail. He just wants to be ready, in case it comes to war, that's all."

"Would you go?" Alaisio asked.

"Me?" Luncas wondered. "No, I would not. I'm done with armies, Alaisio, I can hardly walk anymore, and my strength isn't what it once was. I'm counting on the three of you to help lead the Free Army— that's what they're calling the army now— if it comes to war with Laen, you know. There's a reason I always kept you close."

"Because I'm the next king," Bendoraun said. Luncas smiled. "Precisely."

"Keep mocking me," said Bendoraun, "I'll hurt you!"

"Would you?" Luncas said daringly. "Well, I think I have enough strength left to handle you, anyway." Bendoraun laughed.

"I'll be ready," Gendorn said gravely. Surprised, the three others looked at him with a sudden interest. "I will. And I won't wait. We're going to Laen, whether or not King Centreal tells us to. I have my men ready. They aren't waiting either. They don't want to."

Luncas looked angry, and for a moment Gendorn saw the captain as he was on the first day of their meeting, looking at him as if he were a child unaware of the world. "You would jeopardize everything, Gendorn."

"Jeopardize? They are jeopardized every day, while we sit here! They die every day!"

"Don't tell yourself you're the only one who cares!" Luncas retorted, "You are all Gaolnian, remember— everyone has their Kamiras, and most have a lot more than that. Some of these men have entire families in Laeolin. King Centreal knows what he is doing."

"Won't you help me?" Gendorn asked, gazing at Luncas. "Won't you help me gather the troops? We're not launching an invasion, captain, we're just launching a mission. All we need to do is sneak inside Laeolin. I snuck around Skaen for half the war, making up so many different stories, and visiting so many places, and having so many covers— I know what I am doing, and Bendoraun does too. We survived behind enemy lines for a hundred days or more. Remember?"

Luncas smiled. It was so like him, Bendoraun thought— whenever he had been worried that Luncas would get most angry, the captain always smiled, from the very first week the four of them had met when they divided up into their regiments. The captain looked at Gendorn as if he were suddenly proud of something, and scratched his chin as he thought. "Yes. You do know what you are doing, don't you?" No one replied, and the captain, after the pause, continued— "Well, I suppose you should get to setting sail, then, if you are so intent on doing this."

"Does that mean you'll help us?" Gendorn asked.

"Maybe. I still think it is the wrong decision, Gendorn. But I will trust that you know what you're doing. If you will set sail, you'll take no more than one ship, and your crew should be as able as you, Gendorn and Bendoraun, when it comes to hiding themselves and sticking by their disguises. I am not saying that I will help you. I am saying that I will not tell King Centreal. You'll need to come up with a flawless excuse for that eye patch, though. And the men you've recruited for the other two ships will have to go. Choose the best men between the three of them."

"Thank you, captain." Gendorn said.

"We should pick our men, Gendorn," Bendoraun said. "The sooner we set sail, the better."

"I'm not done yet," said Luncas, the smile still on his face. "What, precisely, will happen when you walk into Laeolin and free the prisoners? I suppose you will have armed escorts waiting to take all one hundred and fifty thousand of them back to Skaen? And a thousand ships waiting for you outside the city, to depart upon your command?"

"Well," said Bendoraun shyly, "we hadn't worked out all the details..."

"Well," Luncas said firmly, "I suggest you do."

As the two younger friends were leaving, Alaisio got up to follow them. On the street he stopped them, and pressed a paper into Bendoraun's hand. "If we get many more papers, we'll lose track of them," Bendoraun said smartly. Alaisio smiled.

"This one is important, so remember what I say. Ciso. A name. He is my son, and he would be eager to help you. He studies in Laeolin. You are kindred souls destined to meet, it seems," a smile crossed his face, distant but warm, "so remember Ciso. The Academy of Laen. Do not ask for him. It would put both of you in grave danger. But find him all the same." Bendoraun opened the paper, and saw there were no words on it. *Just as well*, he thought to himself, *it's not as if I can read*. Instead, there was a picture of a man with dark hair half-way down across his forehead, and a warm smile and narrow eyes alight. Of course his father would see his son in such a way— was this what Ciso really looked like? Bendoraun shrugged. He could only hope.

Bendoraun and Gendorn were left alone, and Gendorn turned to address his friend.

"When we get to Laeolin— "

"Assuming we get in."

"— and we have the prisoners freed— "

"Assuming we haven't been shot full of arrows."

"We can lead the prisoners immediately outside the city— "

"Assuming the guards won't have blocked the gates and set off the alarms— "

"As it will be in the middle of night, Bendoraun, there is a lower probability of that, especially once we have taken control of one of the gatehouses and disposed of the guards. We won't be working alone, you know."

"I know that you know what you're doing, Gendorn. It just sounds ridiculous."

"Of course it does. But I know you won't run off on me, will you?"

Bendoraun sighed. "No, I won't. Let's decide who we'll be taking and be done with it all."

- Chapter Two -

As the prisoners in Laeolin waited for relief or for death, the gulaus-heroes of Gaoln gained a reputation in Doneaihr. Their cover was that they were recruiting to sail down to the islands as the first envoy of the Free Kingdom to the Territories of Bautaulan, to see if they could find allies and trading partners, but it was understood among those who were finally selected for the journey that their journey was far more dangerous, and much more important, than all of that. They became the most popular men in town in short order, and the only man more recognized among them in the port was the king's own commander.

Luncas's home had progressed quite nicely in a matter of weeks. The porch was the first thing to be complete, and he made sure to spend his afternoons watching the soldiers sparring across the street. Every now and again he would get up and yell at one of them for some thing or another, and then sit back down. The Commander of the King's Division, just as quickly as Gendorn and Bendoraun had risen in popularity, was soon referred to as the crazy old porch man who genuinely expected every man to fight like a born hero.

Affairs went along much the same for the first five or six weeks. By the end of that time, the harbor was a bustling center of trade with a firm seawall, pullers all around, and a swarm of smaller fishing vessels as far as the eye could see. A land wall was going up to enclose and secure the city, and the foundations for towers had been built. Brick and stone buildings rose out from the streets pulling away from the seaside, and men hurried about in every direction with crates and boxes and barrels and ropes and smiles on their faces, sweating under the sun. Homes went up by the block, the whole block, and new stories were added after that. It was an incredible feeling to have— the feeling of having a country, a home, a place to belong. It was not quite complete. Not yet.

That was Gendorn's first source of pride. It was what lay behind him. The second was what lay before him. Thirty sailors on the decks and ropes, swinging with excitement instead of fear, with eagerness devoid of hesitation, with dreams and the strength to follow them out from the darkest tumults of war. Every man of them was a hero, and for them to call him their leader was a title he hardly believed he deserved. After six weeks of recruiting he had these men to show for it, and he could not be even the smallest bit prouder of them.

It was no idle speculation. He had heard their tales. One of them, Harrkal, had snuck inside Gensballa prior to the arrival of the Gaolnian forces in order to measure the strength and type of the garrison there. He snuck a report over the wall. When battle was joined, he had ran out to the walls, thrown on his Gaolnian rags, picked up a sword and joined rank with the rest of them, receiving fire from both sides. Another, Gurien, had already lost his entire family. They had died in Gaoln of the storms and the sickness and the starvation, before rebellion was ever whispered. "What made you fight?" Gendorn had asked. "Their memory. It's all that keeps me alive." Gendorn supposed that he himself was a troubled youth, but here, truly, was a man whose world was already destroyed, a life left without purpose. Somehow, when everything had been taken, he still found something to hold on to. This mission was life's greatest work for a man like that. He could never call himself a hero next to these men, and his position as their leader would never seem proper.

Bendoraun, however, easily assumed his position as first mate. He never hesitated to give an order, and he hesitated even less to crack a joke or share a drink with his crew. Gendorn was not quite sure how he did it, but he supposed Bendoraun was just being himself, and that there was nothing more to it. He was likeable enough, at any rate. He never lost respect among the crew, never incurred a loss of loyalty, and even for those old enough to have had him as their son, they listened as they would have to a father. It left Gendorn with most of his time free to consider the logistics of this journey, and that was a truly baffling thing to be done.

He pushed away his sigh of doubt, and found a note of confidence somewhere deep inside. *But it will be done.*

On the first day of the seventh week, Gendorn woke early. He caught the sunrise through the verdant greens of the forest outside the city, the forest he had seen covered in snow when landing on these very same shores. Well, enough of that. His dream was not a reality yet, but he found an energy in his step these days. It would be soon.

The sun was bright that morning. It shined on every man there, on their ship, their harbor and their town, on their kingdom and in their hearts. Its light was still and graceful over the ocean when the crew set sail, and it shined strong in a clear blue sky for every second of that day.

- Chapter Three -

It was at about this time, by which time half of Trest had almost gone and the new Gaolnian constructs were visible all throughout the nation, when Joel, Gonaka's Director of Ambassadors, arrived on the back of a litha in Freetown and requested an audience with King Centreal. The two met inside the town center, in a secret room built into the underground where no one would hear them. "King Nowhawna sends a message," Joel told King Centreal, "he advises King Centreal to keep his army ready and his men prepared for battle. He says that if negotiations do not improve, and if things do not go the way we hope them to, it may be necessary to use our soldiers to rescue the hostages from Laeolin. We will need to be ready to act quickly, and be ready to seize Laeolin. We should begin planning for this course of action, in case it becomes necessary. Have you been trying to win over the Skaelin?"

King Centreal nodded. "We've had great success in that within Free Kingdom territory. Keeping mixed garrisons and stationing mediators in each castle has delivered incredible results. There is the occasional murder, but given the situation, things have been the best we could hope for. Outside our territory it's been more difficult. There are a considerable number of Skaelin companies who refused to surrender and continue attacking us from inside Skaelin lands. As for the preparations, tell the kind King Nowhawna that he underestimates his friend and ally. We have already prepared for the possibility of immediate departure, and will be moving most of our forces south in the weeks to come, in case the Council of Nations is not able to release the hostages. We will be ready."

Only a short time later, as they were preparing to adjourn, the town bell rang. Centreal and Joel heard it right over their heads, hardly three floors above them, and it was deafening. Someone burst into the room, and shouted, "King Centreal, a party of Skaelin fighters has surrounded the settlement."

The king seemed to take the news quite calmly. He looked at Joel. "Care to join us?"

Joel bowed in acquiescence. "I would be honored, king."

When the king and the ambassador reached the enemy with an entourage of one hundred armored Freemen, they were given no notice at all. The Skaelin speaker, holding a flag and no weapon, had been addressing a crowd of Freemen, and he continued to do so with the king present.

"...holds them hostage, and will return them only if these wrongly conquered lands are first returned to us in full! We have presented our demands before and you have refused to comply. We offer you the same chance again, but the offer will stand only this once. The king is tired of the ineptitude and the foolishness of the Council of Nations. We will not wait for negotiations in Laeolin. We will settle this ourselves, or King Seagraul will settle it on his own accord. You have no choice. Go now, people of Gaoln, and your families will meet you back home."

"You've seen that land before!" One of the Freemen cried out. "You've been there. Out of pity, do not demand we return. No one should have to call that land 'home'."

"I am not authorized to pity," said the swordsman. "So what is your decision?"

"Were you sent by King Seagraul?" asked King Centreal.

"Our message comes from both Laen and the Skaelin."

"By direct order of the King of Laen?"

"Indirect," answered the swordsman.

"Are you to negotiate with us?"

"The time for negotiation is over," said the flagbearer. "The time to decide is upon you now."

"My people have already decided, and have told your messengers our decision. King Nowhawna is clear on where we stand, and your King Seagraul, daft as he is, should recall the decision that my people reached only months ago in Fenidaln Meadows. We have not changed our minds. If you do not have the power to negotiate, we have nothing more to say. If we cannot negotiate a settlement where our families are returned to us in these free lands, then war will come to you, war will come to your family, and war will come to your country."

"You are condemning everyone in Laeolin to death!" shouted the Skaelin flagbearer.

"We fought and died for their freedom, and you have thrown them in chains!" King Centreal replied. "If they die, their blood will be on your swords and by your orders. The sin will be in your own heart. But know that their deaths will be outnumbered by your own."

"War is already here, King Centreal!" A flight of arrows shot out from the woods and took down a number of the hastily assembled Freemen. The Skaelin broke formation, sweeping across the muddy grassland, and met the Freemen head-on. Freemen fell before they had a chance to form lines. The Skaelin did not, however, target and kill the soldiers themselves— rather, they kept fighting their way through the lines toward one specific figure, allowing them to immerse themselves deep within the Freemen lines. At this, their intention became clear, and King Centreal knew it— that this was a suicide mission in an attempt to kill him, the King of the Free. And in that instant he had some hope— *they're trying to find a new king for the Freemen, someone who will negotiate. They don't want to kill the hostages in Laeolin*— not yet.

It was a stunned and bloodied king that survived the attack, fallen to the ground and dazed, his sword in the dirt beside him. Two men were on the ground beside him, their hands and feet bound, looking bloodier and angrier by far. Joel, standing beside the king, was cleaning the blood from his sword. He waited patiently while the king regained his senses, and abruptly the king realized there must have been three or four dozen Freemen waiting for the same thing. Centreal rose, and spoke first to the ambassador:

"Thank you, Joel, for saving my life."

"The Freemen saved you as much as I," Joel whispered. He spared a look for the men he had captured and bound, and then returned the look to King Centreal. "Seagraul was involved," The ambassador said in the same soft whisper. "He is using the resistance fighters as a proxy army to kill you."

"I suspected. We need hard proof, though, if we are to argue that in front of the Council of Nations. Fly to Doneaihr, and tell the men there to prepare. Fly back the Fortress of the Free when you are done there, and do the same, and from there to Gatsesilli. We will send word to Gonaka and ask them to beg for our families in Laeolin, and do so ourselves as much as we can, but we cannot beg when the sword is to our heart and the man behind it is without a heart of his own. We will raise the swords in Doneaihr. We will be ready, if we must bring war to Laen." The men nodded. They had been listening closely. It was a fair assessment. "War must come when hearts no longer heed one another, and Seagraul has lost all of his senses in that regard." He turned to Joel, and spoke only to him: "See what proof you can find regarding this link between King Seagraul and the Skaelin Resistance within the Free Kingdom. It would mean a lot to prove this in the Council of Nations, and on the evidence we have gathered so far, it looks hopeful for us that we may do so. The Council might even force Seagraul to resign and surrender the prisoners. That was good work, binding these men. They had no time to get their senses together. If they had, they might not have answered you. I am sorry that I lost my senses myself. I cannot remember much of it all."

"It was a hammer, my king, on your head. You will want to avoid resting. Be vigilant and stay awake. Keep men around you at all times. Keep questioning them. There are men here who will do a fine job of it."

"Oh, sure." Joel's eyes narrowed. Centreal definitely had something wrong with his head. "Well, then. We should get packing. Farewell, Joel, and good luck in your missions."

"Good luck to us all, good king."

- Chapter Four -

Commander Luncas felt older in his chair, rocking back and forth all through the day, criticizing the young folk for their lack of skill with the sword, limping around his home and stumbling up the stairs with difficulty. It was one of two possibilities. First, it could be that inactivity was causing his leg to be more of a bother, or that activity kept his mind off the leg, either in which case he must find some activity with which to preoccupy his time. Second, it could be that he was growing older, and his age was causing an already bad leg to weaken further. Well, that couldn't be possible. It must certainly be the first of the two.

From the corner of his eye he saw a litha flying overhead and land somewhere in the center of the city. Luncas rose and almost ran toward the spot, along with most of the other workers and residents. There was no pain in his leg then, nor any memory of it. A man leaped off of the litha, tall and stone-faced, his eyes grave but laden with emotion and understanding. Luncas, though not close enough at the moment to observe the light in his eyes, could tell as much simply by the way the man moved his head this way and that, the way he carried himself. Whatever news the man bore, it was grave indeed, and there was no doubt of that— for Commander Luncas knew the man by name. Joel. Gonaka's Director of Ambassadors. Joel had been an enemy to him once, when the commander found himself serving under a different king. Now, he suspected, they would prove to be allies.

Joel leapt off the litha as it landed, and seemed to be waiting for something— for more people to gather around him, Luncas realized. The soldiers surrounded the man soon enough, but it took a while for the workers to gather from all ends of the city. Alaisio was one of the last people to get there, but his tall figure had no difficulty seeing Joel as he spoke.

"Citizens of the Free Kingdom, news from King Centreal. Freetown has been attacked, and its inhabitants slaughtered." There was nothing but silence, profound in its own right, from the crowd. "The king escaped with his life, and now leads the few remaining villagers into another, safer location. Soldiers are being sent from the garrisons to secure Freetown. The invasion was carried out by the Skaelin Resistance and was an attempt to assassinate the king. It was accompanied by a message from Laen.

Laen again demanded that the Freemen return to Gaoln, where their families would meet them, and relinquish all claim to any territory outside Gaoln. If the Freemen refused, they would kill the prisoners in Laeolin. The people of the village agreed on their fate, standing by the original decision of the entire army that was reached in Fenidaln Meadows. The ten surviving Skaelin attackers are being interrogated by the king himself, and travel with the surviving villagers from Freetown. We are certain that this assassination attempt, although carried out by the Skaelin Resistance without explicit permission from the new Skaelin king, was a ploy of King Seagraul of Laen. It is our firm belief, and the belief of King Centreal and King Nowhawna, that King Seagraul and the new Skaelin King, Celonis Sabero, who calls himself King of the East and stays hidden in the Eastern Mountain strongholds, are using Skaelin resistance fighters in inland Skaen as a force to kill King Centreal and put up a new king who will agree to surrender the Kingdom of the Free."

The crowd was restless. Cries of "War! Laen wants us at war!" could be heard from every mouth, and "Attack Seagraul, kill the king and free the hostages!" echoed from every corner of the open market square. A man next to the commander shouted: "If Laen is already killing us, why aren't we killing them!?", but Luncas remained quiet. After the initial shouting, there seemed to be a veil of silence that befell the entire crowd.

The birds went on singing, the sun went on shining through the gaps in the clouds, which kept on passing in the sky. The cool winds of early Trest went on blowing. And it dawned upon them then that their families and friends held hostage in Laeolin might actually be harmed, that King Seagraul, tired of negotiations, might actually make a demonstration out of some of those hostages. Some of the men walked away, silently and solemnly, heads bowed to the ground. They returned to their work of building Port Doneaihr, letting their preoccupation with their work steal them away from their grief for a moment's time.

There was a feeling of despair that pervaded the city, and of either doubt or restlessness, the city divided between those who wished to continue negotiations and those who wanted an invasion of Laeolin. Yet they all knew the men in Freetown, lying dead now on the grassy earthen hills, had made the right choice, and would have it no other way. This war had been fought for the freedom of not only themselves but of their children and grandchildren and of everyone who was to come after— it had been fought, and they had died, to end Gaoln. There was no outcry from the crowd when Commander Luncas, representing the city, held firm to the decision not to forfeit an inch of the Kingdom of the Free.

Joel swept across the countryside, alerting all the major towns, cities, and forts of what had occurred. When the news had been spread, he began asking questions about the resistance fighters, and any foreigners they might have seen who looked to be out of Laen. He found the natives to be rather uncooperative with the man who had helped engineer Gaoln's invasion of their lands. But he did connect a few lines on a map, going from the west of the Free Kingdom into Cavfurt, and from there to both Seun Bastion and various locations in Laen. It was something to follow up on. The investigations took nine days, all told, but soon he was flying to Fort Gatsesilli, where King Centreal had just arrived with the survivors. Gatsesilli, since the end of the war, had become a major stronghold for the Freemen, who had already connected it with Bellford and Gensballa and stationed a large standing army inside the fort and the surrounding area. Joel landed in the evening-time, and as he entered the room where King Centreal sat with his advisors, on the first floor of the castle, he spotted Kio sitting there, right next to the king. They sat around a long table shaped like the head of a spear, and King Centreal sat in the cove where the base of the spearhead would have been attached to a rod of wood. From this position he could see the face of every advisor and commander who sat at the table, as the two sides of the spearhead-like table always moved inward to a single point as it got further from where the king sat. This was a very old design for a table, something that had emerged in Skaen centuries ago, although Joel had only seen a few of them still left. It was the table where a king listened to the council of his advisors, from the time when Skaen was only a warring collection of eleven kingdoms. "Joel," Kio began, beckoning him to enter the room, "come join us, we've just begun."

"Kio has just arrived from Gonaka," King Centreal informed Joel, "to deliver news about the hostages. And to alert us of something that has just happened, that was quite…unexpected."

"And that is?" Joel inquired.

"Well," Kio said, "only that there seems to have been some sort of misunderstanding along the border between Kale and Laen, and that somehow a battle ensued, and several soldiers on both sides were killed, and hostilities are now even more intense between Kale and Laen, and between Laen and Gonaka, and that Las has stepped in to defend Laen, and that Phenen is calling it an offensive move on Kale's part and has also started defending King Seagraul, but at the same time the emperor wishes the hostages to be returned, and that, of course, King Seagraul still adamantly refuses to return and hostages."

Joel looked at Kio as if he had gone mad. "*Only*. Of course…"

"We are not going to wait forever," King Centreal said firmly. "If Gonaka and Kale go to war against Laen, The Kingdom of the Free is going with you."

"Stupid," said Joel, "absolutely stupid." King Centreal turned to Joel, plainly offended.

"And why is that?"

"Because if The Kingdom of the Free goes to war, Seagraul will kill the hostages. Outright kill them, there are no questions about it. It is already too risky to have Gonaka and Kale go to war with Laen— we cannot resort to war."

"He's right," Kio agreed, "We know King Seagraul. If he thinks he's going to die one way or another, he's taking those hostages down with him. He has no regard for human life."

"Then there'll be a rescue mission!" The king demanded. "I have men ready to set sail at a moment's notice in Doneaihr. They may have delayed, having received your message, but I can send them to Laeolin straight away."

"We have to make sure that it succeeds, if it comes to that," Joel told the king, "and we are working on it."

"I want Laeolin, Joel, and my people need to see their families. Tell King Nowhawna that we plan on bringing them to Skaen safely, with or without some master plan of his. I am considering sending the men on their way to Laeolin this very week."

"I will relay your message. But I urge you to be patient— I believe we can end this without further violence, and this is too delicate a situation with which to act rashly."

"I will accompany you," Kio said to Joel.

"Have you found any more evidence to connect the Skaelin Resistance to King Seagraul?" Centreal asked Joel.

"Not enough. I need more time."

"Well, keep looking— I appreciate your efforts, Joel. Fortune be with you both."

Kio and Joel landed at the Palace of the King of Gonaka, where guards in their armor and townsfolk in their plainclothes and servants in their very finest all bowed before and greeted them. With such an entourage they ascended the great blue stairwell that led from the entrance hall up to the main reception room, and there the king came out to greet them. "Kio, and Joel! What news from the Kingdom of the Free, and to what purpose do I owe the honor of both your presences?"

"News we have, my king, and Centreal has requested that either I or Kio return to him with an answer regarding a question he had," said Joel.

"What question is this?"

Joel looked at Kio, who understood more deeply the situation in Skaen, having been sent by Nowhawna to work with Centreal. Kio nodded and addressed the king. "King Centreal was attacked by a force from the Skaelin Resistance. We have strong reason to believe this particular force was arranged as an attempt on the king's life by the government of Laen. The king hardly escaped with his life— thanks largely to Joel here— " he said, at which point Joel swatted his hands, and claimed if it hadn't been for Big Litha's child, the whole village would have died. "…and took the few surviving villagers to Gatsesilli, where they await our word. The Skaelin force, before they went in for the kill of the king, delivered a message which we suspect comes directly from the Lonin government. The same demands that Seagraul has stuck to the whole time— he wants all the Freemen returned to Gaoln, which will again become a penal colony, and threatened to kill the hostages. Rightly, and thankfully, the Freemen refused this offer, and the resistance then said that every Gaolnian inside Laeolin would be executed. Centreal observed that many of his people wanted a rescue mission to try and recover their families and friends before they are killed. He emphasized also his desire, his need, for the mission to be carried out with great care— strength, speed, and stealth, if possible. He realizes the situation is extremely fragile, and seeks any opportunity to recapture the Gaolnians alive from Laeolin. We wonder, my king, if such a thing is possible following such news?"

"If it is not," Joel added, "I believe King Centreal and his army will feel the need to act on their own accord, which, although not their intention, would of course jeopardize the lives of the hostages. He does have teams assembled and waiting to embark from Doneaihr."

King Nowhawna thought for a while before making a reply. "I shall confront Laen on this the next time we meet, which should be as soon as possible. Joel, stay with me, I need to discuss some things with you, and I want you to go over these connections between the Skaelin Resistance and Laen. I presume Kio has told you all he knows. Kio, will you confront Laen immediately? Don't be too rash or bold— remember, this situation is very delicate. Handle it with great care. Find out if the prisoners have been executed or not, and if they live, ensure— on your life, on the life of King Centreal, on the lives of all the Gaolnians and Freemen— that they remain alive. Try to convince him to let the prisoners go. We will call a truce if the prisoners are set free and the Skaelin Resistance stops threatening The Kingdom of the Free, and if Laen stops threatening them too, but otherwise we will prepare to retaliate against Laen's offenses with the full force of our army. Make that clear. Good luck. I implore you to appeal to him as best you can, for everyone's sake," said the king. "As far as a rescue mission sent by King Centreal. Well, he will do as he sees best. If we cannot secure the safe release of the hostages, perhaps it is time to let him act on his own accord. We will not interfere, though our advice will remain unchanged."

"Certainly, my king," answered Kio. "What ever did happen with that skirmish between Kale and Las and Laen?"

"Ah yes," said King Nowhawna. "Laen lost no time in striking back— I dare say that it seems we are on the brink of war already. But we sent some aid to Kale and, along with Kale's forces, have seized the border posts in both Las and Laen in that sector, and even now Kale's ships are ready to blockade the coast of Las and take control of its ports should the conflict continue. So far it has not spread south, so the entirety of the Kale-Las border is peaceful still. Laen has not admitted to attacking Kale and so refuses to negotiate peace, as if it is some secret. The islands have received word of the situation, and Phenen joined with Las and Laen— they are trying to even the sides out so that we will feel the need for the conflict to end. We await a signal from them that they wish to end this unforeseen conflict under the terms we determine to be proper. If they do not provide such a signal, and forego a ceasefire promising such terms, we will attack. Of course, we all know Phenen is a great opponent of a Kingdom of the Free, even if they say that they are only marginally involved and that they are only against the keeping of hostages in Laeolin. The Skaelish are, as of now, out of this dispute— they saw what happened to their neighbors, the Skaelin, and want nothing to do with the war— of course, they are as much an enemy of the Skaelin as the Gaolnians were. The Skaelin will probably continue their small-scale attacks on the Kingdom of the Free, so some Freemen will have to remain behind, but the Skaelish may come to the defense of the Free Kingdom simply to prevent Celonis Sabero from retaking land west of his mountains. For the moment we are at an advantage, as the Skaelin have stalled and Phenen has not sent any actual soldiers or ships. Use that, temporary as it may be, as leverage in the debate, but don't flaunt it. He knows better than that. Be on your way now, the next Council begins soon," said the king.

Kio bowed. "Farewell my king, and farewell, friend Joel."

Joel bowed to his friend. "Good luck on your mission."

"Thank you. I hope I have it."

Kio was strapping in his legs and arms, about to leave from the palace, as King Nowhawna turned and spoke to him. "One more thing. Tell Las and Laen, and Phenen if you need to, when you reach the Council of Nations, that if Laen does not return every villager to The Kingdom of the Free unharmed, then as our armies will not stop. We will take Laeolin itself, without barter or negotiation, and will rule his country as a vassal. I won't risk Seagraul staying on that throne unless we come to terms. Say it as a simple fact, as I say it now." Kio hesitated, looking at the king with surprise, and Joel almost spoke up, but Kio did so first.

"They won't believe it. Seagraul will know you're just trying to scare him."

"He would be wrong!"

Kio shook his head. *As if Nowhawna would ever do such a thing.* The thought was ridiculous. "Laen holds the hostages, what if they threaten to execute them all at the first sign of you carrying out such a plan? My king, I assure you, as well as Joel and I know King Seagraul, we swear by it he will not cave because of this. You only do ill, my king. And if you did, it would mean the return of the Great Wars. This is not something we should even be talking about."

"I agree," said Joel. "Neither Las nor Laen will believe you would do such a thing, and they will execute the hostages if you ever attempt to— Seagraul would not stand for it. Please, do not issue this order."

King Nowhawna scratched his long, bearded chin, scrunching his face in thought. Kio and Joel were his two top advisors when it came to foreign affairs. Both of them adamantly agreed against him on this point. "We should consider this. Let us delay our coming, the Council does not start for some time anyway. Let's discuss this with Sela and the others. I want to establish a plan. If all else fails, we will aid King Centreal with a rescue attempt in Laeolin, but we must also ensure The Kingdom of the Free is safe in the absence of its king, should Centreal choose to come along. We cannot allow the Skaelin Resistance to seize power. Come— let's get on with it."

The room inside was dark, unlit by the passing sun to the south of the palace. King Nowhawna sat around the wide, round table, looking around at his advisors. "That is preposterous," one of the king's advisors proclaimed, "King Seagraul is, for all of his character flaws, a sane man. He would not execute the hostages, nor would he dare to say to the face of the King of Gonaka that he does not believe you have the audacity to raze his countryside and take control of his cities. He would not dare risk the lives of millions of people, the stability of the world as it is, hardly able to keep itself from war!"

"He certainly would, because he thinks he would win. He is sane, and wise— this is how he knows that Nowhawna would never dare to risk another Great War," said another.

"I assure you, I am willing to do this if I must!" said King Nowhawna, quite tired of reasserting himself. The advisors were silent, staring at their king with the same skepticism they had shown throughout.

"You're lying. Surely you don't intend to do such a thing? It would be worse than the murder of the prisoners at Laeolin!" said one of the advisors to his right.

"King Nowhawna," began one of the advisors across the table and to the right, "this is, as you know, a delicate situation. We cannot go in with arrows nocked and swords ready when they already have their weapons drawn. We are winning the war, if we're calling these border skirmishes a war now, but if you push too far, too fast, we may lose the hostages. That is, after all, what this so-called war is about— the hostages and the legitimacy of the Free Kingdom."

"I know, Sela," said King Nowhawna, addressing the advisor, "but sometimes to resolve delicate situations, you have to be very not-delicate."

"I don't really agree with that at all. I think we should develop this plan to seize Laeolin from the inside. We must make it flawless. That is the solution, my king, not more threats. Not the next Great War. If the hostages themselves are endangered, they will be moved, and so their captivity is risked. If we threaten them with words and deeds outside of Laeolin, if they see their leverage does not deter us from being monstrous enemies, that leverage will be executed," said Sela. Kio and Joel nodded.

"He is right, my king," said Joel. "You paint a bad portrait of yourself for the world if you do this, and you risk the survival of the hostages, not to mention the survival and well-being of the natives of Las and Laen, many of whom are secretly enemies of King Seagraul and could potentially aid us in the future. Seagraul will only keep the hostages alive as long as he sees them as useful leverage in his dealings with Gonaka and the Free Kingdom."

"What we need to do," said Kio, "as we have clearly established, is facilitate a swooping invasion of Laeolin, in collaboration with revolutionary Lonins already inside of the city, to carry out the swift and flawless escape of the hostages. We should prepare transports off the coast, and as we move in slowly on foot, the ships will draw nearer. It must be timed perfectly so that Seagraul does not expect to lose, and will therefore see no reason to forfeit his leverage. Ideally he will not even identify the disguised troops as such, and will not be aware of their gradual invasion."

King Nowhawna nodded. "We must meet with the Council of Nations. It seems the strong majority side against me. I will therefore withhold my threat to Las and Laen. But they must be confronted about their involvement with the Skaelin Resistance, which Joel has just briefed us on. This must be stopped— above all, the legitimacy of The Kingdom of the Free must be established, and the Council must recognize it. The entire Council, eventually, but I have other messengers and envoys working on that. For now I heed your advice, but I do not withdraw my plan entirely. We must take care of many things over the course of the coming days, and change a lot of opinions in the Council of Nations. We must not fail, and make no mistake— we will do everything in our power to ensure we do not."

- Chapter Five -

Every week Ciso would leave the academy with one of the seven fellow conspirators, and the two of them would scout the entire area where the hostages were held. In the hottest part of Trest, there was only a brief moment some time before the dawn when the city was asleep, so as the days grew hotter their missions became shorter. Every night two of the eight left together, and brought back a report. Sometimes they would scout the far-away barracks in the northeast of the city, to note the sleep schedules of various officers and regiments. Sometimes they would venture in the immediate vicinity of the tower to plan escape routes. Most dangerously, they would scout the tower area itself, to see precisely where the guards walked, how they moved, what might distract them, who they reported to and where that person went and for how long and what their habits were. The studies were intensive, exhaustive, and most of all very, very exciting.

They met in the small room in the basement of the academy one night every week to exchange these reports by the light of a single candle, their voices soft as hushed whispers the entire time. They would leave their dormitories at night, when they could not be seen sneaking through the dimly lit corridors, and return when the rest of the academy's students had fallen asleep.

One night Ciso was wandering through the halls, on the way to this weekly meeting, when he saw a familiar figure— a man of medium height and medium build with a long white beard, who stood there motionless as a tree, watching Ciso. Ciso turned around, and was sure, at once, of who this man was. "What are you doing here?" he whispered.

"Your mission is endangered," Menuld said, as if it had been obvious. "Do not go into that room tonight. Do not use my name. Do not talk about your friends."

"Are you still working for— "

"Hush!"

"But we have to do something, we can't— "

"Can't give them an excuse to act prematurely, and execute the hostages, is what you mean to say," Menuld said in the softest voice he could manage. "They overestimate your ability and the probability this mission has for success, not to say that your actions aren't admirable— but in their misled fear, they may feel the imperative to execute a number of the hostages as a demonstration."

"They won't if we free them."

Menuld smiled, but there was nothing in it of reassurance. "Your friends are safe," Menuld said, "and you will meet again in another location, at another time. The mission is not over. I would not let it be over. But you must not meet here in the academy— the new location must be out of your way, something which no one would suspect, and which is also quiet and not well-known."

"Have you made any progress yourself?"

"Progress, you might call it— we will act when the time is right. We will let you know. It will be soon, before the breaking of Sen."

"The breaking of Sen is still far away, and there are prisoners dying every day— "

"The breaking of Sen is the earliest possible time when we will be able to act. Seagraul will see that the prisoners are given more water in the meantime, to avoid ridicule while the diplomats tour Laeolin in preparation for their meeting. I will say no more. Our aim is to act before the breaking of Sen. But circumstances may delay our action, circumstances which are not under our control."

"How are the others doing?"

"Alive," Menuld said, as if that were satisfactory enough. "You should return to your room. I will find you later."

Ciso nodded. "Thank you."

It was the next week, around that same time of night, when Ciso returned to his room to find Menuld, Furnarwa, and Letharal sitting around in a circle, their heads hung low and their eyes set toward the floor. When he entered, they looked up only briefly, then returned their gazes to the ground. Ciso shut the door behind him, leaving the entire room immersed in the darkness. And then Menuld spoke.

"The Council of Nations is meeting just outside Laeolin at the breaking of Sen." Menuld waited, as if that simple statement could have explained everything— when he saw Ciso's curious eyes, he continued. "That is why we must wait until the breaking of Sen before we act, Ciso."

"We have friends in the Council," said Furnarwa, "powerful friends. And when they convene in Laeolin they will be giving us the chance to execute a real mission. At the same time that our own people, yourself included, will be freeing the hostages, our friends in the Council will be investigating King Seagraul and attacking him publicly in the Convention of the Council. We also know of those who might be interested to learn about how to break in to the area where the hostages are held."

"And that is why we need you," Letharal interjected, turning to Ciso. "Because you have that information."

"I will be coming to get you," Menuld told Ciso, "when the moment is right. And I need you alive to present information to someone who I think will be valuable in our rescue attempt. You have to stay alive, is what that means, Ciso— we cannot attempt a rescue until the Council of Nations meets, even if they do not meet until after their planned date. As it is, we will be waiting for some time."

"But," Letharal added, "we have a lot of work to do in that time."

"*I* have a lot of work to do in that time," Menuld said in the most exasperated voice he could manage.

Furnarwa smiled. "You really do. But we have our work too. Ciso— *your* work will be very important. It is imperative that you and your friends continue to monitor the area where the hostages are held. Menuld cannot join you. If he were caught, the political implications would be unimaginable— and myself and Letharal, well, our work requires us to remain shadowed in even more secrecy than yourself. Setting up underground safe houses is very dirty business."

"So," said Menuld, "in conclusion, keep doing exactly what you are doing. When the Council of Nations meets, be it fifty days from now or a hundred days from now, we can move forward. Until then, keep your followers under the cover and do not let them act."

Ciso nodded, and for the first time in the entire exchange, spoke. "I will."

- Chapter Six -

The shores of Laen were oddly beautiful. Much as he wanted to hate this land, Gendorn could not deny that fact. They looked almost similar to the shores of Port Tekal on a warm, cloudy afternoon, the gentle sort which was common for that part of Trest in their corner of the world. The white summer flowers were knee-high beside the grass that covered the earth, jutting out only a few feet above the sea. That was the only incline needed for the ocean to end and the land to begin. There was not a soul in sight.

It was discomforting to find a place of peace in a country which must be so wicked. Strangely nice, the young gulaus thought. Did the people who lived in such a quiet place know of their king's evil? Did they know of their part in allowing it?

They continued sailing east, within sight of the shore, until they came to the port of Eihar. Eihar, which guarded the mouth of the river as it fed into the ocean, was where they would find a boat going south along the river toward Laeolin. As the river ended just north and east of the city, they would travel the remainder of the journey by land. For the moment, though, they needed to pass inspections here on the shores of Laen.

Gendorn and Bendoraun both stared at the town with the most pensive of thoughts. One year ago they would have had their mouths hanging open and their eyes bulging wide at the sight of this place, yet now it seemed no more than a town. A town full of wicked men, at that. Aside from that, it was not altogether different from a town in Gonaka or in Skaen, but for the colors of the buildings being more blue and grey and the people themselves seeming colder. They moved very differently from the Freemen the two boys had left back in Skaen. These men were not as happy, their smiles not as broad, their eyes more cynical— what right had *they* to be so cynical, men who were born and raised free?— and, aside from all of that, there must surely be some darkness in their hearts. To serve a king so evil could leave no man with his innocence.

Inspections took the rest of the day. Everyone landing on the shores of Laen was being questioned, the harbormaster explained. Gendorn and Bendoraun, now being referred to as "Captain Gendorn" and "First Mate Bendoraun", had prepared for this. When the harbormaster had some of the crates opened up, he found timber and ale and metalware, sacks of grain and rolls of parchment and goods that must have been collected from half the known world. He nodded in approval.

Every man was questioned, and every man passed with his story. A random "Where are you from!" or "What is your profession?" or a deeper question following one of those two would receive an immediate and well-rehearsed answer. The most difficult question struck them hard enough. "What do you think of the rebellion in Gaoln?", the answer to which was universally: "Politics is not my business, good master." A nod of approval, and the man had passed the test. Then it was on to the next.

After the questioning was done, it was too late to set out. They spent the night by the docks, split between three different inns, and slept soundly without event. As the animals of the night came together in their chorus, Gendorn was again struck by the sharp contrast between the grace of this land and the malice of its people. How could people so blessed and fortunate behave with such cruelty? How could they harbor such cynicism, when they knew so little suffering themselves? *They don't know*, answered something in the back of his mind. *They don't even know*.

In the morning the men reunited. It was a smooth journey down the river, across the land, toward the heart of the nation. It turned out that this country was full of farmers and people who seemed to be regular enough. Some of them looked on foreigners with disgust, others smiled and waved and said "good day!", but most gave a curt nod and went about their business. There was a castle at one point, Benin if the maps were correct, which guarded the main harbor of the river as it led south toward Laeolin. Benin looked formidable enough, but there was no question about it. The Freemen would take the fort without difficulty, so long as Kale and Gonaka did their part in putting pressure on Laen's south and west and east and the garrison did not have the force to lead a counter-strike. And then would come Laeolin.

At Benin Harbor they changed ships to a sleek riverboat that carried them just to the north of the capital. It did not take more than four days, all told, to get from the ocean to just north of Laeolin. When they unloaded on the fourth day they proceeded with a large group of merchants who had taken the same route as they, and a good many of them were Skaelin. Gendorn and his company spoke as little as they needed to. No use putting themselves in a dangerous position.

But somewhere along the way they all took their own routes. Laeolin was a large city, and cargo of any sort would be headed to a different part of the city than cargo of another sort. So it was that when the city finally came into view, Gendorn and his company were alone.

The north gate was placed at the very bottom of the hill that rose north of the city. It was not a significant hill, but among the vast plains of central Laen it distinguished itself and managed to hide the city from view before their caravans stood on its summit. And from there, they could see practically every corner of the city.

Laeolin was like nothing they had seen before, and to be sure, they knew not a greater city existed on this earth. It was a great swath of civilization, an endless mass and chaotic clutter of houses and shops and winding streets of all sizes, of harbors streaming both sides of the River Aios that they could see clearly from their vantage, of fortresses and castles small and large, palaces and great towering embassies where foreign dignitaries lived in permanent residence, warehouses three stories tall but wider still than any warehouse they had ever seen, hundreds of them along the riverbanks. Hundreds! *God*, Gendorn thought, reverting to thinking as a strategist— *this city would never be starved out. Not unless they've enough millions of people to get through those warehouses.*

There were great manors and mansions of the rich on one end, the west and north corner of the city, and on the edge of this wealthy neighborhood was the complex where the Council of Nations would meet, a great circular building surrounded by the finest townhomes reserved for diplomats. But this elegant sight, and all the others put together, took up only seconds of their attention.

The tower in its shining blackness scarred the bright sunny sky as surely as anything ever could. It was a pinnacle of night defying the mid-day light, and there seemed to be a storm surrounding it, challenging the calm of Tun-Trest. It roared through the clouds and the empty sky both, high above the towers and the castles and the palaces, its shadows moving like the hands of a great clock over harbor and river and wide boulevards with shops and stately homes. It counted down, Gendorn knew, as surely as any clock ever had. Whether the men thought so or not was a matter for each on his own to decide.

He stared at the tower, and the men stared at it with him. They would attract little attention, as they had a rather panoramic view in any case, and people were sure to stop on top of this hill every now and again. There were no words between them, but this was surely no idle silence. Each man present looked at the tower and saw his children or his wife or lover, or his parents, or those he lived beside and grew up with. They were there, inside that tower.

How might they escape with nearly one hundred and fifty thousand prisoners from the middle of the world's most populated city, even after they had managed the escape from the tower itself? Looking at the size of the city, at the hundreds of thousands of people bustling about, Gendorn could hardly believe it might even be possible. But it had to be. If there was a way in this world, he would find it. If there was not, he would make a new one.

But it was an intimidating thought, all the same. As such, no man brought it up for discussion. They would take this one step at a time, or else the gravity and the impossibility of their task would overwhelm them. That had been the decision.

It had not been so between Gendorn and Bendoraun. Every night, along with the real ship captain, a Skaelish man by the name of Orax, they had brought up questions, discovered answers, and dismissed possibilities. Their escape from this city would be no wild improvisation doomed to failure. It would, in fact, be a significant advantage to have so many people rescued all at once. The king himself would not find the courage to stand against them. Not against one hundred and fifty thousand Freemen in the heart of the city. Not against two hundred thousand, Gendorn assured himself. With a smile, he imagined what it might be like. *We are not as weak as you think.*

- Chapter Seven -

The men had been four days in the city, and they were not altogether sure what to do now that they had gotten inside. Some of the men had volunteered to walk about the streets at night and frequent some taverns, just to measure how many people roamed about in the late nights and early mornings around different parts of the city. The whole experience of it was still rather new to them. There were entire roads where there was nothing but coppersmiths, entire boulevards where all they sold was jewelry and fine gems, entire districts where people were arranged by their trade and craft. *We will have to build something like this when we return*, Gendorn thought. Assuming this all went to plan.

The fifth day was the most interesting among them by far. Gendorn was walking alone just after mid-day when he saw a man who looked somehow familiar to him. The man approached him, broke into a broad smile, gave him a hug and spoke as if they were old friends. "How have you been, you sad lost soul?" The man exclaimed, and he put his arms firmly around Gendorn. Very firmly. Gendorn did not think he could escape if he had wanted to. "Let's spend some time and catch up, yeah?" Gendorn shook, but he could not break free. "I'm sorry if we left on bad terms, but would you forgive me if I buy you a few drinks?" The man was shoving him down the road.

Gendorn twisted around and replied, "No, I don't think I could forgive you. If you will stop bothering me, I have business to get to. I do not care to see you again." He was sure the people around him had heard. It was just enough to garner attention from passersby, but not quite making a scene. The man should have taken the hint, but he did not.

"I have a proposal you will be interested in, and I am sure you will forgive me when you hear of it." The man gave the slightest nod toward the tower, and looked at it for a moment quite pointedly. Gendorn examined the fellow, for no real reason, just to appear as if he knew what he was doing. And the fellow seemed all the more familiar, for some reason.

"I'll consider your proposal when I hear it," He said to the stranger. "Show me the way."

Which is how he ended up on the third floor of an artifacts museum sitting around a table with the Director of Ambassadors for Gonaka and a short old man with a long white beard.

The man on the street, it turned out, was Joel himself, and of course once Gendorn heard the name he remembered the face. The Gash were tall and well-built people, so his height and size alone did not distinguish him from his countrymen. But it was apparent, on closer inspection. His eyes, most of all, which could only be called awake. Those eyes never blinked. They always watched.

The short elderly man spoke to Gendorn: "You are looking for a man named Ciso, but he is already ahead of you. He has finished drafting his plans to rescue the prisoners. It is a matter of waiting, at this point, and of making sure we can house them all safely underground. They will not be leaving the city, except for perhaps a few of them. We simply cannot fit enough ships into the rivers, it is a matter of physical space, and anyways all of the ships are already booked and the harbors will be full. Are you wanting to meet him right away?"

Gendorn's eye must have been quite wide, and his expression something to see, because Joel actually laughed out loud. "Gendorn, this man's name is Menuld. He is a dear friend and he tends to rule most of the world either by convincing a king to do what he wants or subverting his rule when he refuses. He is here to help us get the prisoners safely out of the tower."

"Oh, good, well, good. Yes, right now, I guess. That would be fine." Joel's smirk was still prominent.

"Forgive me, Gendorn, I had forgotten to introduce myself. Yes, I will be here, but I am somewhat of a public figure you know, so I cannot go around talking with some dissident here and some "merchant from Skaen" over there, and colluding with them in common places. I will not be able to be in contact with you. I have been briefed on your story and I will help you reach Ciso. You have a message from his father, I am told."

"How in the world do you know all of this?"

"I was in Doneaihr just after you left," Joel explained to Gendorn. Gendorn was still confused. "Menuld knows everything that I know."

"As soon as you know it?"

"More or less." Gendorn gave up, at that point, and let Joel continue. "We will be taking you to see Ciso now, but we will not stay to talk. We will also be providing you with some things to merchant with in the markets, so that you do not attract suspicion. The rest of it will be up to you and Ciso, until the time comes for us to move openly." Joel rose. "With that, we should be off." Gendorn rose too, and Menuld followed.

"One more thing, young man, and listen well. If something goes amiss in the days ahead, war may come. If something goes horribly wrong, then it will be genocide and war to follow, and you will lose the sense of why you live. You will be tempted to take revenge on people, and do horrible things, and you may even become a terrible, frightening man. I have seen this happen to good people, Gendorn. Seagraul was one of those people. He was once a student of mine, and a good man, a promising man with vision and inspiration. Do you see what he has become? You fight a great evil, and in doing so it will be hard not to be evil yourself. Evil lives in the heart of every man. Evil can grow in the heart of any one of us. Evil exists inherent and it cannot be banished from our souls. The most terrible and most dangerous thing you can do to this world is to pretend like that evil does not live inside of you. Can you remember that for me?"

Gendorn, taken aback at the suddenness of it all, could only stammer a response, genuine though it was. "Of course, I will. I will."

Menuld nodded. "Good. I hope I will see you again." Gendorn turned to walk outside with Joel, but Menuld waved for Joel to stay. "A moment, Gendorn. We will be out in a moment." The gulaus nodded and went downstairs to wait. Menuld shut the door.

"What is it, Menuld? We shouldn't put the boy out there alone, it's dangerous." Joel took a seat, and Menuld did the same.

"You know what it is, Joel."

"We can't tell him. Not until all of this is over."

"We will tell him when we are ready. You will be seeing more of him than I will."

"I don't know nearly as much about these things as you do, Menuld. I wasn't there for most of it."

"No, but you know by secondhand, and that is good enough. If I ever have the chance to explain it to him myself, I will take it. After this war is over and I can share a much longer conversation with him in peace. That will be the time for me to tell him."

"Then what is this about?"

"This." Menuld reached into his bag and pulled out a great tome, a grey and black titan of a book with silver thread lining. The thing was half a foot tall and wider than the frail elder. There was only a single word on the cover, centered and italicized and in a rather small font for such a huge work: *Revolutions*.

"You don't intend on giving it to him, do you? Will he figure out that he is the child? He can't remember any of it. He couldn't possibly."

"He may figure it out, or he may not. I want you to tell him, Joel. If anything happens, I want you to tell him. I want you to give him this book."

"When? Not now. Not before the war."

"It is everyone's right to know who they are, and to know who their parents are. It is every slave's right to know why he or she was raised as a slave in a prison colony, just as much as it is their right to be free from that slavery. The right thing to do is to give him this book. It is the right thing to do."

"Think of the prisoners. They are depending on this man. We cannot give the book to him. Not yet. I will give it to him later, I promise."

"Make sure it gets to him."

"I promise, I will."

- Chapter Eight -

Joel led Gendorn out of the museum and southeast through the city. He was silent the whole time. "Ciso will teach you everything you need to know," he had said. And he must have been quite serious about it, for nothing else was said.

They reached the Academy of Laen while the afternoon sun was still hot and high in the sky. It was a large complex with a great face to it, circles of stained glass and statues carved into the whole exterior. The great oak and iron doors were surrounded on each side by a small carved alcove where a statue held a stone candle. Balls of stained glass served as the flames, and they glistened with a thousand colors all together. Gendorn did not recognize the statues holding the stone candles with the glass flames, but Joel must have. He bowed to one of them deeply, while the other he met with a glare.

When they entered the halls, it was as if a cool breeze had come right down from Skaen, and they both shivered. Gendorn's mouth almost dropped to the floor, and he felt like a fool at this point for how many times that had happened.

It was some of the most decorative stonework he had ever seen, that was for sure, surpassed perhaps by the palace in Gonaka and its Glorious City, or by the Great Hall of Gatsesilli. Every inch of carving was deliberate. The stone columns that held up the arches were wider than he was, and they reached fifty feet high before they hit the arches. The ceiling was as tall as a mountain. From the outside, it had been apparent this building would be nice, but every part of this building inside was as intricate as the statues outside. Great chandeliers hung from the centerpoints of the crosses, and they cast their lights all about one certain square of the grand hallway. Where one ended, the next one picked up precisely. There was not a flaw in this design, not one.

To his disappointment, they took one of the first turns down a side hallway, and could not continue walking down the great hall.

Each wooden door was only about Gendorn's own height, and they were packed closely together, so the rooms could not be all that large. They winded their way down the corridor and stopped abruptly at door number sixteen, so said the sign hung haphazardly upon it. Joel knocked, and a young man answered, whose face Gendorn recognized in an instant, and he could not hold his tongue. "Ciso!"

"Do I know you?"

"No, but I know your father." Ciso's eyes grew wide, though he looked skeptical. Joel rushed Gendorn inside the room and closed the door behind him.

"Ciso," Joel told the boy, "this is Gendorn, he served with your father's regiment in Skaen." Ciso's eyes lit up, and he gave his hand out to shake Gendorn's.

"An honor to meet you, then. Are you one of the slaves? You've come here to help free the rest of them?"

"I am and I have," answered Gendorn. "I'm told you can help me do that."

"I can and I will." That brought just about the biggest smile to Gendorn's face that he had known in a long, long while.

"Well," Joel interjected, "you two have to get to business, and I can't be seen snooping around the students' quarters or too many questions will be asked of us. I'll leave you two. Gendorn, I will have Bendoraun notified of your having found Ciso, and I will get word to him that he is to direct your company until you return. Ciso can see to your reunion when your time with him is done, and it would be wise if there is no contact between the two of you, after that, until the time to begin the mission has come."

"Thank you, Joel," Gendorn said, and Ciso thanked him too. Without another word, the ambassador bowed and left the room.

The man did not think that he had been seen, but Joel was not one to miss such a thing. As Joel entered the great hall, the man appeared to just be leaving from the same corridor, but instead of taking a right, he took a left. Now, that was a rookie mistake, and it gave him away as a spy on the spot. The corridor looped around, so it would have been pointless to return to the great hall, walk down its length, and re-enter the corridor from the opposite end, when one could simply continue down the path of the corridor and come to his or her destination that way. The individual did not look over his shoulder to see who was behind him, but Joel was so close at one point that any normal person would have out of sheer curiosity, if not alarm. Those two signs were irrefutable. Someone was reporting on Joel's whereabouts. *Or worse*, the ambassador thought, *they are reporting on Gendorn's*.

- Chapter Nine -

Gendorn was eager to get on with the recuse attempt, but Ciso took the time (and a lot of time it took) to convince the young hero that Menuld's plan was always the best. The Council of Nations could get the prisoners out safely. They were the will of the world embodied, and they could not be defeated by the madness of a single king once their voice was victorious in vote. Should Ciso and Gendorn fail in even the smallest regard before that time, the alarm would be raised in Laeolin, and, more likely than not, a great many of the prisoners would be killed. A rescue attempt would be made, but only if it appeared imminent that the Council would fail. Not too late, of course— before anyone would suspect it, but after the Council had made their best efforts and were near failing, if it came to that. No one would harm the prisoners while the Council still sat in Laeolin, because if Seagraul allowed it he would be forced to forfeit his kingship. But, this delay was a blessing, Ciso contended, for it allowed them to chart the movements, the character, the habits, the contacts and routines of every single individual who they needed to avoid or bypass in an attempted rescue, and it also let them memorize the safehouses and the code names of those arranging for them. Without this delay, their chances of success would not be so high. Ultimately, all of these arguments won out, and Gendorn told Ciso to show him the maps and charts and lists of information they had compiled so far. And so it was that all night long whispers passed between them, and even on into the next day they shared the ambitions of their noble young hearts and made plans to save the world.

Ciso spent a great deal of time copying the lists and charts for Gendorn's crew. Gendorn himself, raised a slave, could not read or write except for what Gulaus Kanel had taught him, so the copies were for his comrades who had spent their younger years as free men around the world. When Gendorn finally emerged from the room so many days later and reunited with Bendoraun, he told his men of all these plans, and he gave them the charts and figures. "We will begin the mission when the word comes from inside the Council," Gendorn explained to them. "In the meantime, let us pray that there is never the need for word to come, and that our families are returned to us safely sooner rather than later."

So Gendorn and his crew spent the weeks pretending to be merchants looking to set up a new permanent shopping area in a middle-income market district, something not too lavish to attract notice, but certainly lavish enough to justify spending weeks on end inside of the walls, and also to justify scouting different areas throughout the day and night so as to judge how visible one area was compared to another, in case any of them were questioned on the matter. In fact, they were able to lend a great deal of help to Ciso's associates, who could not get away with an excuse as legitimate as Gendorn's. And if there was a question about his eye, well, he lost it in the Southern Seas to the Pirate Confederation, and he hoped they all burned in Gaoln for it before the year was through. Gaoln had rebelled? Well, good for them, but to hell with those pirates all the same. "Politics is not my business, good sir," and that was the only proper way to navigate Laeolin in these times.

The days grew hotter, and then they grew cooler. In Skaen, the winds from the south did not come so often, and the winds from the north threatened to approach. The men there went about building their castles and their cities and making room for their futures to thrive, with all the faith in their hearts placed in the valor of their heroes to save their loved ones, while the women waited in a dark tower across an ocean cold where storms gathered at Trest's end. Those in Laeolin went about their days almost as if this Trest were any other Trest, smiling and laughing in the daylight because they knew that soon the cold winds would come to silence and still all the world.

Gendorn could not pretend those winds would not come, and he thought of them more as they drew nearer. Up to the highest reaches of the Black Tower the gulaus would look, and he would feel the wind cooler every evening, and know that one of these days there would come a wind more dangerous than the rest. It was all well and good to wait on the whims of some council, he thought to himself on such nights, but if no council would remove these people before the snows come, then remove them his own self he would.

One of those nights, the cold wind did come. Commander Luncas, on his porch in Doneaihr, rubbed his chin and rocked back and forth, and cursed the soldiers for rushing inside, cowards that they were. A whole war fought in a blizzard and they wouldn't train another day in the cold wind! He cast a sigh into the air and watched it turn into a cool mist. Sen was coming. Where was that stupid boy?

Alaisio did not know, but he hoped he had found Ciso and that his son was still fighting for what he believed in. Well, that was not the whole truth. The whole truth is that he wished he was back in the islands with him, that his son was young again and not so full of such foolish ambitions. Maybe, then, they could spend all their days together not worrying about whether or not they would ever see each other alive again every time they said goodbye. He wished a great many things had gone differently, and the cold wind on this night did not bring him back to those islands in the Southern Sea. All they did was remind him how far away from those days he had come.

Gendorn, well, he stood beneath the Black Tower, with Bendoraun beside him, and he knew that from another location, Ciso looked upon the tower as well. This wind was the first of the freeze-winds, those winds that came to mark the gradual end of Trest and which encouraged the farmers to harvest the last of their warm season crops. They would not be the worst of the winds yet to come.

As for the people of these countries, whether in Skaen or in Laen, those who had the company of families huddled together before fireplaces and cookpots and dinner tables where they shared their hearts and their harvests to warm themselves from the wind. And those without such comforts huddled inside alone, or beneath blankets in the alleys, and they turned their backs against the gusts. It would have been a dream for the weather to turn warmer, and to be sure, it would be temperate the coming day and for weeks still after that. But time moved only in one direction, and cold days followed close on the heels of cold nights. There would not be warmth again, once that time had come. Not unless they could whether through the cold.

PART THREE:
THE COUNCIL OF NATIONS

- Chapter One -

It was the first snowfall since last Sen in the city of Laeolin. It did not usually come so soon in the year. Juron was outside, watching the snowflakes fall upon the buildings and cover the land in white. How the snow fell around the perfect shining blackness of the towers in the city's heart seized his breath, and somehow it made him feel small, a momentary thing in a world more lasting. It looked rather majestic, he thought to himself, this tower of black rising out from the white snow. The snow would be gone in a few hours' time, of course, as this was only a cold morning toward the end of a warm season, and the day was sure to heat up even before noon. But while it lasted, it looked almost beautiful.

There was a feeling of peace about it all, and the peace lasted a long while. But anger followed quickly when peace began to waver. Anger was strong. There were many things at which to be angry.

Juron slammed his door shut behind him, and started to move to his desk when Menuld's voice came out from the other side of the room. "Haven't changed your mind, then?"

"No," Juron answered quickly, "and I do not intend to."

"Such a shame. It seemed to me, as I was watching you look up at the tower, that you may have reconsidered your...ambitions."

Juron's ears perked up, and his eyes grew slim as he turned to look at Menuld. "Ambition is a dirty word around here,

Menuld, in no small part because of you. And why would my ambitions have changed?"

"Not changed, no— reconsidered. The difference is that when one reconsiders their ambitions, they may realize that their ambitions are not, in fact, what they have been working toward, whereas when one changes one's ambitions, one realizes that the ambitions one once held are no longer applicable and makes the decided effort to pursue new ambitions, which tend to be in contrast with the older ambitions. I am not suggesting you change your ambitions, Juron. I am suggesting you reconsider them."

"Have you been in Laeolin this entire time, Menuld?"

"Where I have been is not your concern."

"And what have you been doing?"

"Also not your concern."

"Who have you been working for?"

"When, in all my years, Juron, have I worked for anyone, anyone at all, other than myself?"

"At least you answered one of my questions."

"You needn't have asked it."

"Thank you, again, as always, for your advice, Menuld."

"I suggest that you consider this as something more than advice, Juron."

"More than— what, are you suggesting I take it as a warning? Are you threatening me?"

"I am not strong enough for such a thing. Juron, we all make mistakes, but to make a decision already knowing that it is the wrong decision to make is sometimes unforgiveable. I would not forgive you, of course— but you should realize, also, that you will never forgive yourself." Juron's eyes, which looked more wary now, met Menuld's own, and in that instant Juron saw in Menuld's eyes the patient wisdom which let him speak so softly and kindly to a man who, by all accounts, he should desperately hate. Juron's stern face relaxed, and he looked at Menuld sincerely, as if looking at a dear friend.

"Menuld, I cannot forgo my duties. If I stepped down someone else—"

"If you stepped down, Juron, King Seagraul would rethink his strategy and realize that his tactics have been detrimental to his own interests— that they have come at the expense of popularity not only with his citizens, but with his most reliable officers. And that is a very good thing for him to have to consider."

"Be that as it may, this is my job, my duty."

"Your duty should be to Laen, to the country and its people. At the moment you are placing your priorities with the king at the expense of the nation and its people."

"The king is the will of the nation and its citizens, he dictates the national interest as the sovereign of Laen, and he is wiser than any citizen."

"We have debated on government enough times before, Juron. We should not concern ourselves with it any longer— it is not as relevant, anyway, to what you know is the right thing to do. You can talk yourself out of doing the right thing, convince yourself all you want, go over all the reasons in your mind. Or, instead of talking to yourself, you may listen. And I think you will find that it makes a very great difference indeed."

Juron nodded again. "Thank you, Menuld. I appreciate your time."

"I hope it is not wasted, Juron."

"I hope so too."

- Chapter Two -

The Council of Nations sat in a circle around a large brown and yellow table. Envoys, ambassadors, councilors, queens, presidents and kings sat side by side. There must have been at least forty people in the room altogether, with at least one person from each of the eleven nations in Fengorian. There were three envoys from The Kingdom of the Free and another two who represented the Skaelin Lands in the Eastern Mountains under

Celonis Sabero. There were even two emissaries from the Skaelin Resistance inside what was now the Free Kingdom, sent to argue their case to the world. There was also one ambassador who represented what were once the United-Independent Territories of Bautaulan, an archipelago in the southwestern corner of the world which had, over the course of the past sixty years, devolved into a set of colonies ruled by the more powerful nations. UIT-Bautaulan was not really a nation at all, but they were counted as such in the council out of respect. There were three councilors from Kale, King Nowhawna and Joel of Gonaka, King Seagraul and his chief advisor representing Laen, The Emperor of Phenen and his chief ambassador— nearly every leader of the world was present in the room on this morning, eagerly waiting to assess the prospects for their futures and each hoping they could shape them to their liking.

As Aniania, that massive island in the southern end of the Warm Ocean, was seen as being the most powerful nation to remain relatively uninterested in the Gaolnian-Skaelin and Gash-Lonin conflicts, and Aniania's leader, Acahna, had decided to remain uninvolved in either side during both of these conflicts, at least in these most recent years, it was her— President-Queen Acahna of Aniania— who would be this year's President of the Convention— the Convention, of course, being the assembly of the Council of Nations, known commonly as the Convention of the Council. She rose and welcomed the nations, and then told them to begin the proceedings. Beginning the first session, President Lokiey of Las addressed the entire assembly.

"Friends from far and near, I— we, welcome you to this Convention of the Council of Nations. Let us begin with the more important matters at our immediate hand— the war. King Seagraul and I have been swapping thoughts back and forth, and passing them on to our fellow officials. We believe it is time for this war to end. We are willing to negotiate, but only to certain extents. King Seagraul, you have something to say?" said the president.

"I do. Thank you, my friend— and let me also extend my own welcome to yet another assembly of the Council of Nations. I am willing to negotiate on many terms, and I have become more lenient on issues I was once adamant about— but let me reassure you all, I have not changed my stance regarding the government of New Gaoln. This Gaolnian government is an usurpation of the rightful ruling Skaelin, who for thousands of years inhabited the continent of Skaen. King Centreal is no more, in truth, than a governor appointed by myself, and for that I take blame, that I could allow such a risk to become reality. I did not think he would seize power and take arms against me or my allies, your friends. But so this is upon us, and I will— I say again— not compromise on this point. We also are firm on our decision to hold the Gaolnians in Laeolin until the government of the Skaelin Lands is returned to the Skaelin," said King Seagraul.

King Nowhawna was about to speak, and Joel, to Nowhawna's left, was very tempted, but both restrained themselves. The Free Kingdom envoys were visibly anxious. Nowhawna had asked them all to be silent, as they really knew nothing about the council or about Seagraul, and the King of Gonaka was more than confident in his own ability to deal with the King of Laen. Seagraul continued. "What we are willing to compromise on is our status in relation to Gonaka and Kale." He seemed disgusted to utter these words, as if they would poison him and everyone in the room, as if he were swallowing his own soul and imprisoning all his will and desire. "We are willing," the king went on, "to give to Gonaka and Kale our sincerest apologies, in several forms. We offer ourselves to rebuild the ruined parts of Kale we took in these recent offenses, and to send leneis to combat the ill we have done to both Gonaka and Kale."

Finally, King Nowhawna smiled. King Seagraul was surrendering, and offering to pay tribute to Kale and Gonaka. It was obviously a bribe, and nothing else, to keep the powers from intervening in this Gaoln affair. Nowhawna, seeing Seagraul had momentarily finished, spoke up. "What kind of aid do you speak of? How much, how often, when, and how?"

King Seagraul turned to King Nowhawna. "We are open for negotiations. We had a rough plan of a sum of 100,000 leneis a year, and also to extend our forces to help in any construction projects you desire. We offer teams of men who will aid in whatever purposes you require them for. We offer also food in time of famine, medicine in time of plague, and additional leneis in times of crisis, when and however possible."

President Lokiey spoke again. "And Las offers Kale and Gonaka annual reparations of 80,000 leneis a year for the next five years, and also our help rebuilding your lands. The division and return of land from and to both of our sides shall be discussed in depth, we decided, at some later time, if we can agree on these loose terms."

The Freemen looked openly worried by now. King Nowhawna scratched his beard, but he spared a reassuring wink for the escaped slaves. Joel whispered in the king's ears, while far to the right, several councilmen from the Council of Kale were talking amongst themselves. The Chief Councilman of Kale looked at Nowhawna, who shook his head no. The Chief Councilman agreed, signaling his fellow councilmen, who had arrived at the same conclusion.

"I am sorry, President Lokiey, and King Seagraul," began King Nowhawna, "but it seems Kale and Gonaka are also adamant on the issues of the hostages being held in Laeolin, and of the legitimacy of the new government in Skaen. We are simply unwilling to compromise on these points. The release of the hostages and guarantee of their safe passage to The Kingdom of the Free must be secured. The government in the old Skaelin Lands now under Centreal must be at least half Freemen." The Freemen nearly failed to hide their smiles.

Seagraul was quick to answer. "We will not compromise on this issue. We have made that clear many times before."

"As have we," declared the Chief Councilman. "King Seagraul, you swim against an overwhelming current. You resist the very movement and destiny of time and fate. The Kingdom of the Free is legitimate. It is not a question. Stop calling it 'New Gaoln'. The Freemen rule there, and they will continue to rule there. Gaoln, the prison state as we knew it, cannot exist any longer."

"And the Skaelin Resistance will trouble them no further," said King Nowhawna. "That, also, is one of our terms. Do not think your operations to topple The Kingdom of the Free and instate the Skaelin Resistance as the rulers of Centreal's lands goes unnoticed. They do not. Your direct involvement and support of these movements is well known. Also, we thought you should know, King Seagraul, that your attempt to murder the King of the Free in Freetown was foiled. Further attempts against the kingdom are being tracked and thwarted even now."

"I never did such a thing!" declared King Seagraul.

"Well, that isn't true," said Joel. Seagraul looked at Joel defiantly.

"I did not!" declared the king.

"Joel," said King Nowhawna, "perhaps you could explain to the Council the connections between the Skaelin Resistance and the government of Laen? And Las, at that."

"I would be glad to inform the Council, my king," said Joel, rising from his seat.

"Fellow men and women from across Fengorian: Three months ago King Centreal of The Kingdom of the Free was attacked. The force that invaded Freetown was highly trained, and they carried the banners of the Skaelin Resistance. They delivered a message to King Centreal. They said that if Centreal did not surrender the government to the Skaelin Resistance, the hostages in Laeolin would be killed. This is the first point that connects the Resistance with Laen, directly with King Seagraul, who has the sole authority to order such an execution. No authority in the Skaelin Lands or among its associated resistance movement in the west could threaten to kill the hostages, are those hostages are in Laen and quite obviously outside of Skaelin control," said Joel. There was a great deal of twitching and shifting about the assembly. Joel kept his smile to himself— he prayed he would gain favor for Gonaka and Kale with these arguments. They needed more support from the Council, if this was to work.

"And the second point is that the attack was an assassination attempt. The commander, from the start, issued orders to trap and kill the king. They did not want to weaken the strongholds, nor did they want to tear down the fortifications that were being constructed. Instead they wanted a new man on the throne— a man who would agree to their terms, who would leave 'New Gaoln'. The Skaelin Resistance was, before this, extensively tracked by King Centreal and Commander Denelu, prior to his death at Seun Bastion. Their hideouts are known, their supply lines established— and this brings up yet another point. I myself aided in the investigations to track the supply lines and sources of the Skaelin Resistance. What I found, along with Commander Denelu's successors, was that the supply lines were stemming from the east and the south— not the mountains, but the coast. They were coming in from ships sent from Las and Laen. Laen was the primary source, supplying large amounts of weapons, armor, food, maps— even men! Lonin tacticians and strategists were brought in, and several of these men lie dead in Skaen. We can show you the bodies, if you need more proof. Until the attack on King Centreal and the discovery of those bodies, the connection that binds all these points and incriminates King Seagraul and President Lokiey was only speculation. At this point, it is indisputable fact.

"What made me certain was what I discovered after the battle at Freetown. King Centreal was about to be killed by two

Skaelin soldiers, who were quite well-trained, when I arrived and rendered them useless, seizing their weapons. I proceeded to interrogate them separately, and though one, as expected, said only a few useful things, the other talked in great detail. He had been a captain in the Skaelin Army, at one point in charge of three separate regiments. Since before the death of King Sendroun, he had been scheming and working with the Skaelin Resistance. He was one of the top coordinators who ensured the Skaelin Resistance had a steady supply of goods after Sendroun's death. He noted several key locations that Commander Denelu and myself had already confirmed, and connected them to sites in Laen and Las, which we had also identified. But then he told us even more. In Las, it turns out, the provincial governors of the states of Leknus, Dwosur, and Fengar were all supplying the Skaelin Resistance. Through both state and personal funds these governors, along with their respective lesser officials, channeled goods and men into ships bound for Skaen. Here they were unloaded to specific people at specific points, where they were taken up into the hills or the eastern mountains— or in some cases other parts of Skaen. I have brought some of the shipping and processing papers for you to view and pass around here at the end of my narration. The situation in Laen was similar, except it was not only the provincial governors who schemed. King Seagraul himself ordered and coordinated the funding and channeling of goods to the Skaelin Resistance. By working together with less than legal contacts, some of whom held provincial positions under the governors, and one of whom— Governor Kleans— was a governor himself, Seagraul was able, for a time, to conceal these operations. I have many more details, and can go into further depth on these points— if the Council desires?" concluded Joel.

"You ass!" Shouted one of the Skaelin emissaries. Joel's mouth very nearly dropped to the floor. "You facilitate the sweeping invasion of my country, your allies burn my towns to ashes with the people inside them trapped—"

"Your country burned my people! Your country starved and raped and froze my people until they died by the thousands as slaves in Gaoln!" One of the Freemen chimed in, every bit as boisterous.

"Your people are nothing but pirates and barbarians!" The Skaelin man returned.

"Your country deserved to burn for what you did to us!" Said another of the Freemen.

King Seagraul rose. "Quiet!" He ordered, and the lot of them fell silent. Some of those gathered continued to shift in their seats, but most of the members were silent and dumbstruck. "You were the only one who knew of these things?" Seagraul said challengingly to Joel. "The only one who interrogated the man? The only one present who can verify those papers and those orders? Tell me, Joel, what happened to this man you supposedly caught, after he confessed these things to you. Did you take him to King Centreal, so that he could repeat his confessions— or did you kill him, deciding it was best you were only one to hear these words?"

"The man made me promise only one thing before he confessed to me, and that was that I would release him immediately after he told me these things," answered Joel. "I kept him bound, and released him when it was clear he would forfeit no more information."

The king laughed, and several members of the Council smiled. "So all of this relies, then, upon the word of one man?" inquired Seagraul.

"Not at all— far from it. King Centreal would testify just the same, as would all the surviving soldiers in Freetown, on the accounts of the attack and the message. Commander Denelu's closest ties can verify the source and drop-off locations, and the supply lines themselves, that support the Skaelin Resistance. There are many others who know, whose testimony may yet be heard— but for their protection I do not reveal their names. Least of all to you, Commander of the Skaelin Resistance," said Joel.

"I do not command them!" Protested the king. "You're one to talk anyway, to accuse me of supporting the resistance— you facilitated the escape from Gaoln in the first place! You gave them the ships, the food, the blankets, and training for their officers— you're the reason why this war began!"

"You are the reason it cannot end reasonably," Joel answered him.

"Enough," said King Nowhawna. "The Council of Nations has heard the testimony. Do they need further detail?"

Kings and ambassadors exchanged glances and signals throughout the room. The answer, it seemed, was no. Some of the members visibly scrutinized the papers Joel had brought, but none among them said a word. Joel's testimony was accepted, but not by the King of Laen. "How can you put so much trust in one man, one who is so clearly biased on these issues?" he demanded. "Surely he would contort your opinions for the sake and goodness of his beliefs, what he sees as the sake of his nation?"

"King Seagraul, we pray you be content," said Acahna, the President-Queen of Aniania. "It is well known throughout Fengorian, and throughout this Council especially, that Joel does not lie and that he has not in the history of his career. Questioning his bias and his character is, therefore, useless and irrelevant."

President Lokiey stood. "I wish to assure you, King Nowhawna, and you, the Council of Kale, and most of all you, Freemen, that if we can manage to come to some accords, to settle this war between us, I will do everything in my power to see any involvement Las has with the Skaelin Resistance ceases immediately. Those responsible will be brought to justice, if we manage some peace between us."

"I thank you, President Lokiey," said King Nowhawna. The Freemen, all of them still fuming, nodded in thanks, but otherwise kept quiet.

"Kale thanks you also," said the Chief Councilman. "But we wonder, is Las as adamant on those other terms of peace as Laen is? Perhaps, if they are not so destructively set in their views, we can arrange a peace?"

King Seagraul looked at President Lokiey, who seemed thoughtful for a moment. Finally, the president spoke. "We should discuss this further. Perhaps after this Council is adjourned," he said. The Chief Councilman nodded, as did Nowhawna. The Freemen and the Skaelin and the resistance fighters, all too angry to continue in a civil manner, nodded in agreement.

"I assure the Council I myself am not connected with the Skaelin Resistance, whatever those fools who tried to kill Centreal may have indicated," Seagraul protested. "If there is any government involvement, it most certainly is not on my level. You may review the financial records from my own offices—there is nothing I have set aside to support the Skaelin Resistance," said Seagraul.

"The evidence suggests otherwise, but in any case you still granted permission for those below you to support the Resistance, and so you yourself supported them," said Joel. "Because you knew of it and allowed it to take place, because you in fact ordered it, even if you did not allocate the funding, it happened."

"Those fools would have tried to kill Centreal anyway! They hate the Freemen to the bone, man! They would have sent their own armies— "

"Enough," said Joel. "King Seagraul, you have been discovered. Your plots are known. Your stance is clear, but your vision is clouded. You lose this war. You lose land and people and power and wealth. You betray the goodness of your country by not allowing this war to end. Let the Gaolnians go, King Seagraul, and cease immediately your support of the Skaelin Resistance."

King Seagraul stood up. "You dare to accuse me of violating my own people? You are the one whose armies march now to prepare for an invasion of my own land! Your soldiers frighten our citizens on the border, and you——"

"Must I remind you," Nowhawna interrupted, "that you began this conflict with us by attacking Kale three months ago, around the time that you invaded Freetown?"

"I will not stand here," said the President-Queen Achana, President of this Convention of the Council of Nations, "and listen to you two argue back and forth. We have a lot of business to attend to, and unless we can agree on something and stop our fighting, we must dismiss this day's deliberations and meet again tomorrow when we are of a cooler temper and have had ample time to consider these revelations."

"Then I call this meeting dismissed!" Seagraul shouted. "I will not stand here and listen to this man——"

"king——"

"insult me and accuse me of treachery and conspiracy! This meeting is over, and if I should decide I have any further interest in the Council of Nations I will return sometime this week. Goodbye!"

And with that, King Seagraul turned away and stormed out of the room, followed by his two officers. The Freemen and the Skaelin were not speaking with each other. Kale and Gonaka both ignored Las, which showed no interest in any of these parties. Phenen's delegation looked as if they wanted to leave right away. The President of the Council surveyed the room and found not one person bold enough to speak, or of a cool enough temper to say something useful. And in such a disagreeable way ended the first day of the Convention.

As the King of Laen walked down the hallway toward the exit, he looked over his shoulder and yelled at one of the men: "Get Juron. Tell him to meet me in my office. I need to see him immediately."

It was just after the breaking of the Convention, as King Seagraul was speaking with Juron in the Palace of Laen, when

Menuld appeared again in Ciso's room. Ciso, who had been about to go to sleep, saw him standing by the open door. The door closed, and Menuld lit a candle. When he spoke it was in a strange and hurried voice that Ciso had never heard Menuld use before. "Tonight," Menuld said. "King Seagraul has left the Convention of the Council. He stormed out of the room and demanded an audience with Juron. I am very afraid that it will be tonight, Ciso, when King Seagraul makes a demonstration and executes some of the prisoners. It would show his resolve— yes, I am certain, some of them will die tonight."

"Should I move? Should we gather together— "

"There is no time for gathering together all your followers— we will wake up anyone in these dorms who is in your group, there should be four of them? And move out tonight, Ciso."

"And where will you be going?" Ciso asked, already out of bed and getting his clothes on.

"I will go to the Council of Nations, and see if I can intercept those whom I most need to speak with, and if I can we stand a chance at averting a tragedy. Pray to Fate for me, Ciso, and may Fate be with you. I will see you in the morning, when hopefully the news we have to report will be good news. If you see anything out of the ordinary going on about the tower, send word to Gendorn and his men, and they know how to reach the individuals I have been working with. You can have a small army beside you, if you just say the word. If anything at all looks anything except perfectly normal, send word to him, and he will come right away after dispatching a messenger to those who have been arranging the safehouses."

Ciso nodded. "I understand. Thank you, Menuld. We'll leave immediately."

It was hardly an hour later when Menuld burst into the Palace of Laen. The corridors were very dimly lit, and there were no sounds inside the building. Menuld rushed toward where the council had convened, and threw the doors open. The room was dark. Every seat was empty. The Council of Nations had been dismissed.

Furnarwa came up behind him, and Letharal behind Furnarwa. "You know where he is staying, here in the city, of course, don't you?" Furnarwa asked. But the question was not needed— Letharal and Furnarwa could tell by the expression on his face, that solemn and grave look, and by the fact that he had suddenly stopped moving, as if his mission had ended, that Menuld did not know where the representatives of the Council of Nations were staying.

"I do not. They keep every representative's location a secret, and they have doubles disguised as the representatives living in different locations throughout the city. These doubles, and the representatives themselves, change residence twice a week, according to an irregular pattern, and also randomly switch themselves with the doubles disguised as them. We need to find Joel, but he was unexpectedly given a new residence when the Council convened and I have not established contact with him since. I do not know where Nowhawna is, or Seagraul, either."

"So we'll go to every location, and break down every door!" Letharal said. Menuld turned to Furnarwa.

"Furnarwa, go set up your system. The time to act is tonight. I do not know if any order has been given, or if Juron will, in the end, execute any of the prisoners. I pray he does not. But something is going to happen tonight. Make sure the safe houses are ready. Go now." Without a word, Furnarwa turned and left the room.

"Menuld," Letharal persisted, "give me the locations— I swear I will search every one of them."

"We do not have the locations."

"Why not?"

"Because the man who was tracking these locations and their arrangement has been captured and killed." Letharal was silent, searching for words she could not find. "King Seagraul always intended to kill the Gaolnians, can you not see it? He never intended on negotiations. This was what he wanted all along, an excuse to kill them. He's going to do it tonight. I know it. They're going to die tonight."

"I will search the palace if I have to— "

"No. You and I will both be spending this night around Laeolin. You should help Furnarwa direct the Gaolnians to the escorts who will lead them to safety, if there is a confrontation tonight that ends in some sort of escape attempt. I will be searching the buildings and offices around the center, looking for evidence of where this man might be staying. But if it comes to it, I will join you and Furnarwa in directing the escapees to their escorts. Ciso will be sending word from the tower itself to you and Gendorn. Be ready to move with them."

"Menuld...yes, alright. Good luck."

"I hope it may be ours tonight."

- Chapter Three -

Kamira was worried. The guards had not come in that evening to give them their daily meal. It was the first time they had ever not shown up. There was talk among the prisoners that they had been left to starve here, that King Seagraul had given up and wanted them all dead. It was the quietest way to go about it, by just keeping them locked up in this tower. The public would find out eventually— but it would be too late.

There was banging on the door that night. The prisoners on the ground floor were trying to escape. The guards, outside, were yelling something at them— Kamira couldn't tell what it was. Word reached her that the prisoners on the ground were going to make a run for it— they were going to tear down the door and run out from the tower. Kamira knew it was the right choice— she, herself, was already on the verge of starvation. The first snow had fallen, and it would not be long before sickness spread in one form or another. They would die here or die trying to escape, and that was it. Waiting was not an option.

Sometime in the mid-night the door burst open. Out from the tower, a horde of Gaolnians rushed into the courtyard. Kamira could not see, but there was a woman by the window, watching it happen. "There's archers everywhere," the woman told them, "they're being slaughtered!" She whispered. She froze in mute horror, and an elderly man shoved her rudely out of the way to see what she had seen. The woman, still mute and frozen, started to cry. The man spoke with authority: "They're being slaughtered, all of them! They're shooting them even before they come out from— They're coming inside! They've got swords all bloody and they're rushing inside the tower!"

Kamira could hear the screams from below, and the sounds of people struggling for their lives, an unarmed and half-starved mass against a small group of armed and well-trained soldiers. The tower was a scene of total chaos. Some people were trying to rush down the floors to fight the soldiers, or to try and escape between them. Others were trying to reach the top floor, thinking the soldiers were only retaliating against people who were trying to escape, and that they would be safe at the top. People could hardly move at all. "Go down!" urged Kamira. "Down to the bottom, they're trying to come up to kill us all! Run!"

Juron stood numb and at a distance. How could it be that so many died so quickly? Was what he saw even real? The frail and the sick fell by the hundred. The armored soldiers of Laen ran over them as easily as they would have run over a green field of grass.

King Seagraul had lost his temper, finally. "You have to march in there, Juron," Seagraul had told him, his voice deceivingly calm, "and kill them all. We can't risk an uprising. They must die."

"They are only banging on the doors, my king."

"They're banging on the tower doors, Menuld is looking for my door, and the Council wants Laen to roll over and die. I can't do this anymore. Kill them, Juron. Kill them. They mean nothing to these great advocates of freedom and humanity, nothing at all. All they want is their land and their money. Their demands would be the same if the prisoners were dead, and frankly I don't care for them being alive. You have your orders."

"My king, I am sure they will stop banging, even if we make an example of just a few of them—"

"Make your examples, then, and if your example does not suffice, then you have your orders and you will obey them."

"I serve and obey, my king. I always do."

Serve and obey. Blood had starting running through the cracks in the stone. *Serve and obey.*

What had happened? Some of the prisoners were shouting curses and banging on the doors, and Juron followed orders. He took out a small group of the protesting hostages and had them executed, but instead of filling the rest of the hostages with fear, they hadn't even been able to close the gates and lock them back down. The prisoners poured out in the hundreds, the thousands, an endless streaming mass, and the soldiers, well, they panicked. They filled them all with arrows, volley after volley after volley. Then the panic died, and for some reason it kept happening. A few of the guards found their friends dead outside the tower. They went inside the tower, and Juron could hear the effects of their intrusion. And somehow Juron found himself frozen in the tower courtyard with screams and dead bodies everywhere.

Beside him, the five students they had found were pinned to the ground. Two of them had already been killed. Three others— Nadur, Ciso, and Jiheh, Juron had learned— were being kicked and rolled around in the snow, their hands bound behind their back. "Who else is coming!?" The interrogators demanded, "who set this up, who sent you? Who knew this was happening tonight!?" But none of the students answered. Ciso rolled his body around so that he could look at Juron, who stood there quietly, and waited for their eyes to meet. He didn't say a word, he just stared at Juron. Then Juron tore his gaze away, and looked at the interrogators. "Kill those two," Juron told them, pointing at Nadur and Jiheh. The soldiers shot an arrow into both of them, and they became motionless, their blood spilling into the snow. "And now," Juron said, turning back to Ciso, "could you tell me, in words, what your eyes almost told me just now? Who sent you, Ciso?"

Ciso saw, out of the corner of his eye, another three students, who had come as a separate team. They were waiting in the shadows behind the buildings, and he knew that after he himself died, those three figures standing in the shadows would make sure the Gaolnians were set free. They would have already sent a runner to Gendorn, and another to Menuld. From the corner of his other eye, he saw his four dead friends beside him. "I act on my own accord," Ciso answered. "which is more than you can ever say for yourself."

Juron's eyes and ears flared up in anger. Without any hesitation, he issued the last command— "Kill him."

The soldiers took the tower, floor by floor. Kamira could hear them as they drew closer, and as she fled down the stairs. "Come on!" she urged everyone as she passed. "They don't have our numbers!" There was only a small group following her, but she led the way. When she got down to the sixth floor, she stopped in her tracks. Three swordsmen were blocking the stairwell down to the fifth level, and no one else was there— everyone was dead. Behind her, the rest of her followers came down and looked at the soldiers. From the stairs below them, they heard more soldiers coming up. But there weren't any more Gaolnians coming down.

The bows were aimed right at them, and Kamira stood motionless and in shock. From behind the troops one single bloodied Gaolnian came up the stairs, and threw himself on the soldier in the rear. The archers looked away, and the Gaolnians dashed forward. But when they realized it was only one man, the archers turned around quickly, and fired into the crowd. Two fell dead. They jumped on the archers and took their arrows, but the swordsmen fell upon them swiftly. More soldiers were coming up the stairs, but now another wave of Gaolnians— a larger wave— had come down. They jumped the swordsmen and wrestled for their weapons, while Kamira's group kept fighting the archers with their own arrows and their fists, making sure the others didn't get shot. Two of the Gaolnians got swords, and they stabbed the archers, then Kamira picked up a bow and some arrows, and the others did the same. They turned and shot the guards in their exposed necks— Kamira did not hesitate for a moment on the first person she killed.

The Gaolnians rushed down to the fifth floor, where they saw that another group of Gaolnians had taken some weapons and claimed the floor. They were holding up at the stairwell down to the fourth floor with some archers, and the guards could not advance. For a moment, Kamira didn't know what to do— they were locked in a stalemate. She knew the longer they waited, the more guards there would be to fight— but if they charged, they would be massacred on the stairs, one-by-one, shot as they came down. Some more Gaolnians came down now, most of them unarmed. "There's more of us on the two levels above, and some coming down from the top," said an elderly man with a stern and aggressive face. "We're ready to push when you are— we can't hold up here forever."

"Do we have enough people?" wondered another elder.

"We have more than a thousand now, between all of us willing to fight, and another two thousand at the least looking to escape. We have to rush them now, before they get reinforcements," the first man answered. Some of the others nodded. "The rest of them, the ones who won't leave now— they'll come later. As soon as they comprehend what is happening right now, they'll risk their lives fighting to get out of here. They are in denial, still— telling themselves they won't be killed. But they'll come to their senses."

"Let's go then. On three— and we can't pull back. We'll have one chance to make this work, and that's it— no retreating from here." Everyone nodded. Another crowd of Gaolnians

came down. The man counted to three, and some Gaolnian
archers ran down the stairs, arrows nocked and ready to fly, with
the infantry behind them, followed again by more archers.

Kamira followed them down, caught in the middle of the
rush. She saw the dead bodies of the people who had gone first,
some of them girls her own age— but she had no time to stop
for them. She trampled over them with the rest of the crowd and
tried not to get her feet caught between the arms and legs
crossing one another as she rushed over them. A number of
people tripped and fell onto the bodies. At the bottom of the
stairs she saw five bodies of the larger, armored Lonin soldiers.
There were a few more coming up the stairs, so she took aim,
ready to shoot them as they came. But someone pushed her aside
as they were coming down the stairs, and as the soldiers came up
Kamira fell over. Right where she had been standing, an elderly
man with a bow took aim, but the Lonins were faster, and they
shot him in the heart.

The soldiers rushed them, but there were far more
Gaolnians now, and they came running down the stairs as a mob
flooding the room. Men and women and children as thin as bones
threw themselves by the dozen onto strong men with sharpened
swords and polished armor. The Lonins pulled back to the next
stairwell, and the Gaolnians regrouped again. Their numbers
were higher— in spite of all the people who had already died,
then, they were stronger— that meant more of them were
fighting. More of them were working together. They took the
next stairway in the same manner, though the fight was harder.

Kamira and the rest of them almost stopped in their tracks
in sheer terror as soon as they began to rush the third floor.
Twenty arrows loosed all at once. Elders and children and
women of all ages fell dead where seconds ago they had been
living and breathing before Kamira's own eyes. It was only
because the archers needed to reload that the Gaolnians found
the courage to continue their assault. But the archers drew
swords. Each Lonin soldier could fend off seven or eight of these

emaciated prisoners. The Gaolnians were tossed about like pebbles and cut through. Time after time, Kamira's life was saved by mere chance. A body fell on her and took an arrow that had been meant for her. That was when she faltered, and her heart, at last, nearly gave out. But she, like every Gaolnian on that night, pressed on.

The stairwell after that was well defended, and they lost more than they counted— but soon they were on the bottom floor, fighting for control of the base of the tower. Kamira stood toward the front— those who had previous experience with swords and bows now insisted on going in front of all those who hadn't, which was the vast majority of them. But Kamira followed right behind them, hollering for those behind her to hurry down and pressure the Lonins. The Gaolnians raised a shout: "We're taking the tower!"

They pushed the Lonins back, Kamira firing from behind the front lines, until the last armored swordsmen walked backwards out of the door. The Lonins closed it quickly behind them, and locked them in, then they barred the door. The Gaolnians smashed against the barrier like the ocean upon a rocky shore, but like the waves their single charge made no difference. They hit it again, and again nothing happened. They tried again— nothing happened. Some of the archers shot at the old doors, but with their limited supply of arrows it soon became obvious this was not the best solution.

Some older swordsmen hit their swords against the sides of the door, trying to prop it open. Others went up to the second floor, to see if they could escape through the window. But the window was locked and sealed from the outside— at some point this building must have been rebuilt to keep prisoners inside— and the door would not budge more than an inch. Kamira ran up the tower with a small group of people, to see if anyone had found another way out. None of them had. They had been locked in and could not escape.

- Chapter Four -

Gendorn was making good work of it, but it wasn't good enough to satisfy him. They had intercepted both messengers that had been sent from the tower to ask for reinforcements from the barracks, and Bendoraun had left men at the interception points to find any who might be sent after. The only fighters in the city who would arrive to help would be his own men.

Ciso was not responding to the messages. He could not be found. Three other students had been found dead. Five of Gendorn's men had been found dead. Now twenty-two of them moved together with Bendoraun and Gendorn, swiftly and not caring about who saw. The screams that had come from the towers gave it away. No one would ask questions about a band of armed men running around the city after hearing those screams. They would be inside with their doors locked and their eyes shut tight. The entire city was hiding from the night, doors locked and lights out, pretending like they could not hear the screams, like they didn't know what was happening. It was enough to make Gendorn want to kill them.

There was something odd about the perimeter of the Black Tower which made him call his men to a halt. There had been shouts and screams before, the kind of noise people made when they were killing and dying. The only shouts now were orders between officers, and the only noise from the towers and the buildings surrounding them was a terrible, horrible, sad and desperate crying. The fighting had ebbed. Was it over?

He looked over at Bendoraun, who was alone edging along the side of an adjacent building. Bendoraun slipped back beyond sight of the guards, and flashed fingers at Gendorn. Fifty-two. Fifty-two soldiers. If Gendorn and Bendoraun rushed them now, they would need to kill three men for every one they lost just to have two men surviving to open the doors. They might have managed on a night when the men were less alert, but these men had eyes as wide as the moon. They would not make it into the courtyard without being stuffed full of exactly fifty-two arrows, and not a single one less. Bendoraun had flashed that too, with a simple signal that meant *do not advance*.

Gendorn, in any other scenario, would have listened to his best friend. But as he was settling down and considering his next move, there came a great crashing noise from the Black Tower. Gendorn looked at Bendoraun, who signaled *I don't know*. Gendorn signaled back. *Prepare to advance*.

Everyone heard it— the loud crashing sound of shattered glass. One of the women hit the glass with her sword again, and the window fell to pieces. An arrow came right up from the ground, as soon as the glass fell, and hit the woman in the right breast. She fell over, and died in an instant. Kamira, who stood right behind her, almost vomited— the woman's head had almost landed on her feet. She turned and ran back down the stairs to the first floor, just in time to avoid a stream of arrows coming up through the broken second-floor window. Everyone either ran up to the third floor or followed Kamira to the first, with the exception of only a few brave marksmen— a group of three women and an elderly man— who fought back, firing down on the Lonins. Within minutes, they had either fled or been killed— there were too many arrows coming in.

Kamira heard screams from the floors above her— people arguing violently, but she couldn't make out the words. Some of the others ventured up to the second floor, and all but one of them made it to the third floor alive, through the stream of arrows. Kamira went up, but paused at the top of the stairwell. The woman at the other end shouted to her: "They've taken all their clothes off! They're trying to make a rope to climb down to the ground from this broken window!" Kamira shook her head in disbelief. They were all going to kill themselves!

"Tell them they're all going to get killed!"

"That's what they're arguing about," the woman replied.

"They can't climb fast enough, and there's too many archers!" Kamira told her.

"I know!"

There was a shout from below, and then the first floor exploded in noise. Kamira ran back down to see what was happening— just as the door opened up and the Gaolnians in front of her rushed outside.

Kamira did not follow them. She was about to, when she saw what happened to the first rows of people who escaped from the tower. The first wave of them rushed out like all the ocean, sweeping across the courtyard— and then the entire mass of them fell into the snow, and the blood poured out of them— they had been shot full of arrows, all of them. There were lines of Lonin archers posted on the sides of the courtyard, one behind another, firing at the Gaolnians as they escaped. Every single one of the people who ran out from the tower got cut down by the volleys, and Kamira found that soon she and three others who had remained behind were the only ones alive on the bottom floor. Together, they turned and ran up the stairs. The arrows had stopped coming in on the second floor. And Kamira knew in an instant what they had to do, if any of them had a chance of getting out alive.

By now, almost everyone in the tower— just less than twenty thousand of them— had resolved to escape and try to overrun the Lonins and get out of Laeolin. There were several ex-military captains, and one old ex-Lonin commander guiding and dividing different groups. Kamira was assigned to one of the groups that would run out from the base of the tower, which was the larger group. They would take a left out of the tower and attack the archers on the side who were firing in, and call for reinforcements if the Lonins had posted additional archers further around the tower— no one knew if they had encircled the tower or just prepared to defend the gate. Several smaller groups would provide diversions by climbing down the clothes-ladder from the second floor and by firing out the window, defending themselves with the few shields they had taken from the soldiers.

Kamira stood back as the first wave of Gaolnians ran out from the tower and as the Lonin archers mowed them down. But the second wave ran down from the floors above and closely followed the first wave, so that the Lonin lines didn't have time to fend them all off or reload. Soon after the second wave departed, Kamira ran out with the third wave, and turned a sharp left, where there were still some archers alive.

The courtyard was littered with bodies. Some of them were naked, and had fallen dead from the rope. Some had weapons— most did not. They were all dirty, and their brown bodies covered in their grey clothes sat almost naturally in the white snow. The rain was coming down, it was cold and hard, freezing as it fell, packing the snow. Kamira could hardly see, but she saw the old woman in front of her as she fell over backward and did not get up. Behind her more Gaolnians were rushing forward to overtake the lines. But as they fell upon the tower guards, a formed line of Lonin infantry stepped up to confront them.

She stood back where they couldn't get her, firing her arrows as the sword-bearing Gaolnians ran to the fore. Everywhere she looked, the snow was hardly visible— bodies were piled atop one another. She ran forward when there was a break in the Lonin lines, just after the infantry stepped up. "Don't break the line!" shouted a Lonin commander from afar. "Keep them enclosed!"

Kamira was already out and on the other side as he shouted this. There were others all around her, maybe a hundred of them in all, but then the soldiers closed the line and beat back the prisoners on the opposite side. Some archers were firing at them from another location, but they couldn't make it out in the freezing rain and the black sky. Somewhere beyond their immediate vision there appeared to be armored men fighting other armored men, soldiers fighting soldiers. Whose soldiers would dare?

"They're only concerned about us, see?" said Kamira. "That means the others are already dead. In the other towers and the

buildings. They aren't going inside there. They must be dead."
Her pace slowed a little, but the old man behind her pushed her
forward.

"Keep going," he said, "we need to find a place to hide.
They'll be after us immediately." So the lot of them, less than a
hundred all told, ran into the first building they could find that
wasn't being watched by the Lonins.

Kamira could hardly even pay attention to what she was
doing. *They're all dead*, she couldn't stop thinking. *That's why they
were only focused on the Black Tower. Everyone else was already dead.
They were already dead.* She kept thinking this, still she could not
understand.

None of them knew where they were, actually. They were
all sitting on a cold stone floor, shivering. They huddled together
as closely as they could, still drenched and frozen from the rain,
and their bare feet were completely numb from the snow. It was
an old, abandoned building, down one of the alleys away from
the central area where the tower stood. There wasn't anything
for a fire around them, and it was getting darker. "We won't be
able to walk, if we wait too long," one of the women said grimly.
"That happens when your feet get too cold."

"Where can we go?" asked the old man, "does anyone know
this city?"

None of them did. "We should go now," said Kamira. "The
rain has stopped, and it's still dark. The soldiers will break free
from their engagement and come after us when they do." Who
were those other soldiers fighting them and keeping them from
this building?

"What about warming ourselves? We need a fire now— we
need to find someone who can help us," said a young girl.

"There isn't anyone," a younger boy told her.

"They'll be searching all around here," the old man said.

"That's right," said Kamira, "no one lives here— they'll
come here first, because they know we wouldn't have risked
asking for refuge with this many people."

Some of the others nodded. "No one will give us refuge," the young boy said sadly.

"We can give ourselves refuge," Kamira told him, "we just have to get out of the city first."

"Are you mad, young lady?" an older woman said to Kamira. "We've got no shoes, we've hardly any clothes— some of us are stark naked! We have no food, and we can hardly make a fire out in conditions like these, when the whole forest is wet, iced over, and coated in snow! We wouldn't last the night out there!"

Kamira lowered her head. The woman was right. "What does that mean?" she asked them all, "should we split up, and try to find houses that could offer us harbor?"

"I don't wanna leave," said the little girl, "I want to stick together."

"I'll stay with you," said the younger boy. Kamira could not smile, but she would have in an earlier age. She wanted to look after them both— but she knew what they had to do. She turned to the woman next to her, who was maybe ten years her elder.

"We should assign each child to a woman, and each man too, if we can— and match their ages. We have to make them look like families," Kamira said, "no one could refuse refuge to a family out on the streets, if all they ask is for a night. Even if we are Gaolnians, and even if everyone in the city knows by now what has happened." The woman nodded.

"The girl is right," said the old man. "we need to split into family groups. And whoever's left over can pose as odd groups— a grandparent and grandchild, or something like that. It's the only way we could all be rescued. But where will we go after that one night?"

"We can't meet up again," said Kamira, "it would be too dangerous and suspicious. We just have to see what we can do."

"We could try meeting outside the city," another woman said, "and leaving the country, to Kale. Kale would give us a place to live, once they hear what we've been through."

"Do you really believe that?" asked an older man. "They sat by generation after generation while we all suffered in Gaoln.

They did not do anything to help us, through sixty-five years they've just watched us. Why would they care now?"

Another silence ensued— the rain was picking up, and it got even darker. "We need to go now," said one of the women, "and we can't meet again."

Kamira nodded. She took the hand of the young boy, who turned to face the little girl. "Good-bye," he told her. The girl looked very sad.

"Good-bye," she said.

As soon as she and the young boy left the room, they saw a tall figure standing in the snow, staring at the house, and Kamira, wasting no time, let go of the boy and charged at the figure. The figure caught Kamira and held her still, then whispered into her ear: "There is a man who will guide you to your safe house. He is standing behind this building. He will not speak to you. Follow him, and do not talk. Grab the boy before he runs away, he's frightened."

"I'm frightened!" Kamira replied, "who are you?"

"Leave."

Kamira took the boy's hand and led him behind the building, where another shadowy figure was running through the snow, without looking back. She followed him in silence. She could not feel her feet touch the ground as she and the child ran through the snow. She knew they needed a fire quick— or a bucket of very warm water, as one of the elders had advised them to use instead. "Not too hot", she remembered, "just very warm". That sounded good right now, and it was all she could think about as she wandered through the city.

The whole alley was deserted. She didn't see the first torchlights until she came upon a small street. There were some porches along the opposite end, and under the roofs a few torches still burned. She walked across the empty street— the guards weren't anywhere. And then she realized she couldn't find the man who was meat to lead them to their safety, and she started to panic. The boy looked up at her, expecting her to keep moving, to keep taking him to safety. She smiled down at him, and resolved to find a house to stay in, shadowy figure to guide them or not.

She came upon one house— a two-story white building with a patio on the second floor and a covered porch beneath— and knocked on the door. There wasn't an answer, so she knocked again, and eventually a young man of perhaps thirty years of age came to the door. He looked angry to be disturbed, but when he saw the poorly clothed, clearly starving, and almost frozen girl and child, with blood all over them, his face softened. "What happened to you two!?" he asked. He even asked it as if he did not know. As if he had not heard those screams.

"Please— we need a place to stay, just for the night," said Kamira. "We have to get inside— our feet are frozen and we'll die out here in the rain."

"But why on earth are you out in this rain!? And what are you doing on my doorstep!?"

"You know why. This boy needs shelter. If you cannot take a grown woman, than take a young child."

"This house is full."

"I'm sorry," Kamira said defiantly. "I thought you were a decent human being. We'll seek shelter somewhere else." She took the hand of the small boy, who was on the verge of tears, and turned away. The man stood on his porch for a moment longer, with his torch hanging above him, before he turned and slammed the door behind him.

The boy began to cry. It was snowing now, which wasn't quite as dangerous as freezing rain. But the two of them were still very wet, and they knew they did not have long. Even in Gaoln when the storms like this hit, they always had the shelter of their huts— being soaked was the most dangerous part of these kinds of storms, and they usually didn't have to worry about that. But Kamira knew that they would die tonight if they could not dry themselves off— she had seen it happen back in

Gaoln, and she would not forget the look of frozen, hollow eyes buried in the snow and dirt.

There were one thousand of them, two thousand, three thousand. Every man, woman and child rushed out of the Black Tower and the more than a dozen buildings surrounding it, and either ran for their lives or threw themselves into battle. Gendorn tried to direct them, but more than once they mistook him for a soldier and tried to attack him. Bendoraun was leading the line of Freemen against a formation of Lonin guards, who were unpleasantly surprised to be facing off against veteran fighters with armor and proper weapons. Gendorn was arranging the Gaolnian escapees who had found weapons into teams and throwing them against tight knots of Lonin guards. The guards were overwhelmed, and unarmed Gaolnians escaped, but that did not last long.

From behind the buildings one regiment came, and then another, and another, and still more. They encircled the courtyard and cut down anyone who tried to run. Even those coming from the buildings on the courtyard's edge were cut off from escape. Somehow word had gotten out. Lonin soldiers arrived in dozens from every side, and then again. Bendoraun's line was being surrounded, and it would be ambushed soon enough by one of the approaching regiments. Gendorn was running out of prisoners to direct. How was he running out? He spared a moment to really look around and assess the scene, rather than to just find guards to attack, and when he did so he was almost paralyzed with disbelief. There must have been ten thousand, twenty thousand bodies in the courtyard, thirty thousand, how many? He could count forever! They were stacked in piles and thrown in heaps and their blood was up past the tops of his ankles. The courtyard was literally running with blood, in currents moving this way and that as the freezing rain hit it. Slaughter everywhere.

The distraction nearly cost him his life. A guard swept across him and one of the Freemen soldiers intercepted the attack, or else Gendorn would not have lived long enough to notice. He was enraged. Gendorn threw himself at every guard he saw in reckless and thoughtless abandon. He took one man down, and another, and another, and another after him, and he fought two men at once, three men at once, four. He took a cut on his arm, a cut across his face, a mace almost split his skull, a sword cut his leg and it bled badly and he ran with a limp, he felt something crack against his back, someone slammed his head against the stone floor, someone bashed his face with the hilt of a sword. There was blood in his eye, ringing in his ears, and nothing but madness and rage inside of him. He killed and killed and killed again, and it did not occur to him as important that he might be killed. Two men, three men, one more.

Bendoraun brought back the line and picked up Gendorn off of the floor. "Fall back to the safehouse, back to the safehouse!" Bendoraun shouted. His men followed him. They cut a path back the way they had came while Gaolnians rushed out of all the towers and all the buildings now at once to overwhelm the guards. More soldiers were coming in from the streets. They numbered in the hundreds. Bendoraun spared a glance to see how many men were left alive from his line, and a part of his heart gave out. *Three men.* He didn't understand. He had to look again, he had to see it again. *Just three men.* And Gendorn, limping, spitting blood, somehow without his shoes, his leg running blood faster than a river, his scalp sliced open, *Spirits*, Bendoraun thought, *Spirits, save us!*

Kamira saw him again, the tall man in the robes, standing further down the alley, and she almost yelled at him for leaving. But when the figure saw she had seen him, he turned and ran, and again they followed. The figure stopped in front of a house further down the next street, and Kamira approached it, still holding the boy's hand. When they reached the doorstep, the figure bowed, and ran back toward the Tower of Laeolin. Kamira knocked on the door, and a woman answered, maybe ten years her elder, and in the background she saw a small boy and knew she had found the right house. Without saying a word, the woman ushered them in. "Come in, dry yourselves off," she said, "I'll put on a fire— we've still got some dinner left. Are you hurt? Do you need anything more?"

Kamira hardly heard the words. It hardly made sense that there was a person speaking to her. Every time she closed her eyes to blink or try to relax, she saw the bodies lying in the snow outside of the tower. She couldn't even think of the magnitude of what had just happened— of how many Gaolnians might be left now, of how she might ever get over such an experience— of whether or not any of the Gaolnians would ever see each other again. All she could think of was those bodies in the snow. She saw them fall over dead to the ground in a wave, like someone pushing back their hair, all full of arrows. She saw them naked, climbing down the rope of clothes and getting shot half-way down. She lay awake sweating for the whole night, cradling the child in her arms, thinking of the nightmare that she never saw— it was the end of it all, every Gaolnian piled dead in that courtyard, completely covered by the falling snow. The Lonins weren't there any more, they had done their job— they were coming for her and the boy, but she didn't know where they were, or how to evade them. But in reality, the snow was still falling. It was still night. *People are still dying, and I can't do a thing.* She drew the child in closer and realized her shirt was soaked in his tears.

- Chapter Five -

There were four odd things next morning in Gruso, the wealthiest district of Laeolin which was walled off and guarded from the rest of the city, and they were surely not coincidental. The first was that people had awoken in the night to hear screaming from far away in the city center, a great deal of screaming from a great many people. The second was the smell of death. Pervasive, provocative, gut-wrenching was the smell, suggesting a crime of tremendous proportions. The third was that sometime in the night the gates to and from Gruso had been sealed off. No one was permitted to enter or to leave the city. Not even the morning criers were allowed in to give the news of the past day and night. The forth, and actually most troubling of them all for the astute young diplomat from Gonaka, was that Menuld had been sealed inside the city, outside of Gruso and so beyond contact. What in the world had Menuld been doing in the city center the night before, under such damning circumstances?

Well, it was not altogether impossible for Joel to deduce that there had been a Gaolnian uprising and that many of them had been killed. The stench of death alone said as much, from so far away. But too many questions remained for him to denounce Seagraul at the council. How big was the uprising? Whose fault were those deaths? Had the Gaolnians instigated the violence? Was there a group of guards, drunk and careless, who started the killing? Did Seagraul even know about it, or did he in fact order it? Far too many questions, and too many possible answers, to lay any substantial claim against the King of Laen himself.

But, Joel thought with a shrug of his shoulders, *that does not mean that one cannot try.*

The President of the Convention, Achana of Aniania, stood before the gathered rulers of all the nations two hours past sunrise on the third floor of the council's building here in Gruso, a quaint room whose windows looked out upon the open green expanse to the north and to the west. Their view of the south and the east was shielded by the wooden panels all along that side. *What would we see*, Joel wondered, *if those windows looked down on the city, instead of these farms?* The President-Queen cleared her throat.

"King Seagraul, you have an explanation to give us of the night's events, and you know to which events I refer. I will leave it to you."

Seagraul rose as if he had been expecting this. "An uprising in the night resulted in the death of several hundred Gaolnian hostages. We are cleaning and preparing the bodies for burning so as not to contaminate the remaining Gaolnians or the guards posted with them. The incident was triggered by a number of Gaolnians who had escaped the Tower of Laeolin itself. These prisoners, I suppose thinking they would be shot, attacked the guards as soon as they escaped, and were put down for their assault. The prisoners who tried to attack the guards were killed, and most who did not were put back in the tower. The tower doors have been resecured. We have shut down the city and closed off the neighborhoods to locate a small number of Gaolnians who got free and who we were unable to find in last night's search."

"Does anyone challenge this story?" Asked the President-Queen.

Joel rose in sync with at least four other members of the council, but he did not let them speak. "Seagraul, what you say may be the truth of the matter, or you may have slaughtered everyone in those buildings and left their bodies locked inside to rot until we leave Laeolin. We have no way of knowing because you have barred access to our district. Let the news vendors into Gruso, let the criers and heralds through every district's gates, so that everyone in this city may know the truth of the matter. Your prisoners will not be disguised as newsmen. Let the newsmen in here, so that we may know the truth."

"The newsmen of Laeolin are renowned for many things," The king answered, "but while fearmongering and rumormongering are among them, objectivity and foresight are not. The newsmen will cause a riot and they themselves have no sense of what actually occurred. The scene lasted only a fraction of the night and none of them were there to bear real witness. They will only be trouble, and this is no time for trouble."

"King Seagraul," Achana interrupted, "Unless I am mistaken, I do believe it is the will of this council that you allow us to personally investigate the matter in the city center itself. Do I speak for the council?" There was loud agreement from nearly every representative. The Free Kingdom envoy, who had fought as a captain against the Skaelin, was on the verge of killing the King of Laen right there, and the ambassadors near him kept hand on him to keep him down. "Then, by that decree, I order you to allow us access to the city center."

"President-Queen, I do not mean to anger the council, but did we return this morning just so that you could wrest control of the city from me?"

"I don't know, Seagraul," the queen replied testily, "did we return to find the hostages killed?"

"Have we nothing else to discuss?"

"You will allow us access, Seagraul. It is a decree of the council."

"Three votes can veto the decree."

"Because you are the subject in question you are unable to be counted as one of the three, which leaves only two objections."

Seagraul looked at Emperor Sealibahd III, but the ruler of Phenen gave no indication of his thoughts. "Emperor, will you not speak in my favor?"

"I want the truth of all this, Seagraul. Before I cast my lot in with you for good."

"I have given you the truth!"

"Why are you afraid to show it?"

"I will not discuss this further!"

The King of Laen had not realized how loud his voice had grown until the stunned silence came after that statement. The rulers of the world looked expectantly at this one unruly king, waiting for an explanation, but none came. The President of the Council proceeded:

"King Seagraul, you will give us permission to get into the city or we will use our authority at the gates to overrule your own and proceed into the city ourselves. It will be done, and that is enough talk about it. We will learn the truth of the matter before the day is through.

"There is another matter of equal importance, and in this matter we require your explicit agreement.

"Together with envoys and officials from Phenen, Laen, Kale, Gonaka, Las, Keay, The Council for the Territories of Bautaulan, The Kingdom of the Free, the Skaelin Lands, the Skaelin Resistance inside of the Free Kingdom, and the Skaelish, I and my officers have been working on a draft of a treaty hopefully acceptable to all. You will notice the officials working on this treaty were drawn from every nation in Fengorian and from the Skaelin now under Freemen occupation. Fellow leaders of the world, I present to you all the Treaty of the Free Kingdom."

King Seagraul almost spat at her when he heard this. The queen, ignoring him, continued. "The Treaty of the Free Kingdom outlines the conditions of peace between the four of you, and also deals with the issues inside the Kingdom of the Free. The conditions are these: One, The Kingdom of the Free will be recognized by this Council and, therefore, by each individual nation of Fengorian. This kingdom will be a legitimate government, run as the Freepeople see fit. Two, the Skaelin Resistance will immediately cease all attacks on the Kingdom of the Free. This includes all attacks, whether or not they be sponsored by another foreign entity or not," she said, looking at King Seagraul.

"Three, in exchange for this peace, the Kingdom of the Free will agree to allow certain members of the Skaelin Resistance inside Free Kingdom territory to join in their government, with positions roughly equivalent to the positions these officials held under the government of the Skaelin Lands. These native Skaelin representatives should hold some of the highest offices in government and have wide resources available to them. The specifics of each representative and position may be worked out subsequently after the passing of this treaty. Four, there shall be no espionage whatsoever— the Skaelin Resistance will forfeit their plans and hideouts and integrate peacefully with the new monarchy in the kingdom. The Skaelin Lands, still ruled by the Skaelin in the Eastern Mountains region of Skaen, will not spy on the Kingdom of the Free, and likewise the kingdom will not spy on Skaelin forces. Five, Laen will provide ships, food, and clothing for safe passage for all Gaolnian hostages taken during the Invasion of Gaoln to the towns of Port Doneaihr, Port Sesbuina, Port Tuyhaln, Port Tekal, and Port Daturna. Further provisions to ensure as many families as possible are reunited will be made after this treaty. The ships will be under the command of and stationed by the Army of Gonaka. Six, all the nations of Kale, Gonaka, Las, and Laen, will return any and all territory gained within the past three seasons to their previous owners: This includes the return of the coastal areas of southeast Kon to Las, the return of all land in southwest Kon to Kale, and the return of all lands in what was very recently southwest Laen, currently under the control of Gonaka and Kale."

The crowd listened intently, absorbing the points made by the President-Queen of Aniania. She took a breath, then continued her presentation. "Seven: Kale, Gonaka, Las, and Laen will all decrease the size of their respective military forces. Disarmament will begin immediately; The Council of Nations will ensure that this is followed through by every one of these nations. This will be done using a combination of Anianiese, Skaelish, Keyanese, and Phenese forces. The forces will not be armed, but rather they shall be mid- to high-level officials of their respective nations, and will take a vow of honesty before the Council. These forces will inspect and monitor the respective armies. Eight, The Kingdom of the Free and the Skaelin Lands both will not posses more than a basic military force; there shall be no excessive buildup of arms, warships, or soldiers. The level of their military will be in like regard to the restricted militaries of the four nations of the continent of Kon. Nine, any movement made by the nations of the Free Kingdom, Gonaka, Las, Laen, the Skaelin Lands, or Kale that indicates any sign of aggression towards any other of these above nations will be examined by the Council of Nations, and, in short, will not be tolerated. This will be enforced through economic sanctions, and if necessary full-out blockades or military intervention."

"Ten: Any aggressive movements made by any other nation toward the above six nations, seeking to in some way exploit, take advantage of, or otherwise use for their own benefit the military restrictions imposed upon these nations will not be tolerated. These movements will be likewise examined by the Council of Nations, and if any such movements are permitted without agreement of just cause as dictated by three-fourths approval of the Council of Nations on at least three-fifths of the occasions these votes are taken, the nations of Kon and The Kingdom of the Free and the Skaelin Lands have full right to defend themselves from such actions, if they so choose. Eleven, on account of any and/or all of these preceding conditions, and or on account of the reactions by the various leaders of these nations present at this Council of Nations, or also because of preceding actions or conditions, no government shall be deposed from their current state, excluding the Skaelin Resistance, which will merge either with the new government in the Free Kingdom or the remainder of the Skaelin Lands in the Eastern Mountains depending on the individual choice of each member of the Skaelin Resistance; Upon the mutual and expressed consent of the Skaelin Lands and the Kingdom of the Free this clause may be revised or rewritten. If the new government in the Free Kingdom fails, the Council of Nations will meet with Freepeople and Skaelin representatives to address the problems promptly and ensure there is peace and cohesion in the new nation. Aggression from either side will not be tolerated."

Acahna took another breath before she presented her final point. "And finally, if any of the parties, should this treaty be passed, refuse to follow through with any of the above conditions, the Council of Nations reserves the right to intervene, if necessary, through military means, or to strip any of the privileges granted by being a member of this council."

For a while after her presentation, the room was silent. No one among the Council spoke. And King Nowhawna's voice filled the room: "I accept." The Councilors of Kale talked among themselves, and everywhere people broke off into discussion. Finally, the Chief Councilman of Kale spoke.

"We agree," he said.

"As do I," said President Lokiey of Las. King Seagraul looked at his ally and friend with a look of betrayal, as if shocked that the president would ever agree to something so rational and pleasing to the country of Las, and in doing so abandon the efforts of Laen. Lokiey, for his part, was excited to be presented with a treaty so favorable to Las, who had lost an important part of their territory in the recent skirmishes, and he was eager to regain this land.

King Seagraul was as close to giving in as he had ever been on these issues since the outbreak of war. He seemed calm and considerate, and instead of answering, he thought deeply on the opportunities— and limitations— presented. Finally, he sighed, and looked up at the Council of Nations. He seemed about ready to speak, but then he lowered his head again. Still, he made no reply. President-Queen Acahna took the opportunity to give Seagraul more time to think it over— worrying, rightly so, that he was on the verge of denying it, so set he was in refusing the ideas brought forth to him. "Perhaps we should continue this tomorrow?" she asked. King Seagraul looked at her, then across at the various envoys and officials from throughout Fengorian.

"Keay agrees to the Treaty of the Free Kingdom," said a tall dark man, standing up to address the Council.

"Aniania agrees," said the queen.

"The Skaelish agree," said a tall white man with a long blonde beard.

"The Kingdom of the Free agrees," said the Freemen captain— a shorter man with thick black stubble, clothed in a red shirt with a tree stitched into it to declare him as the chief representative of Centreal.

"The Skaelin agree, as long as the conditions are fully obeyed and further negotiations concerning Gaolnian reparations to the ravaged Skaelin Lands are addressed," said another man."

"The conditions will be met, but realize The Kingdom of the Free does not have the funds to repair Skaen," said the Freemen envoy, "so the army will engage in reconstruction when the new settlements are finished." The Skaelin representative nodded in agreement.

"That is fine, then," said another of the Skaelin, this time one of the resistance fighters. "The Occupied Skaelin Lands also agree."

"Laen agrees," said the king. The representatives looked at King Seagraul shockingly. "I concede."

"Good then," said Acahna. "I believe that is all for today. We shall return to further discussions tomorrow after sunrise. We are adjourned."

- Chapter Six -

The streets were clear now— the snow which had fallen the previous night had completely melted, and today was already rather warm, considering Sen had already begun, even if it was only the first week of the season. Everyone had expected Trest to last another few weeks, but as the beginning of Sen was marked by the first snowfall, the cold season had technically started, even if it was going to be warm for another thirty or forty days. The buildings towered high above Joel, their upper parts bathed in the light of day, as he explored the largest and most beautiful boulevard in Gruso. He returned a few nods, smiles, grunts, and threatening scowls, as he made his way down the street and through the various shops. This part of the city was very showy, and there was hardly a shop without some fine stone or precious metal showing on the exterior.

There was one particular orange gem at a jeweler's that glowed brilliantly, even in the dim light of the shop. Joel examined it without expression— he had seen more beautiful jewels before, but this was an exceptional one. It had depth, yet maintained a surface still glossy. Inside of it, millions of separate lights could be seen, if one only had the eye and the sense required for them.

"Joel?"

Joel turned around to see a rather shady looking man with a hood over his head and a hunch in his back. If he was trying not to be noticed, he had the opposite effect. "Who asks?"

"I shall protect my name. But I will not guard my knowledge," said the man quite softly. "Would you perhaps accompany me to a more private place?"

Joel's scornful look grew more intense. "I am protected by diplomatic immunity, you know. The Council of Nations is quite a powerful force to reckon with. Needless to also remind you of my sword."

"I know your sword, and I know the Council— I even know of the agreement of the Treaty of the Free Kingdom. I also know something you would be most interested to hear, and that me and my fellows would be most pleased to inform you of— in a more guarded place," said the man. He nodded upstairs with his head, indicating a red and brown wooden staircase. "Please."

Joel's eyes were still sharp and his ears were perked up, the way they got when he regarded someone with his full attention and caution, but there was something that drove him to listen to this man— he needed to hear what he had to say. When the shopkeeper turned his head to other matters, Joel accompanied the stranger upstairs to an empty room. They went up yet another floor, which appeared to be a bedroom, and then yet one more. This last one was an empty store, decorated with various items and artifacts. There were swords of some older metal no longer used, and some pocket-sized navigation devices Joel did not understand. "Is this some kind of museum?" asked Joel. "Why are there so many museums in this city?"

"What I have to tell you, you did not hear from me," replied the man.

"I haven't yet anyway," said Joel expectantly. The man smiled.

"I am very glad we finally have the chance to get this out. It was not easy getting through from the city center."

Joel was nothing but ears then.

The man sat back in his chair and outstretched his arms and hands, tapping his fingers on the table. Abruptly, the tapping ceased. He sighed. "Joel, the hostages inside the Tower of Laeolin were executed last night."

Joel stopped breathing, his chest tightened, and the air itself froze inside his body. "You are telling me......all of them?" The man nodded. A full minute passed before Joel could speak again. "Sir, I simply do not believe you."

"I was there last night. I took part in the killing. I was ordered to. I killed more than fifty of them by myself."

Joel took another minute. "Was it by order?"

"I cannot tell. I hear two things. First, I hear that Seagraul did in fact give the order to kill the hostages. Second, I hear that there was an uprising in the tower. The guards did not feed them their dinners, so the prisoners believed they were scheduled for execution and decided to make a move. What I can piece together is that the guards did not prepare the dinners after hearing word of Seagraul's orders to kill the prisoners, and before the killing could begin the Gaolnians attempted to escape, thereby providing the guards with an excuse to use force. Of course, to kill one hundred and fifty thousand people you must have the intent of absolute annihilation. There was nothing retaliatory about it, whatever Seagraul will try to tell the Council. He pardoned the perpetrators. King Seagraul decided it was best to continue as if nothing had happened, to pretend the hostages were alive. His plan was to make the agreement regarding the Free Kingdom as if all were fine. He planned to make it appear as if the hostages were executed afterward, against his will, and was going to execute those responsible for the attack. We have frantically been searching for anyone involved with the Council of Nations to contact— we cannot trust our own representatives."

"Have you any proof?"

"If I had the Tower of Laeolin, where twenty-five thousand bodies lie dead inside, stacked atop one another, I would present it to you right here," said the man. "Or any number of buildings with ten thousand bodies or more."

"They have not been disposed of?"

"No. It's part of the cover-up— they can't drag out one hundred and fifty thousand dead bodies from fifteen different buildings in the very center of Laeolin without word reaching even Gruso. It would be quite a noticeable labor. They doused the bodies with something that neutralizes bad odor, and locked the doors," answered the man.

"Didn't anyone hear?"

"Everyone heard. How could they not? One hundred thousand voices screaming and crying and dying and shouting orders? It is a shame upon the people of Laen that they pretended that they did not, and those who acknowledged what they heard, in any case, took no action against this evil deed."

"What was the exact order? What words came out of the king's mouth?"

"King Seagraul said to kill them all. And, well— "

"Who received this order?"

"His highest officers. They agreed that the order had been direct— King Seagraul said he would not speak with the officers again until the Tower of Laeolin had gone silent. And the officers understood this as an order to execute every hostage."

"Well," Joel said with a sigh. "I will speak with King Nowhawna. I will tell him I must go to the center of Laeolin immediately, to confirm these reports. I'll make a public scene of it. Seagraul will not deny me. And I will be ready by the meeting in the morning. It will not take long. Who are you, man?"

"I will be dead soon, so it is of little importance. I once was a friend of King Seagraul's, and in his highest confidence. But I can no longer pretend that what we've done is acceptable. When the time is right, I will present myself to the Council of Nations and testify against the king. But until then, it rests in your hands."

"I can vouch for what he has said," came a strange voice from another corner of the room. A man who had been hidden in the shadows stepped out from where the voice had come, and Joel smiled— was there anything Menuld did not see, anything he did not know? "He is telling the truth, Joel. And we have a lot more to say. You will take this mission, of course?"

"Of course," Joel answered.

"Good— "

"Menuld, who is this— "

"Not important." Menuld turned to the man who had brought Joel upstairs. "Leave us." The man rose, nodded to Joel, and left the room without a word. Menuld waited until he could see him in the street from the window before he spoke.

"We have been monitoring the movements of the guards around Laeolin," Menuld said to Joel, "there was a group of students at the academy here who were adamant on their helping me to rescues the hostages. Unfortunately, our efforts came too late— we could not have imagined that King Seagraul would execute the hostages the very night after the Convention of the Council."

"It is true, then," Joel said.

"Yes. But I cannot say this before the Council of Nations, and you must not let anyone know about this meeting. I came to look for you that night, Joel, but I could not find you. They were massacred. But you will need to see for yourself— speak with King Nowhawna on the matter, and he will agree. You may confide in him. What I came here to give you is the information gathered by the students at the academy, before their deaths. Sit down."

Joel sat, and Menuld explained to him, for a rather long time, precisely how the guards moved and at what times and how many would typically stay at which buildings, and which ones would wander off and converse with the other guards. He handed Joel a large bulk of papers that had been copied from Gendorn's that had been copied from Ciso's. When the meeting was over, and Menuld dismissed Joel, it was already sunset. Menuld sent Joel off, and he sped down the stairs.

Menuld sat silent in the room for some time before he heard the other man returning from the street and coming up the stairs. The man stopped in the doorway and spoke without even sitting down: "I am sorry."

"I am disappointed in you, Juron."

"I am disappointed in myself," Juron said weakly.

"I told you that you would be. Your refusal to understand, to listen, came at the expense of one hundred and fifty thousand lives. You are weak."

"I was not given a choice. Were I to have refused, I would have been killed for it. There were too many officers around me. They would have finished the job."

"What makes you think their excuses are any different from your own? Isn't it a shame that you never dared to find out?" Silence. "You can make sure that Joel's mission succeeds, Juron. You know the movements of the guards as well as Ciso did. And you can command them to do whatever you say."

"I can and I will."

"Do not let Joel see you. He will presume you are an enemy, and for his sake he should consider you as much, as should I." Juron nodded, and without another word he turned to walk down the stairs.

Joel found King Nowhawna speaking with a group of senior emissaries near the building where the Council was meeting, at the end of a long, disgustingly over-decorated hallway. He was standing between the President-Queen of Aniania and the President of Keay, also receiving guests. The king saw him from where he stood, and Joel nodded to him, beckoning sideways with his head, then disappeared from view. It took some time before the king was able to excuse himself, but eventually he emerged and looked, quite angrily, at his friend and messenger. "What is so important that you had to disrupt me from this meeting?" asked King Nowhawna.

"The hostages," said Joel. The king raised an eyebrow and looked at his friend with renewed curiosity.

"Where shall we go? The rooms upstairs are vacant."

"Let's go then, two floors up, just in case." The king nodded, and they continued down the hallway and up the stairs.

The two men sat across from each other on the long side of one of those spearhead-shaped tables. Quietly and collectedly, Joel recounted his day, relaying the words of the man he met at the shop. The king expressed much interest, but seemed unimpressed and unconvinced, until he mentioned Menuld. "I am not sure who this man is, or what he truly seeks. He may be trying to undermine Seagraul's newfound ability to compromise so that the old positions are retaken, or it may be entirely true. Even Menuld can have faith in the wrong people. The only way to find out, really, is to see for ourselves," said Nowhawna.

"Do I have permission then?"

"You have my permission. Do not take the litha. Do not make a scene out of it. Instead, be as hidden as you can be. Wear whatever it is that people wear in this city and do whatever it is that they do. If you are asked by someone who can put a name to you, use the pretense that there is a certain item you seek in Laeolin, a specially crafted sword I told you about. Look for it in the arms quarters, near the tower, and on your way back, sneak in. It must be at night— tonight— but even then, guards are sure to be surrounding the place. You cannot be discovered, but if all else fails and you must reveal your quest, do so with steadfast fervor. Refuse to give up your errand until you yourself have walked through every level of the Tower of Laeolin. If the authorities refuse you, that is proof enough. Still, it is best for our relations, and for accuracy's sake, if your mission is unknown. I expect you back as soon as possible. Until then I will ensure that the Council of Nations remains in session, and no one returns home— you can rely on me for that. But don't keep me waiting too long, I can only complain about so much, you know."

"Yes, my king," said Joel, bowing his head as he stood. "Farewell."

"Farewell, my friend, and good luck."

- Chapter Seven -

Night did not end when the sun rose. The blood was still wet. The child in her arms was still crying and had been sick to his stomach now that he was out of shock. Kamira's eyes were still fixed open, glossed over and staring at nothing but unable to shut. Had those eyes truly seen what they had seen? Had her heart begun to feel it? Night would not end until those feelings had come and gone, until she did not see blood when she closed her eyes, until she no longer heard screaming where others heard only silence. Night would never end. Not until the very end of all their days. Not for her, and not for this child. That much she knew already.

The boy rested his head on the palms of his hands, propped up against his knees. Being sick had exhausted him. "Are we ever going to see them again?"

Kamira shook her head. "No, we won't. They've gone away."

"To where?"

"We don't know— they're okay though," she said, "they can take care of themselves. Do you have a family?" The boy nodded shyly. "Were they in Laeolin?" Again, he nodded. Kamira's next question came much slower, as if she were afraid to ask it. "Did you see them when we escaped from the tower?"

"Yes," the quivering voice answered, so soft that Kamira could hardly hear, and then he started crying again. He kept trying to say something, but he could not get any words out, he could only keep crying. "I saw them outside, near where we were running…" he said between bouts of tears, and then the crying came back. The boy started sobbing so intensely that he could not finish his answer, through he opened his mouth to try and speak time and time again.

Kamira drew him closer. "What's your name?"

"Pas," he whispered.

"I'm Kamira. I'll take care of you." His grip on her tightened.

The woman who had taken them in, whose own son was sound asleep, came down the stairs. She made a good effort at finding things to say, although she seemed to have some sense of the uselessness of words in such a time. "Are you okay?" Kamira could not even respond to that. Was she actually supposed to? The woman— Iuna was her name— drew nearer, and asked Kamira to the kitchen. Kamira squeezed Pas's hand, and followed her in. As Iuna drew closer and brought her into the kitchen, she asked Kamira how many had survived the night before. Kamira did not answer, and Iuna did not ask again. "You can tell me when you're ready— and don't worry about what happens next, we'll take care of you until we figure that out. Let's make some breakfast."

Kamira, in all her life, had never tasted anything other than degln, bread, and water— and, when necessary, snow, rocks, and dirt. Bird meat was the best thing she had ever eaten. Did this woman actually know anything about Gaoln? Was Kamira expected to cook?

"Sure," Kamira said, as if it was the most natural thing for her to cook every morning, "let's make something. And go get Pas. He needs to do something." Iuna looked happy, or even proud for just a second, and then she went to fetch the young boy.

Cooking was good. It helped them pass some hours, even if nothing of importance transpired. Pas would help out with whatever he was asked to do, except that every now and then he would break down into tears and he would not be able to do anything. Kamira would go hold him, and on occasion she would join in the crying, but Iuna carried on as if everything were okay, with a smile and a whistle and a caring eye. Iuna's son, Faero, would join from time to time, but he must have understood something about what had happened the night before. Iuna had never seen a look of such sympathy on her own son's face.

At some point they had finished, though Kamira hardly noticed. She certainly did not notice much of what happened after. Life was unreal. It did not make sense. Something happened, and her mind seemed to skip.

And then, all of a sudden, she was clean and in fresh clothes and she was sitting on a porch in a home in Laeolin with a strange woman and her son, and a strange young Gaolnian boy. "This whole week will be warm," Iuna had said, "Laen does this when it transitions from Trest to Sen. It won't be cold every day for some weeks to come." Kamira looked down at her new clothes, a dress of gray and blue, with the small Gaolnian boy next to her, also dressed in blue Lonin clothes, a deeper blue that the boys wore. They felt as soft as pillows to Kamira, used to the rags that she had worn her entire life. Her skin was lighter now— she had been amazed at the amount of dust and dirt she had accumulated in her years in Gaoln, and in her time in the tower, which the bath she had that morning helped to wash away.

In this safe house inside of Laeolin, with her clean body and her clean clothes and her food, Kamira felt very disconnected from the prisoners she had almost died with— it was easy to feel that way when one's life changed so abruptly and in such important ways. She knew, without giving it much thought, that Gaoln was gone forever, and with it the Gaolnians. But whatever clothes she would wear, a Gaolnian she would be. And she would raise the boy to know that he was Gaolnian just the same as she.

- Chapter Eight -

Night came again. As soon as darkness enveloped the city, Joel set out on his mission. Juron led Joel through the gates and instructed the guards not to whisper a word of it. Whoever this Juron fellow was, these guards certainly listened to him without question. They continued past Gruso, through the north end of the Middle Market. Joel spent his time weaving through tall buildings and cluttered market areas filled with the sounds of people and the smells of foods. He wove in between stalls, trying to appear as if he were searching for someone he had only just lost sight of. Anyone who recognized him seemed to be fooled by this guise, for soon the markets were all behind him, and he was nearing the end of the Middle Market. Down through the north end of the south borough and the west end of the east borough Joel continued, and by that time Juron had trailed off. He would not be accompanying Joel, but Joel had his writ of permission to re-enter Gruso if he needed it.

The boroughs were just as lively, with people celebrating and the sounds and smells of cooking, fires starting inside and their warm smell coming through the chimneys. Mostly it smelled of fish, spices, and no small amount of alcohol. Children and their parents met in the streets and paid no attention to the tall stranger wandering between them.

Then he came upon the great boulevards that separated the tower courtyard from the rest of the city. Whenever someone passed him along the wide whitestone streets, Joel would resume his pretense of looking for someone, and he was never disturbed. Only when he neared the tower, when it loomed above him so high it seemed to break the boundary of the sky itself, did he give up this pretense in favor of true stealth.

Silently Joel slipped around the buildings surrounding the Tower of Laeolin. His sense of smell was always keen, so he knew without entering the tower that at least a good number of dead bodies of some sort or another lie inside— and indeed the vast majority of dead bodies would have been in the buildings surrounded by the tower itself, which was why, with his back against one of those buildings, the scent was so strong. But that would not be proof enough if they were to refuse the Treaty of the Free Kingdom on these grounds. He had to get inside, and this posed a significant problem, because as Joel scouted around the Tower of Laeolin, which, out of necessity not to appear suspicious, took the better part of an hour, he noticed that a large number of guards were stationed well beyond the tower base, but around the tower itself the area was devoid of guards. He had to slip past the guards broadly surrounding the tower, and once he was inside the ring, find a way to enter the tower unnoticed.

Joel was quite good at thinking on his feet when occasion required. He returned to one of the earlier shops he had visited— an empty shop four stories high. He climbed to the top from the rear, which was guarded from view by taller buildings, and kept low to the roof, crawling to the edge. There were a few guards in front of and below him, and several times he barely avoided their gazes. He waited for a long time, hoping the guards would tire and slacken as the night progressed. They did not. He considered presenting himself and demanding entrance to the tower— was it really a bad idea? After waiting for some long, unknown time, Joel was glad to see two of the guards resting their backs against the buildings. By then Joel was actually doing the same. But for his purposes, the position of their sitting only made them see right where he needed to go. He waited even longer, until the guards started conversing as lively as if it were high noon. Joel cursed his luck— Seagraul had chosen his guards well, they might all be insomniacs, for all he knew— it seemed, indeed, they were not tiring, but, if anything, growing more lively as the night went on.

Then his luck changed. A man was strolling down the street, toward the tower, and upon seeing him, several of the guards abandoned their posts. "Henya!" exclaimed one of the men. Henya, a tall, islander-brown-skinned man with long black hair flowing beneath his shoulders, embraced the guards, and they talked quietly in a circle, though their laughter rang loudly through the sleeping city. Joel couldn't help but smile in satisfaction as he slipped quietly down the side of the building, and walked right up to the tower. He waited until one of the guards turned his head, then, fast as lightning, opened the large tower doors, went inside, and shut them, all before they had enough time to squeak on their many age-old hinges.

He gagged before he closed the doors. Twelve bodies, rotting already in the damp insides of the tower. He nearly vomited before he realized how horrible the stench really was. He pulled his thick sweater-shirt over his nose, and went up the stairs. Thirty. He went up the stairs some more. Forty? The next floor, there were nearly one hundred corpses. He could not count them there. Piles, that was all they were. Piles without numbers and without names.

Tears streamed down his eyes as the odor burned into his pupils and bore through his skin. He coughed again before catching his breath, breathing shallowly through his nose to minimize the gut-wrenching smell as much as possible. The victims were only recently killed, it seemed— not even all of the blood had dried, and the air inside was damp. Faces were cast in place, faces of terror and sorrow, whose only relief would be the slow decay of time. Cautiously, Joel made his way through the levels of the tower, climbing stair after stair as he ascended, eventually, above the clouds themselves, and into the open space of the universe beyond. But the scene did not change. Each level was filled with bodies stacked on bodies, drenched in blood that dripped down the stairs and wetted the bottom of his pants and boots. Every single floor was like this, even the topmost level where normally soldiers would be stationed to watch over the city and ensure the tower's security. No one was there.

He had seen death before, but death was nothing next to this. He had suffered nightmares and gone long weeks on end without sleep, but this was surely out of the depths of those terrors, and a not a fact of the living world.

Joel took a deep breath of the air as he opened the doors to the balcony overlook circling around the top of the tower. The air was offensive and corrupt here all the same, but it was breathable. He looked out and under himself as he patrolled the railing. The guards, it seemed, were all talking to this Henya fellow, and not concentrating much on their duties. Unfortunately for Joel, they were sitting directly in front of his path of escape. This fellow had not been in the plans that Menuld had given him, and, based on the information Menuld had relayed to him, the situation left him with very little chance of escape. He knew he could not remain alive inside this tower for very long— the attack of the odor was simply too harsh. Not to mention that he would certainly lose his sanity if he stayed too long tonight. An objective and rational thinker, Joel knew this as a simple matter of fact. The place deserved a lifetime of reflection, but he could not manage to stay one second longer.

As he watched the guards talk in their circle, he raced through plans and desperate gambits, trying to find some way that would lead him out safely and without being caught. Again he returned to the possibility of revealing himself, truly thinking now that it may be the best way to deal with his situation.

Joel ran down the stairwells— and there were so many that this effort made him dizzy and disoriented— and reached the base of the tower, opened the door swiftly, and peered out into the dark. As he had hoped, the time he spent waiting inside the tower for the guards to disperse had provided him with a darker sky than the sky of mid-night, for now it was nearing the morn, in that small time when the sky above Laeolin was most dark, as the early-risers were putting out their night torches. Under the cover of this darkness Joel slipped out of the tower and quickly shut the doors behind him, as he walked silently through the streets, briskly heading away from the Tower of Laeolin. At that moment the guards that had once convened together outside the tower were changing shifts with another set of guards, and as he, one lone figure in the darkness, slipped through the buildings, very few of the guards paid any attention, assuming him to be another one of their own. The only guards able to see him were the guards assuming the shift, not the guards being relieved, so it would have been understandable for them to make the assumption that he was among the guards relieved and that rather than talking he preferred to go straight home. Joel certainly did carry himself like one of them and looked more authoritative than themselves. That was the impression he had meant to give. All Joel really did was walk very regularly and not appear hurried or concerned, and hold himself with confidence. Soon enough, the guards were behind him, and the darkness that crept in between the tall and tightly packed buildings hid him as soon as he was out of the courtyard area.

The sun had risen again on his return to Gruso. Joel had not been sure that it would, but it had, and so he sat under its light with the King of Gonaka and a great silence between them.

Nowhawna took a hard breath. "You know what this means?"

"I know. We must report to the Council of Nations at once, and…well, then we will deal with King Seagraul."

"We'll have his head by the end of the day— he will never surrender power, I know him."

"I thought I did too, but I never imagined him doing this."

"He was never in his right mind, Joel— the man has no 'right mind'. There is no end to his wickedness and treachery," said the king. "He is truly mad."

"What is done is done. Some monsters may only be defeated by those who become monsters to defeat them. I wonder, if King Seagraul ignores the decisions of the council, will we find ourselves in another war? Is that the way this is meant to end?"

"Are you suggesting I simply let this pass? What kind of message would that send?"

"My king, Laen is willing now to accept The Kingdom of the Free as a sovereign nation in Skaen. They agreed to cease their support of the Resistance, and the Resistance agreed to assimilate themselves into the new government or leave for the Eastern Mountains. Las has agreed, Kale has agreed— we have agreed! We and the Council of Nations will take care of King Seagraul. I cannot imagine us letting him escape, or getting away with this— he will not! I would kill him myself before letting him get away with this!" Joel insisted. "But we cannot let what has happened become a pretense for war— that would only mean more horror, more bloodshed. We can resolve this now, without further violence, hard as it may be for us to do so."

"I do not like war, but I don't like King Seagraul either, nor do I like what has transpired these past few days. I think Seagraul's treachery runs deep, and I suspect this mass slaughter was no mistake in his mind," said Nowhawna. "I will do anything in my power to take the very life out of Seagraul, and after today, I know everyone in the Council of Nations will feel the same way. There will be no need to talk of war, Joel. We will strip his support out from under his feet, and leave him falling blindly into our hands. We will leave him alone and incapacitated, and powerless. And dead."

"Your foes are evil people, and it is easy to assume that the only way to destroy them is by evil means. Take care not to become evil in dealing with them— sometimes it is hard to resist that, and to maintain clear sight when circumstances and fate seems to cloud everything around you," said Joel.

King Nowhawna sighed. "All those years you spent with Menuld are wearing off on you, Joel." Joel smiled. "I will turn this information over to the Council of Nations today, before the council meets. We will have our answer today."

- Chapter Nine -

Alaisio sat across from his old captain, in the armchair that Luncas had built for himself. The windows behind Luncas, which Alaisio stared at as he was sitting there in silence, looked out toward the docks, where Gendorn and Bendoraun used to sit talking about their plan, as they had done every day until they left. Now there was a new group of soldiers preparing to set out in their wake. How many more would set out on their own? They were not leaving Centreal with a choice. It would be war by his decree or war without it. Luncas shifted in his seat, and as soon as Alaisio turned his eyes to look at him, he spoke. "You're sure you're going with them?"

"My son Ciso is there," said Alaisio, "I know that he will be working with someone to try and set the prisoners free, and I have to see him. I'm either going to get him out of the city, or, I suppose, I will be joining him in his work. I can't be wasting my time here. I should have gone with Gendorn in the first place."

"You three are leaving me at last, then," said the captain. Alaisio smiled. "You'll be the new captain of the 53rd, of course. Those two boys, Alaisio, when they came here, do you remember how childish they were? How disobedient and naive? They used to wander off every night, without any regard to our need for secrecy. And now they are trying to be secret, and they've got everyone else doing the same thing!"

"I remember," Alaisio said with a smile.

"You take care of those two. The king likes them. So keep them close, and train them."

"I know, captain, and I will."

"I'm not your captain anymore, Alaisio, you're the captain. Don't forget that."

"Of course, Luncas."

"I am a commander. That is much more important."

Alaisio laughed. "Of course, commander."

The emissaries and officials from around Fengorian took their seats around the table, glimmering under the light of the sun through the windows in shades of brown, gold, and amber. "Before we get started again," began the queen, "I have been informed that King Nowhawna has a development which he would like to share with us all."

Clearing his throat, King Nowhawna nodded at the queen, then rose from his seat. "Fellow leaders of the world, yesterday morning one of my most trusted advisors received a tip from an anonymous citizen of Laen. This citizen made a very outrageous claim, the truth of which we decided to investigate. I sent Joel, in secret, to the Tower of Laeolin. Inside that tower Joel found twenty-five thousand corpses. Throats were cut, chests were pumped full of arrows, children were lying dead and naked in their mothers' arms. Brief correspondence and additional investigations showed the hostages in the surrounding buildings had also been executed. The number of the dead approaches, and may equal, the number of hostages brought into this city only months ago. The Gaolnians, who were to become the Freepeople, have been slaughtered."

At first after he finished, no one spoke. There was a sort of heaviness in the air, after this report of one hundred and fifty thousand deaths had been delivered, the sort of heaviness which none of them felt worthy enough to break— what could they say, what was worth saying at all, when their reactions were so obvious, their disgust so plain and visible, their disbelief so clear upon their faces? How could one possibly react? It was those least disgusted among all of them who first spoke.

"It was not my wish," King Seagraul began, "for this to happen. Truly, I was outraged when I heard of the executions. If truth be told, at no point throughout these councils have I planned to murder the prisoners of Gaoln, rather than return them. For the good of all our countries, I wished them to remain alive."

"It was you, King Seagraul, who in a fit of rage ordered their execution," said Joel calmly.

"I ordered no such thing— I said something to the likes of 'why don't we just kill those Gaolnians', but I meant it not as an order, which, sadly, it was interpreted as," replied Seagraul, in the same calm voice. "I never wanted them to die."

"If my sources are correct," Joel answered him, "your orders were far more plain and explicit than a simple rhetorical wondering. You gave the order to kill them, Seagraul, and nothing less. It was always in your plans to execute the hostages if you felt it necessary."

"Your voice is heard and considered, Seagraul," Nowhawna added. "Nonetheless, they are dead because of you."

"One hundred and fifty thousand unarmed and innocent women, elders, and children, slain because you could not control your temper," said Joel.

The Freeman captain's eyes were fixed at some nothingness and his mouth hung half-open. He looked at Seagraul, disbelieving, without anger or any hint of another emotion—only and completely disbelief. And he whispered: "You killed them?"

"They are dead," was the King of Laen's only answer.

The Freeman captain and his two fellow Freemen remained dumbstruck. Without even raising his voice, without any indication of the capacity for any emotion at all, for that matter, other than a somber and quiet defeat, the captain nearly whispered to the Council: "I move to dethrone the King of Laen and to charge him with conspiracy to commit the highest of crimes, and to ask that he and his officers be hanged for those crimes."

President Lokiey of Las shifted uneasily in his chair, unsure how to respond but certain that he must. How could he possibly retain his alliance with King Seagraul after this? The Councilors of Kale took no time to respond. They agreed with the Freeman ambassador's motion to dethrone and execute the King of Laen.

"Does anyone require time to consider their position on this matter?" wondered the queen.

"I think it would be best, Queen Acahna, if we took at least a short break," said the President of Keay. "So that we may speak with our own peers on this, and arrive at some consensus as to how we may react."

"Agreed," said the queen. "Hereby, this meeting is temporarily adjourned. We will meet back in this room at high noon. If any of you attempt to leave this facility, you will be arrested, and it will be taken as an implication of conspiracy."

The meeting resumed when the sun had risen to its apex in the grey sky. The first one to speak was King Seagraul, addressing the whole of the Council of Nations.

"First off, I would like to apologize for this incident, not only for its atrociousness but for the personal offense that it causes every one of you. I also extend my apology to all the people of Gaoln, whether they be right in their actions or not— for, without argument, the execution of the one hundred and fifty thousand Gaolnians was a wicked and shameful deed, one which in no way I am supportive of. I assure you those involved are being punished, several have been executed already, and those awaiting trial will most surely be found guilty as well," said King Seagraul.

President-Queen Acahna of Aniania was next to speak, and she spoke firmly to King Seagraul, her gaze locked upon him. "King Seagraul, your apology does not aid our situation. Not only is it your own fault that this mass slaughter happened, but what's more, you attempted to conceal this whole affair from the Council of Nations. Even worse, you held the pretense that the hostages were still alive, and signed a treaty regarding their release! The penalty for that is severe, as you know, but the dishonor gained by this is far greater. I have spoken with the other leaders from across Fengorian, and we have come to a very clear consensus."

She sighed as she closed her eyes. When she opened her eyes, she spoke to the Council as a whole, shifting her gaze from one individual to the next. "All in favor of ousting King Seagraul from power, placing Seagraul and his officers on trial for the mass murder of civilians, working with the Lonins to place a new king in Laen, and maintaining all presently applicable terms of the Treaty of the Free Kingdom, speak," she said. King Seagraul felt his body grow hot with fury and terror both. The queen thought that the King of Laen might jump up and tackle her right there. But he held his tongue. One by one, the leaders of the nations spoke their word, and some of them a little more besides. The final tally was nine to two. Las and Phenen, two of Laen's most trusted allies, voted against King Seagraul. The Skaelin Resistance was the only vote other than Laen, represented by Seagraul himself, in favor of not ousting King Seagraul from power. Even the Skaelin Lands, who had seen more than half of their territory taken by Centreal, voted against the King of Laen on that day. When the score was final, King Seagraul, overcoming his shock, found that he had plenty of things to say.

"You have no right to oust me! I have the support of my people—I have always done the best I can!" proclaimed the king.

"You are a tyrant and a paranoid fool!" said King Nowhawna. "You are malicious to your citizens, unappreciative of your friends, unaccepting of new allies and possibilities, and deaf to reason and wisdom!"

"So is King Nowhawna!" protested Seagraul.

One of the Councilmen of Kale rose to the defense of Gonaka. "King Nowhawna did not try to make fools of the Council of Nations! King Nowhawna did not keep information from us that ought to be known to the whole world! King Nowhawna did not systematically exterminate one hundred and fifty thousand hostages!"

"It is true," agreed Queen Acahna. "Both of you need to relax, but King Seagraul is the only one here who ever attempted to deceive us so. Never in our history has the leader of a nation attempted to conceal so grievous a crime against all the world. You undermine the very cooperation that enables this council, the honesty that is crucial to its success, and the human values it was built to protect. Your leadership is no more, King Seagraul. You are not fit to rule."

"I am fit to rule, ask my subjects, my officers, my citizens— they support me! What gives this council the right to oust a government supported by the people from its rightful place of power? I am not unwanted, I will not cease to lead this nation simply because you think I am a poor king. My people think otherwise!"

"Your people fear you, Seagraul— we do not!" explained the queen.

There was loud and unanimous agreement throughout the room.

"You would if you were wise!" said the king.

"Temper, temper!" said the Emperor of Phenen. "Calm yourself, friend. The council has spoken, and so have I. You may not agree, but you must heed."

"Your officers no longer support you, King Seagraul," said a voice which came from the open door. King Seagraul whirled around in his chair, and his mouth dropped open in shock— Juron was there, standing right in front of him! At the Council of Nations!

"What are you doing here, Juron!?" Seagraul demanded.

"I have come to tell you that the Council of Nations is not alone in its decision. You are not fit to rule this country, Seagraul, and we will no longer allow you to do so. Laen votes against you, and you not speak for our people."

"We? Who is 'we', Juron? You were my best officer— you, you yourself killed those hostages! You were the one who ordered their execution, Juron, you were the one who stood outside the tower that night, who stood there in the snow, and watched their bodies fall to the ground— you were the one whose hands are stained in their blood!"

"I have not come to debate that. I have come to aid the Council of Nations in escorting you to your new home, where you will be guarded by the army of the transitional government."

"Which you will be commanding, I suppose!?"

"No, I will not be working with them. That army is under the command of the Military Board of the Council of Nations, and so answers to the Joint Commanders of the Council. I will not be involved."

"Then what do you gain, Juron— trying to clear your conscience, are you? You've already killed them, and there is nothing you can do!" King Seagraul yelled.

"Be quiet, Seagraul," said Acahna, who had risen from her seat. "Be quiet, and sit down."

King Seagraul locked his gaze with the queen. Regaining his composure, he looked across the table. "You are seizing my kingship?"

"You are no longer a legitimate king," explained the queen. "The one who follows in your stead will require both our approval and the approval of a group of Lonin figures popular with your people. Our guards will escort you to a home, where you will be watched. Your actions will be noted, every word heard. You will resign in public, or you will be executed and your power seized from you by force. I hope that is clear enough for you to understand. Your reign is over. If you make any attempt to revive it, you will be killed, and your government will be punished for any support they give you. Severely." Seagraul nodded.

"Very well then," said Seagraul, managing as much pride as he could find, "Escort me." At these words the guards who had been standing outside the building came in, lifted Seagraul up, and led him out into the hallway with the tips of their spears pointed at his chest. Juron trailed behind the procession of guards that surrounded the ex-king, and an ambassador from each nation of Fengorian, and whichever heads of state had attended this Convention, including King Nowhawna and President-Queen Acahna, walked beside the entourage.

When they walked out into the daylight, there was hardly anyone in the streets. It was a hot day— the last hot day they would have before Sen really set in and the weather turned cold for the season, Seagraul was sure. The thought only came for an instant, before it was gone— *Will I see the snows of Laeolin melting again at the coming of Trest? Or will I die before the coldness flies before the sun again?*

The streets were becoming more and more populated as the guards marched the ex-king onward. From the townhouse towers above him, the six-story buildings that contained a separate house on each floor, Seagraul could see scores of people coming out to see him. They would stand on their porches and lean against their balcony rails, or climb to their rooftops. Most of them stood there and gawked in silence, and then it dawned on them, it must have dawned on them, that King Seagraul was no longer a king, for at once the crowds erupted into noise.

Some of them yelled at the guards, and demanded he be set free. "The revolution has died!", some of them lamented, or they cheered "save the savior of Laen!" and "Long live the revolution!". Such cries echoed through the streets as these people threw stones at the guards and hurled curses at the ambassadors, and looked upon their king with pity and adoration. Others yelled: "Let the wicked king die! The new revolution has come! Laen will be free!" and, in turn, threw stones at Seagraul himself, or at those who chanted for Seagraul. Some yelled "Murderer!" and "Criminal!" and tried to break through the crowd to attack the deposed monarch. The people were thus divided not even by neighborhood or by street, but even on the floors of individual buildings. Every single residence and place of business, and everywhere the ex-king went, fighting broke out in his wake.

The guards held the eyes of the king, and were distracted by nothing. They arrived at the home where Seagraul was to remain under their watch, and led him into the entrance hall. President-Queen Acahna came up to the ex-king, and stopped in front of him, their faces only inches away. "Seagraul," she said softly, "I can have sympathy for you no longer. Your reign is over. How did you come to this— how did this happen?"

"It's those Gaolnians, Acahna, they're the ruin of this earth!"

"No, Seagraul, it is people like you who are the ruin of this earth. Myself and my predecessors have striven against you or worked with you, depending on their interests— but I now know that they were wrong not to assess you as an individual, and see you as the monster that you are."

"We were friends once, Acahna— "

"I did not know who you really were. Now I do. An entire world that you deceived now sees you as you are. You will remain inside this home, and if you attempt to escape you will be killed. The Council of Nations will decide what to do with you, and we will return when we have decided. I advise you against trying to escape. This city is not a safe place for you."

"My people will always believe in the revolution— "

"There is no revolution!" The woman shouted as loud and angry as she could, as quick as a bolt from a crossbow and every bit as sharp. She continued more calmly: "Your 'revolution' is over, Seagraul, and if you attempt to cling to power, a new revolution will strip that power from you. Remain here, or you will die. Goodbye."

They all left him standing there alone with the guards who had been assigned to stay with him, except for Juron, who stood by the doorway. Seagraul, when he saw Juron standing there, looking at him, almost lunged for him, but the guards held him with the points of their spears. "What have you done, Juron?" Seagraul asked.

"Me? What have I done?"

"You, yes, you! You killed those prisoners without my order!"

Juron shouted in reply: "You told me to kill them all, Seagraul, and don't you think of lying!"

"You killed them, Juron, you killed them all!"

"By your order and on pain of death! Don't pretend to care! The Gaolnians are what's wrong with this earth, remember? They are the nothingness, the dirt that we are meant to purge— or do you not recall your mouth saying those very words?"

"I have never considered them anything other than human beings— "

"'An infectious cancer upon the world that we must cure' is how I remember you describing them!"

"I was referring to— "

"Human beings," said Juron, "yes, well, I have gone along with your wickedness and downright insanity long enough."

"You cannot clear your name, Juron, you can never do that after what you've done, and you will never be able to clear your hands of the blood of one hundred and fifty thousand!"

"Don't put this on me, Seagraul."

"Do you really believe that it isn't upon you, that it isn't your fault to bear whether or not I put it there?"

"No," Juron said boldly, "but it is just as much your fault, Seagraul. You knew what would happen."

"Knew that I would be deposed by the Council of Nations!? No, I cannot say I knew that would happen. Leave me, Juron. I would not like to see you again." Juron did not obey.

"I have one last thing to say, that whether or not you are enough of a man to take the shame of your mistakes, those mistakes remain and they will always be yours. I hope that before you die you truly understand what you did while you lived. I hope you pray to everything sacred for forgiveness, and I hope no one ever answers you." Then he turned and left the once-king by himself.

When no one was watching, Juron slumped down in a thin alleyway and he let the tears come out. It was hard to say those last words for only one reason, that once he said them to another man, he had to live with them himself. He had tried to already. He had turned Seagraul in, he had testified against him, and he had said those last words that he had been so eager to say. It all wasn't right. It could never be right, save for one thing, and so that meant that there was one more thing he had to do. After he was finished with crying, Juron rose and set out with a heavy heart to do that last thing.

The night was still. Overhead, the clouds drifted slowly through the darkening sky, and the noises of the night's activities— creatures foraging for scraps in the streets, people laughing as they strode through the alleys— faintly filled the air. Seagraul looked out the window, onto one of the large stone-floored circles that served as one of Gruso's marketplaces and gathering places. He was tired, yet he did not wish to sleep. He was sad, yet he could not bring himself to concede to such emotions. Rather, and not really meaning to, he clung to the embarrassment he had suffered during the council, and to the anger that had surged through his whole. These things he could not escape, and for as tired as he was, he was by far more restless in his mind.

As the king paced around his room, two teams of thirteen men snuck through the sparsely traveled alleyways and the winding streets of Gruso. Dressed all in black and travelling with muffled boots through the slimmest and darkest of alleys, they were quite impossible to see or hear or stumble upon, and although they were prepared to kill anyone who had taken notice of them, they did not expect that anyone would. One of them signaled to another, who ran around the dark side of a building and came out the other end. Anyone who was keen enough to notice a large group of men dressed in the camouflaged colors of the night would probably have been smart enough not to inquire— but the fact that it was merely hours from dawn's breaking meant few people were wandering about. The group came, eventually, to a large building surrounded by guards. The venture had taken them several hours— they had to evade many guards stationed around the city to guard this building, and it was a tedious mission. At last, though, they surrounded the large four-story house. Assigning three men for every outside guard, the group moved instantly and as a whole. Before any alarm could be raised, the guards were executed, their throats cut or their bodies pierced with arrows, and the group entered the building.

Seagraul stood in the corner of his room, his ears alert and his sight focused on his surroundings. From the floors below he heard sounds of struggle— plates crashing, people smashing into things, muffled shouts of pain, the cracking of bones, and feet rushing down the halls. He wasn't sure if he should try to escape— he was worried this was an attempt on his life, but there was also a small chance of rescue. He knew one or the other would come. At last the sounds were outside his room. Suddenly the door burst open, and four men covered in black rushed in and surrounded him. They took him by the arm, but one of the men bowed before him, and looked at him through his mask. "King Seagraul," he said with a smile. "Welcome back to kingship. Let's get out of here, and quickly."

- Chapter Ten -

President-Queen Acahna cleared her throat as she rose and addressed the Council of Nations. "Last night, Seagraul escaped from the house in Gruso. A large contingent of men dressed in black escorted him out of the district, and he has seized power over Laeolin from the city center. Their position is weak; many rebel against him, believing he is no longer the legitimate king, but many parts of Laen follow his orders directly. He ordered the entire nation to step up their war efforts. His intentions are clear: We will recognize him as king, or he will fight us all, if need be, with all his power. I must emphasize, if Kale and Gonaka choose to resume this war, they can likely overpower him. A great deal of support will come from inside of Laeolin, where many people want Seagraul dead. And further support is not impossible— I know for sure that Aniania would be willing to send supplies, if not troops. Those answerable to the Council of Nations will, of course, fight for the Council of Nations and not for King Seagraul, which will give us large tracts of the countryside. I advise our continued efforts to arrest or kill King Seagraul, but this does mean plunging Laen into civil war. I see few other options— he has a powerful base of support that is blindly and dangerously loyal to him and his beliefs. The thoughts of the Council?"

The Chief Councilman of Kale rose and addressed the Council of Nations. "I propose we suspend the Treaty of the Free Kingdom, for clearly, after these incidents, it may require some revision— although Kale pledges its support of a peace arrangement, once peace may be found. A joint government should still be established in Skaen immediately, but the other clauses seem impossible for the present time, in light of these events. I also propose we waste no time at all in pressing the offensive against the territories and forces loyal to Seagraul. We cannot allow such a dangerous and evil mind to regain power over a unified Laen."

"I agree," said King Nowhawna. "We must press against his power everywhere we can. Joel, take Big Litha and notify The Kingdom of the Free. It is your unfortunate duty to relay to them the sad events that have taken place in this vile city. See if they will join us in this endeavor— I think they will. Aeron," the King of Gonaka continued, turning to the Freeman captain, "I ask that you and your associates remain here inside Laeolin to organize and lead a team of the Freemen who have arrived in this city. They will be needed when war comes."

"Phenen objects," Emperor Sealibahd III said suddenly. Concerned and curious, King Nowhawna looked at the man. "We believe Seagraul should be recaptured and punished according to his crimes. But to resume war to is revert back to that which we have striven so hard against. We are adamantly opposed to this," he explained.

"Your empire's loyalties have been in question for some time now. What side are you on, I wonder?" inquired King Nowhawna.

"We are concerned about what has recently transpired— it seems you are seizing any chance you can, Gonaka and Kale, to gain more land and power and wealth. Will it end with Laen, I wonder— and when Seagraul is deposed once and for all, will you then return Laen, which you will control, to a nonexistent yet-to-be-devised government? It would be more beneficial and easier to simply govern the land yourselves— I worry of your motives."

"As do I," said President Lokiey of Las. "My advisors are wary of your actions. You embraced the treaty, and that comforted us— but now you wish to suspend it, perhaps indefinitely, and resume the war."

"Once Seagraul is dead, the Treaty of the Free Kingdom will be enacted," said King Nowhawna. "The occupying forces, whoever they be, will govern the land until a proper and agreeable government can be devised."

"President Lokiey, surely you do not support Seagraul's kingship?" wondered the Chief Councilman of Kale.

"I do not anymore, but I still worry about Gonaka and Kale. He is paranoid, yes, but killing another however-many-thousand people and starting a new war will not solve that. If we are to have peace, we must solve this problem with greater care and discretion than you are giving to it," answered Lokiey.

"Those would be wise words," Joel whispered beneath his breath, "if we lived in wiser times or among wiser men."

"Seagraul will not embrace peace!" objected King Nowhawna. "He is mad! You are with us or against us, President Lokiey. As is the Emperor."

"King Nowhawna, do not be so aggressive," warned Queen Acahna.

"I grow tired of your insolence, King Nowhawna, and your ways of solving your disputes through murder and deceit. I, personally, believe it is you who is not fit to be king. Does that answer your question?" said the President of Las.

"I too grow tired of these things," said the emperor. "I am intolerant of arrogance and bloodlust, both of which you display openly and in excess, King Nowhawna— and you as well, Councilman Keleanas."

"Then the sides are drawn!" said King Nowhawna.

The Council of Kale, whose members had been speaking with one another throughout the entire affair, ceased their discussion as their leader rose. "We support King Nowhawna in this, and we agree to fetch The Kingdom of the Free and to recruit their eager help to depose Seagraul and eliminate his wickedness from the earth," said Keleanas. "King Seagraul will not be removed peaceably. He refuses. War is the only way. We will bring war to Laen."

The President of Keay threw up his hands as if in defeat. "Why don't we just assassinate him instead!? It's not like we don't have the power!"

"His loyalist government is too strong for that," said the queen. "He has successors posted in almost every part of Laen. It has all happened rather quickly, which leads me to suspect that King Seagraul has in fact been planning this for some time. Assassination will put another Seagraul in his place. We have to make sure there is no place safe for Seagraul or for anyone loyal to him. We will prosecute all of them. The magnitude of the crime requires it."

"The sides are drawn then," agreed the President of Las. "If war is the only answer, so be it! Let you both remember, Gonaka and Kale, that Las and Phenen both wanted to resolve this peacefully— but your insolence was your downfall!"

"Patience comes at a heavy cost, when a mass-murdering tyrant is on the throne!" retorted King Nowhawna. "We have no time for more bargaining. Seagraul is not fit to be a king, and it is our responsibility to overthrow him. It is your responsibility as leaders of this world to do so as well, but you forsake your duties!"

"These people will fight until there is no one left!" The Emperor of Phenen proclaimed. "You know that, and you know that when you've won the war it will be you, Kale and Goanaka, who decides who will rule over Laen. The Treaty of the Free Kingdom— "

"Is no longer enforceable," the President-Queen interjected. "It is obsolete and inapplicable under the present circumstances. It is non-binding given recent events and so long as no king rules in Laen. King Seagraul must be caught and killed."

"I will not see Laen disappear, and I will not see the loyalists in my own country rise to the defense of King Seagraul at my expense," said Lokiey. "Those who support the Las-Laen alliance would have me killed for declaring war on him. And I do not trust Kale and Gonaka to lead the war themselves."

"The Council of Nations will lead this war!" King Nowhawna declared.

"But you, King Nowhawna, and you, Chief Councilman Keleanas, will be the driving force behind it."

"That is not true!" Protested the Chief Councilman. "This war will be led by the Council of Nations and the Council of Nations will set up the government— "

"The Council of Nations may only go to war if there are less than two dissenting nations, and there are four in this instance. My own country, our allies in Phenen, the Skaelin Lands, and, we may assume, the Skaelin Resistance both reject the idea of war," Lokiey explained, his voice rising again, "Seagraul's support cannot die with his loss in war."

"You must concede, there is no choice!" The Chief Councilman of Kale asserted.

"The Council does not have the authority! If there is no other way," said Lokiey, "then I suppose this means war."

"War!?" Exclaimed the president-queen. "War— you talk of war so lightly! Las, Phenen, and you Skaelin of all sorts— do not behave so rashly— Kale, Gonaka, consider how they think of you. But President Lokiey, I must say that if you and your allies choose to aid King Seagraul even after the Council of Nations has decided to strip him of his kingship, then you, too, will find yourselves at war with the council and likewise stripped of your right to rule."

"I will not let Kale and Gonaka take over this entire continent, there is hardly anything left to stop them from ruling the world," Lokiey retorted.

"And don't you dare threaten the sovereignty of Emperor Sealibahd III of Phenen!" Added one of the Phenese ambassadors sharply. Emperor Sealibahd III remained silent.

"If you intend to treat us as if we were unfit to be kings, unfit to make our own choices, then you, President-Queen Acahna," Lokiey said threateningly, "will find yourself at war with Las and Laen and Phenen and the Skaelin!"

"You are as blind as Seagraul, Lokiey!" Nowhawna screamed. "And you will meet the same fate!"

"We will see," the President of Las replied.

The Freemen had remained silent the entire time. It was not lost on them that this was the beginning of the next Great War. Of greater importance to them, and the subject of their silent thoughts, was the noted absence of all the representatives of the Skaelin Resistance.

PART FOUR: INTO THE GREY
MOURNING SKY

- Chapter One -

The snowfall was light. There was a grey sky above the grey city, a sky which left a grey mist atop the grey stone streets of Laeolin. The world was encased in grey, and only the pure white snow dared to challenge it on that day, along with the pure white dress of the mourners who had come to display their anger toward King Seagraul, and their disapproval of the genocide he had committed. There was one other color to break the grey. Far above the clouds the Black Tower reached. It was captivating, mesmerizing, but Kamira's attention was elsewhere. Kamira stood there amidst all of them, indistinguishable from the rest. She wore nothing but the long, thick, warm, and billowing white gown which covered her entire frame, from the hood which covered her head to the lowest threads weaving around just above her ankles. There must have been almost ten thousand there on that day, come to watch the burning of the bodies.

They were piled in heaps in the center of the courtyard, all around the smooth black Tower of Laeolin. Two hundred guards were dragging out bodies by the dozen from at least twenty different buildings. From every direction, all around the courtyard and beyond, the guards dragged bodies by the couple, dragged them by the hands or feet. Sometimes all there was to drag was an arm or leg or head. Thick sacks full of body parts and fluids were thrown among the corpses. The mourners stood all around them. A line of them surrounded all the buildings that the bodies were in, but Kamira and hundreds of others surrounded the tower itself. Still, some groups of mourners went out to the middle so that they could face the guards and obstruct their path. Every one of them wore the purest white, the same color as the lightly falling snow. Every one of them looked solemnly at the guards, daring them to look back. Few of them did.

The bodies piled up quickly. There were ten of them, twenty of them, fifty, one hundred, two hundred, two thousand, ten thousand— the entire courtyard became a mountain of bodies in the snow, just as Kamira remembered it. She looked around the crowd. She had no doubt that all the surviving prisoners of Laeolin had come to witness the commencement of the cremation of the one hundred and fifty thousand who had not survived that day. She felt alone for a brief instant— these Lonins around her, however sympathetic, could never feel what she felt. But she knew beyond any speculation that every one of those alive who could feel what she felt, who did feel what she felt, was with her on this day, even though none of them could know the other's face or hear their voice.

They could not burn all the bodies at once, as large as the courtyard around the tower might be. When the mountain of bodies was large enough and a flammable chemical thrown atop them, three of the guards came forward and threw torches along the top. The fire was slow to spread, as there was a light layer of snow upon the corpses and they were wet in any case, having been locked away in the dampness of the tower and its surrounding buildings. But the fire caught onto the clothing as soon as it dried up, and quickly it had spread to the other bodies. It took a lot more of the chemicals and only a short time before the corpses themselves were burning. Kamira, in her gown of white billowing in the wind, watched in an utter, dumbfounded silence. Not a word among them was spoken, not a muscle twitched in the crowd of mourners, and the guards stood rigid at their posts, watching the bodies burn.

The mountain lost its top, the bodies having been burned to ashes, and as the mountain devolved into a hill the guards set out for more bodies. They emerged again from the buildings and the towers, flinging the bodies onto the fires, dousing them with a

dusty compound or a glistening viscous liquid, and continued like
this for many more hours. Throughout the entirety of that day
more and more bodies were thrown up onto the mountain of
fire. Toward the end of the late afternoon the clouds thinned out,
and though the sky was still overcast, one could see the traces of
yellow light hidden behind the barriers in the sky. The fire behind
the clouds burned its way through to the fire in the snow, the fire
spreading from corpse to corpse, and all the while the snow
continued to fall, and the ten thousand mourners stood just as
still, just as silent as when they had come that early morning
before sunrise.

The guards stood at their posts again. Suddenly, they had
ceased their bringing out of bodies. The fire was roaring, and
already mountains of ash lay around the mountain of fire. Hills
of ash, indeed, were hidden in between piles of bodies— ash was
everywhere. When the wind blew, the ashes would be caught up
in its gusts, and displaced. Sometimes the black ash would fall
upon the mourning gowns of white, and would leave their stain.
Other times the ashes would fall upon the faces of the guards,
who remained expressionless. Many of the ashes were borne
high up by the wind, and thrown throughout the city. In every
corner of Laeolin the ashes fell that day, when the dying gusts of
wind had decided they would carry them no more. And there
was not a single pinch of snow left to its pure whiteness, without
the stain of the black ash.

Ashes and bones were all that was left. One heaping and
endless mound of ashes and bones which encircled the Tower of
Laeolin and towered above the heads of the guards and
mourners. Kamira stood there entranced. She felt the wind grow
bitter, the air become colder, the sky grow darker around her.
She felt the tear cold upon her face and the urge to fall down and
weep, to throw her hands and feet upon the cold stones of
Laeolin and cry forever. She remained standing, while the tears
and the hours passed uncounted.

At some point she realized that, but for a very small group of people standing alone in different places throughout the courtyard, she was alone. All of the mourners around her had left. Iuna had taken Pas back to the house. The guards had departed. The billowing white of the mourning gowns could only hardly be made out through the sudden darkness of deep night. Two of the mourners left, then three, then four and five. And then she was alone with one mourner, who remained on the opposite side of the courtyard. She knew that this must be one of the survivors, and without another thought she approached the hooded figure.

"What is your name?" Kamira asked as she grew closer.

"Juron," came the sturdy voice. At once, Kamira knew she had been mistaken— this was the voice of a healthy man who would have sailed away to Skaen and fought for Gaoln's freedom. It was not the voice of anyone who would have almost died in Laeolin.

"Why do you stay here so late?" Kamira asked.

"To think."

"Of what, may I ask?"

"Of what we are capable of doing," Juron answered, "in the name of and the service to king and country."

That was an off answer. "Who are you, really?"

"I am nothing but a man, and a bad one at that."

"Why would you say that?" Kamira asked gently.

"Because it is quite true."

"Are you not curious to know who I am?"

"I have already decided for myself that you must be one of the very few survivors of that fateful and tragic night."

Kamira's eyes grew wide, and her forehead tensed as her ears perked up. She took a step back and examined the man. "And how did you know that there were any survivors? What makes you think that?"

"Because I killed you. I killed everyone in these towers and these buildings. I am the one who broke the dreams and the promises, and stole the lives away from those who had never really lived. My name is Juron, as I have said. I was the Commander of the Guard of Laeolin, and Acting Commander in the mission to capture the hostages and return them to Laeolin. I led the men into Gaoln and I took you bound to Laeolin. It was I myself who, acting on the order of King Seagraul, ordered these hostages to be executed. And so I saw them die, young lady, and I saw those few lucky ones escape alive."

The silence lasted forever. How does one react to such a thing? How can the heart bear it to understand? At some point Kamira looked up into this man's eyes, and saw his face. She had wanted to see this face for a very long time. In the days since her escape she had pictured this face as something contorted, twisted and inherently disgusting— something ridden with scars and with only one eye and an ever-present scowl. The voice would have been rough and deep, and always aggressive. There would have been no remorse in this man's face, indeed no emotion at all except that of unabated hatred. But upon this face there were none of these features— this face was gentle, calm, and even somewhat youthful in appearance. The voice did not carry hatred— it carried regret. Unending regret.

There were children running in her mind, and naked women scrambling through the snow, being shot down by arrows. There was blood running through the stones, and in an instant she turned around, and saw that the blood ran everywhere— it was creeping up on her white gown, reaching toward her face. The tower doors opened, and piles of freshly-killed elders and children faced her, their eyes still gleaming and almost alive. People fell from the floors above by the dozen. Everywhere there were screams, and there was one voice— could it possibly be the same voice?— issuing the orders— *do not let them escape. Kill them all. We have our orders. Kill them all.* It was the same voice. It was the same man.

It was quiet again, and Kamira realized that this was not that fateful night. She had seen those bodies burned tonight, and now the man responsible for the massacre was right here in front of her. After all this time, the thought registered. This was the true face, the true voice of the man she had dreamed of. She looked into his blank eyes, and he looked back, and then she spoke to him, just as calmly and as softly as before. "I have to kill you now."

Juron pulled a dagger from under his white gown, and offered the hilt to Kamira. "Then kill me," he told the woman, "and see that my body is not given as much honor as the bodies burned today."

Kamira grasped the hilt, and held the blade flat, pointing toward the man's face. "This cannot be the same man that I heard that night. It cannot be the man who killed everyone, every one of us. It is not the same man."

"I swear to you," Juron assured her, "it is the same. I have regained my senses far too late, after the deed has been done and Seagraul's wickedness made clear and indisputable. After my own wickedness has been made just as clear. My life is forfeit, and I do not have the right to even know your name. I should not know the name of my killer, it is too much for me to even have known your face."

"You're wrong," Kamira proclaimed. "You deserve to know everything about me. My name is Kamira. I was born in Gaoln, and I do not know why that I was not born free. I was raised by my mother and father who were placed in Gaoln as enemies of the President of Las. I lived for sixteen years on rotten degln and bad water, if it can be called living. I survived for sixteen winters with two shirts and one blanket. I saw everyone around me, including my father, die of starvation and dehydration and hypothermia and disease. Then I saw the man I love sail away to Skaen, to fight for our freedom without any weapon in his hand and only hope in his heart, and I had nothing left but my mother. Then you came, and I saw you and your guards chase my mother off, and I have not seen her alive since that day. Then I saw everyone around me, every Gaolnian left in Gaoln who had survived all their trials and tribulations, locked away in a prison in Laeolin. Then I saw every one of us murdered in one night, by such a small group of such heartless men— I saw our life disappear, our dream fly away. And that rests upon you, Juron. May that guilt always rest upon you.

"Were justice to be done, you would have known the story of every single person who you have killed. You would have seen the faces of their grandparents, and you would have heard them talking softly between themselves about the hopes they held for their grandchildren. You would have seen the brothers, sisters, lovers, children, and parents of those you had killed. You would have known every one of them for their entire lives. Images would have flashed before your eyes of who those children might someday be. You would see a proud man, tall and strong, standing before you upright and noble. Then the image would fly away and you would see the body of the five-year-old boy who you had killed, the boy who could never be that man. You do not deserve the innocence and the blindness of not knowing us. You deserve to know every single one of us, to know every human that you have killed and every family that you have ruined. Were this world a just place, Juron, you would not meet your dying day until you had known all of this."

The silence came again. In his mind, Juron heard Menuld's voice proclaiming in that peculiarly soft but confident tone: *You are weak.* The tears were cold on his face— he could not look at Kamira, could not possibly speak to her. He wept softly at first, and then loudly, and then he fell to his knees and looked up at her. "Kill me," he begged, "kill me, and do not tell anyone who I am or what you've done."

"Were I to kill you, I would tell absolutely everyone what you had done, and I would tell them who I was, and why exactly I had killed you." She spoke as if speaking to some unintelligent child who had disobeyed an elder. Juron lowered his face again, and continued to weep.

"Just do it, please." Kamira looked at the dagger, and leveled it, preparing to thrust it into his heart. She felt an almost irresistible urge to kill him right then, to cut his head clean off, to stick it on a pole and place it in front of the Tower of Laeolin. It would be the smallest measure of justice, she knew. But it would be more than nothing. But as much as she wanted to, she knew that it would not mean any great deal. She would still have nightmares of this place. She would still see the children running through the snow, and falling dead in front of her as she fled. She would not ever escape that— the killing of this man, Kamira knew, would be of little or no use to her.

There was one additional fact. A dagger through the heart was better than this man deserved.

Suddenly, she dropped the dagger. "Kill yourself," she said boldly. "You have the blood of one hundred and fifty thousand on your hands. You have the blood of another hundred thousand, for you let us die in Gaoln while you went on living in Laen. What is one more life?"

"But does it not give you satisfaction?"

"If you had not been groveling at my feet, it would have given me satisfaction," she answered spitefully. "I have wanted to take your life every moment since I fled. In my dreams we met in opposition. I declared you my enemy, I told you who I was, I shoved the faces of the dead into your own face, made you scream in anger. I would bind you to a pole, and set the body of a young child in front of you, and make you stare at the child for hours while the snow covered you and you froze to death in the cold. I have killed you in my dreams many times, Juron, as I have killed Seagraul and all of the other guards present on that night. But I will not kill you when you cry at my feet. If you are to die by my hand, then you will rise to meet me."

Juron gathered himself and stopped crying. He rose to his feet, and stared at Kamira. "I will stand to meet you, then. But I should die by your hand, Kamira, I must die by your hand, and by the hand of no other." Kamira raised the dagger and thrust it toward his heart.

Juron threw up his hands and stumbled backward, and screamed "No!". The dagger had cut into his arm, and he clasped the wound with his good arm. He fell to the floor again, and resumed crying.

"Stand up!" said Kamira.

"No," Juron cried, "no, I can't."

"You're weak, Juron." Juron stopped crying in an instant. He rose again to his feet, and walked up to Kamira. He nodded at her, and stood still. Kamira held the dagger in front of his eyes. Juron did not move. In one swift movement, she plunged it into his heart, twisted it, and pulled it back out. Juron's eyes started to float, and he collapsed onto the stone floor. Kamira let the dagger drop beside her. The red of Juron's blood was the same color as the red of the blood that Kamira had imagined creeping up her own cloak only moments before. "Others might have been more patient with you, Juron, they might have shown you some mercy. But they have not experienced the extent of your vileness, your relentless evil. I could never face the survivors of our kind, and try to explain to them why I had let you live. I could never have looked in a mirror, and explained it to myself. You will rest in the snow, Juron, where a hundred and fifty thousand have lain before you. May their spirits haunt you forever."

Kamira's mourning gown was no longer white. It was stained both with the black and grey ashes of the cremated dead, her fellow people, and with the red blood of her enemy. When she turned around, she saw the Tower of Laeolin rising before her into the darkness. The courtyard was empty, and there was not a single person around these buildings. The wind was sharp and the air was freezing. It was into such a silent night that the black tower rose before her. Every time she blinked, she saw the bodies lying there, she saw the blood running through the snow. It was a different face every time, a different body, a different pair of eyes. She gathered herself up, and fought back her tears. Then she set out through the snow, stepping on the bodies in her mind's eye and ignoring the shouts and yells from every direction. There was one man she took notice of, one man in the background screaming commands and directing the guards. He wore a white mourning gown, and his heart was bleeding. She looked for only a moment, then she averted her gaze, and continued on her way back to the house, where Pas and Iuna would be waiting for her.

The sun was out the next day. It shined on the city, and Kamira hated it. The sun should not shine on such wicked people. But it should shine on this house, and on all those who would stand by her— the shadow should cover the rest. The snow melted that afternoon. It would come again, the fragile white of the snow, but fragile things died in such a world as this. The snow that was white to others was forever red for Kamira, forever black and grey, forever ashes and blood. The white snow, the gentle snow, the fair and soft and fragile snow that covered all the earth in a blanket of glittering light, that snow would never fall again. Not ever. And that world would never shine, under any moon or stars or sun. Not ever.

- Chapter Two -

Commander Luncas and Alaisio were among at least two thousand people gathered in the Doneaihr city circle, a great open courtyard in the heart of the port town. They had made a clearing for the messenger to land. The people of Doneaihr had seen the tall man in the robes of Gonaka once before. When the man spoke it was in a slow and solemn tone, the tone of someone who has chosen every word and recited something many times before.

"I have just spoken with your king," Joel began, "about some events which have taken place in Laeolin. It has been a very fateful city as of late, a very unfortunate place. It is my first duty, and my most unpleasant obligation, to inform you all of the murder of the one hundred and fifty thousand hostages in that city." He stopped speaking, and looked into the eyes of the men. He saw, in their faces, a most disgusting sort of twist, the mark of having received news which they could not begin to understand or internalize. Some of them fell to their knees and looked upward. The silence was grave. To Alaisio, it all moved very slowly. People had begun to fall to their knees too soon— he himself could not even consider that the Gaolnians were dead. In his mind, he was still going to set sail tomorrow morning with the next ship to Laeolin, and join his son Ciso. Wasn't he still going to sail?

"There was only a small group of people— only a few thousand among the one hundred and fifty thousand, at most, and perhaps less than one thousand all told— who survived the systematic execution, which had been ordered by King Seagraul himself. Those very few survivors are now in hiding in the city of Laeolin." Joel paused again. "The Council of Nations has declared Seagraul unfit to rule and has stripped him of his kingship, a move which has plunged Laen into civil war. When Seagraul proclaimed himself king and refused to yield the parts of Laen still loyal to him, the Council of Nations broke out into factions. Laen, Las, and Phenen decided that they could not trust Kale and Gonaka to lead the expedition into Laen. Seagraul's Laen, Las, and Phenen are now, once again, at war with Gonaka, Kale, and the Council's Laen. Aniania has joined in on the side of the Council of Nations, and, earlier today, King Centreal showed his support for joining what everyone is calling the Alliance for Freedom, or the Free Alliance. It is assumed the Skaelin Resistance will continue their attacks, that the Skaelin may lend aid in that effort, and that the Skaelish will come to fight off the Skaelin here in the Free Kingdom."

"So I ask you, as is again my most regrettable duty, Freemen of the Free Kingdom: Will you join Gonaka, Kale, Aniania, Council-controlled Laen, and the Council of Nations in war against Seagraul's Laen and his allies, Phenen and Las and the Skaelin who still resist?" Most of the men remained silent. Most of them looked down toward the earth, or up toward the heavens, or their eyes were blank and uncomprehending, and stared at something distant or near. Some people wandered off away from the crowd. Some wandered to the sea, some to the forest, but between them all not a word was spoken. A few solemn eyes looked up at the messenger from Gonaka, and a few heads nodded in agreement. It was a silent consensus, the consensus of a group of people who had not yet had enough time to react to the news— they had not even been given enough time to hear the news. But Joel was patient, and as he waited more pairs of eyes met his own, more heads nodded their agreement. Alaisio traded a look with Luncas, and then he too nodded. Luncas, after lengthy thought, nodded as well.

"Men of the Free Kingdom, we are going to war," Joel continued, "and we will set sail immediately for Laen. Gonaka and Kale have wasted no time in capturing more land from Las and Laen. When we land in Laen, our route to Laeolin will be brief and direct. I have the deepest sympathy for every one of you. It is very regrettable that I must bear such news— it should never be anyone's burden to carry with them such words. It should never be our burden to have to hear such news and know it to be true. It should never be anyone's burden to endure the hate of one man so mad and cruel, and of a group of people whose willingness to follow that man costs the lives of hundreds of thousands. But such is the situation we face today in Laen. Such is the situation that we must confront with the same sword and shield that we brought down upon the Skaelin Lands. King Centreal's troops move south. This city will be one of the locations of departure. You will remain here until you set sail. The survivors of Laeolin are safe and will remain safe through the war.

"I would urge you, on a more personal note," Joel continued, "not to give up hope. We have weathered through the most difficult storm. We have little left to lose. Most of you have lost your families, your friends and loved ones, after having just won your freedom, the freedom which you as a people decided to risk everything to obtain. There is little left to risk but your own lives, which now to many of you may seem senseless and irrelevant— what is a life, after all, when everything that gave it purpose is snatched away? When everyone you've cared about has left you for Sendeilta or the Great Beyond?

"But what little is left you risk for something great. The leaders of Las and Laen and Phenen are convinced that King Seagraul cannot be deposed, because they are afraid of Gonaka and Kale becoming too strong. We risk what we have left so that we may tell them: It is not how much power one has, but how one uses that power. Seagraul cannot be king because of how he used his power, regardless of how much power he has, or how much power other nations have— he has taken the lives of one hundred and fifty thousand children and elders and women, and he has said to the world that he believes he can do this, that he believes he, as a king, has the power to do this. We risk what is left of our lives to say that he is wrong, and answerable not to the dictates of his own deluded sensations, but instead to the dictates of human conscience and to the goodwill of the people of Fengorian. He, in his rage, has denied the importance of both. And we rise now to correct him in front of all the world.

"You still have your freedom, the freedom which you have just won only recently. You still have the choice to stay here, where, certainly, you will be far safer, where you can integrate with other populations, where you can create new lives, maybe even form new families someday. Should you bear more children, as many of you will someday want to, someday years after these awful affairs, they will grow up in a land where they are free and able to make something great of their lives. But that is the future. Today we face a less pleasant truth and a less pleasant task. We must go to war and announce to the world that what happened in Laeolin will never happen again."

The people were nodding fervently now. Almost all of the men were in tears, but, crying or not, they looked up at this messenger and nodded in agreement, that they would go to war. Alaisio nodded in assurance to himself. They would be setting sail, after all— and bound for Laeolin. But they would be sailing with eighty thousand men.

- Chapter Three -

Gendorn was on a ship out at sea, and the mist that engulfed all the world kept him hidden. There were men everywhere around him, starving and overworked men with smiles on their faces and the light of the sun in their eyes. They were always talking about the same things. What it would be like to live in a real home. How soon the war would end and they could come back for their families. What they would do once they had settled down in a quiet castle town. It was all the same. The stories they shared, the songs they sang, the dreams they held waking and sleeping, all of these things were held in common among them. When they looked at one another they saw their own eyes and their own smiles, with the same great aspirations behind them, and for this they were closer than brothers.

The mist grew a little bit darker, as if the daytime were waning. There were less men about the boat. The wood started to creak. The waves became rougher. Night came.

There weren't any men about the boats now. Had they ever been there, or had Gendorn set sail alone? It was a poor choice of a ship. There were holes everywhere and water coming up through the hull. The rigging was torn. The crates of food and water were empty. The rudder was warped, badly enough so that the ship seemed to be veering about wildly as the waves hit it with growing intensity.

The ship lurched, and it did not right itself. Gendorn was closer to the sea, and then closer still. And when he looked up into the fog he saw a thousand faces looking back at him, blowing with the wind to make way for a thousand more and a thousand after that. The faces swirled around him as he felt himself sinking into the Cold Ocean, and he was too shocked to move. The ocean swallowed him, and when he opened his mouth the water poured into him and froze his insides. In the dark of the ocean as his life fell away, he still saw the faces swarming him. They were the very last things he saw.

Gendorn coughed and his eye shot open. He saw Bendoraun, and no ocean, and blood everywhere, on bandages and on the floor and on the door and on himself. He coughed again and blood came out. Bendoraun handed him a bloody tissue. Gendorn took it, and he looked at his friend with the most solemn face that the boy had ever seen.

"They're dead, aren't they?"

Bendoraun gave him the saddest of looks in return, and put his hand on Gendorn's shoulder. "Yes. They're dead."

- Chapter Four -

Commander Luncas's home was finished just in time for the cold season to begin in earnest. Alaisio was in the central room, where one enters from the outside porch, sitting on an old wooden chair by the window. Having heard the news, the ship captains had made the choice not to set sail until the army was ready to embark, and as such Alaisio found himself nervous and anxious more days than not. The commander, meanwhile, was quite busy corresponding with the ship captains and the regiment captains, which meant that Alaisio made greater use of Luncas's home than the commander himself. So it was that Alaisio was already sitting inside when his old captain returned home from the barracks. The commander did not make it far. Alaisio was not reading anything, he was just sitting there thinking, which meant something was off. "What is it?" asked the old captain.

"Captain..." began Alaisio. "Do you still have that note...from Seun Bastion?"

"Yes...do you want it?"

"No..." replied Alaisio. Luncas sat next to him. "Makes you think..."

"It does..."

"I feel oddly disconnected. All those people fought for their freedom, and they ended up losing all their loved ones in the process. But I came from the islands, from Bautaulan, and I didn't sacrifice anything, I wasn't fighting for my freedom or leaving my loved ones in a penal colony. I only suspect that Lendah was thrown in Gaoln, and I know that Ciso is well hidden. You and me, Luncas, we're not going through what the rest of them are, you know."

"What does that have to do with the note?"

"Well, nothing, really. Except that I sometimes wonder if whoever wrote that note would still preach to us about the uselessness of our war, after looking at every dead and motionless face in Laeolin. The triumph and glory..."

"It wasn't about choosing sides, Alaisio."

"I know..."

"So what makes you think about that note?"

"Honestly, captain, I just wanted to reassess our motives for joining the Gaolnian Army. I know they are rather unique, as most people who fight for Gaoln are of course from Gaoln. And, well, I was hoping that by talking about our motives, I might convince you to lead our regiment again. You know, I do not like leaving jobs unfinished. We will need you in Laen. The men, all of them, they will all need you."

The silence was thick. Luncas looked down at his leg, then at his arm, and then looked at Alaisio as if the man had lost his senses. "What makes you think I can do that, Alaisio?"

"I just thought I would ask."

"And why would you want me to? My way of war is too ruthless for your liking."

"I know. But I would like to know that we can count on you to kill Seagraul. I know you'll be able to get the job done, Luncas."

"Well, you know I will say yes. I belong on the battlefield, I always have. I am meant to die on the battlefield, and my death is long overdue. This house, well, it was just a dream anyway, you know. I am glad that I finally was able to build the thing. I had been meaning to for far too many years. It was nice to spend some time in it, but I can't stay here. I can't die here, and to be honest I doubt I can even live here, now that I have finally accomplished the goal of building the thing. I wrote the plans for this house with a girl I used to run with, back when I was younger and had a prettier face. Have I told you that already?" Luncas laughed. "It means a lot that I finally did do it. It really does. It's something like completion. I suppose I might redeem something of myself by killing Seagraul, would I?"

"They'd sing songs in your praise, captain. You can't be complete while Seagraul still lives after what he has done."

Luncas nodded. "Well, that's true enough. It would be something to face him, wouldn't it? I'd like to see his eyes when I tell him I am the Commander of the King's Division of the Free Kingdom. I'd like to see him realize that no sane leader in this world still believes in him. Then I'd like to see him die, but only then."

"That's a yes?"

"It's a yes."

- Chapter Five -

Iuna sat in her rocking chair on the porch, knitting a sweater for the coming cold. She had taught Kamira enough so that she could start something of her own, but rather than knitting an item for her own self she had begun working on a sweater for Pas. Iuna had enough clothes to spare some for Kamira, but the young boy had nothing to fit since they had burned their prison rags in the fireplace two nights ago.

"I can teach you some basic sewing," Iuna explained to her, "and as long as you can sell your things in the market I'll be able to keep you for a longer time. We agreed to harbor those who escaped, you know, but you'll have to help provide for yourself. We simply aren't that well-off. I do wish we were."

"You are a seamstress?"

The woman nodded. "My husband owns a bakery down a few streets. But he probably stayed inside last night, with the storm and what not, and won't be back until the afternoon. But I'm sure he would be alright with this, as long as you can provide for yourself— we just have to teach you. We will be able to provide for the boy, you know, but you need to start eating some real food now that you're a free woman, and real food doesn't come as cheap as a basket of degln. You need to get healthier, otherwise the cold will kill you."

Kamira smiled. This woman knew nothing at all about surviving in the cold, but it was sweet of her to think of it. "Thank you," she said gratefully. "How long will this sunshine last, do you think?"

"We can have sunshine into deep Sen, when we are lucky, but don't let that deceive you. Our blizzards hit hard, and when the cold comes it will not relent. This is going to be a cold Sen, with the sun or without it. We may not get as much snow as Skaen, but there will be days when you'll find it hard to open that door and trudge your way through the streets. The first thing you'll have to make— and I'm sorry it will be so difficult— is a thick winter cloak. We've got boots for you. And I will help you make it— maybe I should just make it…"

The warm spell lasted for three days— and to call it a warm spell is really just to say that it was sunny, as the wind was always sharp and chill and bearing tidings of deep Sen— before the snowstorms returned with renewed force. After that point, Kamira stayed inside sewing with Iuna, while Pas would play with Faero and the neighborhood boys and Komu would hike back and forth to his bakery. On some days Pas stayed inside and would not leave his bed or speak with anyone. On others he acted as any other boy his age might. Iuna and Komu passed Kamira off as their far-removed cousin and Pas as Kamira's nephew, as Kamira had a rather small frame and a youthful look and would not have passed as the mother of a five-year-old. The fact of it was that Kamira was not healthy enough to have survived childbirth, and she never would be unless Iuna and Komu helped provide for her. Like Gendorn, she was still only in her seventeenth year, so it would have been a difficult thing to argue in either case.

Five weeks passed like that. They would hear news from the outside every day, talking about the war. It was always something good coming from the army— "we've taken control of the towns to the south, and driven Aniania from the coast" or "Gonaka has fled before us and we've planted spies in the main camp of Kale, we know all of their movements". But then there would be the merchants or the travelers, who would say things like "Seagraul's forces are being driven back to Laeolin, we can't hold the coastlines" or "they're going to invade Laeolin"— and that was a common one, from what Kamira could tell.

Throughout this time Las lost the lands west of the River Las, but gave no ground beyond that river, guarded as it was by bridges and ships and towers and armies alike. The combined navies of Aniania, Kale, and Gonaka overwhelmed both Las and Laen along the shores of the Endless Water of the East, until Phenen arrived with ships and beat back the Alliance forces to impose a temporary stalemate. Laen's battles continued to be fought in the streets of every large town and city, and in the hills and dales of the country where citizens clashed with one another in unorganized mobs. The Alliance for Freedom worked relentlessly to disrupt Seagraul's trade and supply routes and to isolate Laeolin.

After the immediate breaking of the Convention of the Council, Seagraul's forces converged in Laeolin and forced those against Seagraul out of the city. Rebels left by the thousands as loyalists rounded them up night and day and forced them to leave by the tips of their swords and spears. The rebels besieged Laeolin from the outside, but the siege was constantly broken by loyal forces coming in from further out in the countryside. In this way most of Laeolin and its hinterland came to be held by Seagraul, and his opponents withdrew into hiding.

After two weeks the Skaelin fighters arrived on the shores of Laen and reasserted control in the north, east, and south of the country. When Seagraul dug his battle lines, only the west had already been lost to the Alliance, with only small pockets of resistance elsewhere.

Meanwhile Phenen and Aniania had checked each other— each had blockaded the others' ports and had placed large armies on the islands off the coasts of each other's' nations. Each was afraid of sending their troops so far north, fearing the other would launch an invasion of their homelands in the south. Aniania withdrew their troops to the southern coast of Las, and Phenen sent only a small team to Laeolin and kept the rest of their army and navy engaged with Aniania's main force in the Southern Sea after their initial defense of Las.

So it was that by the close of a few weeks there was fighting from the northern end of Laen all the way down to the warm waters of the Southern Sea. The world was again at war.

Back in the Kingdom of the Free, the Free Army assembled in Freetown. There a great castle was being built, a new testament to a new age in the history of Fengorian. The Fortress of the Free, or Freetown Castle as the soldiers called it, was built on designs that derived from Gatsesilli's plans. Gatsesilli was the strongest castle in the Free Kingdom, so Centreal had found the architect who worked on maintenance there and hired him to build an even better one. The fortress was to be a magnificent compound apart from Freetown, with its own killing lands stretching out beyond a moat as wide as Gatsesilli's. The walls were of the same build as those at Gatsesilli and of comparable dimensions, but with wider killing fields in between them. Inside the innermost walls there was enough storage to last a double garrison for a full year, and the civilian population besides. This was the finest strength of the castle, as Gatsesilli's reliance on constant caravans from the countryside outside its walls was what led to its defeat at the hands of the Gaolnian Army. It was a lesson the Skaelin had learned the harder way, but that the Freemen would remember just as well.

King Centreal had led his army south and east from Gatsesilli to greet the soldiers as they showed up at Freetown Castle. One by one, caravans and wounded soldiers arrived at the fortress. Having received the news of their families, these men banded together with the intention of remaining there until the active soldiers returned from Laen. They could not function as soldiers and neither could they live in a world apart, where their families had died and no one around them understood what they had been through. So they became the best of friends inside these walls and prepared to spend the entire Sen together in what was to become the capital of the Free Kingdom.

Joel had lent Big Litha to help defend the fortress, and Kale had sent a team of their best swordsmen. Gonaka had sent archers and engineers. The Skaelish had sent troops there too, and to Gatsesilli, Bellford, Doneaihr, and the Thin River Highlands, to help defend against any Skaelin who had not gone away to Laen. That came with a warning, from the Skaelish to the Skaelin, that in the case of continued conflict the Skaelish would side with the Freemen. Deiknahr had promised King Centreal that he would remain as one of the men who would help run the Free Kingdom in Centreal's absence, and Nowhawna had also made Deiknahr an ambassador between the two nations. So Deiknahr had taken up residence inside the Fortress of the Free itself.

It was on one particular afternoon toward the end of this great migration that Centreal, Joel, and Deiknahr found themselves propped up against the outside of the castle walls, surveying the land and the people before them and inspecting the caravans as they arrived. Trest was much longer this year— although Sen had already technically begun more than a month ago, there was only a light coat of snow upon the ground, and the day was rather nice. At almost this same time last year, Centreal recalled to Joel and Deiknahr, the snow had been up to their knees as they made their way out from Port Tekal to Bellford. "Why you ever thought to take Bellford so early, I will never know," Deiknahr said, "dumbest thing that Denelu ever told you to do."

"Pure luck that you won," Joel added.

"There was a great deal in that victory other than luck," said Centreal, "and there will be still in the victory ahead." How Centreal could use such a word as victory in the aftermath of such unimaginable loss, neither Deiknahr nor Joel could understand.

The King of the Free went about these days, in his inspections and his meetings and in just about everywhere, wearing the official glistening white and brown robes of the Free Kingdom, which he himself had designed. The last tree in Gaoln, the Lonely Tree— that withered old thing on the hilltop by the sea— was emblazoned in brown against the white backdrop. Brown, the color of the earth of Gaoln, was originally chosen as the background color, with a red sky set behind the tree, but both the earth and sky became white, the color of mourning, after the execution of the Gaolnians in Laeolin. Centreal had suggested the idea— and everyone he talked to embraced it. So now the withered tree, the last symbol of life in Gaoln, stood alone against the white that remembered death. And everyone he chanced upon remembered it beside him.

Kio had arrived in one of those caravans and explained that he had ordered fresh uniforms from Gonaka to the Freemen troops preparing to embark from Doneaihr. They had been designed after Centreal's own robes, with the brown tree of life against the white of death. Remembering both and to do them justice, the soldiers of the Free Kingdom would set sail for Laen.

King Centreal held a meeting that next morning after breakfast, with he and his men all bedecked in those robes. The king took his seat at the center of the table, where the spearhead would be attached to the pole, and looked out across his audience of advisors and commanders and ambassadors. This particular table was one of the original of its type, ancient and beautiful and decoratively carved, from the Age of the Ten Kingdoms many

centuries ago. There was a particular material the ancient
Skaenish had used to build this table— the Skaenish were those
who lived in Skaen before the civil war divided them into Skaelin
and Skaelish, and it was also the term used for the ethnic Skaens
who lived here from ancient days. The material was called seiln,
and it was the most beautiful mix of bronze and amber hues. It
was soft, and no good for war— but the taletellers said that it
trapped the sunlight and kept it inside to be released on darker
days. It always shone, even in the total absence of light. Centreal
had moved this table from Gatsesilli just a week before— it was
to be the physical center of government in the Kingdom of the
Free.

Kio and Joel sat to his left and right. The two of them argued
about strategy the whole time, and most of what the king did was
listen to the two sides of their dispute. There were enough ships
to get everyone in one load, but it would be very crowded, and
they would need to borrow some Gash and perhaps Kanish ships,
as they had done to get here in the first place. But many fleets
had anticipated this, and had already been dispatched to help
transport them. Once they set the date for departure out of Port
Doneaihr— two weeks from that day— the king's table was
dismissed.

- Chapter Six -

And so two weeks from that day there was a crowd of more
than fifty thousand soldiers, with more still on the way, gathered
before the King of the Free in the green fields to the northwest
of Doneaihr. From atop a hill the king addressed the swelling
crowd, and there could not be more pride in his voice. "People
of Gaoln, Freemen," the king announced to them, "you will need
rest. When we land on the shores of Laen, there will be no time
to waste. Make sure you have ample time to recover from the
voyage before we land— some of you will, of course, have the
guard shift when we land, but make sure you are well rested
beforehand. The Lonins may greet us at their shores. They may

do so with open arms, asking for aid against Seagraul, or they may do so with their swords. We will come and be ready all the same. Upon landing we will set out for the fortress of Benin. Benin lies to the north of Laeolin and is held by Seagraul's loyalists, one of the last strong outposts he holds this side of Laeolin. Once we have taken Benin, our march to Laeolin is straight and will not be impeded. Benin guards the river going south that stops just north of Laeolin, so we can control access to the city from there. Kale and Gonaka lay on the other side of Laeolin, and together we will besiege the city and, if necessary, enter it by force. This will leave Seagraul confined to the southeastern quadrant of Laen, where he will be vulnerable to attack by the river warships of Aniania, Kale, and Gonaka. Our victory is already at hand, Freemen, as support for Seagraul crumbles and falls away from every corner of his old country. Our vengeance will be swift."

That night all the supplies were loaded into the ships, and a good while after the sunset had faded into night, the ships began to take off and await their fellow ships outside the town. All that night and the next day the ships were loaded and set out, and all that night and the next day as well. Just before dawn on the third day of preparations, the last crew set out from the harbor, and the Army of the Free Kingdom set sail for Laen.

The most novice warriors were put in charge of operating the ships during the night. They would arrive on shore in two to three days, and this would allow the more skilled fighters to rest for a good amount of time before battle, if they would encounter loyalists on the shore. It also let them retain their normal sleep schedule.

Most of the sailors were quiet throughout the journey. It was the same sort of feeling that had come over Port Doneaihr after Joel had landed and relayed his message. Men wondered why they sailed, why they got up in the morning for that matter, when all their reason and understanding lay dead in Laeolin. The silence was pervasive, and it was all the sound that men required in such times.

The journey was easy and without any unruly storms or swells. Midway through the second full night, the captains ordered the men to suit up. They would land at dawn.

Back in Laeolin, Gendorn sat upright on a cot in a small stone cell that had been given to him as his room. He stared at the wax figure on the wall, wearing the set of full orchalin armor that he had obtained in pieces throughout the war. He stared down at the helmet he had found all the way back at Port Tekal, the one he had picked up after he had first killed a man. He had acquired a lot since that time— in addition to the armor, he had a sword and shield that he had become familiar with. His shield, like the shield of every Gaolnian, had been emblazoned with the emblem of the Free Kingdom— an image of that barren tree sitting atop that one hill in the vast dirt plain of Old Gaoln, set against a backdrop of an almost overcast red sky. It was outdated now that King Centreal had changed the background to white, but Gendorn liked it better this way. "It reminds me of when we sat there, on the hill under the tree," he remembered explaining to Bendoraun. "It reminds me of when Kamira was alive— and not…white." Bendoraun had nodded and remained silent, allowing Gendorn to work things out for himself. At some point he had left. And now Gendorn stared down at the shield for a long time, and in his mind he drew two figures sitting on top of that hill, holding hands and looking out across the ocean to the north.

For a very long while he sat motionless, mute, and unable to comprehend his own thoughts or to understand the gravity of his own heart.

Then he picked up the sheet of paper that had been delivered to him that morning. Unable to read, he had asked the courier to read for him. *We are coming. Signed, the Captain of the 53rd.*

As his gaze shifted to the array of weapons and armor, he reminded himself that the men he would meet in battle were the same men who supported Seagraul even after he had killed Kamira and all the other hostages. The enemies he would meet in battle were his own enemies, as true as enemies could be. When he thought of Behk and Synla, he knew that what laid behind in Skaen was some old and more distant conflict— and whether or not Gaoln had been right to invade the Skaelin Lands was no longer a relevant question. Bendoraun kept reminding him of this, but it only know struck him as true. This was a different war, Gendorn knew— and in this war he would be fighting the men who supported that monster of a king, the loyalists, the ones who had killed Kamira. Everyone who did not support Seagraul would be fighting on the side of the Alliance for Freedom. He nodded, but did not speak a word. He put on his armor and picked up his sword and shield.

- Chapter Seven -

The men were in full armor as the ships prepared to land, and the red metal glistened bright as the ocean beneath them. Sixty-five thousand men had sailed, and in those moments sixty-five thousand men all in full red armor burned as the fire of the sun itself. Commander Luncas and King Centreal stood next to one another, at the bow of the first ship, and when they looked back they were nearly blind. "Spirits, Luncas," the king whispered. "Look what we have become. We are death, and death only we bring. Everything we wanted to save has been taken from us forever. Death only can we bring."

"Then let us bring it, and get out of this nasty hot armor."

The king smiled. "Good. I was hoping you hadn't softened on me."

In full armor they tied the ships to rocks by orchalin chains, and secured them with wooden posts and planks. The men set up camp in the sandy valley and along the grassy plateaus above, but extra supplies were kept on the ships. It appeared as if their landing would go unhindered by Seagraul's loyalist army.

King Centreal stood up on a rock, addressing the large crowd of people who had gathered upon the grassy shore. "Fellow fighters of the Kingdom of the Free, this camp is for the ship and camp guards, who stay behind to defend us and to escort any and all survivors of Laeolin back to the Free Kingdom. Proceeding with the plan, we march now for Benin." And with that the army set out to begin their war against Seagraul and his Laen.

The marching went on for nearly thirteen hours before the army set camp. The 53rd had been reformed with new soldiers and placed under Alaisio's command, but tonight the Commander of the King's Division was with them. Luncas did not like when Alaisio used the formal title, so Alaisio used it often.

Alaisio tossed another log on the fire. "Tell us a story, Luncas," he said, "one we haven't heard before." It was a common request, but this was anything except a common night.

"Since when am I your storyteller?"

One of the veterans in the regiment, a man who had joined them after Tekal, took the chance to be plain with his old captain. "Since you became an old man— somewhere between Bellford and Gatsesilli."

Alaisio and the commander both smiled. "Well," said the commander, "I used to be a guard in Gaoln, of course. Plenty of tales to tell from those days." The men went silent. One of the logs broke on the fire, and a few embers scattered outside the ring. Alaisio was stunned. Luncas had ordered that to be kept a strict secret! "I've come to terms with it. I told King Centreal, and I told you, Alaisio. But I don't see why I should keep it a secret." He looked across the faces of the men around the fire, the men who once served directly under him. "I was an orphan in Laeolin, just a boy in the aftermath of the last Great War. I joined up as soon as I could and I never left the military— I just changed countries. When Seagraul rose with his revolution, I saw opportunity, and I took it. I believed in him. Centreal himself was the man who turned me. I spent three days wandering Gaoln disguised as a prisoner, and I haven't been loyal to the King of Laen since." They were waiting for him to go on.

"Well, I have a good number of stories besides that one. I fought in the Skaelish March. I saw him die, Lenien the Victor. On the very eve of the end of the war, as the Great March was ending."

"Were you at Liono Den?" asked Alaisio. Luncas nodded. "Gendorn and Bendoraun met a man who fought for the Skaelin at Liono Den. I wonder if you saw him then."

"The battle lasted three days, the actual fighting that is," said Luncas, "it isn't unlikely. When did they meet such a fellow?"

"Back when they were in that village they found," answered Alaisio. "He was the one who sheltered them and took them in. His name was Behk." The flames flickered as the wind swept across the camp on the plain.

"No, I didn't know any Behk."

"You were really a guard in Gaoln?" The veteran wondered. Luncas nodded. "That's one of my earliest memories— watching the last of the guardhouses fall and King Centreal— who proclaimed himself king on that day, atop that mound of ruins, if I recall— watching him give his speech, and saying that we were so close to our freedom."

"We all thought we were," said one of the men around the fire.

"It's getting colder," the first soldier said, reaching for a blanket.

Alaisio nodded. "Tun-Sen is cold up here. And it will come quickly. Down in Goba, just off of Bautaulan, you know— west of the mainland— it's warm the year round. The cool winds will just be grazing the warm lands this time of year, and the smell of the ocean will never be too far away. It's a different smell than this— it isn't so bitter to the senses."

Luncas got up and threw some sticks on the fire, and a small log on top. He knelt down and blew on the embers and coals, then sat back and warmed his hands by the flames. "I bet it's nice to live down there."

"I dream about it every night, that I'm back in the warmth of Goba. But I couldn't bear it any more— the whole house reminded me of Lendah. It was such a nice house, too! It was tucked away, deep in the rainforest, and I cleared this nice little path to get to the town and back. You could see the Little Mountains, just to the north of the house through the forest, where upon the foothills the mists would gather each morning. There was always the fresh smell of rain in the forest. This time of year it would be slightly cooler, and the elders in the town would be in their blankets, but I could never bear to wear such thick clothes.

"Anyway," Alaisio continued, "I couldn't bear to think of Lendah, who was either dead or in Gaoln, sitting in that dust starving to death while I sat there in our old home. And my son Ciso, he is such a brave man— he went to Laen and appealed to King Seagraul himself, you know. And of course the king dismissed him— appeals were quite common— but Ciso has been fighting for the Gaolnians ever since. I couldn't stay in that house, because I just didn't belong there anymore, and that was it, really."

The man next to him looked up curiously. "Did you ever look for her?"

Alaisio regarded the young warrior with a sad sort of expression. "I look for her every day, every time I turn around in bed and every morning when I wake up. I find her every night when I sleep, but she disappears again in the morning." Some of the men smiled at that. Alaisio knew why. *They know exactly what it's like.*

A heavy silence followed this confession, unbroken and hanging in the air. Finally, someone commented: "You know, I bet your boy and your woman, well, I think they would be proud of you. If they could see you here fighting beside us, for no other reason than because you believe. I think they would be proud. And you, Luncas. Whatever family you once had, I think they would break down in tears if they knew your whole story today, if they understood why you chose to fight for Gaoln when you could have just retired. You are good men."

"We all of us are, and the lot of you more than me," the commander answered. "You've all suffered great loss. You have gained things with your blood and tears I was born with and took for granted, and everything dear to you has been stolen forever. You are writing the history of our world with your sacrifices and with your dreams. If your families could know what you had done for them, well, there would not be a happier people in all the world."

That was what caused the real silence. Not a man spoke after that.

- Chapter Eight -

Laen had erupted into total civil war.

Every city was divided into sectors. Some revolutionaries even fought other revolutionaries, trying to install their own heroes as the next King of Laen. Most, however, banded together against the loyalists, and even without the aid of Alliance forces many of these bands expelled the loyalists from their villages and towns and castles. When Kale and Gonaka arrived in force they pitched their battles against the Skaelin and forced them into retreat. They and the Council had troops to spare besides, and with their aid the rebels were able to put the loyalists on the defensive.

Aniania and Kale, meanwhile, forbid Phenen from landing any troops on the continent of Kon by engaging them with their warships at sea. Thus the Kanish and Anianiese together were able to advance against Las without having to fight against Phenen on land or in the rivers, and so President Lokiey was, for the time being, unable to dispatch additional forces to Laen. The defenses in Las held up well, and the Alliance gained little ground. But they kept loyalist Laen isolated from significant reinforcements, and that was all they needed to do for their plan to work.

Gonaka and Kale, along with the companies of Freemen that had already arrived on their own accord before Centreal sent orders to invade, and together with the revolutionaries, prevented the loyalists and the Skaelin from arriving in Laeolin. Through their victories they cut off Laeolin completely, and by then King Centreal with his Free Army had set his sight upon the high walls of Fort Benin and was ready to secure firm control of the north of Laen.

Yet Seagraul's hold over his city was as firm as ever before. Laeolin, a city of more than one million residents, among the strongest and boldest cities humankind had ever seen. That city, as one, would answer the loyalist call to arms, or they would face down death as their punishment.

King Nowhawna, noble leader of Gonaka, understood that a full assault on a city of one million people would be impossible. Insurrection from the inside of Laeolin was one possibility. But the King of Gonaka was not ready to stake hundreds of thousands of lives on that one possibility. Too many had died already. He had an alternative solution in mind.

On one quiet evening King Nowhawna and King Seagraul met in the Fields of Alarai west of Gruso. The Fields of Alarai, two hundred years before, had been the site of the First Great War's most terrible battle. Today it was overgrown with wild grass and patches of pale flowers under a cloudy sky. The grass was firm, as it should be so deep into Sen, but it was altogether a cool and temperate day. *A day made for peace*, mused King Nowhawna. But peace would not come today.

In the Alarai War, called this because the battle here had in fact gone on for months, Gonaka had defeated Laen. Seagraul, the coward that he was, would never have agreed to duel Nowhawna, the King of Gonaka supposed. But how could Seagraul refuse a duel in such a place as this? He would lose all credibility with his people if he refused, and Laeolin would expel the loyalists no matter the cost in blood. By choosing this location, Nowhawna was forcing Seagraul to accept the duel.

Seagraul had made quite the entrance. He appeared on a large black and purple litha, bedecked in armor and baring its teeth. Its wings were transparent and the sunlight near bore through them on those few occasions when it made its way around the clouds.

Nowhawna had himself come on his litha, in his polished red armor with white jeweled lining. He was not normally a man for vanity. But he wanted to look good when he killed the King of Laen.

The armies had not come to Alarai. There were only farmers here and there with their fields large or small. No rebels and loyalists, Freemen and Skaelin, no Kanish or Gash or Laese or Lonin or Phenese or Anianiese. Just farmers and their fields and the slow moving clouds over the Fields of Alarai on that day, and two kings, worlds away from one another, who could find no other way to settle their dispute.

Only four had come to bear witness and officiate the duel. Commander Amrusak, who oversaw Gash forces in the war effort, and Amrusak's top officer represented Gonaka. The captain of the guard of the Black Tower and the City Defense Officer, who had authority over civil defense inside Laeolin's walls, had come to represent Laen. They stood removed from the battle, all four of them together and in silence watching from a hilltop.

Sword and shield. That was the weapon of choice. So with sword and shield in hand the two kings advanced.

The farmers that day heard only every now and again the sounds of swords clashing or beating against shields, sometimes a cry or yell. It was not unexpected in a time of war, so they continued about their business as usual.

The officials watched with patience. Up and down the smallest inclines they fought, up and down a larger hill, through fields of grass and flowers, in sunshine and in light cold rain. For twenty minutes they fought and stabbed at each other, and they both bled in no small amount. By the end of twenty minutes they were panting and faltering, and looking quite unlike kings to anyone who might have seen.

When King Nowhawna fell over backward and Seagraul put the sword to his neck the Gash officials tensed, and the Lonin officials prepared to fight them if anything occurred.

The kings exchanged words for some time in that position. The officials could not hear from so far away. The farmers certainly did not hear. The soldiers, miles away in their respective camps, did not hear. Whatever words they exchanged thus passed between them in secrecy and then were lost forever.

The King of Gonaka lay dead in the Fields of Alarai, his eyes, in an instant, hollow and devoid of life.

On the next morning Joel assumed his place as the King of Gonaka, standing before the amassed army just west of Alarai. He led them through the fields by the tens of thousands, with their swords and spears and axes and shields all shining and red under the sun in its open sky. They moved south and united their force with the main invasion army of Kale that had come up from the southwest under the direction of Commander Kenfus. Together from that point, now numbering larger than the Free Army, they marched east to Laeolin.

The Skaelin, meanwhile, had managed to reinforce Laeolin. Every night with the loyalists and soldiers from Las, they hunted down self-organized teams of revolutionaries and Freemen soldiers. Freemen, horribly outnumbered, fled Laeolin and organized themselves into small armies in the countryside that attracted revolutionaries in the east and south, or they met with King Centreal's forces in the north or the Gash and Kanish in the west. But from Laeolin they were purged.

The Fields of Alarai lay quiet once again.

- Chapter Nine -

There wasn't anyone there with a clue of what to do. There were five of them left, three besides Gendorn and Bendoraun. Umani, a south islander who had been acting first mate for the actual ship captain, now deceased. Jahro, a west Kanish man who had fought pirates before being imprisoned and branded as one himself and transferred to Gaoln. And Veir, a fisherman's son from Keay, of all places, who had been abducted by pirates as a boy and, like Jahro, mistakenly thrown in Gaoln as a pirate himself. Umani was the only one never to have been captured by pirates. He was also the only one who refused time and time again to admit why he was in Gaoln. Whatever the reason, he knew a good deal about ships, and that was enough of a clue for Jahro and Veir to dislike the man.

There was plenty of time for the men to get to know one another. They stayed more or less in one place, because Gendorn couldn't really move in his condition. His hamstring had been cut severely and, although he could stand, moving the muscles inside the leg caused a horrible pain. So most of the time they spent in a glum, overbearing silence inside of a small dark stone cell in the basement of someone's home.

The home was a safe house set up by Menuld, and that was all they knew of it. Menuld had told the residents that the men he would be harboring would be particularly wanted, and that contact was to be minimal for their own safety. Nonetheless, the man had introduced himself as a trader originally from Aois, a man who had witnessed the events of the revolution that brought Seagraul into power firsthand, first in Aois and then in Laeolin. That was the only excuse he gave for harboring them. His name was Meceré, a Laese name from south Las, not belonging in Laen, but he offered no excuse for that either.

There was remarkably little to do.

One night, Gendorn decided he could not remain underground forever. When the men were sleeping, he got up and walked outside. He could not move well, so he did not try. He would have liked to walk in the woods outside the city, but he would have collapsed before reaching the gates. Instead, he sat down on the porch and looked up at the sky. He breathed in the night air and counted the stars, and he wondered if they were watching him too. He breathed out and in, just to know that he was alive, just to see that his breath hanged on the night air and then fell away, just to feel the cold when he inhaled and to know the world was still here. With his one eye, he fixed his gaze on the brightest star.

He took in another breath, and then he spoke for anything in the world that might listen, for his own self, and for that which was lost and gone forever:

"I know that you are sitting on the shores of Gaoln right now, or upon the barren hill underneath the Lonely Tree. There will be no one around you, unless your mother has joined you, and you will be looking out toward the ocean, toward that spot in the sea where you saw my ship disappear— where my waving hand was lost in the mist, and I will be staring back.

"I hold you every night when I close my eyes, and I feel you when I sleep. I hear your voice after the voices of the day have died. I belong with you, Kamira, and I always will. I do not know when I will come to Sendeilta to be with you upon the shores of Old Gaoln, or when we will pass together into the Great Beyond. But until the day I die I will walk upon this earth, which your body, your memory is now a part of— and I will think of you always."

He watched his breath freeze and then disappear, not fully aware that he was alive, not at all caring. But surely aware of those who were not. He moved down to beneath the porch, where the earth was exposed. Then he whispered: "You rest in the earth and in the memory of the world, Kamira." He dug a hole with his hands, though the earth beneath the porch was hard and cold. On the slip of paper handed to him by the messenger, he drew a picture of two children sitting under a single tree. Next to it, though it made him cry, he drew a picture of two figures holding hands walking through a verdant forest with high boughs over their heads. He placed the paper in the hole, covered it up, and sealed it. "And my love rests with you."

He stayed there beneath the porch until he saw the light of the sunrise make its way through the streets and rooftops. He could not smile at it. Not under such a sun, not in this place and not in these days. Tears still falling softly down his face, Gendorn forced himself up and returned to the darkness of the stone cell.

- Chapter Ten -

Those first nights on the shores of Laen, after the taking of Benin, were when most of the men broke down. Benin had been enough for them. Benin had shown them how much of their sanity they had lost. Benin had shown them more than they had wanted to see. Far too much to understand.

It was a massacre. An absolute massacre.

Laen put up heavy resistance when the Freemen got within range of the boulder and the bolts and arrows and the firebombs, a forbidden weapon that the Lonins had not used since the Age of the Great Wars. Everywhere Freemen were crushed, bombed, burned, filled with arrows, and laid to waste. There was outrage that the Lonins were using the firebombs, but it was only an excuse for a hatred that had been boiling since the messengers arrived in Skaen. When, after such awful losses, the Freemen scaled the walls, they could not even push the line forward. When they got to the top, they would be filled with bolts from the huge war machines that reloaded as men climbed, and they would be thrown off the side of the castle by the force of the shots.

It was dark, and nearly dawn, when the Freemen finally advanced. The blood they paid for that advance was comparable to nothing but Seun Bastion. It would not be the worst of things to come.

Alaisio was not among the first to scale the castle, so when he made his way down from the castle, he saw only the aftermath of the hardest part of the struggle. The Lonin men were cut into pieces, which was not all that unusual in the course of war, but these cuttings were deliberate and needless. They were not killing blows. Men were cut so severely, so many times and in so many places— it was apparent that the Freemen had cut them up even after they were dead, cut them in anger and frustration and in madness. Men had been cut and mashed so thoroughly that their parts could not be distinguished, so thoroughly that their bodies and masses had become a liquid mush, no longer made up of bones and muscles and limbs but instead of a red, viscous paste that was a combination of multiple bodies, bodies without faces or anything to identify them as such. They were not bodies, really. It was just one sprawling heap of dead human matter, mashed and beaten and ground up, floating on a pool of red blood.

Alaisio vomited. He had not vomited once this entire campaign, not through all the bloody sieges and the starving cold and the murder in Skaen. Not once. He vomited again.

Some of the men beside, grim and steadfast, trudged through as if there was nothing there, and made their way down into the castle where the fighting continued. Others stood there for as long as Alaisio, and together the lot of them went down in absolute silence.

An arrow hit the wall in front of his nose, and that is when Alaisio registered the scene. That is when he stopped seeing what he had seen replay in his mind.

Commander Luncas was at the top of a stairwell shouting something down to men caught in a battle in a narrow corridor of the hall, where only two men on each side were actually fighting. The Lonins had put good men up there. They actually gained ground up the stairs. Another team was off fighting a similar pair in another stairwell. Alaisio went to where some Freemen had found an open hallway and had cast some ropes down to the floor below. They were shot as they descended the ropes, but they descended quickly and it did not take all that much time before they controlled the floor. The men caught on the stairwells in between surrendered, seeing themselves surrounded, but the Freemen shouted at them to keep fighting or die like cowards. Two of the men put down their weapons and the Freemen ran through them. The Lonins shouted for mercy, and more threw down weapons, but all were run through, until the last of them picked up their weapons and fought to the death.

The gates barged open, and Freemen entered the main hall. From that floor and the floor above the Lonins cried surrender, having forfeited every escape. The Freemen everywhere accepted no surrender, however. They hacked and they chopped and they sliced and they cut, some of them even bit the Lonins and tore parts of their skins off, they beat them and crushed them until they were as indistinguishable as the bloody mass of material on top of the castle. And when blood ran like rivers down the steps of the castle the Freemen, content and nothing else, opened the gates again and stepped into the day.

The world was lighter out here. A rain had fallen overnight and had turned the land to a great swamp, pools laying between small rises, pools more red than not, with blood and pulp and human parts everywhere, as much a mess as any other scene Alaisio had seen. The sky was starting to give way to the dawn, and the morning fog covered the whole of the swamp. It concealed most everything, but every now and then, like out of the depths of the most horrible nightmare, the fog would dissipate and reveal a mountain of hacked limbs and guts and brains and blood that surely once came from beating and feeling hearts. In moments the fog would cover it again and it was lost, but a scene just like it would appear elsewhere. Alaisio bent over and opened his mouth into the swamp, where a face, severed from its body, looked up at him— but nothing came out.

The only thing he could make sense of after that moment was Commander Luncas shouting at him to get back to camp, to get away from Benin. Why was the commander so anxious, so angry about the orders? There was a heat behind him, and Alaisio turned to look back. The castle was a titanic fire, with everything inside burning, everything on top, everything around, a great roaring inferno. Bodies, that was the scent that filled the air, bodies being burned.

The swamp was on fire. The swamp itself! Body parts burned in pools of blood. Heaps of people burned on the hilltops. Freemen scrambled to gather the notes of their dead friends. Anyone who was not concerned with such things ran wildly away from the swamp. Alaisio was not the only man sick among them.

Not by any means. The whole thing was a nightmare. None of them had a sense of where they were running to, and it was as likely as not that any one of them would wind up alone when the mist cleared and find themselves surrounded by torn up corpses. It happened to Alaisio once, but the commander was still shouting, calling him back through the fog.

The men did not have fires when they returned to camp at sunrise. They cried and they cried inside their tents, they fell asleep on the bare earth outside in their own tears, they looked to Heaven and found no answer there and they cried some more. It was all nonsense, all a blur to Alaisio, nothing sensible and nothing remarkable, just a numbness, a hollowness, and a stalling of time.

Alaisio regained his senses two nights after Benin around a warm campfire when the crying had stopped. That was when the nightmare ended and he realized that it had been a reality. Time moved forward again, after stalling for those two or three days. He could feel and think and be alive again, but not as much as before. Not by far.

That night, all the men in Alaisio's circle went around and talked about who they had left in Gaoln. Some of the men spent more than an hour talking. Some spoke for less than ten minutes. Some spoke of grandparents and parents and siblings and lovers, others had one or two people to remark on, and Alaisio, he had just Ciso and Lendah. Some of them were quieter, and some were louder, but when the embers died they all looked at one another in the eyes, and they held each others' hearts as much as they could. The circle did not break from the fire that night. Most of the men did not sleep. They stayed around stoking the embers and muttering a sentence or a story about someone who had been left in Gaoln. It was understood that all of these people were dead now, but it was their determination to keep them alive between themselves, and such a task allowed no time for sleep, not on a night like this.

It was the next night when the men wandered off by themselves. Some were gone for most of the night and only returned for a few hours' sleep. Now that their families were gone, their notes had to be completely rewritten, as most of them had been addressed to loved ones now deceased. So they had spent all their hours writing new notes, but in truth most of them had nothing to write. They buried the notes in the ground or cast them into the river with a prayer, and went on without any notes at all. Some wrote accounts of their lives. Some could not write at all, and stayed in the fire circle for another night. Alaisio spent his hours with these men, listening to another night of them unloading their memories.

None of them said a word about what had happened at Benin, but as the men went on about who had died in Laeolin, he began to understand even without their explanations. He did not bring it up with Luncas. There would not have been any point in it. This, for once, was not one of the old captain's awful and inhuman ideas. This was just men who had lost everything in their lives, and had lost their minds because of it. It was really as simple as that.

He learned a lot about the prisoners who had died in Laeolin. The way they smiled, what made them laugh, where they were from. He made an effort to remember them, names and stories both. He himself did not speak much during these days, but he noticed the men speaking more and more. They had found something in one another that was worth fighting for, something worth staying alive for, rather than allowing themselves to fade into silence, obscurity, and loneliness. Many of the men did succumb to that, all the same.

- Chapter Eleven -

Meceré came down one night with a peculiarly solemn look. Gendorn was fast asleep, with orders not to get up. Meceré had treated his wounds with a sharp and rather painful ointment that immobilized him for a brief time, but he insisted it would help.

So he lay there on the bed while Bendoraun and the others received Meceré's message.

"The noises you have been hearing are men being force-recruited to fight as loyalists for King Seagraul," Meceré explained. "Some men have taken together to resist the recruitment, and have even met the loyalists in the streets with swords. It isn't safe for anyone to go outside. Men of your age would be forced to fight for the first person who lays eyes on you. That's all there is to it. I will update you if something happens, but for now, we are staying in here."

The news did not go over well with Gendorn when he stirred, but he did not have much choice in the matter, being in bedrest. So he conceded and went back to sleep.

He was hardly conscious enough to do much about it. But Bendoraun and the rest of the men were restless. While Gendorn slept, the four of them slouched against the walls, never sleeping and never waking, time as an endless torture to them and this cell their prison as much as Gaoln. If they could escape it alive and get through to the gates to open them for the Free Army, maybe the war would be won. If they could not, and the loyalists came to relieve Laeolin? Bendoraun had no answer for that, except that their only choice was to try, whatever Meceré might say to the contrary.

PART FIVE: HEROES AND VILLAINS

- Chapter One -

Before the close of ten days, the Free Army joined the armies from Kale and Gonaka at their main campground west of Laeolin. They shared information on the troop movements in Laen and word reached every regiment there that the renowned Joel was the new King of Gonaka, and that Kio was to follow. Kio was now High Commander of the Armies of Gonaka, and the closest and highest-ranking advisor to the new King Joel. Word had also reached each of these regiments, although Centreal had tried to put an end to it, that the two young heroes of Gatsesilli, still only in their seventeenth years and having not even acted as captains of regiments before, were to be the ones who would hand them the city of Laeolin from the inside. The excitement over Joel's new kingship was matched perfectly with the widespread disbelief of this second rumor.

They waited for another week while the last of the Kanish and independent Freemen and rebel companies arrived, and by that time Laeolin had been almost totally cut off for more than thirty-five days, and its provisions were already very low. The day before they were set to leave for the final push in the siege of Laeolin, King Joel summoned Kio into his private pavilion, and spoke with him alone in the long hours after most of the men had already gone to sleep.

"I have been considering this very carefully, Kio," Joel began, "and I am quite sure of my decision. If you would accept the charge, it would please me to allow you to lead the Army of Gonaka as both the Director and High Commander, jointly with myself. I will remain in Gonaka to lead our country from home, while you will remain in the field to lead our troops as King Abroad. I do this because I would like to watch over Gonaka myself— there are some things that I must see to. But I would trust this war to no one else but yourself, Kio, and I will not dare to return to Gonaka until this war is over should you refuse this appointment. It is entirely your choice, of course. But as good a fighter as I am, I know that you are better with the strategy. You are a better commander, on and off the field, and I would like to know that our coalition has someone like you to direct it while I can focus on directing Gonaka inside Gonaka."

"And you are worried about Gendorn."

"Of course I am, who is not? It will be upon you and Centreal to make sure that he receives word at the correct time to open the gates for us."

"I will accept your appointment, Joel, but I do not accept it lightly. How are we to get word to Gendorn?"

"Speak with Centreal. I must return to Gonaka for a few days and set things straight there, to make sure everyone knows that I am king. I will return in time for the final assault on Laeolin, but until my return you will have my powers as King Abroad. And after Laeolin, should it be necessary to remain at war with Phenen, you will again assume that position as I return again to Gonaka, unless circumstances demand my presence on the field."

Kio nodded. "I have been preparing for this day all my life, King Joel, and I assure you I will meet it with strength and confidence. We will have Seagraul in our arms shortly, and this war will be behind us."

"May the Wind guide you to good fortune, King Kio."

"May the Spirits guide you to the good fortune of all our people, King Joel."

- Chapter Two -

The armies of the Free Alliance arrived the next night at an old outpost once used by scouts to guard Laeolin. It was abandoned now, since their gathering was known, and the forces had pulled back into the city itself as the Alliance's advance teams had begun to engage them in battle just the day before. They spent the night there, in that old post outside Laeolin.

Even Commander Luncas had never seen such a vast gathering of soldiers. There must have been more than two hundred thousand men on these grounds, armed to the teeth and covered in armor. They covered the western part of the country almost in entirety. Some of them were rebel farmers and traders and ordinary folk in hard leather armor and spears they had made themselves. Some of them were just boys with bows and arrows. But there were columns and columns of men while they marched, stretching for miles and miles and miles, shining in full orchalin with greatshields and greatswords and double-edged axes, men who carried lumber and stone for giant war machines and cloth that could put out the fires from the enemy bombs, ladders to scale walls and giant sacks of dry foods. Of this sort of men there were at least one hundred and eighty thousand, all told. Every one of them was a fighter. There were some who carried wagons or wheelbarrows full of armor and weapons for those who were preoccupied carrying other goods. Alaisio, who knew more than most how such weapons could be used, did not like to look at such things. But neither he nor his old captain could tear his gaze away from such an incredible mass of people in every direction.

Some of them were Freemen and looked almost as weak as the day they set sail from Gaoln. Others had been trained soldiers from childhood. But from the farmer to the nobleman they stood side by side with level eyes and a common goal as they marched toward the rising sun.

The next day, following again the rising of the red sun from its resting place deep in the earth, they set out to attack the city itself. The pale green grass was stiff enough in the cold that it got crushed under their boots. Commander Kenfus, the leader of the Second Division of Kale, gazed ahead. He was at the fore of the Alliance's advance toward Laeolin. He would be the first to face combat, and his men must be the toughest of all, else they would not survive.

There was a pause when the loyalists on their walls became visible through the light cover of trees to the Kanish troops approaching from the forest. Lines of men in the thousands stared at one another and were alive, and each of them realized quite suddenly that in a few moments that may no longer hold true. No one fired, or shouted, or charged. Each man stood silent, still, and alive.

And then war began. It came first from deeper back in the forest. No man who saw the eyes of his enemy began this battle, and perhaps they would not have, in the end. But from afar the war began.

Boulders pounded against walls and gates and towers or landed on the ground. They tore up the earth and flung men into the sky. The Lonins responded swiftly. Fields caught on fire as the loyalists threw their small handheld bombs, but the Alliance was quick to put out every fire. Arrows in the hundreds, in the thousands flew in each direction. Orders could not be heard. Shouts and cries could not be heard. The rending of the earth doused every other noise, the swoosh of thousands and thousands of arrows, the explosions and men shouting and rushing to put out fires. There was not an order among all this mess that made it through.

The gates opened. Out of them came masses of loyalist and Skaelin soldiers. The Skaelin met the Kanish in battle, while the Lonins made a mad dash for their enemy's artillery.

Thousands of heavily armored Kanish swordsmen stepped up to defend their artillery, and the Lonins faltered. From further back another four thousand Gash soldiers approached, and another three thousand Freemen, all heavy armor men to defend the catapults and trebuchets. Alliance men continued to arrive, and they were so numerous after a time that they formed into three teams and surrounded the Lonins that had come to dismantle the artillery. The loyalists retreated, and they took the Skaelin with them back through their gates.

There had been oil splashed on the grounds outside the walls, and when the Alliance soldiers were packed tight in their pursuit of their enemies as they returned to their gates, the Lonins released a volley of firebombs. The land lit up as if it were nothing but a thin sheet of paper. The water and fire blanket crews rushed forward and met the men as they ran out from the flames. As soon as they left the inferno, they would be drowned with water and would roll around on the cold ground. Some men took of their armor and were shot full of arrows from afar. Plenty of men did not escape the flames.

The outermost wall of Laeolin stood firm without evidence of being assaulted, and beneath it roared an inferno, a wall of fire more dangerous and more insurmountable than any wall of stone might be. The Alliance retreated.

When the flames died, the Lonins had reinforced the outer wall and it appeared as if no assault had ever been made. It was the most demoralizing thing to see, Commander Luncas knew, but if there was a victory ahead for them it was through such trials as this.

They renewed their attack.

After two full days of combat the Alliance expected that the defenders would be too tired to continue. But on the third morning a loyalist division tried to break through the siege, just before sunrise when it was hoped the siege would be weakest. The Alliance routed the loyalists, but the loyalists had traps set up in the forests, and as the Alliance pursued them they fell victim to murder holes and tripwires and ambushes. Men would dash through the woods and in a moment disappear altogether. They would fall six or seven feet and impale themselves on spears. They would collapse, as whole regiments, into thin ditches laced with the flammable compound, and a single Lonin archer would set them all alight. Whole regiments would be ambushed by a hundred men or more out of nowhere. Thick chain nets fell from the treetops and held down half a dozen men, and there were nearly one hundred of such nets. Again, a single

Lonin archer could sit there and kill every one of the trapped soldiers. The whole forest became a scene from the darkest of nightmares, and the sun rising with slow grace did not belong in such a scene. The fire was brighter than the sun, hotter, more real. The spears and the tripwires and the ambushes were all more real. The loyalists of Laeolin were defeating the largest alliance of nations since the Age of the Great Wars, and they were doing it with incredible ease.

The Lonins, exacting a heavy toll on their enemy, retreated further and further into the woods, but the fires and traps and ambushes did not end.

At the end of the day the Lonins went back to their wall. There was no ground lost and no ground gained, but a great number of people dead, and strikingly few of them loyalist.

It was not until the fourth day that the Alliance took the outermost wall, after another fifty-hour assault without end in which the smaller number of defenders were simply defeated through exhaustion, and even then the Alliance could go no further. The Alliance had been able to rotate men, but this smaller, more inner wall required fewer defenders, so they would be fighting a rotating defense in their next assault. Furthermore, the killing ground in between the third and fourth walls had been evacuated and filled with the same flammable substance, and there were enough loyalist archers with braziers on the third walls to keep the Alliance from taking risks. The Lonins feared that the Alliance would remain there until Seagraul surrendered, which he would not do until every last person in the city had starved, while the Alliance worried that the Lonins, allied with the loyalists in Las and Phenen, would rout them if they remained in siege for too long. But for the moment neither of them had any advantage to press, and combat lulled.

- Chapter Three -

Menuld sat in the dark brown chair, as large and intricately carved as a throne, under the dim light of the two candles before him struggling to light the vast emptiness of the living room. Before him sat Letharal and Furnarwa, pensive and solemn, their faces cast in the same dim of the candles as Menuld's own. The silence between them hovered but for an instant before Menuld broke it again.

"We cannot allow the siege to go on," he said plainly, "and that is the end of it. We must find a way to let them inside three sets of walls, not just one, not even two— three. Seagraul will have everyone inside the city starve to death before he surrenders power— the siege will not present any problem for him. And right now, the Alliance will be content enough to let the siege go on as it is, possibly for weeks. But the citizens of Laeolin will not long survive this Sen, already cold as it is. Our food has been cut short for fifty days. Sen grows deeper. And now there are no roads leading in or out of the city that are not controlled by the Alliance. There is no question to it, really— we must find a way to unlock all three walls and allow them access in a single move."

"How could we possibly do that?" Furnarwa blurted out. "I am sorry, really, but do you even think such a thing is possible? We may as well lead an army out there and take control of the walls ourselves."

"Precisely," Menuld said as if that were the most obvious conclusion.

"What?" Furnarwa asked in shock. "You're mad. You're too old— you're losing your mind."

Menuld smiled. "Or perhaps you're young and have yet to find yours. I assure you we are quite capable of the feat. Letharal," he turned to Letharal, who had remained silent the entire time, "you will take control of the first western gate, the kings approach from the west and so that is the direction we should set our sights on. Furnarwa, you will free the second set of walls. I will lead a very small team of people to take control of the third wall, and when I have opened the gates I will send the signal back to you, Furnarwa, and you will send it back to

Letharal, and you will both open your own gates even as I open the outermost circle still controlled by Seagraul. When the Alliance sees all three gates open, they will not hesitate— Kio will know what has been done, I trust, as he has met in confidence with myself and Joel on several occasions and should realize that we are behind this plot. I will have our young Freemen associates come with us, and they can explain the situation to their leader while we coordinate the resistance to keep the loyalists from closing the gates back off."

"You must be mad!" Furnarwa repeated.

"Okay," Letharal said calmly. Furnarwa turned to Letharal.

"What? Letharal, are you serious?"

"Quite," she said, just as calm as before. "Menuld has clearly concluded that this is the only viable option available to us, and I am inclined to trust him."

Furnarwa looked from Letharal to Menuld, and then threw his arms up in defeat. "If it is the only way, Menuld, then I am with you." Menuld smiled at his two co-conspirators.

"Good then," he said. "We should be leaving in a few nights."

"A few nights!?" Furnarwa exclaimed. "No— I won't say anything. I should not still be surprised by your schemes, Menuld. Just tell me when we are leaving."

For four days and four nights the siege lay at a standstill. King Centreal stood on the ramparts with King Kio, Commander Kenfus of Kale, Captain Alaisio, and Commander Luncas, surveying the field. Centreal heaved a sigh as he saw the sun ascending on the city. "I can't figure it out, Kio. I just can't. It's as if they want us to enter the city. They're not even trying to break the siege."

"I know, and I don't understand it either." Even as the five of them examined the wall, they saw the Lonins withdrawing from their positions, as if they had suddenly decided that it was a brilliant idea to outright abandon one of their walls. "It doesn't make any sense. Kenfus, you haven't heard that horn again, the Phenese?"

"I have not, good king. I had expected that, were there any Phenese forces, they would try to break the siege at the earliest possible point, when our forces are still spread thin. They have not done so— it is as if they are all waiting for something. Then again, I stand by my opinion that the Phenese have not come, and that the sound was false, something to make us more scared than we ought to be."

Luncas threw an arm around Centreal, and whispered in his ear: "If, for some reason, they want us to enter the next section, between walls two and three, then they will open the gates. It will be framed as an attack, but they will let us push them back. It could even happen tonight. We must not take their bait— there is no sense in abandoning a wall while they have the men and the resources to defend it. Seagraul is not the sort of person to surrender a position without any fight. It must be a fire trap, and nothing else. Should the gates open, we must not enter them."

Centreal nodded. "I agree. But what if it is some subversive plot within those who were still loyal to Seagraul? What if this is the product of some sort of fighting within those who once held the same beliefs? Seagraul must be losing support inside that city, it is only natural."

"You misunderstand Seagraul's regime. He will not be losing support, because there is no one who opposes him who still has a voice. They will be defending him more fiercely than ever before."

"It doesn't make sense."

"Well, neither does Seagraul."

Centreal nodded. "That is true."

- Chapter Four -

It had been almost ten days, and Gendorn could walk quite fine. It did not mean that he would be in shape enough to do what he had to do on this night. But it did mean that he refused to stay behind.

The message had come from Meceré that they would be leaving tonight. Without any idea of where to go, the five Freemen left Meceré's home an hour after sunset.

A single crew of three men came quickly into view, young and able-bodied fighters by the look. That was good, Gendorn thought. Let eight of them travel together, and maybe the rest would be too scared to try and recruit them at such a late hour. It would not be worth the risk. At least, that was the hope.

The men embraced and talked loudly as if they were old friends, and wandered off down a road as if on a stroll, not taking any measures to keep quiet. The ruse worked. The gates had not been so far away, after all, and when Gendorn saw them he did not quite know what to do. What, actually, was he supposed to do with these giant gates and their many loyalist guards, when he had only seven men beside himself?

The night was as quiet as it was cold. The last regiments of the loyalist forces had run by the house hours ago, and now Kamira stood outside waiting. Down toward the end of the alley, off to her right, she saw three cloaked and hooded figures approaching. From behind her the door opened up, and Iuna and Komu stepped out. The three figures came up to them. One advanced ahead of the others, removed his hood, and spoke frankly: "Our mission may not allow us to survive. We must hold the western gates open for as long as we can, and it is likely that we will come under attack. We have men posted to help ward off the Lonins who would attack us, but it is dangerous all the same." The man's voice was raspy, clearly affected by the cold, and his long white beard was littered with snow. He threw the hood over his face and disappeared, then the raspy voice came out again: "Follow me."

The six of them walked briskly through the empty streets. Their own part of town was tightly packed, and every building was at least three stories high, most of them having shops on the bottom and then two floors of housing atop them. As they moved through the city the buildings became taller and more decorative, the streets were thinner, and the city seemed more tightly packed. At one point it thinned out, and seemed again to be similar to the area where Iuna and Komu were living. As they neared the innermost western gate the buildings became wider, and they saw things like factories and blacksmiths and workshops of various sorts. The entire journey was undertaken in total silence, and they avoided every person they met along the way.

It rose sharply in front of them, as if carved randomly in between the buildings and the alleyways of Laeolin— the first set of walls. The gates had been left open, for traffic, King Seagraul had ordered, should remain unhindered while two adjacent sectors were still under their control. The six of them passed by a larger group of cloaked and hooded figures, standing hidden next to the gate, and the bearded man exchanged a nod with them. Kamira followed as her five companions led her into the next part of the city, and from there onto the next. They passed through the second innermost set of walls easily enough— their hooded escort simply designed some story about a delivery of orchalin ore that needed to get through and that the blacksmith's family was coming with him to visit whoever it was they were going to see.

The next section was filled with large and spacious houses that would have had room for a hundred people or more in the center of Laeolin. By now, however, many of those properties had been divided into separate homes or storefronts. There was a harrowed silence and a complete absence of activity here. No one remained between the second and third walls except for soldiers. Those giant buildings and the many smaller ones roaming between them all alike were abandoned. Various items lay strewn about the cobbled roads. Kamira, had she anything left to be afraid of, would have turned back right there.

By the time they reached the second outermost wall, the buildings had become newer-looking, and could be only two stories tall on occasion.

This wall, the third innermost and second outermost in all, was thicker than any before. It rose steeply and cut into the sky with its superbly tall crenellations. The crenellations here were smooth and melded into the wall itself, as if the wall were only some gentle rolling sea composed of small waves. "It's so that climbers cannot land a hook atop the wall, and ladders have a hard time finding a place to rest," the bearded man explained to Kamira. "But be silent now." He ran to the side of the gate and without any further delay began twisting the wheel that controlled the portcullis, while at the same time signaling for the five of them to unlock the bars that kept the door closed. Worriedly, Kamira asked the old man where the guards had gone, and he smiled back at her. "Our friends have taken care of the guards for tonight. There will be no need to worry. As long as you are a fast runner," he added, with a hint of humor. Kamira could not find it at all funny.

The gates opened. Gendorn stood there atop the wall, gazing into the dark gloom where he could see the slow movement of the large wooden doors and the drawing up of the portcullis as it reflected the soft light of the moon in the clear sky. And he suddenly knew what he was meant to do.

Hoods over their heads and cloaks wrapped around them, the five Freemen and their three mysterious companions walked through the open gates and into the barren killing fields. It may have been the most dangerous thing these men had ever done, but not a one among them felt fear. There was no room for fear in such an exciting moment as this. No room for fear where triumph was so near. If they failed, there was death. If they succeeded, then maybe someday they could smile again. And that would be a very nice thing to do.

They were intercepted by a man from Gonaka. Gendorn removed his hood. "Gulaus Gendorn of the 53rd Regiment of the King's Division of the Kingdom of the Free," he said.

Bendoraun removed his hood. "Gulaus Bendoraun of the 53rd Regiment of the King's Division of the Kingdom of the Free."

Umani removed his hood. "Umani Eram of the 14th Regiment of the King's Division of the Kingdom of the Free."

Jahro and Veir took their hoods of at the same time. "Jahro Bane, of the 19th Regiment of the Second Division of the Kingdom of the Free."

"Veir Set, of the 42nd Regiment of the Second Division of the Kingdom of the Free."

One of the three strangers that had come with Gendorn's company removed his hood, and the Freemen were taken aback— the man had scars, visible even in the night, across his entire face, as if some rabid animal had diced it into small parts and the skin had someone patched itself back together. His voice was grave in a way one might expect from such a man: "Donestus, son of Gaoln and Secretary to the Free Kingdom Ambassador to the Council of Nations, here to verify that this is not a trap and that the gates are open for you. Gulaus Gendorn and Gulaus Bendoraun lead this company. I am being followed and must return to Gruso immediately." The man turned abruptly and left with his hood now lowered. His two affiliates, silent and hooded the entire time, followed him. Gendorn and his four friends were dumbfounded into silence and staring.

"The gates are open for us?" The man asked. The five Freemen nodded.

"Be quiet about it," Umani told the man, "until you control the wheels themselves and can defend them. Send someone light, someone who won't make noise, and be quick about it."

The man from Gonaka smiled. "I think I have the crew for it. Stay behind the walls, and you can show them the way."

King Centreal raised a finger, and one of the soldiers came dashing toward him. "What is it, my king?"

"Send the order to Captain Alaisio and Captain Urhaun. The gates have been opened. They are to secure the passages while we march in. Our runners will be on standby just before the entrance, and should they have need of anything they need only to send word and we will be there immediately."

"Yes, my king."

"Bid them good fortune."

"Of course, my king!"

From his post atop the wall he watched as the light-armored 8th Regiment led the way toward the gates at a very fast run. Behind them, and at a slower pace, ran the 53rd, in heavier armor and led by Captain Alaisio. Luncas stood on a part of the wall that allowed him to see everything as it happened, and his eyes could not blink even once.

Alaisio led his regiment down and to the gate, and there he saw five cloaked and hooded men waiting as still as stone. His sword out, he whispered to them, but when one of them raised his hood Alaisio almost laughed loud enough to alert the loyalists. "Gendorn," he said with relief. Gendorn smiled, and Bendoraun removed his hood. "Bendoraun, too. You two do some amazing things. And all I have is the title of a captain."

"There's no time for a reunion, but it's nice to see you, captain," said Gendorn.

"Lead the way, gulauses, and my men will follow."

They saw the 8th Regiment stop and remain still ahead of them. Gendorn signaled for the men following the 8th to gather around him. They walked together up to where the 8th Regiment lay still, and saw that at the front of the regiment a small number of the men were conversing with six more dark-cloaked and hooded figures, standing on the opposite side of the open gate.

One of the six walked out from the rest and removed his hood. Captain Urhaun of the 8th gasped, but no other man recognized this bearded figure. "Menuld!" exclaimed the captain. "It isn't a trap, then?"

"No, my friend, no trap at all, and if you have any sense you will go fetch your army right now! Go and tell them to make haste to the inner reaches of Laeolin. I will keep the men here in defense of the gates. All the gates lay open before you, but they will not be for much longer. At some point the loyalist guards will discover they've been deceived by their comrades. Run!" Captain Urhaun turned around and led his regiment back to the wall to pass the news. Alaisio stepped up to address this man.

"Where may we stay, Menuld, that we may guard you until the army reaches us?"

"Out of sight!" Menuld answered in a quick whisper. "Get behind us and keep yourselves against the wall, and stop talking!" Alaisio, taken aback, raised his hand and signaled for his men to do as Menuld had bid them to do. In silence they stood there with their backs against the wall.

Kamira knew it. It could be no mistake. This boy of the medium build, surely a man after all he had seen and done— this one with the matted helmet hair and the starstruck face and the eyes that looked like the leaves of the forest— this was Gendorn, and no other. Even with one eye covered with a patch and the other open, even with a limp in his walk, even if he had an edge to his voice that he had never had before— this was Gendorn.

Gendorn and Bendoraun stood next to Alaisio, and they watched anxiously as one of the six figures twitched his head, and took a few steps toward them. The figure looked at Gendorn. A rough voice came out from under the cloak, hushed and urgent: "Speak," the voice said. The figure was now right in front of Gendorn, and from eyes hidden beneath the hood must have been looking right at him, he figured.

"Do I know you?" Gendorn asked on the verge of hostile, quite unsure of how else he should respond.

"Gendorn," the voice said in a much softer and more feminine tone.

Gendorn regarded the figure with disbelief. "Who are you?" The figure removed her hood. She stepped out from the side of the walls and into the light of the moon, and in that instant all the noise of the soldiers rushing behind Gendorn through the gate disappeared. The glimmer of her smile under the moon struck Gendorn breathless, and her voice— that beautiful voice— left him still. This mirage, as it must be— it must be a mirage!—

stood before him as some soft and beautiful part of his past, some fraction of his imagination, and he could think of nothing else. He could not tear himself away— then Kamira drew closer, and she kissed him, and rested her arms around him, and looked into his eye. Was it real? Kamira was here— Bendoraun saw her too, she must be real!— and Gendorn opened his mouth. Not a word came out, not a sound. His eye was left unblinking, and he could not take a step toward her if he had tried. Kamira kissed him again. *You've lost your mind— you need to go sit down. Tell Alaisio to take command of the regiment back, he can take Laeolin as well as anyone*, was some distant thought in his mind. Then Kamira shifted again, and her eyes moved, and Gendorn was lost again.

"...Kamira?"

"Yes..."

"Kamira?"

"Yes!"

Gendorn stepped back. He tapped one of his guards next to him. "Do you see that girl? The one in front of me?"

"Of course," said the man, "she's right in front of you!"

"Gendorn!" Kamira said firmly, "I am here, and I am not an illusion!" Gendorn almost fell backward. He looked at her curiously, then he broke into a smile wider than Bendoraun's, who had been thoroughly enjoying Gendorn's confusion.

She said nothing. She threw her arms around them both and Gendorn was amazed at how wide she could hug. She squeezed the both of them, then hugged them each apart, then kissed Gendorn all without a word.

Gendorn looked into her eyes and he never looked away. She was crying. He was too. What else could they do? There was certainly nothing to say, nothing more than this. They held each other, their arms around their backs and their heads on each other's shoulders. He remembered a day when they held each other like this on the shores of Gaoln. He would be able to hold her, just like this, somewhere far away when peace was in the world. He would! And no words were worth the silence of such beautiful thoughts. So they held and they cried. And everything around him, well, it could continue without him, anyway.

Kamira, she was crying for something else, and Gendorn did not know what it was until she whispered between sobs, her arms as tight as they could squeeze him: "They were all killed, Gendorn. All of them. There were only one hundred with me. Just one hundred."

Gendorn nearly wailed. Instead, he held her closer and moved his hand to the back of her head, and said nothing. Armor clanked, boots crunched behind him, regiments poured through the gates and it all was nothing. Swords clanged somewhere in the distance. It all was nothing.

Kamira whispered something else, and Gendorn's heart fell to the pit of his stomach. "I shouldn't be alive, Gendorn."

"Never say that, Kamira. Everyone who survives does so for a reason. Keep your heart up. The three of us are still alive, of all things! Who could ever have imagined that we would meet in Laeolin, after all of this?" Kamira nodded gravely. "None of this was your fault, and Fate has ordained that you live— so you must live!" Kamira nodded again. She kept her head on his shoulder, though, even as she spoke.

"Thank you. I hate to say it— I didn't really expect to see either of you sailing home to Gaoln. And when they came into the tower, I can't..."

"You don't need to say anything, Kamira. With any luck we never will see Gaoln again. We'll go back to Skaen— it's so beautiful there!— as soon as we get out of this damned city, and this war finally ends. Kamira, you will be so amazed— it is such a beautiful place. It's just like the picture I drew you when we were kids."

"I bet it's just as beautiful as those lines in the mud," She took his hand and squeezed it, then let it drop. "Okay— what are we doing now?"

"You need to stay here where you are safe, away from the fighting, or with the family that has been protecting you. Not with us."

She squeezed Gendorn again. "I know." She made no effort to leave. "I know." An age passed before she whispered again: "I'll be waiting— I don't care if you have to come back to Laeolin alone— you find me. I will be outside the tower when you take the city. And if you don't take the city, then I will be at this gate everyday before sunset."

"I'll build a home with you in Skaen," Gendorn said suddenly. Kamira's face twitched on his shoulder, and Gendorn thought she must be smiling. "A real home. Keep low— we'll find you soon."

But even as he spoke these words, the army came rushing past them through the gates. Bendoraun stood still, and signaled for Kamira to wait. Menuld was there suddenly, and his face revealed that their time to reunionize had run out.

Menuld took Kamira and showed her where she could hide inside the walls, then Gendorn and Bendoraun sprinted forward to catch up with the rest of the forces. They were running as fast as they could, but they could not catch up— Alaisio was too far ahead. One of the riders, sitting atop a chuel, stopped in front of Gendorn and got off. "Take it," the man said, as he turned away. Gendorn and Bendoraun jumped on the small furry creature, who could hardly handle the weight of two men, and took off toward the inner gate. Gendorn smiled. It was nice to be among men who remembered him, nicer still that they respected him. But what were they expecting of the gulaus who had opened the gates for them? Too much, the hero of Gatsesilli feared.

The poor animal almost collapsed when they reached the front lines. The regiments gathered around Gendorn as he ran with Bendoraun deeper into the city. Alaisio, when he saw the regiments approaching, turned around. "We're surrounded, Gendorn. What did the runners say of the others?"

"Kale and Gonaka are advancing to our north, and Seagraul has taken the south. We are cut off— we need to rejoin the forces to the north immediately."

"Well, I had assumed that much," Alaisio said plainly. "Alright, we'll withdraw and hold them back near the gate. The other forces are coming in from the other parts of the city, the other circles of walls, aren't they? Seagraul's forces, I mean."

"Yes, and coming quickly. We need men on the walls."

"We'll have them."

They pulled back the line until they were surrounded by the main contingent of Amrusak's division, which included many of Gonaka's finest fighters and was to lead the assault. More experienced than Luncas's division in street fighting, Amrusak's men would act as a shield while Luncas's men secured the area in their immediate control. Luncas had vocally objected, but had relented when Centreal allowed Luncas himself to still be on the front lines.

The Alliance had taken control of most of the western Middle Market all the way up north to the walls of Gruso, and as far south as where the South Wall district began. Such a large swath of homes and shops meant that they could move half of their main army inside of the city, even if it was a bit crowded, and they kept another quarter on the walls, leaving only one quarter exposed to attacks from outside, but even them with support from the walls. Even when the loyalists were mustered they could not take back the streets that the Alliance had won.

The battle still continued through the night, with neither side gaining a lot of land and neither side giving up after that initial invasion. Seagraul had tried to move his forces around the outside of the city to surround the Alliance, but the troops that the Alliance had left outside the city had held Seagraul's forces back, again with support from Alliance-controlled walls. When the morning came it dawned upon a city converted into a war front, with barricades and patrol lines and no sensible people out in the streets.

The battle had died down by then, and everyone was resting. The Alliance took control of all the buildings they could and used them as shelter, under the direct order that they not destroy the buildings as they converted them into temporary houses and fortresses. King Centreal himself took a very large five-story stone building, where he, Bendoraun, Alaisio, Gendorn, Luncas, the 53rd, the 52nd, and one other regiment— the 10th— stayed. He was on the ground floor, at his own choosing, with the men of the 53rd, while in the buildings all around him the other regiments of the Free Kingdom worked to set up a perimeter and to fortify their positions. Several times that day Gendorn heard reports of Seagraul's forces attacking them, but it was mostly Kale's forces that fought that day, and Gonaka to their south as they tried to catch up to the Free Kingdom.

It was in the evening when there came a knock upon Centreal's door. The king rose, and went to open it. Before him stood a stocky man with a long white beard and beside him stood the tall, strong and slender form of King Kio. "King Centreal," Kio began, "Menuld has arrived to deliver a message."

The old man stepped up into the doorway. He smiled to see Gendorn and Bendoraun inside, and gave a polite nod to Luncas and Alaisio. "King Centreal and King Kio, I wanted to tell you this together, and I hope you will relay the message to High Commander Kenfus of Kale. There are one thousand and two hundred swords under my command, my good kings, should you need them. It is a small number in a battle fought by the dozens and dozens of thousands, and for a city of perhaps one million, I know. But, all the same, we have a sort of influence among the population, and several among our number are in a position of, well, relative power, we can say." Menuld smiled cunningly. "At any rate, we are able to take control of the third outermost northern gate, the fourth outermost eastern gate, the innermost eastern gate, and the second innermost southern gate. Should you send the word, Kings Kio and Centreal, I may order all the gates shut down or open as you please, and the orders that Seagraul gives will be, let us say, unclear. I can cause a great deal of confusion among Seagraul's troops as to what they should be doing and what their orders are, and effectively open or close the city."

"This man is truly amazing, Centreal," Kio said, "the most resourceful man I have ever met. And he is good for every word of what he says."

"Where is Kamira?" Gendorn asked. The two men looked at him quizzically.

"Safe. In her home. I understand your concern, do not worry. It is our highest priority to protect those who have survived. Should you need to send word to me, Kio or Centreal, or Gendorn," he looked from Gendorn to Kio, "simply send a runner to the Tower of Laeolin. We will be watching it. If you cannot reach the tower, we have a runner placed at the innermost western gate, firmly under your own control. He is inside the walls, you will find the door just along the edge of the gate. We will not let Seagraul escape this city alive."

Just then there came another knock came upon the door, and Centreal jumped up again from where he had been resting. Kio came up beside him, and together they opened the door. There before them stood a figure not altogether different from Kio, except slightly more lanky and with much darker hair. "King Joel!" Kio exclaimed. Both Kio and Centreal bowed their heads before him.

Joel walked into the room, turned around, and looked at them both, his face set like stone and looking rather angry. "Seagraul is somewhere in this city," he said, "I have come to strangle him with my own hands, if it is alright with you."

"I'd like to kill him myself, actually," said Gendorn. Joel smiled at that, of all things.

"Really," Centreal said, "I presumed I would be the one to kill him."

"I'll let one of you do the deed, so long as I take the credit," Menuld added.

"Well," Joel conceded, "four swords, or four thousand for that matter, will be better than one, in any case. Kio, join if you'd like. We need to split our forces. I want to seal off the innermost part of Laen as quickly as I can. We have the outside surrounded, but I want him to feel our swords all around him. We cannot risk his escape. We will renew the attacks tonight. I have already set up the scouting divisions, and they depart at sunset's end."

Kio nodded. "I am of the same opinion. We leave tonight, then?"

"Yes, but we cannot travel together, or we would be discovered."

"Excuse me," Centreal said, "where exactly are you planning to go? I would like to plan my attack around your own."

Joel took out a huge map of Laeolin and sat down on the floor. "Join me, every one of you, if you'll please."

- Chapter Five -

Alaisio, Gendorn, and Bendoraun snuck quietly through the night. Around them, the stealthy figures of the 8th Regiment scouted the thin alleyways and broad boulevards of Laeolin, while the trio of friends advanced in the middle. As the three of them moved through the darkness they could not see or hear anyone else— these men, Gendorn thought, may as well be ghosts, for he himself could not detect them. There was one peculiar sound which ran out in the night, and which made them pause in mid-step— the soft sound of someone trying to push the blood out of their throat and get off a shout or a scream— followed by an abrupt silence.

Gulaus Gendorn signaled behind a building, and they sat along the edge for a short while. He saw a figure on the rooftop above, one of the 8th Regiment, Gendorn figured. But the figure picked up a ready bow, and aimed it at Gendorn. Bendoraun shoved him inside the buildings and scrambled in after him— Alaisio was already there. They heard the arrow bounce off the wall, and then the three of them dashed into the open boulevard, and Gendorn shouted into the night: "To me!"

At the sound of his voice fifty soldiers of the Free Kingdom came out from hiding, but there must have been two hundred others who were not of the Free Kingdom, and they swarmed the soldiers of the Free Kingdom along every rooftop of every building and down every thin alley which ran between them. "To me!" Gendorn shouted again. Alaisio and Bendoraun pushed him back in the direction of their base, keeping him under cover while they ran. In front of him, as he ran back, Gendorn saw an army of regiments dashing toward him, with a single runner boldly sprinting far ahead of the line, shouting to Gendorn, "It's the Phenese! Phenen is attacking us!"

One thousand torches exploded in light, and the city was suddenly alive. From every rooftop regiments of Phenen's archers revealed themselves, and began firing down upon the forces of the Free Kingdom. Alaisio grabbed Gendorn with his one arm and tossed him inside a building for safety, then shut the door on him. Gendorn tried to open it, but found that Alaisio had blocked off the door from the other side. Bendoraun had made sure that the story of Gendorn's fighting at the Black Tower made it around the campfires and through the streets as a heroic tale, but the consequence of this was that people were quick to protect him, assuming the fool boy would get himself killed in an instant. Alaisio was the worst when it came to that, but every Freeman was more than just anxious to protect the hero who had defended their families on that night.

By the time Gendorn hacked down the door and opened it, he walked out into a street where he was surrounded by other soldiers of the Free Kingdom. But from every doorway Lonin soldiers emerged to attack Gendorn's men, from every window they shot at them, and from every rooftop and alleyway the allied force of Phenen and Seagraul's loyalists poured out and assailed the Free Kingdom.

Gendorn couldn't see Alaisio or Bendoraun anywhere. From the middle of his forces he took command and directed the runners to fetch the rest of the Free Kingdom's soldiers, as many as Centreal could spare, and to order them around the flanks.

Gendorn's own flanks were falling and the middle itself was hardly holding as Phenen and Laen put more and more pressure on every side. Everywhere he looked, Gendorn saw his people dying. He grabbed one of the captains nearby, and brought him by his side. "Send word to Kio, Joel, Luncas, Centreal, and Kenfus. Send a runner to the innermost western gate. He will find another runner hidden just inside the walls, in a small room carved into the stone. Tell that runner to send word to his master that the time has come. There will be no more pauses in this fight until Seagraul is dead, and this city is ours. They are trying to push us back. Tell them all!" The captain nodded and bowed his head quickly, then ran off in the opposite direction.

In no time the soldiers of Phenen and Laen had gathered their forces and pushed into the center of Gendorn's force, almost splitting his five hundred men into two separate sections. Kio and Kenfus had sent forces down to aid Gendorn, but they would not arrive until later. Amrusak was held up elsewhere. Luncas, however, had nearly arrived with a force almost equal to the one they were fighting. Gendorn's own force continued to come in from the west, but the enemy soldiers soon cut Gendorn's line into three sections, only one of which could be reinforced by Luncas. If the two groups of roughly nine regiments each were to survive, Gendorn had to find a way to break through and relieve them. In the sky above he saw a flash of green and white reflecting under the moon, and in a second the litha landed there next to him. Joel dismounted, and looked at Gendorn gravely. "They're coming," he said. "Not our friends. We need to hold them. I have most of a division nearly here. With Luncas's men, we can relieve the rest of your men and hold them."

So Joel and Gendorn ran through the night, leading their companies in assault after assault, and yet they could hardly gain any ground at all, and before the dawn they found themselves right where they had begun. From all sides the attack against them grew even stronger. In the very late night, just before dawn's light, the Phenese and Lonins made another push, and cut off Joel and Gendorn from the center of their forces.

Joel whisked around and took Gendorn by the arm. "Gendorn, you must hide."

"I am going to— "

"They want you and me dead! They're going to divert all their pressure against this force until we both lie dead in these streets. Then they're going after Luncas, Centreal, Kenfus, and Amrusak. I need to find my litha, and get out of here, and see what may be done— and you need to stay hidden until I can come back for you."

"I will rejoin— "

"Gendorn, you don't understand how valuable of a target you now are. After Seagraul knows who you are and what you did. You must hide. We've gone too far east, we are too deep in the city. Luncas hasn't got half his men here, and less than half of mine. It could take us days to regain this position, and this position is at most two hours away from collapse. Everyone you see here will be dead before the dawn, and there is nothing you can do about it! Hide yourself. I know what I am doing, please trust me!" Joel showed him into a building, and walked inside with him. "You will not stay here, because they are watching. You'll sneak out back and hide somewhere further south. As the battle dies down, move north again and eastward until you are near the center of Laeolin. If you do not hear from us, and if you are unable to rejoin our forces, meet me outside the Tower of Laeolin three dawns from now, counting this coming dawn. Do not put yourself in danger."

"Joel, I have given the order for Menuld to close the gates."

"I received your word. It was a good decision. This battle will end with our victory, and with nothing else. We can reopen them for our men and deny the gates to Seagraul, if we find Menuld's men are as reliable as we hope."

"Where is Centreal? He should have relieved us with his men."

"Centreal has left command to Luncas and Amrusak, and he himself leads just four men in the shadows. They are seeking out Seagraul to kill him and end this for good. Tell no one. I will take care of this and do everything I can to save these men, but I can fly, and you cannot. Stay here. Do you understand?" Gendorn nodded.

"Well, Fate bless Centreal. I hope he succeeds."

"Time and Fate be with you, Gulaus Gendorn."

"And with you."

Gendorn watched the battle from one of the rooftops far away, immersed in the darkness cast by the shadow of a higher rooftop, and kept hidden from the wandering of the torches and the moonlight upon the city. Half of Luncas's relief team and half of Joel's relief team meant that they put up a good fight altogether. The line dividing his army was growing thicker, and Seagraul's forces continued to come from the east. He was now too far away to see the main contingent, but he could see the Lonins and the Phenese as they arrived by the thousands. He could see his team of men growing smaller and smaller. He saw as they became trapped in, and could not escape, and watched as they were slaughtered by the dozen. A flurry of arrows came down from the nearby rooftops, and the Lonins surged forward on the ground, and just like that another thirty of them had died. The first light of dawn had not even struck when he saw the last of them die, and he wished he could have killed Joel for telling him that he, their fabled hero, could not die with them.

Now, had Bendoraun and Alaisio made it out of that mess? And if they had, where were they?

Innumerable Gash regiments under Joel, along with some Kanish, had taken up position around Luncas and his Freemen as he marched to relieve Gendorn and his separated army, and they made their way through the Phenese forces, collecting as many of their own soldiers as possible and relaying commands to every captain they encountered. Their force grew and grew but was halted immediately at a barricade erected at the end of the

Middle Market District. The men had charged and found the barricade covered in the powder, and before they could fall back the barricade had exploded and the buildings all around were on fire. It took only a few hundred loyalist archers to make sure the men did not advance through the fire that now spanned at least a third of the whole inner city from south to north.

Luncas stood there, his face a stone. This was it, then. Fortune be with the men on the other side of those flames. He, himself, would not be.

Alaisio had taken command of a host of regiments whose captains had been lost, and managed to regain one of the major streets that had some of their bases on it. But when enemy reinforcements arrived from the other side of the city, Alaisio's own regiments were cut off and surrounded by both Phenese and Lonin forces, and Kio, now just to the north, could not reach them. Desperately, they tried to make a breach and return to the center, but much of the center had already collapsed, and those outside were unable to get to them. The Phenese and Lonins closed in around them and pushed them back and forth, forcing them even deeper into the city, toward the center where Seagraul's forces were still unchallenged. Alaisio knew they could not let that happen— the deeper they went into the city, the more impossible it would be to get out alive. Yet as the night went on they had no choice— they lost man after man, and still they were being pushed eastward.

Commander Amrusak arrived, as if from nowhere, in some dark hour of that night. "We've channeled more regiments this way, Alaisio. We're trying to reconnect the army but the connection is very thin and about to collapse. I need you to go and tell Gendorn what is going on, and he is in communication with Kio's runners now— have him tell Kio that we need him here, or our position will collapse and we will all die." Alaisio nodded— he knew that the commander, by sending him on this mission, was saving his life. Without a word he signaled to Bendoraun, and the two of them took off. Throughout the night

Amrusak battled in the streets and between the alleys, in the houses and on the rooftops, trying to reestablish connection with Luncas or Joel or Kenfus or even Menuld's men. Throughout the night his numbers grew smaller and smaller. No messenger made it through alive to tell Kio of the urgency of their fight. Men from Luncas came too little and too late after the fires had died down. Alaisio and Bendoraun, frantic in their search for relief, never returned. Before the dawn shed light upon the city of Laeolin, Commander Amrusak and all of his regiments, the greater part of an entire division, lay dead upon the stone streets of the city.

- Chapter Six -

Bendoraun and Alaisio hid behind the counter of a store, waiting for the regiment of enemy archers to pass by. When their sounds grew distant, they revealed themselves once more, and continued through the dawn to work their way cautiously back to the Freemen lines. It was just a moment later when another regiment came by, and the two of them rushed into another building, hiding behind another counter, waiting again for the sounds to grow distant.

Gendorn wandered alone in the early dawn, sometimes posing as a Phenese soldier to get by a large group, having stolen one of their uniforms and tucked his clothes from Behk into his armor. Other times he posed as a spy for the Phenese, waving them off with small bits of rather useless intelligence. He found himself trapped, eventually, between a Phenese regiment and a Lonin regiment who were exchanging plans and information about their enemies. He waited for a tormentingly long time before they finally left. The sun had already begun to appear in the east when the opportunity to make another run presented itself.

The calm of the wind passing through the streets was deceiving, as were the peaceful lights of the dawn as they rose over the city. They cast a beautiful light, and Gendorn thought it unfit for such an unforgiving city. The footsteps of soldiers rarely ceased, and Gendorn was constantly on guard. He paused only for a moment to look at the red and orange lights rising over the tall buildings and winding their paths through the alleys and down the broad white stone boulevards, and to ponder this paradox. They looked like fire to him, and as well to let this city burn. With such dark thoughts he resumed running through the streets, avoiding any possible encounter.

Alaisio and Bendoraun stood as still as they could, hardly able to maintain a steady pace of breathing. The men on the other side of this counter were tired, but a few of them were still quite lively.

"It better be an inn. I need food, and I need drinks," said a man, approaching the counter. Another man walked upstairs.

"I need water," said a third, as he searched the cupboards.

As the second man came in to view on their side of the counter, Alaisio sprung in to action. With the hilt of his sword he smacked the man on the side of his head, which was left bare, and the man struggled before Bendoraun stabbed him and he fell to the ground. Alaisio, by that time, had already tackled another man, and quickly cut his throat. Bendoraun and Alaisio quickly killed the third, and prayed the first man hadn't heard— but he had, and came running down the stairs. He was dead soon enough, but, as they also feared, there were many soldiers outside the building, and their scuffle was not unnoticed. The two of them ran out of the building as fast as they could and wound their way through the streets. They were surrounded on several sides, and had to take an alleyway between two sets of buildings, but as they were about to emerge, three soldiers appeared at the end of the alleyway. Behind them, at least a dozen approached, and on the rooftops above archers pointed their nocked arrows down at them. Without thought of escape, Alaisio and Bendoraun lowered their weapons, kicked them away, and fell to the floor. "Good men. You'll fight for Laen now. Good soldiers, I think you'll be," said the man in front of them. Looking at the men behind Alaisio and Bendoraun, he shouted a command. "Bind them!"

Gendorn watched the line of men forming a large sort of semicircle around the perimeter they had established. How could he ever breach the perimeter without being discovered? It was amazing he had made it as far as he had. He still had a long way before he reached his own lines, he knew. Then the opportunity came— there was a distraction behind him, and many soldiers rushed off, as Gendorn hid behind a trash dump. All he had to do now was wait for the soldiers to pass— but instead they only intensified their watch, being more vigilant than they had been at night. Gendorn almost shouted at them to get out of his way, he was so tired of remaining hidden and having to sneak through the streets! He almost didn't notice the two captives being led through the streets just behind him, and if he had been any less aware, he would not have noticed the sounds or sight of his friends, Alaisio and Bendoraun, as they were escorted through the city.

The day was cloudy and still. The sun began to descend from high noon and a light snow fell off and on, the clouds never clearing. Bendoraun almost smiled as he stared down at the snow, forming clumps of white between the bloody streets. It was an odd thing— snow, to him, was a peaceful thing, something light, soft, delicate, and beautiful. It was not quite as dangerous as a cold heavy rain, which leaked through rooftops and had killed many people back in the penal colony days of Gaoln. As the snow fell and mixed with the blood of other people, it lost something of its luster, but it took on another note, as the white-blue crystals became red and clear. It became a representation of what had become— of this world, really. Of how such beauty and grace had been transformed through the vices of people to the world as it currently was. Of how something so frail and wondrous could be so easily corrupted, if only it came into the slightest contact with something wicked. That was the blood, of course. It made enough sense when there was nothing else to think of, at any rate. He stepped in the footprint of the man in front of him, and out of instinct, paused to look down at it for a moment. Before he could ponder much of it, however, the soldier behind gave him a shove, and with a sigh, Bendoraun raised his head, and continued walking.

His would-be-enemies blinded by the fog and snow, Gendorn managed to track the group of soldiers escorting Bendoraun and Alaisio from the rooftops. They stopped in a building after a few hours— why they were taking so long to do whatever they planned to do with them, Gendorn could not figure out. But as the day neared night the snow grew more intense, and when he decided the time was right, he struck. The men had just split up, and could not see one another in the storm. A few of the soldiers had gone off into one building, taking Alaisio and Bendoraun, while most of the men went into several others. They thought they were safe and were taking shelter from the storm, Gendorn supposed. When the doors of the other buildings were shut and locked, he climbed nimbly down to the street and ran into the building where Alaisio and Bendoraun lay.

Gendorn burst through the door and charged straight toward the three soldiers, taking one of them with his shoulder, hitting one of them in the face with his shield, and turning around to fight the other, who had taken out his own sword by the time Gendorn turned to fight him. Alaisio and Bendoraun wasted no time— they threw their bodies at the soldiers from behind and kicked them in the shins, doing whatever they could to distract them. Gendorn killed the man he had been fighting soon enough, and the soldiers looked as if they were about to strike down Bendoraun and Alaisio, when Gendorn charged them, his shield out in front of his face as he knocked one of the men down. His sword met his enemy's axe, but as it did Alaisio and Bendoraun threw their bound bodies at the man, and the soldier could not even get his axe up to strike again because of the awkward angle at which the bound men had tackled him. Gendorn killed the second soldier, then turned to the third, who tried to turn around and run to alert the others. Gendorn ran up to him as he was running for the door, and cut his throat from behind.

Gendorn set his friends free then they armed and suited themselves up from the gear of their dead captors. A worried, and almost angry "Why are you here?" was the first thing out of Alaisio's mouth. "You should be back at the lines, not rescuing your friends from enemy bases!"

"You're welcome!"

"It's irresponsible!"

"Well," Bendoraun said quietly, "I appreciate it." Gendorn nodded. They snuck back out, and by the cover of the snowfall made their way west through the city.

There was no relief for them. Everywhere they looked, even through the now thick snowfall, troops of Lonin or Phenese soldiers moved east and west and north and south. Entire regiments patrolled the rooftops, and they could hear the calls all around them: "Two prisoners have escaped! The Alliance's soldiers must be near! Find them! They are hiding!". For most of that day, it was the three of them who were forced into hiding. They found themselves on a rooftop at one point, and in the cellar of a warehouse the next— strolling along an alleyway one moment, and diving underneath a broken bedframe the next. They continued like this throughout the day— but it was slow, and when the sunset came the three friends found themselves not far from where Alaisio and Bendoraun had been held prisoner. They realized they were cold and wet, without fresh blankets for the night— thirsty, without water, hungry, without food— and, worst of all, the snow was letting up as the sunset began to clear the clouds from the sky. Their cover had been jeopardized, and they would become clearly visible under the light of tomorrow's sun. Short of facing an army right then and there, things could not get much worse.

The Free Alliance gained a little ground that day, and managed to reunite their two sides to establish a firm hold on their center and on all their flanks. They struggled after that, however, and the outcome of the day proved to be only slightly in favor of the Alliance. Their enemies still pressed hard upon them, and the numbers they lost far exceeded the numbers lost by the Phenese or the Lonins. Much of the day was spent collecting notes.

At the end of that day Joel rested his head in the palms of his hands and sighed. He had no idea where Luncas was. Amrusak was dead. Kenfus was cut off. Centreal, the King of the Free, had not been heard from or given orders in two days. They had come all of this way and made it into the heart of the city itself, and now their alliance was tearing at the seams. He was to meet Gendorn on the dawn of the day after tomorrow. If the Free Alliance did not have control of the tower by that time, would he still find him, Bendoraun, or Alaisio alive? What a terrible mess this was. A terrible, unintelligible mess.

The air was still in the night. The moon cast a silver light upon the grey stones which made up the floor of this part of the city. The alleyway was again deserted, except for that same stocky, hooded character Kamira had seen several times before. He approached the house and stood outside in silence, until Kamira walked up to him. "What is it, Menuld?" she asked the man.

"It is time. I have received word from Gendorn, who I hear is your lover?— anyway, this is not time for gossip, I apologize. My army is ready to seize command of the towers. I fear that Seagraul would just as soon tear down the entire Tower of Laeolin, I would not put it past him— but I do not think he values the lives of his men enough to do that. He'd rather see them fight and die. He will submit to our demand that he fight us for every inch of the tower, rather than risk losing the tower itself. But on with it, then— let's get going. You are coming, right? Iuna and Komu said I would find you here, they've gone ahead to get together some of the others and we are meeting them along the southern end of the city."

"Yes, of course I am coming," said Kamira. "But Pas is here. And where are the men who were with Gendorn and Bendoraun? They were meant to guard you. You shouldn't be walking alone anymore."

"I assure you he will be fine. We will send someone to watch for him. As for the men, they've disappeared. It is likely they lost their lives trying to reunite two forces that became separated the day after last."

Kamira said nothing. She simply fell in line behind the old man and followed him.

The two of them ran through the streets. The snow masked any noise their boots would have made upon the stones, and they kept to the shadows along the buildings or stayed hidden in the darkness of the alleyways. It was not long before they met with Iuna and Komu, who told Menuld they had successfully gathered around two hundred of the fighters. "We will strike at dawn," said Komu, "and seize the towers, and refuse to let them in. From the towers we will be able to create a diversion and a panic, and incite an uprising in the neighborhoods which are less supportive of Seagraul. At the same time, Seagraul will find the gates locked, and all his escape routes denied to him."

"And what if the Army of the Alliance fails to meet you at the towers? What if they cannot push through?" Kamira wondered.

"We do not rely on them pushing through," Komu said sternly, "we rely on our own community, and not some other army."

Kamira cringed— was he insulting the Army of the Alliance? "I doubt your community alone could kill Seagraul," she snapped, "you haven't been able to yet." Komu turned to her, his face a stone mask of anger.

"We have been trying to kill Seagraul since the day he took power, before you were even born, before Gonaka even considered— "

"Komu!" Iuna exclaimed. "Calm down, Komu." Komu huffed and turned away.

"Well, now that we've got all of that out of the way," Menuld said with a smile, as if he were not at all worried about the time or about how much of it Komu and Kamira wasted while arguing, "why don't we go see to those gates, shall we?"

The gates stood tall and strong, dark in the gloom of night. There were large metal spikes sticking out from the sides of the gates, a measure which was meant to repel attackers, so that they could only be attacked by weapons or artillery from afar. They were open when first the band of four arrived. But as Menuld took off his hood, the soldier atop the gates nodded, and he spoke some command to a nearby man. The gates closed and locked. "Our men have been moving in since sundown. They've come from every side of the gates, but most of them come from the east," Menuld explained to them. "The eastern gates will be the last to close, therefore, but the northern gates should be closing soon."

One of the soldiers came down from the walls and walked up to Menuld. "What news, master?"

"He is alive, but will try to escape on this night. The gates will remain closed. He will argue, and will try to escape with his soldiers by his side. We will prevent that. The gates will remain closed until Seagraul is dead. They have been instructed not to harm the safe houses. We will rendezvous at the house nearest the center— " Kamira knew this meant Iuna and Komu's house— "as soon as we are able, but no sooner than the dawn. We will approach singly or in very small groups. Is everything prepared?"

"Yes, master."

"Send the signal. We begin tonight."

"I will send your order to our friends here in the southern sector. Will you be leaving for the east?"

A grim smile crossed Menuld's face, a dark and foreboding sort of smile. "No. We will be staying here with you."

"Why is that, master?"

"Our friends are strong in the east, and they approach the center. They do not need us quite as much." Menuld paused, and then he looked up with heavy eyes, staring at the soldier before him. "And because he comes tonight to escape the city, not to the east, but to the south."

Kamira gaped. "Menuld, you'll bring the army down on us!"

"No," Menuld said quietly, "I think not."

"We need sleep, Gendorn," Bendoraun said, "we have to get some sleep. You haven't slept in two days, and we won't survive a fight like this." Bendoraun was shivering in the cold even as he said this. "We will be even colder tomorrow night, even hungrier. We will not want to stop for sleep— we will want to push on to our own base. You need the rest."

"I agree with Gendorn, Bendoraun— we cannot afford to sleep."

"Thank you, Alaisio," said Gendorn, "Bendoraun, I know you are concerned, but the most important thing is for us to get back to the lines."

"I have another idea."

"And what is that, my friend?" Gendorn asked him. Bendoraun sighed, and took a moment to craft his answer.

"I think we should hold up at the Tower of Laeolin."

Gendorn looked at him critically. "What?"

"Just consider it," Bendoraun persisted, "King Joel will be there two dawns from now— we have this night, the next day, and the next night, and then he will be there. With him will come a major offensive on all sides. Menuld's men, as you have told me yourself, will be making an attempt to take the towers tonight or tomorrow morning at the latest, and with his offensive, the armies of Gonaka and Kale will approach from the north, the south, the east, and the west. If we can stay hidden in the center of the city then we can wait until the forces take command from all around us— and then we can raise the banner of the Free Kingdom, in the center of Laeolin, we, with Menuld's soldiers who have fought for decades to rid Laen of

Seagraul. No one could resist us, Gendorn. The people of Laen will rise up against Seagraul, because they will see every gate closed and every corner of their city controlled by the Free Alliance, and in the very heart of Laeolin, the flag of that alliance will fly from the top of the Black Tower."

Bendoraun let Alaisio and Gendorn consider this a moment, before pushing his argument upon them some more. "Gendorn, you don't yet realize how much power you have. You don't realize what you mean to people, what a symbol you are. You don't realize that when you rise up against Seagraul from the heart of his own city, there will be no power left that can resist you. Alaisio, tell him! Menuld has allies all around the center of the city, and his forces are moving there tonight. They will control the towers by dawn." Gendorn remained silent, and his gaze shifted between the ground and Bendoraun's eyes. Alaisio said nothing— this, he knew, was for the boy to decide, and Bendoraun was making a point that Alaisio had not considered.

"Listen to me," Bendoraun insisted, "if we make as much distance as we did today, we are two days away from getting safely behind our own lines. And then what, we resume command of regiments just because of what we have done, knowing nothing at all about how to actually lead a regiment in a pitched street battle. Two days of hoping that we do not get caught just to serve no purpose. If we leave for the tower tonight, we can be there by tomorrow's noon. As Seagraul's forces meet Menuld's rebels in battle, *we* can meet Seagraul. Don't you understand? He will be there, Gendorn."

Alaisio shifted uneasily. "The boy is right, gulaus."

"I know," Gendorn said softly. "Seagraul will be there, won't he? He will think it an easy victory. And I can challenge him to a duel, and no one will be able to interfere."

"King Seagraul is no amateur swordsman," Alaisio cautioned him, "he did kill King Nowhawna, and King Nowhawna could kill you as easily as he could kill a fly. No one has gotten close enough to even offer the challenge, and more than one hundred have tried. Bendoraun, your plan has some awful flaws."

"I will not die by his hand," Gendorn swore, "but I will have him die by mine. And I will raise the banner over the Tower of Laeolin— I will call the entire resistance out from hiding— and I will tell them that Laeolin no longer belongs to Seagraul— that Seagraul is no longer fit to be king. And this time there can be no escape— there will be no way out of the city for the old King of Laen."

Bendoraun rolled his eyes. "I'll just sit here, then, while you keep talking yourself into it and building it up to make yourself seem like a hero, Gendorn. Let me know when you've come down from the clouds to get the rest of us."

"You gave me the idea in the first place!" Gendorn retorted.

"Enough," said Alaisio. "We travel until daybreak, and then we rest. When we reach the Tower of Laeolin, we will be ready to bring this battle to an end."

- Chapter Seven -

The circle of the sun had fallen against a towering building to the north, and light protruded from the top, left, and right. The sky seemed to be reaching downward, pillars of yellow clouds grasping for the earth, like spires from the roof of heaven come to reach for the floor of the world before it faded into the blackness. Luncas and Kio exchanged glances, and turned to face the light of dusk. Arrows let loose from behind their lines, and another volley came toward them from their enemies. The king and commander ran forward, and all around them Freemen and Gash rushed toward the lines of Lonin and Phenese defenders.

Kamira shivered again. She could not stop shaking— Seagraul was coming here, and he would come with an entire army. What was Menuld thinking? They had thirty men here loyal to Menuld, at most, and as it was they could only keep the gates closed by arousing suspicion and attracting attention. When Seagraul himself showed up, and ordered them to open the gates— what was Menuld thinking? *There is nothing he can do*, Kamira concluded— *nothing*.

There was a lone figure emerging from the shadow. It happened suddenly and all at once— he came out from the darkness, and in the moonlight Kamira could see his robes of blue and white thrown over his armor. The King of Laen walked toward them, and as he did so, one hundred soldiers followed in his wake— then two hundred, then three hundred. *It's an army*, Kamira thought.

Menuld walked out into the moonlight, and Kamira almost grabbed him, and shouted at him for being so reckless— but then he started walking out away from the wall. Alone, he walked toward King Seagraul, and King Seagraul froze. "King Seagraul!" Menuld exclaimed, as if he had been looking for him, "news from the west and the south I do bear! You must be leaving to relieve your forces in the east? I am afraid they have been overwhelmed already." King Seagraul looked as if all he wanted to do was walk up and strangle the life from this old man. His forehead throbbed, his ears perked up, his eyes grew wide, and his face became stiff. Menuld smiled back at him.

"I was," came the king's slow, firm reply, "how clever of you to have taken notice, and to have been so kind as to inform me." He twitched his head sideways, keeping his eyes locked on Menuld. "Never mind. I will still be leaving through this gate, as it will be necessary to reunite with the regiments I left south of here."

"I bear terrible news of those regiments, I am afraid, my old king," Menuld said.

"What news?" Seagraul said, his voice loud and clear, and hardly restrained from a shout.

"They are all dead, I am afraid."

"All dead!? All dead! Well, isn't that a coincidence!"

"Quite a tragic one," was Menuld's reply, calm as ever.

"Well, I will need to come to the aid of those you have said have been overwhelmed."

"The last I heard, King Seagraul, they had already been pushed back toward the middle of the city. If you are to aid them, I should suggest that you take your men and cut them off along the Old Road to the Sea where it begins here in the inner city, for that is where they travel now, last I heard— far from the gates."

"If these reports are true, Menuld— and I know you would never deceive me," the king said— and now he really was almost shouting— "then it is paramount that I leave Laeolin and return with forces from the territories in our southeastern provinces that remain loyal to me."

"I am afraid, King Seagraul," said Menuld, his voice suddenly forceful and every bit as loud as the king himself, "that the forces of Kale have taken position just south of this gate, and they would not let you through alive. That was the latest report I had heard, at any rate. Kale and Aniania have also occupied Aois and have closed that province to you. Surely, King Seagraul, in such a time of dire need, when your people need your leadership, as their city is surrounded by enemies on all sides, as enemies rise from within, even— surely you would not desert Laeolin, and leave your people to fend for themselves?" As he finished, the guards upon the wall turned their gaze to King Seagraul, and they looked at him expectantly. Seagraul could not ignore their glares, or the silence that followed Menuld's tirade. "Your people need you. They are being attacked from the east. Your enemies hold the west and north. Why do you turn to the south? What do you think awaits you on the other side of this gate? Only your death. Those who live and stay loyal to you are here in this city, and they need you!"

"Guards!" Seagraul announced, "I command you to open this gate!"

"Your people die, Seagraul," Menuld shouted, "why do you flee?" The gates did not open. Menuld did not move.

"I commanded you to open the gates!" King Seagraul yelled.

"King Seagraul," cried the voice of an officer upon the walls, "for what purpose do we open these gates? Surely if you send this force to relieve our armies, we may send word to the nearby regiments that help is on the way."

"I have already sent word, and I intend on attacking the enemy to the east, they are fast approaching the gates!"

"King Seagraul," Menuld said, "the gates have already closed behind them. The enemy is inside the city."

"I have not received any word that all the gates have fallen, Menuld, and last time I checked I was the one who commanded the opening and closing of these gates, not you." King Seagraul looked again to the walls. "I will not explain myself any further! You will open these gates immediately, or you will be discharged and sent from Laeolin!"

"Sent to Gaoln, by any chance?" Menuld said quite placidly. The guards on the walls did not move an inch.

King Seagraul looked again at Menuld with renewed rage. "I should have sent you to Gaoln ages ago!" he hissed.

"It is a shame that you were unaware of the extent and the limits of your power when you could have sent me to Gaoln," Menuld said slyly, "perhaps you should be careful not to make the same mistake…again?"

"I am quite aware of my power in this city, Menuld," Seagraul said softly.

"This city has afforded you too many mistakes, King Seagraul. I think it would be unwise to abandon it, to reveal your cowardice in the presence of soldiers who in bravery would give their lives for you." The faces of the soldiers upon the wall became darker— every one of them fixed their eyes on King Seagraul.

"You will stand down and open these gates!" King Seagraul commanded, "Or you will fight me and my men as traitors of your king and country!"

There came a cry of pain from behind Seagraul, somewhere among the ranks of his regiments— and then another, and then a blood-curdling yell, and the sounds of someone gasping for their breath. The king whirled around, and he saw an arrow coming right toward him. He ducked and turned around, and ran back to his men. The arrows had come from the darkness, but from the nearby buildings small groups of men emerged and attacked Seagraul's regiments. "Defend the gates!" Seagraul commanded. "Do not follow them, they try to lead us away! Pull back to the gates, and we can battle them from the gates!"

Menuld looked up at the officer on the wall. He nodded his head, and the officer raised a hand, then let it fall, pointing his finger toward the king. From the wall, a volley of arrows fell upon the king's guard, and twenty men fell dead. Another ten fell dead from the volley which came from behind, and the king's guard struggled to arrange itself while being attacked from two sides. They formed their lines quickly, however, and King Seagraul was there in the center to direct his men. "Kill him," Seagraul whispered to his own guards.

Menuld looked up, and the world froze for a moment. There was the moonlight upon the streets and the rooftops and the figures of men, and the snow gentle while it lay on the cold stones. There were these men before him, these loyal men, who would follow the orders of their king if it meant their very life, much less the life of a hundred who they did not know. There was the matter of the young Gendorn, about whom Centreal had made his intentions clear, and who he would not be able to raise and instruct, who he had hardly ever known. There was the matter of Gaoln, which he thought of for a moment— and he was so happy to have seen the day when Gaoln was Gaoln no more, when prisoners were Freemen in the Free Kingdom. For a moment he was in a stone room in another part of the world an Age ago, a rain outside that beat a bloodstained earth. What a blessing it was to see the end of such an awful story before his own end must be met. And then there was the matter of that tree, that simple tree upon that dirt hill, which would not fall and could not be struck down. And he wondered if it could still grow again and become a symbol of strength for the men who had lived their lives around that one tree.

They fell upon him at once. There was an arrow in his chest, and then another, and two more, and two more— and one in his arm, another in the other arm, several in his legs— his body, in a single, almost graceful movement, fell entirely backward as one, onto the ground behind him. His eyes, so suddenly blank and without any thought in the mind behind them, stared up at the night sky.

Komu held Kamira back. "We cannot fight them," he whispered. He led Kamira and Iuna deeper into the guardhouse within the wall, and they stood up against the edge, waiting. Komu turned his gaze toward Iuna. "I do not think that was a part of Menuld's plan," he said gravely.

"No, I cannot imagine that it was," Iuna agreed, "who will command what is left of the resistance? And who will keep Seagraul from getting out? He'll get through this gate in only a few more moments."

"Keep Kamira safe," Komu said to Iuna, then he turned to Kamira. "Keep Iuna safe." Kamira nodded. "I'm leaving to inform those in the east, you know of whom I speak, Iuna. They have to lead the resistance, and we will make sure that if Seagraul escapes this city, he will not make it far alive. Stay hidden until someone comes to get you. If no one has come by dawn, return to the house and do not look for me." Iuna nodded. "Get Menuld's note. It might have something important in it." Again she nodded. Komu, not waiting for another moment, turned and set off at a run.

"Iuna, we can't just stay here."

"We can't do anything, Kamira. Seagraul's forces will overpower the guards here and subdue the rebels at any moment, and we will be lucky if we go undiscovered."

"But we know that Seagraul is leaving. We know that Menuld failed to stop him, that he is dead— "

"Other people will know that very soon, people who can actually do something about it."

"I can do something about it."

"We don't even know where Gendorn is. His own army hasn't even seen him since the great push into Laeolin. There hasn't even been word of where he might be."

"I know where we can find him."

"That's impossible."

"It isn't. There are only two possibilities. One, he will go looking for me, which will put him next to Bendoraun outside our front door. Two, he could try and draw out King Seagraul to fight him— "

"Not when he receives word that the king has fled, he won't."

Kamira sighed. "No, he won't. But what if he doesn't receive word?"

"He's gulaus, Kamira. He'll receive word, wherever he is."

"Yes," Kamira said resignedly, "I suppose he will."

Seagraul's men ignored the arrows shooting at them from behind. They threw themselves at the wall, upon the king's command— "Take the walls and get those gates open! Draw these traitors out into the field, where we can see them!" The king himself had to keep low, and was always ducking beneath his soldiers. A circle of shields kept him protected. But from the walls a hundred people emerged, who had been crouching or keeping themselves hidden. In the same moment that they rose, they let loose a volley of arrows down upon the king.

Komu dashed into the darkness of the slim alleyway, just as wide as he himself, and took off northward bound. He skimmed the central part of the city, working his way eastward. He sprinted until he had no breath, until he could feel the cold in his lungs contrasted against the heat of his blood, and then he ran some more. Twice he almost ran into an enemy soldier. Once he was discovered, and had to run along some side streets to lose the man pursuing him. And then, after far too long a time, he found what he was looking for— a group of a thousand men spread throughout the city, making their way westward in silence.

He walked up beside one of the men, and before they could subdue him, blurted out: "Furnarwa!" The man stayed his sword.

"What do you want with Furnarwa?"

"Tell him that Komu has come with an urgent message and I must speak with him at once." The man dashed off down another street. Komu waited for some time, and he grew impatient, thinking the man had run off, or was Furnarwa in trouble somewhere? But even as he thought this, he saw them coming back down the same street, and Furnarwa came to meet him.

"What is it, Komu? Are Kamira and Pas in danger?"

"Yes, and so is everyone else in Laeolin. Seagraul has escaped."

"Where is Menuld?"

"He is dead."

Furnarwa, who was not often a man of expression, was struck dumb. He looked hard at Komu, as if waiting for him to say that he had just been joking— but Komu stared back with heavyset eyes and a grim face.

"I see," Furnarwa said slowly, "well, then...I suppose...I will be taking command..."

"And you'll also be sending half your force outside the gates and around to the south, sweeping the woods for Seagraul and his band of two hundred guards."

"Yes...I...will do just that..."

"It is a loss for us all, Furnarwa. Know that we stand together, as Menuld would have it, and together we will not falter."

"No. We will not. I will send the forces immediately. Thank you, Komu."

"Of course."

Through the night the forces of the Alliance battled. In the darkness, when one stood from a distance, it was difficult to tell if a man was an enemy or a comrade, as the light of the torches could not reach the center parts of the wider streets. A bystander would have seen only men, indistinguishable from one another, fighting and killing and dying in something beyond comprehension.

Both sides took advantage of this— the front lines dissolved as soon as battle commenced, and from every side Phenese, Lonins, Freemen, Gash, Anianiese, Skaelin, Kanish, and Laese soldiers could find themselves suddenly surrounded by their opponents. It was impossible to tell when one side gained ground, as on all sides every nation was continually gaining ground and then losing it. It was long after the sun had set, deeper into the night, when the clouds broke from the sky above and the moonlight shined bright, beginning to reveal their positions.

Kio, Luncas, and Joel had advanced deep into the territory controlled by Seagraul's loyalists and their allies. Kenfus had held the lines south, and the Council kept the loyalists from attacking out of Gruso. They could almost reach the tower.

At the same time that Joel tried to cut off the Lonins, the Phenese tried to cut their own enemies off and to bring up their own regiments to gain ground against the Alliance. Joel and his guards, along with the regiments further apart along the same perimeter, held off the Lonin-Phenese advance until Kio returned with more men. The Skaelin had apparently run off to fight some pockets of rebel Lonins who had taken up arms to fight beside independent Freemen groups. So Luncas, leading an assault from the north, was actually able to break most of the enemy line before returning again. By the time half of the night had passed, the Free Alliance had managed to repel their enemy's advance and to isolate the enemy regiments that had advanced into the area controlled by the Alliance.

"We have one day and one more night to get to the Tower of Laeolin, Kio," Joel said to his friend, as the battle died down and a brief ceasefire ensued. "If we are not there by that time, I will have to travel to the tower alone on my litha, and risk my life to get Gendorn and as many survivors as he found out of the central part of the city alive."

"It will be impossible to remain secretive once you have exposed yourself, my king," Kio cautioned him, "Is there no other way?"

"I told Gendorn that I will be there, and I need to find him."

"Joel, I must speak plainly. It is not worth you risking your own life. And there is no chance of you two escaping alive, much less you and a regiment."

"Perhaps not. But perhaps that is not the point of it, either."

"What are you getting at? Have you been planning something?"

"Only weighing the possibilities."

"The weight of your death would be a heavy one."

"It would. But life is nothing but a series of gains and losses, wins and sacrifices— death, to a soldier, is only the last among many, as they say."

"There is no one in Gonaka who could be a better king than you, Joel. Let me go to the Tower of Laeolin, I will take the litha and find Gendorn, and I will get him out— I am almost as good at the sword as you are, you know— you taught me all my life. I used to be better than you, when we were boys."

Joel smiled. "You were never better than me."

"You're entitled to your own opinions."

"Kio, I gave my word— "

"And I give you mine, I will go in your stead and I will return with him safely, or I will die trying."

"You are the better tactician, and I the better swordsman. I must go to the Tower of Laeolin, and you must command the forces further into the city."

"Fengorian cannot afford to lose you as King of Gonaka."

"The Freemen need him. They have hardly any heroes left alive, and little to fight for. You do not understand. I will not discuss this any further. I am going, and you will command the forces."

"I forbid you to go."

"You have no such authority, King Kio, as we share the kingship as co-equals."

"Then I wish you the best of luck."

"That you may do. Advance quickly. Take the towers as soon as you can. Our lives may depend on it. But do not risk your position."

"I have no doubt of our abilities, my king," Kio assured him, "we will see you at the tower."

The king's men fought their way on the stairways to the top of the walls and led King Seagraul up alongside them. From afar, everyone on the walls could see the men approaching from either side along the ramparts, two regiments marching toward the battle from either direction. There was a pause as the men approached— swords and arms fell down as everyone's eyes shifted toward these new soldiers. And then, from the midst of one of these groups, an officer spoke: "What in the name of Fate is happening here! King Seagraul, why are you fighting your own men— a better question, posed to your men— why are you fighting your king! I could hear the battle all the way from my post in the turret just to the west along this wall, and the next thing I know I look over and see the king huddled around a hundred men struggling to form a shield around him! Not a man will move from this place until someone explains to me what is going on!"

"I will explain to you, captain!" King Seagraul answered, "these men along the walls, the ones who are meant to defend our city in the name of our country, have conspired against me! They have been tricked by Menuld into containing me within these gates, and will not let me escape!"

"Is the king fleeing Laeolin?" the captain asked in response. The king's eyes grew wide. *Not him too.*

"I seek to escape these gates to relieve a force of my comrades in the east, and to send word to my correspondents in the south that we need more troops in Laeolin."

"You see?" the captain explained to those along the wall, "he escapes so that he may save Laeolin. Who is in charge here? Who dared to tell the king that he may not leave his own city?"

All the faces of the men drifted toward the body lying in the snow, and those around the body edged away from it, to allow the captain a clearer view. The captain scrunched his forehead and squinted his eyes in concentration. "Is that...who is that? All I see is someone's grey cloak. Was that the man in charge?"

"It was Menuld," King Seagraul told the captain.

"I never did trust him. I knew he would always be an agent of Gonaka," the captain said. "But who orders these troops now? Why do they not stand down? There must be some man here who still commands them to fight against you, King Seagraul."

A man came up from behind the battle lines to stand beside the king. He looked over the heads of the men around him, to find the captain and meet his eyes. "I still command them," he told the captain, and the captain stared back blankly.

"But why? You were so loyal..."

"King Seagraul deceives us, captain," the turncoat captain said.

"You deceived me!" the king shouted.

"You have deceived the good and faithful men who have died for you and for their country, Seagraul, and you have defiled their honor!" the rebel captain answered the king hotly. He turned to the captain who had just arrived. "Captain, the south and east are cut off. The enemy surrounds us. The north and west are controlled by the enemy armies and we cannot even fight our way to the gates there. Seagraul does not leave to fetch reinforcements— he steals himself away in the night without any thought of returning. He is abandoning the city, abandoning this country, and abandoning the sacrifices of your men and mine. His own honor is forfeit, and his goodwill is known now to be as hollow as his denial of the genocide at the Black Tower. Consider your actions before you take them. Tonight we know, once and for all, who this man before us is. And tonight— not on any other night— we must act on that realization."

The new captain came closer, and spoke into the crowd: "I command every soldier here to stand aside. The king is leaving Laeolin to find reinforcements, and any man who stands in his way is a traitor to this city."

"A traitor to this city," came a pensive voice from below. "Such a funny thing to hear, that word— I have heard it too often before, and this city can testify to that."

The captain looked down at the man, and at the hooded figures emerging from the side of the wall. There must have been four hundred soldiers coming up from the east, coming into sight from the far-off darkness or revealing themselves from the shadows of the wall and from behind the buildings just inside the gateway. "Who are you," the loyalist captain called down to him, "and how much longer is this going to take? My shift was meant to end, you know, and I did not plan on killing you tonight. I hate going out of my way for things as trivial as that."

"You'll not have to, if you can keep your wits about you," answered the man who stood beneath the inside of the walls and in the front of the men emerging from all around. "King Seagraul, I think I should introduce myself. You and I have met before. It has been many years since that time, and I cannot begin to fathom what has happened in that great span of years. I cannot tell you how many times we almost killed you, how many times we almost had you under arrest. I cannot tell you how many of my good friends have died trying to end your terror.

"You'll remember me from the First Rebellion and the Pirate Wars. I had some rather close associates who were enemies of yours. I am amazed that you cannot recognize my voice, Seagraul, for it is only by chance that I ever escaped. You'll remember Malia and Ambaru, of course, and you'll remember Furnarwa and Letharal, who worked with them. You'll recall, more than any of these four, two individuals named Ailo and Numini, and you will recall the son they bore, Gendorn. It is a broken history of blood and tears, and you are responsible for that."

"You can't be…it's been so long…" Seagraul began.

"It seems longer to me, Seagraul, as I have been trying to bring you down every moment of my waking life. You do remember them all, don't you?"

"Of course…"

"Yes, then, you should remember me— I am Furnarwa, and behind you, on the outside of this wall, I believe you'll find my best friend and my partner in this life, the lovely Letharal." Seagraul turned around, and, over the side of the wall, saw Letharal coming out from the distant darkness. Behind her trailed a group of at least three hundred— four hundred soldiers. Seagraul looked at them in disgust, and a hint of fear. He turned his gaze back toward the city, where Furnarwa now stood in front of another four hundred soldiers. "It is a shame that Menuld did not live to see these last moments of your life, Seagraul. I can only begin to imagine how much he would have enjoyed seeing this finally come to a close. But there is one thing that he did not tell you, and that I believe you should know before we take your life, and end this for good."

"What is that?"

"Gendorn, hero and gulaus of the Free Army, son of Numini and Ailo, he the son of Malia and Ambaru, is next in line to the throne of the Free Kingdom. The child and grandchild of your worst enemies will rule as a king after you have died as a traitor. Had you taken them into your arms rather than expelling them to Gaoln and taking their lives, perhaps none of this would have happened? You should have listened to me all those years ago. You have no idea how happy it makes me to say this to you in person, Seagraul. I've dreamed about it ever since Aois."

The old king paused for a moment, and then he looked upon Furnarwa with wonder in his eyes. "You must be right— the timing is perfect, he is of the perfect age— the boy never knew his parents and he was raised in Gaoln, thinking he had never had another home until he went to Skaen." He stopped, and his heart beat faster. "How is that possible?"

"Fate has allowed it to be so," Furnarwa said, "Time and Fate have spoken against you. You will never be king again, and your life is forfeit. Those who you have spent your whole life persecuting will take your place as the new leaders of this world. Your time is over, and the Laen that I have known my entire life— we will never be forced to know such a Laen again. Fengorian will never again be forced to suffer under the wrath of such a king."

Letharal walked along the outside of the wall until she was near the captain who had come to the aid of the king. "Times change, captain," she said to him, "Seagraul's time ends tonight. If you remain on the wrong side, you will find yourself out of a job very quickly, and your life will be suddenly in my hands."

"She speaks truly," said the captain who had sided against Seagraul, who now stood immediately behind the loyalist captain. "And you would do well to choose as wisely as your men."

The captain looked around, from his own men to Furnarwa's men, to Letharal's men and to the king. King Seagraul felt his indecision, his wavering loyalty, and before the captain could speak, King Seagraul shouted, with the same sense of command that his voice always bore: "Regroup at the Tower of Laeolin!"

King Seagraul turned and ran without another moment to spare. Behind him, no less than a hundred soldiers jumped down and surrounded him, forming a shield and protecting their king, at the same time that another hundred men from the wall fired down on his band of guards. Furnarwa's four hundred men stood firm, but King Seagraul and his guards formed the tightest of circles and charged them like they had never charged before— they threw themselves at Furnarwa's men, tackling them and pushing them aside just as often as killing them. They had no restraint or regard for their own lives— they broke upon Furnarwa's soldiers like a wave upon the sand, but one which returned again and again, so fast and with such fury that they soon broke the lines and passed right through them, leaving half their number dead behind them and only forty men beside Seagraul, another ten caught in combat. "Capture the king!" Furnarwa shouted, "Capture him, and kill him at once!"

The sky grew brighter. The clouds had come back in time to cover the dawn, but the light of the rising sun bore its mark on the grey clouds, and gave its best attempt to light the city. Gendorn and Bendoraun could hardly keep their eyes open. Alaisio tried to remain vigilant— he would slap himself across the face and force his eyes wide open, and look around as if he might be in danger at that very moment. But Gendorn and Bendoraun could not bring themselves to keep their heads up.

"We'll rest for most of this day," Alaisio said, "You two, especially, need your sleep."

"Don't pretend you're not sleepy," Bendoraun said.

"I am, and I'll need sleep as well," Alaisio admitted, "we can rest here, inside this cellar— it seems to be safe. This house hasn't been used in years, and whoever left it forgot all of their belongings— blankets, clothes, everything."

"How can we make sure no one will come in?" Bendoraun wondered.

"We can't" Gendorn answered, "that hasn't been considered. There is nothing to do about it, Bendoraun, we need our sleep. We'll traverse the rest of the way tomorrow night under the cover of darkness, and believe me when I say the day after that will be a long one. Once we raise that banner over the Tower of Laeolin, we will not sleep until Seagraul is dead and this city is our own. So we better rest beforehand."

"He's right," Alaisio said, "and I am glad we are finally in agreement. I have considered the possibility of our being discovered. But this is the safest place behind enemy lines that we can find. Now sleep, and sleep well. When we wake, we will all need to be well-rested."

The room was silent, but for the thunderous noise of a thousand feet running on the streets above, in pursuit of the king. King Seagraul sat down against the wall and relaxed. His three guards stood on the opposite wall. The cellar was tall, and it was nothing at all except a cellar— there wasn't so much as a bucket or an old shirt in a corner. The trampling of feet continued overhead. It became thinner, then it became distant, then it became something the king had to strain himself to hear— and then it was gone.

The street was empty. A gust of wind blew down it, and chilled Seagraul to the bone. His three guards came up to surround him, and the four of them together set out down the road. There were not a lot of people around who would investigate four travelers in the night-time, this deep into Seagraul's own area of control, but there was no telling how tonight's events might change that. At any rate, no one would stop the King of Laen unless they had a large rebel force at their command. Still, he had to get back to the actual base, and soon. What had become of him, that he wandered in the streets with three guards, fearing for his life and without support in a city divided? *We are a long way from Aois*, the king thought grimly, and he felt rather aged with that thought.

They moved between the streets from building to building, cover to cover, avoiding the light of the moon wherever they could. They were almost to the centermost part of the city when a band of Furnarwa's and Lehtaral's soldiers came looking for them. How many there were, Seagraul could not tell, but they were combing through the streets and along the rooftops in groups of six and seven, battling with loyalist patrols here and there, but the loyalists were not in force enough for the king to reveal himself. What had happened to all of them? Had they pushed so far westward that they had forgotten to leave sufficient forces in the east?

Seagraul caught a glimpse of two separate groups before he and his guards even found a place to hide. One of the guards looked out from a window, and from his very limited visibility where he could see only the rooftops across the street and the street itself, he counted seven more bands of six men each.

"They won't stop the patrols, my king. They want to find you."

"Is there no one in this ancient city who is still loyal to me?"

"There is fighting everywhere— these groups are foolish to come so deep into loyalist territory, my king."

"Which means that it is no longer loyalist territory," Seagraul said grimly.

"No, my king. The fight still goes on. Do you see King Joel here, knocking upon the doors of the Courtyard Offices outside the Tower of Laeolin? Our front lines are holding up quite well. If Menuld spoke truly, and his men have moved in from the east, then that leaves the land to the east of Laeolin unprotected. Once we escape we can liberate those territories and bring aid to Laeolin— we will find a warm reception in Aois if we can wrest it from Kale."

"I know. But if we lose Laeolin, can we ever expect to regain it?" Seagraul wondered. "My journey began in Aois, but will it end there? I cannot lose Laeolin."

"My king, Aois is a more vital trade center, it has almost as many people, and is surrounded by defensible positions. It is in the heart of loyalist Laen. For your own safety, I advise returning there."

"There is no one left to help me escape this city."

"We three are left, my king, and we'll walk with you all the way to Aois, if it comes to that. We'll tell the Skaelin and the Laese and the Phenese to push with all their force, and we can get away in the mayhem to the east."

"Would they abide, if they knew I was fleeing the city? Or would even they take up arms against me? We'll see where this night leads us. It may be that if I leave tonight, the city will be lost to the rebels. I won't risk that. Retaking Laeolin would be impossible."

"They'll never take Laeolin."

The king only whispered in reply: "What if they already have?"

His body lay still. There was not a man around him. Kamira walked beside Iuna out into the open, and stood beside the mound of snow that covered Menuld's body. Together they knelt down, brushed the snow off of him, and looked into his frozen face.

His hollow eyes stared back at Kamira. His face seemed so pale, his body so still. "It's so odd," Kamira said quietly, "for him to sit here so…" there was a very long pause, as she searched for the right word. "…so restful."

"There was always something restful about the man. But then, there was always something restless. It is unsettling," Iuna agreed. "If he had an ounce of life left in him— I can hear it now— 'Seagraul, you child, where are you going? I'm not through with you— come back so I can chastise you some more!'. He meant a lot to us, Kamira. He was the one who really began this movement, all those years ago. He was the first to protest Gaoln, at the very same meeting where the colony was partitioned in the first place, back in the Age of the Great Wars. And it is more than ironic that after all these years, Seagraul would be the one to kill him. If you knew the history between those two…"

"Seagraul will be dead before he escapes this city," Kamira said to Iuna. Then, having only begun to realize who this Menuld was, she turned to the hollow eyes of the old man that stared up at her. "I promise you, as you promised us," she said, holding the gaze of those eyes, "that Gaoln will never happen again."

"Furnarwa and Letharal will take his place," Iuna told Kamira. Then she turned to Menuld. "You have instructed them as their leader for decades, Menuld, but you have been a father to them too. I was hoping you could raise Gendorn yourself, like you raised Joel. But the world does not always turn in the direction we would like, as you say. Furnarwa and Letharal, and maybe even Joel, will do just fine. Time and Fate be with us."

"I cannot believe in Time and Fate," Kamira said. "Not when Seagraul still has his way in Laeolin."

"You may believe it or not," Iuna said, still looking down at Menuld, "but I think, had Menuld heard you, he would have said that you have much to learn."

"I do have a lot to learn," Kamira said, "but I have little love left to hear the pleas of murderers." Iuna nodded at her, and their eyes met for a moment. Kamira knew that Iuna was trying to share some of her feeling, to hold some of her weight— but she can never bear it, Kamira thought. The young girl turned her eyes away.

Iuna reached behind Menuld's back, still wet and red. She reached into a bag inside his jacket, and pulled out not one, but at least three or four slips of paper. "There are a few notes," Iuna explained, "which Menuld always carried with him. His own note is here, if he even had one— he was not a vain man, and I would not put it beyond him for him to presume it selfish to think his own life worth remembering."

"May I see them?"

"In time, Kamira. There is one note here that should belong to Gendorn."

"*Gendorn?*" Kamira exclaimed. "What was Menuld doing writing a note to Gendorn? Why didn't he write one for me, while he was at it?"

"It is his father's death note, but do not tell him before Seagraul is dead. It is too emotional," Iuna said with a smile. "I would like to present it to you and Gendorn together. It would be far more meaningful. Gendorn's parents were close associates of Menuld and his likes. Did you ever find anything of your own mother, Kamira?"

"No. The last time I saw her she was running for her life in Gaoln, about to be captured by Juron's men. Was she also involved?"

"Not to my knowledge, but I am not as closely connected as Furnarwa and Letharal. Ask them. Well, I do hope you have the comfort of knowing what happened someday."

"She died," Kamira said plainly, "everyone died."

Again Iuna tried to meet Kamira's eyes, and Kamira averted her gaze. "Things are not always as they seem, Kamira. I hope that your heart can know some softness once again, even if it may take some time." She paused, while Kamira stared down at Menuld. "We should return to the house. We must check up on Pas, and make sure that the area is still safe." Kamira nodded, and after another moment of silence, they rose, and as they walked they left Menuld's body behind them, to be covered in the snow and buried by the city of Laeolin.

Pas was asleep. His bedroom was quiet and had only the faintest hint of blue light coming in from the window, the light of the moon reflecting off of the snow. Kamira and Iuna stood in his doorway, looking at him. "He'll be raised in a completely different world," Kamira mused in a whisper, "His earliest memories will be these— the crumbling pillars of the old order, the way things used to be. He'll grow up into adulthood as a free man in a free world." Iuna nodded. They never tore their eyes away from the boy. His body rose and fell in some hardly noticeable movement— the quiet movement of a boy in his peaceful sleep. "He won't know his parents, or his grandparents," Kamira continued, "and that will always be the reminder to him of where he comes from— where he once came from, in the earliest of his years. It would be nice, don't you think, to find a way for him to meet the other survivors? There must hardly be any of them, I know. But it would be something nice in this world, and the world needs it."

Iuna nodded. "I would gladly help you make that happen, Kamira, once this war is over. Furnarwa and Letharal will know where to find the other children. But we have to take care of some other things first, you know."

"I know. I have to find Gendorn."

"You will remain here, where you are safe. Gendorn has enough on his mind. You two can have your reunion when Seagraul is dead and Laeolin flies the flag of the Alliance."

"I know you're right. But it's not as easy as it sounds."

"I cannot imagine that it would be. But you must be patient."

"Yes, I know. Let's get some rest. The sunrise will come soon— we do not have many hours left before these streets are swarming with troops, and there is little chance of sleep once that begins."

"I will see you in the morning, Kamira." Iuna left the room. Kamira stood there for a moment longer, looking at the boy as he slept.

"I will see you in the morning, Pas," she whispered, "if Time and Fate are kind."

The morning bore tidings of a soft and gentle snow waiting to fall. The wind was as quiet as it had been the night before. To the south of them, Menuld's body still lay upon the street outside the gate. It would remain there until the bodybearers, whose job it was to remove bodies from the city and to place them in the forests outside, would pick him up. If there were too many bodies to carry, the bodybearers would burn them, although this was less appropriate than placing the bodies in the forest, where they would return to the earth. Kamira thought of these things as she waited for Pas to come down to the kitchen, and as Iuna put on some takul, a spicy tea which wasn't particularly popular in Laeolin, but which Iuna loved. Kamira couldn't imagine anyone burning Menuld. He would be placed gently in the hills far outside Laeolin, and he would be carried with no one by his side, unless Seagraul had his way— in which case his body would be torched where he lay.

The sound of footsteps became louder. "They're right outside," Iuna said casually. "They'll be all around this house, close as it is to the center of the town, until the war ends or Seagraul flees Laeolin. I do hope that Menuld's body will be given due respect. Is that what you were thinking about? Or

were you thinking about Gendorn? King Gendorn, that is—
goodness, it is difficult to realize that he'll be a king and you'll be
queen someday." Kamira smiled. "Don't your kings tell their
successors that they've been chosen? Why wait until death to find
out? Is it because your kings are always afraid of plots against
them? Oh, sorry, I know you aren't royalty or anything. I don't
mean to sound absurd. I hope you don't think so badly of Laeolin
when you've assumed your place of power, Kamira."

How could she respond to that? She couldn't.

"Good then." She took the pot off the large cooking
device— Kamira had never seen it before, but it was a large
block of something which fires came out from, and it had a sort
of drawer in the middle where one could place something inside
to cook, and the largest fire would be lit underneath the whole
thing. Iuna had tried to explain it to her, but it took some time.
The whole thing was metal, so it radiated heat, but the brick
lining contained some of it, and allowed Iuna to stand close by.
"Is Pas still asleep?"

He came out from his bedroom at the call of his name, and
proclaimed "I'm here." He looked rather worn and tired, despite
his long sleep. "The soldiers woke me up. They're very loud."

"Yes," Kamira said, "they'll continue being loud for some
time."

"Are we safe here?"

Kamira was taken aback, and really did not know how to
answer the question. "We will be safe here, yes," she said as soon
as she regained herself, although she herself did not believe this.

"Are those the same soldiers who killed everyone?" Pas
asked.

Kamira almost lost herself. This boy has had to grow up too
fast, she thought. "Yes, Pas. They are the same ones."

Pas's face contorted and twisted itself, and his eyes roamed
around the room. The boy wasn't quite sure of what to make of
this, and did not know how to react. He opened his mouth, said
nothing, then shut it, and walked down the stairs. He pulled
himself up on the chair and sat by the table, very close to Kamira.

He rested his head on Kamira's arm, and Kamira almost smiled, but for her grim mood. "Can we find my mom?" It must have been the thousandth time he had asked that question since the night of the execution almost half a year before.

"Not now, Pas," answered Kamira. "When the soldiers leave."

- Chapter Eight -

King Kio and King Joel rested most of that morning with their armies. The grey haze that descended upon the city made it all but impossible to see, even though the snowfall itself was rather light. It was a warmer sort of snow than they had known in weeks past, and King Joel mused quietly to himself as he sat in the doorway, watching it fall. "This Sen will end with our victory," he whispered to himself, "and with what else, we cannot yet tell."

"The Phenese have a message, my king." Joel looked over his shoulder, and nodded his head, indicating that the man should continue. "It is from the Ambassador of Phenen to Gonaka, representing the will of Emperor Sealibahd III. He proclaims that should King Seagraul fall, he wishes to partake in the choosing of his successor."

"Well, he's changed his mind rather quickly, hasn't he?"

"I do not think so, my king. It is my belief that the emperor simply wishes to keep his hand in the game, even if he has lost the war."

"Do you think it will come to war between us?"

"My king, it has already come to war between us. Do you ask me if Gonaka and Kale will take the war to Phenen?"

"I do."

"Then I believe it unnecessary. Phenen will come to the table as soon as Laeolin falls. I believe that is the purpose of this message."

"That is my belief as well. Send for King Kio."

"Yes, King Joel."

The King Abroad of Gonaka arrived shortly, and stood towering over King Joel, who sat there in the snow. "Joel, are you not cold?"

"Not really. One becomes accustomed to this weather rather quickly. I have been in and out of Laen my entire life, Kio, and have spent several Sen here. When are we to make the final assault?"

"We stand at the ready."

"We should take some more rest, and when we make our attack, we should not relent until we hold Seagraul in our hands and our flag flies atop that old tower."

"Do you believe what Menuld told you about that tower?"

"We will see, Kio. We will see very soon. I do have some news, now that you've come to mention Menuld."

"What is that?"

"Menuld has died."

"...He's died? Menuld has?"

"Yes. Menuld is dead. He stopped Seagraul from fleeing the city last night at the south gate and was killed in the confrontation."

"Will you go to him?"

"No, I cannot spare the time. It is most unfortunate. I would like to see him, really, before he is carried away. I would send a runner though, to search him for notes. There is no telling how many notes the old man carried— one could say he even collected them. He showed me eleven once, eleven! Spread out across four or five pockets. One of them was from the First Great War. The First Great War, Kio, two hundred years ago! And two from the Last Great War, when he was just a soldier. The man carried a library with him everywhere he went."

"I will send someone at once to search for them, King Joel."

"That is good. Send a team of runners and get some rest. I will be ready when you give the word. On your command, we will finish this war."

"The command will come soon."

Joel was left to his own thoughts, sitting there in the doorway. At some point he rose, after he had grown too cold, and shut the door behind him as he warmed up by the fire. He dozed off for a while and slept through much of the morning. A shout woke him from his slumber, and he rose, his fists at the ready, shouting "Who's there!?"

"I am," said the soldier in the doorway. "Kio sends word. He is ready."

The soldiers stood shoulder to shoulder, fifteen soldiers from end to end, marching in order, step by step and side by side. They stretched from one end of the street to the other. On the rooftops above, dozens and dozens of regiments swept through the city from its heights, dancing across tilted tile rooftops and balancing themselves along ledges that stretched across wide boulevards. As these men looked down at the line of soldiers, they could not see the end of it. It stretched back beyond their vision, and forward beyond their vision, and from corner to corner and end to end the soldiers filled the street. Beyond this column were the other streets, winding around Laeolin toward the center of the city, and upon each of these streets marched the tens of thousands of soldiers who had come to take part in the final grab for Laeolin. Among them Commander Luncas and Commander Kenfus marched, each leading a division, resplendent in polished orchalin gleaming in the sun as it broke through the clouds.

The people of Laeolin remained silent. They did not harry the soldiers, and they did not praise them. They stared at them in silence through their windows, watched them, expressionless, as they marched through their city.

Those on the rooftops of the highest buildings could see the soldiers of Laen and Phenen meet the soldiers of Gonaka to their north and dead ahead of them, and the soldiers of Kale to their south. Alongside the soldiers of Gonaka, the Freemen marched in force. When the marching stopped, there was fighting on all sides. From the buildings all along the streets the soldiers came out. Through the mists the soldiers could not see, but they heard the noise ahead of them, coming from the center of the city.

They came from the windows and arrived on the rooftops, and met the rooftop regiments in battle. They came from the rear and attacked the lines from both sides. They came outward from the Black Tower itself, and met all the soldiers of all the nations in battle. For those soldiers stuck in the middle of the battle columns, unable to fight, it was an awkward and tense time, as they waited to be called to the front to replace those soldiers who had died or become too tired. But King Kio and King Joel were at the front of the lines. Commander Luncas was at the front, and Commander Kenfus was at the front. From four different main streets, all leading toward the centerpoint of the city, that great black tower rising like a smooth monolith, they led their men and met their enemies in battle.

King Kio and King Joel stood behind as they let their best regiments take the lead, and kept their reservoirs of energy to best lead this battle, sure to last into the night. The battle began slow. Only so many men could fight at a time, and from behind them archers would fire into their respective enemies' lines. The soldiers would not see the arrows— they would arrive out of the mist as if conjured up by some magic, some spell of the Ancients, and kill indiscriminately.

Along the rooftops the advance was more steady. The Freemen, Kanish, and Gash pushed back the Lonins and Phenese along every top of every building, and they were soon running high above the Phenese and Lonin soldiers who were waiting for battle below. They formed up groups and shot at their enemies from above, then they would hide while their enemies fired back, then reveal themselves and shoot again. As such, they kept their enemies distracted and made them tired, anxious, and less ready for battle. Then the loyalists sent soldiers up in force to the rooftops to push them back. The soldiers of the Alliance withdrew and formed up in lines along the rooftops to meet their enemies as they arrived, and as soon as they could see them, the soldiers of the Alliance loosed their arrows. Their enemies did not waver in their advance— in terrible numbers they arrived and threw themselves at the soldiers of the Alliance, and the Alliance could not hold— they broke and fled back to their lines, where their own soldiers came to the rooftops in force and met the Lonins and the Phenese in battle.

Down below in the streets, the battle still moved slowly. The Alliance gained ground, then would be pushed back, then the lines would not move for time immeasurable. King Joel grew anxious as he observed the day drawing closer to its close.

The sunset was upon them. The soldiers had shifted lines many times now, and the soldiers who had been in the middle were almost to the front lines. The arrows still came out from the mist, although the mist itself was now dyed the yellow and orange of the sunset, soft as it was behind the thick veil of clouds descended upon the streets. The sky became dim, and then dimmer, and then dark, and the night became complete. The moon was completely hidden and its light hardly managed to weave its way between the mist, until the mist began to fade into the air and the soldiers again saw the eyes of their enemies.

Through the night the battle continued like this, with neither side making any great stride. The Alliance pushed forward in force along the rooftops and fired down into the lines of Phenen and Laen as they took themselves deeper into their area of control. Without as many men as the Alliance, the soldiers of Phenen and Laen found the attack difficult to repulse, but with all their men they held their lines all the same. Try as they might, they could not hold off the forces of the Alliance for much longer— there were simply not enough men left fighting for Laen and Phenen to combat the united force of all the main armies of Kale, Gonaka, and the Free Kingdom.

It began at once, and it did not stop. They withdrew and reformed their lines, then the Alliance pushed forward again, and the Lonins and Phenese withdrew again, and then again. They would lose part of a street and reform their lines, then from the rooftops the Alliance would advance and fire down on them again. At one point Seagraul's men managed to break up the rooftop advance and even gained some roofs deep into the Alliance's lines, and fired down upon the inactive soldiers. But the attack was repulsed, and again the Alliance pushed forward toward the center.

The most incredible sight through all of this was to see Seagraul's men collapsing all around him, not in their physical health, but in their loyalty. Entire companies, one as large as fifteen regiments, laid down their weapons before Luncas and Kenfus and proclaimed their indifference toward Seagraul, which meant that their weapons were seized and they were excused from combat. Some regiments declared for the Free Alliance and kept their weapons. North and south, as the Free Alliance moved eastward, packs of soldiers who had sworn to defend Seagraul proclaimed that they were no longer willing to do so, that they abandoned him to his fate, that he was not the king they believed him to be. How much was out of fear, and how much out of honesty, it was impossible to tell. But the speeches some of the captains gave moved Luncas himself nearly to tears, and more than once the commander embraced a Lonin officer he had known as a comrade.

From the highest rooftop, the soldiers could see the Tower of Laeolin rising against the dawn's light, and for a moment they stared at its beauty, unable to tear their gaze away from this thing which emanated power. They saw it but for a brief moment, and then the mist of the morning came in, and they could see it no more, and beneath them the battle raged on.

King Joel stood beside his litha. "I can't promise we will make it back, friend," he told the beast, "but we will try. We have to save whatever men Gendorn has found behind the lines, you see, and Gendorn himself. The men say he is a great leader, though I see only a boy. Let us hope the risk is worth it." He jumped on the litha's back, and looked into the mist. The sun would be rising over the buildings very soon now, but none could tell beyond the haze. "Well, in truth we have two objectives, my friend. We must kill one king, and save a future one. It may be a very interesting dilemma, as the one we must save will be surrounded by enemies, while the one we must kill is nowhere to be seen, and we have the issue of finding him in the first place. But we can draw him out, yes, I believe we can. It is time we begin, then." In a moment, they were off into the mists of the morning, toward the Tower of Laeolin.

"Komu is in danger, I know it," Iuna reasserted. "He didn't return to the gate last night, and he hasn't been here all day. It's sunset now, Kamira, and the troops are all over the city. The battle is almost upon our doorstep, almost to the Courtyard of the Tower itself. Komu would have sent a runner, he would have let us know that he is safe. He would have reassured us. He's just not there. Where could he be?"

"I just don't think there is a lot that we can do, Iuna."

"No? Well, I do." She picked up her thick cloak from the hanger and knelt down to put on her boots.

"Iuna, it's stupid to go out there, and you know it is. What are you going to do, comb the city for one man? He's probably fighting himself or working with Furnarwa. It could be dangerous to try and contact him now."

"It isn't like him, Kamira. If Komu is in trouble, then Faero is in trouble. And it means Furnarwa and Letharal could be in trouble, and if they are in trouble, then all of the survivors are endangered, not to mention the entire network of resistance. We have to find them, Kamira, or the resistance could collapse."

"I have faith in them," Kamira said boldly, "they can organize themselves."

"Maybe, but maybe not. Furnarwa and Letharal are the only ones who know the locations of all the survivors, at any rate. And Komu and Faero, I know they must be in danger— "

"So you'll put yourself in danger, too?"

"You can come with me."

"Think of Pas."

"I know! Were he ten years older, Kamira, he would want to come with us too, and you know it."

"Komu can take care of himself, I am sure he only took Faero south of the city to a safehouse for them to hide. He must not have been able to come back to the house. The streets aren't exactly empty, you know," Kamira assured her. "Sit down!"

Someone knocked at the door forcefully, and before either of them could react, the door came busting inward and slammed against the wall. A line of soldiers ran through the room. Iuna and Kamira shrieked and backed up against the side of the wall, looking at them with fear in their eyes as they made their way toward the top of the building. They kept coming in, not even acknowledging the two women, making their way to the roof. By the dozen they came, then by the score. Kamira and Iuna heard the latch to their roof open up, then suddenly the soldiers were gone and the latch closed.

It took a while for them to regain their senses, then Iuna said "They've come. Those are the soldiers of Seagraul, come to meet the Alliance upon the rooftop. The battle is coming to us. It will rage the entire night, and it won't stop until victory lies in the hands of one king or the other, or until Seagraul flees the city. Go get Pas. We have to find a place to hide until this war is over. Komu better have taken Faero with him, wherever he ran off to. How will he know we are safe?"

"We will find him when we can," Kamira said to her, "we have to hide now, you are right. I will get Pas and tell him what's happened. Where are we going? The storeroom? Any looting soldier will look there."

"No, we cannot hide there. There is a strong safehouse around here where many from the resistance will be meeting. We must go there and hide. Follow close behind me, and do not lose sight of me. And be silent! We have to leave now— the darkness will be upon us very soon, so it is good. Do not make a noise. Now go get the boy."

The three of them left the house just as the night fell. They made their way up to the rooftops, which were still less flooded with men than the streets beneath them. The snow on the roofs made it difficult to run, but the three of them kept their traction as they made their way south and east.

They turned a sharp corner, and Kamira slipped on the snow along the ledge and lost her balance. Her feet dangled from the edge as she caught the roof with her hands, but they were slipping fast— she could not grip the snow. Iuna and Pas turned around, and were about to shout when they heard a voice come from the streets below— "There! Look! A woman— she's going to fall!"

Iuna dashed toward Kamira and gripped one of her arms, trying to pull her up. Kamira pushed herself up as Iuna carried her higher, and the soldiers started running into the buildings. Kamira was on her feet and at once they made a dash southward, urging Pas forward ahead of them. "Kamira," Iuna said, panting, "we cannot lead them to the safety point. I am going to stay— "

"No— "

"And you must take Pas."

"You take him, Iuna— " they jumped across another slim alleyway, "I do not know where it is."

"We do not have time— " But before Iuna could finish, Kamira had turned around to face the soldiers. Iuna did not hesitate— as the soldiers were distracted and stopped in front of Kamira, she led Pas down to the lower roofs and then onto the streets, and suddenly the soldiers could no longer see them. Just like that, Iuna and Pas were gone— and now they had this young woman in front of them, and they closed in around her.

Kamira jumped down onto the street below and landed haphazardly. She laid there for a while, her face contorted in pain— they had been three stories up, and it was no meager jump. The soldiers in their heavy armor looked at one another, and began running inside the building to take the stairs. When they arrived on the street below, the young woman was gone.

They searched the buildings nearby half-heartedly— what could one girl do, anyway? There was no intelligence worth passing along that the soldiers knew of, and they had only intended to capture her for sport. They gave up very shortly and made their way north to return to their posts. When Kamira knew they were gone, she revealed herself to the sights of the alleyway and its towering tightly-packed buildings. She walked briskly out to the streets. She would never find where Iuna and Pas had gone, she knew. There were again those two options available to her— she could wait in the house, where surely Bendoraun would find her, although the house was not safe with all these soldiers. Or she could try to make her way to the Alliance, where she would reveal herself and find refuge. Without any further thought, she continued to make her way north, not necessarily following either of those paths. For some reason, she was drawn to something else entirely, that looming tower which came to haunt her every night. It stood out to her, and like a thorn in her mind she could not escape it. The tower called to her, and there was only one place she could go— the place where her life was supposed to have ended, but for some reason did not.

She crept from building to building. When she found a clearing she would dash through an alley and then hide under a rooftop while soldiers searched for some hardly-heard footstep. She made good time, all told— the darkness covered her, and though the city was thick with soldiers, the majority of them moved along the rooftops and through the wide main streets of the city, and not through these very skinny, one-person-wide alleys which wove randomly through the gaps in the tall buildings that sat in blocks between larger avenues and roads. When she did see a soldier she would sprint into the shadows or some building, and would wait for him to pass by. The darkness in the alleyways was complete and impenetrable— no man, if they were staring straight down toward a certain spot and not even moving their eyes— could have even suspected there was a person in that gap of space where no light could shine.

When the darkness began to fade away into the light of day, Kamira knew she needed rest. But where could she sleep? Where was she safe? Nowhere. There could be no rest. She climbed to the top of a rooftop, risking discovery, and from it she glimpsed the Tower of Laeolin, and it called to her through the mists of the morning light, and she could feel her spirit pulled to this place, where it had been destroyed so long ago. Gendorn was alive, she knew that now. And if he had one place in mind to call out to King Seagraul, to challenge him in battle, it would be the Tower of Laeolin. It was something Gendorn would do, she knew— at least the Gendorn she remembered. She ran back down to the alley as the tower disappeared in the haze, and she crept between the buildings, making her way north.

- Chapter Nine -

Alaisio walked through the thick, tropical jungle. All around him there were leaves as long as his arm and as wide as his body, and trees of that particular kind of wood found only on the small island of Goba, trees which rose high into the sky— wide and tall as the mountain glimpsed through their boughs. He pushed his way through the underbrush and came to a ledge. Beneath him there was a great river, winding and slow, the source of all of Goba's rivers which led to the ocean on all sides. On the opposite ledge there was the enormous waterfall known as the Majestic Falls— they were as wide as a ship was from bow to stern, and the distance between the top and bottom of the falls was at least half the height of the highest tower in Fengorian— if one did not count the Black Tower of Laeolin.

There was a cave behind the waterfalls, only a small one at the base, where children would come and play together or young lovers would flee to when they needed to escape for a day. This was the heart of the jungle in Goba, only a small hike from Alaisio's house. He looked down over the ledge at the base of the waterfall, and he saw two figures playing in the water inside the cave. There was a woman, who must have been about thirty years of age, and a younger boy who could only have been three. The woman laughed as the boy splashed about in a small pool behind the falls— Alaisio could see them through the gap in the water caused by a particularly large outcrop above them.

Lendah was trying to teach Ciso how to swim, but all young Ciso wanted to do was play in that little pool in the cave, flailing his arms about and splashing his mother with water. Lendah sat down and laughed. A man came out from the water— an Alaisio who was younger, stronger, and happier. He ran into the pool next to Ciso, and helped his son who continued splashing his mother. Lendah stood up indignantly, and the younger Alaisio looked up as if he were surprised. Then Lendah smiled, and came to join the three of them in the pool, sitting across from the younger Alaisio. He took her hand and held it as they watched Ciso tumble over into the water, then roll around and pop up again.

The three of them sat there in the pool for a while, and from the opposite ledge high above them, the older Alaisio watched. His face was lined with age and his smile bore the weight of all the sadness of his years. His one remaining arm was clasped to his heart, and his eyes, which still held some faint glimmer of happiness in the memories they recalled, looked onward at this family.

They were cut from his vision suddenly, when they moved away from the pool. They reemerged in the water, swimming around at the base of the falls— one of them would swim while the other would sit along the rocks holding Ciso, dipping the child in and out of the shallow pools to his delight. It was quite late into the day when the younger Alaisio looked to the sky, observed the sun, and decided they should leave. Lendah took Ciso in her arms, and the younger Alaisio led them back to their home in the deep reaches of the rainforest.

As the older Alaisio stood upon the ridge, he saw the water and the forest merge together into some confusion, and they formed again to create new shapes— there were these new people the young Alaisio would not recognize, these new places, these foreign feelings— and then there was just the snow beneath his feet and the cold stone all around him.

The Courtyard of the Tower of Laeolin was completely devoid of life. The buildings and smaller towers along the edges could not be seen through the thick haze, but that one mighty tower of smooth black rock rose out from the mist and grabbed for the heavens, and Alaisio knew that they had arrived.

The five skeletons were standing perfectly still, with that single plate beneath them, bearing that one inscription. Gendorn and Bendoraun stood perfectly still before these skeletons, but Alaisio knelt down and read the plate of the man whose skeleton had been arranged in front of all the others.

~ This is the fate of those who oppose the King of Laen, the fate of the traitor who knows no nation or king. Here rests the bones of the man named Ciso, who worked alongside other traitors toward the downfall of our nation and the shame of our king. Here rest his bones, and behind this man the bones of the four traitors who conspired with him. ~

When he looked up he could see, in front of the skeleton, a young boy dressed in blue and white. His skin was tan from days under the sun in the heat of Bautaulan's Trest. He wore a broad smile— his cheeks were fat, and his eyes wide with wonder. And he looked at Alaisio, as Alaisio looked at him, no smile on his own face. The image changed— it became an older boy who would always take off without telling Alaisio to explore the rainforest or to visit one of his many friends, or, though he would seldom admit it, to escape to those waterfalls where young lovers would run to when they needed a place to get away.

It all happened so quickly— in front of him was a man, leading an opposition, a team of people devoted to freeing the hundred and fifty thousand hostages of Laeolin, a brave young man who could stand against a king and say to his face "you are wrong". He had a faint echo of the glimmer in his eyes that Alaisio had observed when Ciso was a child, that sense of wonder which came from his youth. He had a certainty in his duty, a command in his speech that was very different from the younger Ciso. His skin was still tanner than most— it still recalled the bright sun of younger days.

The image was gone, and in front of him were the bones of his son. And suddenly he recalled why he had been dreaming, why he had been remembering. How long had he been here, in front of this skeleton? When did he even get here?

Alaisio's arm became weak as it tried to bear his weight pressing on the stone floor, and his knees ached. They became cold and numb in the snow before he regained his senses or was aware that any time had passed. His mind returned to showing him images and moving pictures of he and Ciso and Lendah playing under those waterfalls while they taught Ciso to swim, or hiking through the rainforests on their way to explore the deep caverns south of the Mountain. Then the images would shift— Lendah would be cradling Ciso in her arms, singing him to sleep while the storm raged outside and the thunder grew louder— then dawn would come to find the three of them walking together to the market along the beach, the sands of the eastern shore, half a morning's hike from their secluded forest home.

The snow was cold and bitter now, but Alaisio felt devoid of any reason to stand up, to move from that spot. It was Bendoraun and Gendorn who pulled him up and carried him back away from the tower, into one of the buildings, and set him down in a corner. He could not see the worried expressions on Gendorn's and Bendoraun's faces, or the note of haste in their voice. When he closed his eyes, he saw his son, and he wanted never to open them again.

- Chapter Ten -

The Courtyard of the Tower was empty, and rather eerie.
There was not a single person in sight. There were five skeletons
held up with wooden poles outside the Tower of Laeolin, and
small nameplates beneath them. Kamira could hardly see them
through the mist. She could not see any of the buildings on the
other side, only that smooth black spire which was the Tower of
Laeolin. She felt her heart beat inside her cold chest, and the tears
falling down her face as she stood stoic before it. There was no
one around— why was no one here? But her thoughts died out
as the memory of three thousand white cloaks huddled around a
mass of burning bodies came back to her, and then the ever-
present memory of when those bodies were living people, when
they died here, where she now stood.

Distant in the echoes of her mind, she could hear the sounds
of the armies approaching. One was from the west, the other
from the east. On all sides they clashed now— all around her.
But her mind could not register these developments— it was
thrust back to that night. She could see her body lying there with
the others, naked and bloody and hidden by a dozen bodies that
covered her own. It was the same feeling which had drawn her
back to this place, on this very morning, when two armies were
about to collide before the Tower of Laeolin— the feeling that
death belonged to her, and she should have it. The dead Kamira
that she saw lying in the courtyard seemed more right than the
living Kamira, standing there now. Shadows of faces she used to
know roamed around her and screamed at her— they were
bringing her back. And then there was a calm figure amidst them
all, unmoving, not screaming— not saying anything— and he
seemed more real, more tangible than the rest of them.

He was a young man, very dirty and covered in snow, of medium height and a square build. He carried his helmet in his hand— his hair was matted from it, and his face seemed to droop downward. Kamira almost thought it was a Lonin guard— but then she saw the man kneel before the tower. He must be from Gaoln.

She walked up slowly, then stopped when he saw her. The man opened his eyes a bit more, as if he could not quite see through the mist, or if even this grey haze was too bright for his eyes— he seemed struck by disbelief. He came forward, to where he could see her plainly, and then he spoke. "Kamira…"

Kamira's eyes grew wide. "Is that…who is…"

"It's me, Bendoraun…why have you come here? You should wait at the house— this is a very dangerous place."

"Then why are you here?" She asked defiantly.

"Come with Alaisio and Gendorn and I."

"Where are you?"

"We are in one of the buildings— the armies are coming. This place will be overrun with Lonin and Phenese soldiers at any moment."

"Why are you here, then?"

"We have something to do here, before we can leave."

"And what is that?"

"Kamira, please— if you will not return to your house, you must let us hide you."

"Fine."

Alaisio was crouched down in a corner when the two of them walked in and exchanged greetings with Gendorn. Gendorn nodded at Bendoraun, who came to stand beside him. Then he turned to Kamira. "I don't know why you are trying to scare me to death. This place is too dangerous for you." Even as he said these things, he embraced her and held her face on his shoulder. "Stay here, Kamira— there is a basement underneath this building that's old and abandoned, and I doubt many people know it's here. It isn't the one directly beneath us, but you'll see a passage behind the staircase— it must have been an older building that was here before this one. You and Alaisio can stay there until we return."

"What happened to Alaisio? And where are you going?"

"Alaisio's son, Ciso, has died," Gendorn answered. "We are going to finish this now, so please just stay here, and we will be back for you." Kamira nodded, and watched them walk out the door. When they were gone she told Alaisio to get up, and he rose— his eyes still had not met Kamira's own. She led him down to the basement, and then to the floor below, finding the passage behind the stairwell as Gendorn had predicted.

"She can't go inside," said Gendorn, as he and Bendoraun stood before the tower. "That's why she can't come. She can't be inside the tower. She can hardly stand in front of it. We would never get her out alive." Bendoraun nodded, and kept silent. "Well, come on."

They opened the great doors of ancient black metal, which over the many centuries had remained untainted by age. The two friends stepped inside, and at once the stench of death greeted them. There were no bodies left after many long days of burning, but the smell of decay lingered here in the air, and it took no great stretch of imagination for the two Freemen to imagine thousands of bodies piled upon one another, the bodies of their own people. Names and faces they had known. Voices they could still remember whose sounds would not be heard again in this world. They stood there, paralyzed, as their own imagined creations of that night came rushing through their minds. There was an arrow in one corner, a broken sword in another— the men of Laen had done a good job of clearing the place of both bodies and artifacts, but every arrowhead left forgotten on the floor reminded Gendorn of what this place was.

They crept up the stairs. Gendorn led the way. He passed the second level without even looking to see what he would find. He passed the third without turning his eyes from the stairs. He passed the fourth, and fifth, and sixth, seventh, eighth, ninth floor. When he reached some level, high along the tower, he stopped, and he looked out. There was a bloodstain in the center of the room, a very large and deep one that would have been the reminder of many more bodies than just one. Without turning his eye away he spoke softly to Bendoraun.

"We are heroes among our people, Bendoraun. And we should be able to take this in. We should be able to look back at this, and keep it in our minds when we make decisions for our people. We should understand it, comprehend it, so that we can remember it for the rest of our lives." He let the silence take them. "But I cannot understand it at all. And I could never take this in. I could never judge the world because of this, and I cannot keep it always at the front of my mind. If I did, I would know that there is no hope for my people, and I would fail those who live. It is a duty that I cannot ever fulfill, to comprehend what surrounds me, what I am walking through right now. If I understood, I could not wake up in the morning. It is the very end of our people, and of those who kept hope."

"You submit to despair too readily, Gulaus Gendorn," Bendoraun said, in the same whisper of a voice. "There is a reason we have come to this tower, but it is not so that we may mourn those who have died and tell the world that there is no hope for a Free Kingdom."

In the dark gloom of the tower, there was a silence unlike any silence they had heard before. It was a constant, pure silence throughout the entire tower, through all its dark stairwells and its rooms. And when the noise came it erupted in a single moment— the doors swung open and the sound of a dozen soldiers rushing into the tower echoed up the stairs and filled every room. Bendoraun turned to Gendorn, and pushed him upward. "Go!"

They raced up the stairs, careful not to make any more noise than was necessary. They took the steps two at a time, and passed the thirtieth floor, then the fortieth, then the fiftieth. When they reached the top of the tower, the room was small and could hold no more than seven or eight people, and there was a door that led to the outside of the tower, where a balcony wrapped around the highest floor. They walked out and looked up. The spire went up another full two stories in height, and ended in a sharp point where Seagraul's flag still flew. This flag had been designed especially to withstand the wind high atop the tower— it was thick and attached by a stone rod.

Gendorn slung his bag over his shoulder, and pulled himself up to the ledge where the floor ended and the pinnacle began. Bendoraun followed next to him, and together they climbed. The wind was strong up here, though there had been no wind at all along the base of the tower. The air was colder, more bitter, more dry. Gendorn and Bendoraun clasped onto the thin holds along the pinnacle, the small metal clips that gripped the black stone. When they reached the top, Gendorn took out a sword, and with one swing he cut down Seagraul's flag and almost lost his balance. He put the sword away and took out his pack, where there was another flag.

It was a flag of deep brown mixed with red, the color of the dawn and dusk upon the dirt plains of Gaoln. In the center lay that small hill, and upon it the old barren tree painted in a lighter brown, the small and withered thing that marked the point where the Gaolnians had set sail long ago to become Freemen. It marked, also, the hill upon which Gendorn and Kamira spent quiet nights together when the weather was calm, and where the three friends would go to play when they were younger. It marked the place where Gendorn would go alone and stare out at the ocean, when he felt like dreaming of what was on the other side— and it meant much the same thing for most of those who had lived in Gaoln. The red sky was not the color of fresh blood. It was not quite so dark as that.

Gendorn had it strung up quickly, and tied it down, weaving the strings into the stone pole. When it was ready, he let it go, and the flag flew in the wind. They remained in place, looking up where it waved back and forth.

"This was the original flag that King Centreal designed," Gendorn explained to Bendoraun, who looked skeptically at the flag as it began to billow in the wind. "It doesn't have the white background, the white that is meant to remember the deaths in Laeolin."

"Shouldn't you remember them here?"

"Our original dream was in this flag. It was crafted before the dream died. Seeing as the dream died here inside this tower, and in this ruined city, it seems fit that the dream should return and fly on top of the tower now and forever, doesn't it? We're not forgetting their deaths. We're just remembering their lives, and our dream."

Bendoraun nodded, and in silence returned to the inside of the tower.

They climbed back down to the balcony, and crept along the sides to see below, but they could not make anything out through the mist. Bendoraun tugged at Gendorn's shirt and pointed forward, and Gendorn tried to focus. Through the mist in the distance they could just make out the shape of something flying in the sky, some large creature, and Gendorn supposed it to be a litha. It came closer— it was a litha— and closer still. "We'll have to get down," Gendorn said. "That will be Joel coming to take us back to the lines, and he'll not stay long if he doesn't find me."

"Have you sent word to the rebels?"

"They know. They will come."

As soon as they had the doors shut the sound of marching soldiers returned— they were almost to the top. Gendorn and Bendoraun returned to the balcony, and stayed out of sight from the windows. Looking up at the litha, Gendorn prayed Joel figured out what was happening, and tried to come a little closer.

The litha came closer and closer, but it prepared to land in the courtyard. Gendorn saw the red and white robes of Gonaka flapping in the wind, the clear white wings of the litha coming toward him. The doors opened up next to him, and a group of soldiers came out— *No, Joel, run back*, Gendorn thought. He swung around, sword in hand, to fight off his enemies, but the soldiers stood there passively, examining the two boys. One of them stepped forward and extended a hand. "Well met, Gulaus Gendorn, Gulaus Bendoraun. My name is Furnarwa. May I escort you to the field of battle?" Gendorn turned half-way around— Joel was descending, landing in the courtyard.

"Yes, I think you should."

There was an entire army waiting for them. The soldiers were on every floor of the tower, and they came rushing down, pouring in to the courtyard, when the two Gaolnians had been retrieved. When Gendorn emerged he found not an empty courtyard, but one thousand and three hundred rebel fighters arranged before him under the flags of the Council and the Free Alliance. King Centreal, tall and proud with his great cape billowing in the wind, stood there above the crowd, almost as tall as King Joel beside his litha. Everyone went to join the ranks, except for two figures— Furnarwa and a woman of Furnarwa's age, who introduced herself as Letharal. "Gulaus Gendorn, Gulaus Bendoraun," Furnarwa began, "there are another four hundred across the buildings around this tower. We wait for Seagraul's men to arrive. Already Kio, Luncas, and Kenfus advance with fifteen thousand more."

From the mists Joel and Centreal appeared suddenly before Gendorn and Bendoraun. Joel smiled at them. "I was worried I would have more trouble finding you. It was rather easy, as it turns out. But the enemy advances from all fronts. We cannot hold a position here until Luncas and Kenfus and Kio arrive altogether. It would mean our end."

"The flag already flies on the Tower of Laeolin, King Joel. We have no choice but to wait," Gendorn answered.

"Gendorn," Centreal said warmly, "I know you meant this to be a summoning for the rebels, and it gladdens us to know it is up there, but with this fog not a man in the city will see that flag. Look, and let me know if you can even see it yourself, standing right underneath it."

"Then we'll just have to tell them ourselves," Furnarwa interjected. "And see to it that the summoning occurs, one way or the other. I've already sent runners out, of course— I mean, I wasn't going to wait for your permission. Waste of time." Centreal rolled his eyes.

"How many do you expect to answer?" Joel wondered.

"Five thousand in the immediate area. Most of them with weapons. Those without will serve as runners and lookouts."

"Seagraul's men are more, and better-trained, and have real weapons and armor," Joel said, "we would do well to leave a small force here and gather the rebels together, but Gendorn, you and most of these men must leave."

Gendorn turned around. He suddenly noticed that among the four of them there was one person who was absent. Bendoraun was not there in the courtyard. "Where is he?" Gendorn blurted out. The others looked at him skeptically. "Bendoraun— where has he gone?"

Kamira could see them, with their backs against the wall, hiding where they would not be seen by those of the Alliance. They spoke in low, whispered tones, but Kamira could hear— she took the chance of sticking her head out, to make sure she had heard correctly.

"He should have been here already! We were meant to only make the first assault— we've made three charges so far, and we're being overwhelmed! The rebels are coming from every corner of the city."

"He will be here!"

"I'm sending you up."

"You're what!?"

"Sending you up. Go and see if you can see him"

"He will be here."

"It's not a request, I am ordering you to go."

There was a silence— Kamira hid inside the room again, and listened as the footsteps died out. She ran down to Alaisio. "The rebels are coming," she told him, "should you want to join the fray. I am going to follow some men who sound as if they are up to something." Alaisio looked up, and seemed more attentive than he had ever been since seeing his son's body.

"Kamira, you are to stay here with me."

"I'll be back soon," and without waiting for a reply, she ran off.

A few buildings down there was an empty tower that reached eight stories high, and Kamira dashed inside. She ran to the top, circling the spiral stairways up and up, until she was on the open rooftop. She gazed out northward. The Army of Laen was to the north, advancing toward the tower. Just a dozen blocks to the west of them Kio's army was marching in the same direction. Luncas and Kenfus would be nearby. Seagraul's men were ahead, but they were keeping the Gash cut off from the tower area and trying to push them back. Kamira stood up. She threw her hands up and waited until she had Kio's attention, and then waved frantically. While most of the army could not see her, she knew the message had gotten across.

Bendoraun seethed in anger. Kamira was on the rooftop of one of the buildings, waving signals to someone west of here! His eyes grew wide— he knew it must be Kio's men, and that calmed him— but she would be killed!

There was sporadic fighting just outside the courtyard now, on the streets immediately surrounding them. If they were to escape back to their lines, they had to do so now. Bendoraun could not see where Gendorn had gone— *they're trying to keep us separated*, he knew— *and then they'll close in on the famous gulauses and kill us both. He'll take care of himself, and his men will watch him— but they can't watch Kamira.* He started walking toward the building, but already Seagraul's men were converging on the Courtyard— they must have started running here as soon as the flag went up, Bendoraun realized, which meant that they had been lying in wait nearby, and that more of their men were on the way. He worked this out in his mind, but his train of thought was broken suddenly— five Lonin soldiers were storming into the building. No doubt they'd go to the top floor to scout the area— and they'd find Kamira waiting there.

"Why doesn't that girl listen..." Bendoraun muttered under his breath, "her death will not be on me. I told her to stay inside!" He shook his head. He bolted to the other side of the building, to avoid the two Phenese regiments walking down that road, and threw his sword in his scabbard. With both hands free, he climbed the side of the building— they had practiced that in a few of the towns in Skaen, and at Gatsesilli— and pulled himself up to the roof. Kamira turned when he got to the top, and her eyes grew wide.

"Kio needed me!" she blurted out.

Bendoraun shook his head. "No, he didn't, you just wanted to help! You're acting like a child!" Bendoraun went over to the stairwell and stood by the top. "They're coming for you— the enemy. They saw you." He pulled the sword from his scabbard.

"You couldn't see what was happening, Bendoraun. The Lonins and Phenese wove around you on both sides— Kio had summoned all the men back to himself, and there was no one left who could scout!"

"Alright, alright— be quiet!" Bendoraun whispered. He could hardly hear anything over the clamor of battle all around him, but he knew the soldiers were coming.

"Kamira," Bendoraun whispered. Kamira came closer to him, so he could speak into her ear. "Get out of here. Climb down the west face of the building— it's easy. Go now— hurry."

"Escort me," Kamira demanded.

"When you're half way down and I know you will be safe, I will come— trust me, I'd rather I not die here just as much as you."

Kamira nodded. "Hurry!"

"Go!"

Kamira was almost to the side when Bendoraun saw an armored foot just before him. Before the man could run out at Kamira, Bendoraun swung around from the corner and put his sword through the man's exposed neck. He withdrew quickly and grabbed the body with one hand, using it as a shield— he threw it at the next man, who was forced to catch it awkwardly, and cut him under his thighs as he was trying to get rid of the body. The man crumpled to the floor, and blood came pouring out of his legs. "Stay back men," Bendoraun shouted back up to the roof, "I can take them all!" The Lonins looked around at one another and laughed, but the captain, at the base of the stairs, yelled up for them to fall back.

"Archers," the captain called, "Ready and fire!" Bendoraun ducked back behind the side of the stairwell on the roof. Kamira was gone— she had gotten out, then. He threw his sword in his scabbard and ran to the side of the building. He jumped off the edge and grabbed the jagged stone protruding from the wall, climbing down quickly. He jumped when he was just a single story away, and had his sword out when he landed.

Before he turned around, he saw her body lying up against the building, tossed on its side. His muscles fell limp— there was no blood there. How? Could she have fallen? It was such an easy climb! He kicked her— maybe she just hit her head? "Kamira?"

"Bendoraun!" she turned over in an instant, and Bendoraun almost fell over backward. "Let's go! Quickly!" Kamira shot up faster than an arrow and the two of them made a dead sprint down the alley.

"What on earth were you doing!?"

"I had to play dead— there were enemies all around here, and you know I can't run like my mother!"

Bendoraun shook his head. "You are a unique one. Where's Kio?"

Kamira pointed to the south. "They're already gone, I was just waiting— "

Bendoraun grabbed Kamira and covered her with himself, pushing her down. A volley of arrows came crashing to the floor where they had been moments before, and above them, archers made ready to strike again. They got up and resumed their sprint toward safety. "You'd be safer if you had kept playing dead!" said Bendoraun.

"Are you never satisfied?"

"I just worry about you! Why are you not more scared!?"

Bendoraun made the most gut-wrenching sound, a sound Kamira had not heard since the night of the slaughter, and hit the stone floor with a thud.

Kamira turned around sharply. Bendoraun was not moving. There was an arrow in his back, next to his spine. Bendoraun turned his head up. "Keep going!" he told her, before she could speak. "Go to the lines! It's the only place you'll be safe. Run!"

Without a second thought, Kamira turned and ran toward the Alliance's lines. On the ground, Bendoraun's face twisted and writhed in pain. He could not get up, but he could move his head. He looked up again— Kamira was gone. He planted his face down against the stones and cried.

- Chapter Eleven -

They poured in from every alley and street, down from every rooftop, out from every building. Lonin loyalists, Phenese, Gash, Anianiese, Skaelin, Freemen, Kanish, Lonin rebels, Laese, and Council soldiers from every corner of Fengorian all convened together and met in battle in the Courtyard of the Tower and inside and outside of every building in the city center. In every direction, and in a radius that in some places stretched all the way to the inner city walls, people from one nation fought those of another, they of another, and still they of another. The first regiments from Kale and the Free Kingdom were arriving even as the battle started to begin in earnest. On every rooftop they were fighting, inside every room, down every basement, along every stairwell, and under the very shadows of Laeolin and its Black Tower.

King Centreal and King Joel fought side by side, and Gendorn with them. Furnarwa and Letharal commanded teams of rebel fighters who swept through the enemy lines to connect the different allied nations. Yet from every side enemy soldiers had appeared to reclaim their positions.

Gendorn and the two kings fought their way down to the base of another building and re-entered the Courtyard of the Tower. Before them they saw this giant and uncoordinated mess of people all fighting one another, and for a while they stood there, uncertain of where to put their soldiers. Any concept of front lines had long since disappeared— people were fighting one another everywhere in small groups or large circles. Regiments were battling for a hundred different positions, each one of them to counter the last. And in that crowd Gendorn and the kings saw one figure emerge, one figure who had attracted a hundred loyal soldiers around him, one figure who stood before the Tower of Laeolin as if it were his to call his own.

Centreal and Joel ordered a charge, and they swept across to the center of the courtyard in no time. Enemies fled before the contingent of soldiers accompanying the two kings. They arrived at the tower to find Seagraul waiting for them alone. Centreal and Joel stepped out from their company, and their soldiers gathered around them to listen and watch.

"I am quite surprised you did not flee at my sight," Joel mocked him.

"It should not surprise you. But two kings against one, Joel? I would not have thought so little of you."

"You're not the one to give talks on right and wrong, Seagraul," Joel answered dryly.

"I suppose you think that you are, but no matter. We've one way to settle this, Joel— and Centreal? If you value your life, governor, then run away now, and leave this to Joel and myself."

"I've not time for banter after three days of searching for you in these shadows, and a lifetime of serving such a wicked man," said the King of the Free, and he did not even wait for a reply. He put up his sword and charged.

Joel conceded to let Centreal fight first. No man intervened in a battle between kings, not even other kings. As such, he watched every move to see how the King of Laen reacted, and to note the ways he moved and with what speeds. He learned a great deal, or so he hoped.

The King of the Free, once Governor of Gaoln and directly subordinate to King Seagraul, pushed the King of Laen back to the tower's stone. He had Seagraul pinned to the Black Tower, and the Freeman smiled. "In the Tower you rose, in the Tower you committed your crimes, and from the tower you will hang for it. Put down your sword, Seagraul, and you will be spared another day, and your body will be hung for all to see. Put down your sword and you may give your last words to the city you call home."

Seagraul put down his sword, but he thrust it forward as it was lowered, and Centreal stepped back and nearly collapsed. Centreal parried the next attack but Seagraul pressed him back. Centreal struck but Seagraul, with a strength he had not had before, blocked the blow and pushed Centreal back again. "Stand your ground, governor!" The King of Laen taunted him. "Or put down your sword, so that you may hang like the traitor you are from the top of this tower!"

"I betrayed my king, Seagraul. Never my people."

Seagraul's eyes were fire, and with such heat his body seethed in anger. "You are one of them, then? You will die just like they did." Seagraul caught the King of the Free off his guard as the Freeman fell back, and knocked him down. He held the tip of his sword to Centreal's throat, but Central grabbed the tip with his armored hand. Seagraul, try as he might, could push no further. Centreal pushed the blade away and rose to his feet, but as he did so Seagraul's sword came back around and hit him in the side of the head. Central wavered again, and Seagraul knocked his sword off with his own. Unarmed and swaying, Central still looked surprised when the sword ran through him, shocked until his face hit the stone floor of the courtyard.

Seagraul turned toward Joel, a placid look on his face, and spoke plainly:

"Joel, you see these people all around you? The ones who are closing in? This is their city, and I am their king, and even by my death you cannot separate any one from the other."

"Your madness is unending. The tens of thousands of Lonins who have taken up arms against you attempt to sever that tie—they proclaim that you can no longer be their king, and you'll not get away again. They are so desperately opposed to your being their king that they have risked their lives, their families, and their homes to take you off the throne. There is not a city in this world where you could hide, where justice would not find you."

"King Seagraul," Gendorn said, and both of the kings turned to look at him, surprised that he had spoken. "You have been the person who, above any other, is responsible for all the grief that I and my people have endured these past decades. You are the most hated enemy of the Free Kingdom, the most hated enemy of our happiness, the most wanted enemy of justice and goodness, and the person most opposed to this new world order, where all of us are born free. You are my most hated enemy. There is not a creature in this world that I would sooner kill, and I can think of no villain more vile in all the legends that I have heard. You have eliminated my people and tried your best to steal from us everything that makes us human. You have killed our king. You will be dead by the end of this day. Your hollow and lifeless eyes will gaze upon the peak of this black tower while your back lies still upon the stones of Laeolin."

It took only a brief moment for the two kings to digest what Gendorn had said, and then Seagraul reacted with a voice like roaring fire: "How dare you insult me! You cannot challenge me! You are a boy, not a king!"

"I am a man. And if I cannot challenge you as a king, then I challenge you as a man."

Seagraul's mouth hung open, but before he could form a response, a loud and angry agreement came from the crowd of watching Freemen: "I challenge you!" They shouted; "Fight me, Seagraul, if you are man enough!"; "No sword and no armor, put down the toys and fight like a man!", and Seagraul could not help but look scared as all the voices rose all at once. But he faced Gendorn and retorted quickly.

"Do you know how many people have died on this sword? And you, a child, challenge me?" But he did not wait for a response. He attacked Gendorn, who fell back and struggled to parry blow after blow, while Joel was left standing there. "Fight me, then, if you call yourself a man!"

Gendorn could not even attempt to hold his ground— Seagraul was pushing him back time and time again, and it was only by luck's hand that he was not run through with Seagraul's sword. He managed to turn around so that as he retreated he drew nearer to Joel, and by the time Joel was near Gendorn had almost fallen over backward, so fast was Seagraul's attack.

Gendorn did fall backward, and Joel stepped in front of him. He caught Seagraul's sword in the air, and his advance stopped abruptly. Joel pushed him back as soon as he began his attack, and Seagraul retreated almost as quickly as Gendorn had. Joel pushed him toward the edge of the courtyard, where a wide ring of soldiers from every nation now stood watching. Joel pushed him to the point where the soldiers could have reached out and touched Seagraul, and then he let Seagraul take him back to the tower. When they reached the tower, Joel began pressing his attack again, and in only a few moments— in one great and graceful attack— Joel had Seagraul scrambling for the outer rim of the courtyard again. Seagraul was quick on his feet, however, and whenever Joel pressed his attack, Seagraul would block it even as he stepped back to withdraw from Joel's range.

Joel let Seagraul take him back to the tower again. Seagraul got inside Joel's range and tried to gut the King of Gonaka, but every attempt was foiled. When they reached the tower Joel stopped, and did not press his attack again, but instead stayed there, waiting for Seagraul to overstep in his attack or to try and corner Joel against the tower.

Gendorn came up beside them, but neither king paid any attention to the gulaus. "This is my duel, not yours" Gendorn said to Joel. Joel didn't even so much as move his head to acknowledge that Gendorn was there.

Seagraul came in to close another attack when Joel saw the opening in his side. He caught the edge of Seagraul's sword and swept it away with his arm as he thrust his own sword into Seagraul's side with his other arm. Seagraul stepped back but his sword was at the ready, and when Joel came to finish him, Seagraul blocked the blow. Joel pressed his attack again and drove him halfway back to the end of the courtyard before pausing. Seagraul let his arms fall down and his sword hang limp, but Joel kept his sword up, ready for Seagraul's treachery.

"I surrender this battle, King Joel."

"There is something that keeps me from believing you."

"I've no hope of defeating you."

Joel threw his arms up in the air, as if appealing to some higher power to come lend him some patience. He shouted, "Why you ever thought you could resist us, I will never, *ever* understand! You couldn't possibly have believed that you stood a chance!"

Seagraul let his sword fall down and clang on the stones of the courtyard. "I cannot fight you. I submit."

"I do not accept your submission," Gendorn said loudly, as he came up from behind Joel. "King Seagraul, I have made this clear. You will not leave here alive."

"Gendorn! It is only by the faith of your friend Joel that you are alive now. Leave us to finish our own affairs."

"These are my affairs!" Gendorn shouted furiously. "My affairs, you idiot! The death of my people is my own affair! Gaoln and The Kingdom of the Free are my affairs! Your being king after what you've done is my affair! It is my affair to kill you, and the affair of every good man!" Gendorn picked up his sword. "And I will kill you now!"

Joel stepped back, and kept silent as he weighed his thoughts. Seagraul looked at Joel, expecting some comment, but all that came from Joel was a simple "Well, Seagraul, it appears that you have submitted to my authority, but there is another individual who does not accept your submission, and in such a case a duel to the death is the only viable end, if you are a man with honor. If you are a man without honor, then I will run you through right here and deny your submission."

"I'll make quick work of it, then," Seagraul said. Gendorn was ready for Seagraul's sword when it came crashing down upon him. He stepped back behind Seagraul as the Lonin king overextended himself, having missed his mark, and Gendorn did not even try to put up his sword to block the next blow as Seagraul spun around. Instead, thoughtless of his own life and his defense, he kept the sword steady and parallel as he thrust it into Seagraul's side and put up only his arm to swipe away Seagraul's stray sword. Gendorn's blade went in deep.

The king staggered backward and grasped the wound. He hunched over, and fell to the ground. He sat there in shock, his eyes wide, and his mouth open in pain as much as in surprise. Gendorn came to stand above him, and held his sword over Seagraul's head. Without another thought, he let it come bearing down upon Seagraul— and he was quite surprised when he felt it blocked.

Seagraul rose even as he was pressing his attack, and Gendorn stepped backward. He had to step back again and again— Seagraul's attack would not end— his assault against Gendorn was as perfectly seamless as Joel's had been against Seagraul, and Gendorn could not match the offensive. Gendorn was being pushed back quickly, so at one point he stepped aside while Seagraul was running forward to him, and Seagraul careened into a line of people. Gendorn rose beside him with his sword ready, but Seagraul was writhing and clutching both his wounds. "You will never mean your surrender, Seagraul," Gendorn said, "even when death is so near, you fight until the end. You are not wise enough to understand the prospects of peace, not patient enough to hear the outcry of your own people and the people all throughout the world."

Seagraul rose again, and thrust at Gendorn. Gendorn sidestepped and brought his sword up and across. The blade met the corner of Seagraul's shoulder and cut right through to the bone. Seagraul whirled around and caught Gendorn with his sword— the sword cut into Gendorn's arm, and Gendorn screamed. Seagraul would not die!

Once again, Gendorn did not even consider defending himself— all he knew was that this had to end, or he himself would end. In a single stroke, completely ambivalent to the blade sticking into his own arm, he drew back his sword with the other arm and jammed it into Seagraul's stomach. When Seagraul withdrew his own blade Gendorn gripped Seagraul's sword hand and kept it still, and as he drew the blade out from Seagraul he felt the king's grip weaken. He felt the pulse of Seagraul's wrist grow slow and then fail, he felt the rhythm of his blood flow cease. He saw the hatred grow faint in his eyes— and then Seagraul collapsed onto the stones of the courtyard. His face looked skyward— his hollow eyes fixed upon the peak of the ancient Tower of Laeolin.

- Chapter Twelve -

Kamira ran up to Bendoraun, where he lay, and tried to move his head— then Bendoraun let out a moan. "Go get some people to carry me, Kamira, or find Gendorn and have him kill me. I cannot move."

"We're not going to kill you! Bendoraun, I am so sorry! I can't, I don't— "

"You did the right thing. Kio and his army had to know. You saved a lot of men. Find Gendorn, just find him. I would rather die than live my life with my face pressed against these stones."

"You shouldn't joke, Bendoraun!"

"I'm quite serious about that."

"How is the pain?"

"Unimaginably terrible. Talking to you does not even begin to relieve me."

"How are you not crying?"

"Well, let's see, over the past three seasons I have been starved to the brink of death, so cold that I could feel nothing but my own slow heart, unconscious for nearly a week, and had my skull split half-open by a spiked mace. Granted, this is a rather comparable pain. The mace was still worse. But it isn't as if screaming my head off is going to help things."

"We're not going to kill you."

"I won't ask you to do it, Kamira. Find Gendorn."

The entire circle of soldiers— thousands of them— stared in silence. Rebel stood side-by-side with loyalist, Gash with Lonin, Freeman with those who had guarded Gaoln, Phenese with Kanish— they all looked onward, dumbstruck. Seagraul was dead. What did that mean?

It was then that Gendorn recognized Luncas, and, miraculously, Alaisio beside him. They were back further in the crowd. Luncas's men were creeping in around the outside of the courtyard. There were hardly any sounds of distant fighting. The city was waiting.

King Joel stepped into the center of the open courtyard, and looked across all the faces. Everyone's eyes turned from Gendorn to him. "Seagraul's death," Joel proclaimed, "is the end of our struggle. I proclaim that this city is free of the old King of Laen's appointed successors, and that it is now under the mandate of the Council of Nations.

"Freemen, your King Centreal has been killed by the late King Seagraul. He has appointed Gulaus Gendorn to succeed him as ruler of the Kingdom of the Free. Freemen, do you accept this appointment?"

Nothing could have brought more life to men so tired and empty of everything. They shouted and they broke into smiles, they clapped and stomped their feet and cheered and whistled and shouted boisterous praises. They cheered *Gulaus Gendorn* and *The Kingdom of the Free* and *the war is over* and *Seagraul is dead*, all at once and rotating between them, elated with every cheer and celebrating them all as one. For all of this, there was nothing but shock on Gendorn's face. Joel whispered to him: "I could not tell you. By Centreal's own request, your nomination had to be verified by a vote. This suffices. So, that is why I could not tell you, you see. It wasn't really verified, yet."

Gendorn hardly heard any of what this king was saying. Centreal had nominated him? What about Luncas? What about any of the Freemen who had been statesmen in foreign lands? Anyone except for him. Him!?

The cheering stopped. They were waiting for something. *Waiting for me*, the new king realized.

Gendorn stepped forward and stood by Joel's side. He turned toward those same faces, which looked again at the King of the Free Kingdom. "I proclaim," Gendorn stated firmly, "that the flag of the Free Kingdom will fly always and forevermore above the Tower of Laeolin. What we have struggled for will not be forgotten— and neither will what we have lost in that struggle. The banner of the Free Kingdom will hail the coming of each new day from above the highest point of this tower, and it will speak to every human in this fateful city— it will remind them of what once was, and what terrible things have happened under that flag, and it will remind us always of what we fight for. Forever that flag will look down upon this city, in its eternal sorrow, and grieve for those who were left behind. Forever it will stand testament to what we have achieved, to a light we found in man's darkest days."

Joel nodded, and again stepped forward. "But as we remember those who were lost, let us remember this single day for what it is: The end of a terribly long reign of terror, and the first day of a world where we can know peace."

A figure came rushing from the crowd, and the two kings stopped. "Kamira?"

"Gendorn! Bendoraun is dying!" Kamira was almost in tears. "He's just outside the courtyard!"

"He's breathing," said Gendorn, "and his blood is still moving." He started to turn Bendoraun over so he would face up, but Bendoraun made a terrible, painful face, so Gendorn let him be. "Can you talk, Bendoraun?"

One of the soldiers nearby who had come to help the king's friend spoke up: "He's paralyzed— the pain may be a little much for him, he might not speak for a while."

"He was just speaking to me!" Kamira protested.

"It's not that he doesn't have the ability to speak any longer," the soldier explained, "it is just that at times, it is too painful for him to see any reason to move, and as his face is pressed against the ground, speaking will involve moving."

"The arrow would have gone right through my back, and killed me right there, if it hadn't been for him," said Kamira. Gendorn nodded.

"How can we get him out of here?"

"It will be better for him to stay here in Laeolin. We can take good care of him," one of the soldiers assured him.

Gendorn nodded. "He won't make it to the ships, will he?"

The soldier shook his head. "My king, by the time they depart, it will be a miracle if he can cross the street." The soldier turned to Bendoraun. "Sorry, friend."

"You had to go be a hero, didn't you? I thank you for that, friend," Gendorn said to Bendoraun, "If those soldiers had been just a little faster...well, you're a good man, Bendoraun," he gently put an arm on his shoulder, "the best I know."

Kamira put her hand on his other shoulder. "Bendoraun, I owe my life to you, and nothing less."

"I'll come see you, friend," Gendorn said, "as soon as I can. There is one thing I have to do first. Then you, me, and Kamira will sail away to Skaen, where we belong." There was no reply. Gendorn turned to the soldier beside him. "Do take good care of him."

PART SIX: THE OPEN WORLD

- Chapter One -

The fog had not lifted. Though it was noon, the haze was the same as it had been that morning, and it did not move as the day wore on. The Courtyard of the Tower was not fully visible to any one of the twenty thousand Freemen who had come together on this day.

Before them stood their king, Gulaus Gendorn. Inside of a burial basket, with flowers underneath his sword, King Centreal lay asleep. The eyes of the Freemen went from one king to the other, and waited for the younger of them to speak. Alaisio and Luncas looked proudly up at their king. A group of Freemen had snuck Bendoraun out of the infirmary, much to his liking, and they had him on a pillowed litter with his back down. He remained paralyzed, and could not see Gendorn addressing the crowd as their king, but at least he could hear and be present. Kamira stood beside Bendoraun's improvised bed, and she looked prouder than the rest by far. She radiated, she glowed, she was brighter than the sun and Gendorn could hardly look away. Joel and Kio stood in the rear, whispering between themselves. And Centreal looked upon him with the eyes of a father.

"We gathered around this great man just over eight years ago," Gendorn began. "He was, at that time, still the Governor of Gaoln, appointed by King Seagraul and the other leaders whose nations partook in the use and oversight of Gaoln. When we saw him then, and listened to his words, he stood upon the ruins of the last guard tower in Gaoln, he stood upon the ruins of our captivity, and he promised us our freedom.

"He led our nation into a new day, into the very being of a nation. He called on every one of us to be a part of this common dream. He lies before us now having instilled in us the hope that we, and all who come after us, can be free. He lies dead having given us that freedom, for our own selves and our children and theirs and theirs and theirs. As we stand over him now and recall that one moment when he first stood before us, let us say to him, so loud that he may hear us in Sendeilta: We have found a land of our own, where all people are born free, where all people live free, where all people die free."

The crowd agreed loudly, and in their ecstatic furor they almost banished the mist and summoned the sun to shine in its sky. They roared and roared and roared until the silence came again.

"To all of us, what dreams we have seized, what promises we have fulfilled, what hopes we have realized, are as hollow nothings next to those ambitions we held in our hearts when we first sailed for Skaen. The greatest of our dreams will never come for us. When we leave this city, we leave behind us most everyone we love, and we leave them as ashes in the wind.

"But there are those who live. Out from the shadows of Laeolin two thousand survivors have come to us since the Free Kingdom's flag was hung on the tower. More arrive every hour of every day. Among them are elders who will teach our children values and will tell them what life was like in the old world. Among them are children who bear with them such horrible things as children should never have to bear, who will be our future and will one day lead our country. And among them are our brave women, who, starved and cold and naked, fought armed and armored men to escape this tower in the darkest of days when one king deceived all the world.

"There is nothing in this world that will make up for our loss. There is nothing that will bring us the happiness we used to know in our dreams, if never in our waking days as slaves. What is lost is truly lost and gone forever." He paused, and, though he would not show it, he very nearly cried at that point. Before he could, he forced himself to continue. "But we can rebuild, and we can dream again. It will never be the same for us. Never. But for those who come after, it will be better. For those who come after, there will be no Gaoln, no slavery, no war, no hunger, no cold, and no one looking heavenward and knowing that no answer will come. There will be none of that, for those who come after us. There will be only some memory of ancestors whose whole worlds were torn apart and into ruin, and with such thoughts our children's children will smile and know that they are free, that they can be everything in this world that they were born to be. And there is no greater blessing for men like you and me, no greater blessing than that." He was tearing up. He could not help it. The men looked as if they expected more. What more could he give?

"We have given everything in our world for this moment, and because of that this moment means very little to some of us who no longer care to live. But we have to give more. We have to make sure that every survivor is brought back to the kingdom. We have to make sure they are connected with their loved ones, that every survivor finds their home. We have to gather the orphans and find parents for them. We have to gather the widows and see that they are placed together in homes that we must build for them, so that they are not left alone in grief. We must find homes for our own men, whose loved ones have perished, and who also could not bear to live alone. We must find the elders, and place them with the orphans, and make sure that they receive a proper education. We must teach them to read and write, to build great things, and to think of all the marvelous things in this world that they could do. We must teach them that human life is sacred. We must teach them that evil exists in the heart of every man, and the man who does not guard always and forever against his own evil will succumb to it." He spared a glance for Joel. The King of Gonaka looked very, very proud.

"We must burn these weapons of war, and turn them into things that we can use to build a civilization. We must have an end to war, an end to things destroyed, and a beginning to what can grow again after all the fires have burned."

Faint cheering. It was spirited, to be sure. But how many could cheer, when they knew the truth of it, that they would leave behind their loved ones as burnt ashes in the wind?

"There was a man who gave such a speech many years ago." Joel had that proud, fatherly look again. He had only had time for a few lessons before this speech, and it was showing already. "In that speech, at the close of the Age of the Great Wars, a man proclaimed the first day of the Age of Peace. That proclamation was followed by twenty years of peace and fifty years of war.

"It is clear that words are not enough. To say that a new age has come and leave it to come on its own is to forfeit its chance of ever coming. Therefore, the Council of Nations met two nights ago in emergency session. They declared, in unanimous vote, that instruments of war be torn apart and remade into tools of peace in every corner of the world. No man or woman or child shall make a weapon of war, or design a machine of war, or devise a reason for war. War, its instruments, its reasons, its conduct, are, from this moment forward, deemed unsuitable for civilized life and unworthy of production or study. The Council of Nations itself will oversee this global operation, and at its end they themselves will disarm. No more than one man for every ten thousand will be permitted weapons and armor after that point, for the purposes of preventing thievery and discouraging gangs of bandits, and for leverage in keeping the peace. Exceptions will be made only for villages and smaller towns. All armies will be abolished, and no army will be raised. The raising of an army will be grounds for a full revocation of sovereignty."

Joel absolutely beamed. He had taught the boy all of these words and concepts in the last three days, and the boy was doing his best to apply every one of them! Gendorn almost sighed. Was the King of Gonaka even actually listening to what he was saying?

"With these actions undertaken, I and the Council of Nations, with the explicit approval of the rulers of the other ten nations of Fengorian, do declare this day to be the first day in the

New Age. The New Age will be the age where one sacred truth, above all else, is clear to us and shall be made as clear to our children and to theirs: Peace is not handed to anyone, but instead is the duty of everyone to protect and to grow. Peace will live among us, peace will live between us, if every one of us remembers this one thing."

They were still expecting more. Was there something that Centreal had always said, but he was forgetting? Or something Joel had forgotten to mention? Well, he would do the best he could, and that was all anyone could ever do.

"Long live the Kingdom of the Free. To us peace and prosperity, and to all the world before us."

Gendorn looked down at the face of the man who had inspired his dreams when he was just a child. "And to you, my king," he whispered under his breath, "all to you."

- Chapter Two -

Kamira could see the tower from where she stood on the top of the hill. The tip of it was just in between two barren branches from the tree which rose from beneath her. It was a lonely black line in a sky of white and gray, a small, distant rock in the endless snowscape of trees.

She felt a hand take her own, and turned to see Gendorn. His one eye told her everything that his words could not say. She nodded. "I'm just thankful that some of us lived, even if it was only so few of us. Pas will grow up in a better world. And there are those of us who can recall what happened, who can keep that terrible memory alive."

Gendorn nodded. Kamira was right, and there was nothing more to it.

It had been two days since Gendorn's speech at the Black Tower, and for those two days the tower had not escaped Kamira's mind for even one moment. It was more than just worrisome for Gendorn. But he certainly had no clue what there was to be done about it. *Time*, came the answer in his mind. *If there is anything at all, it is only time.*

They wandered out from the small camp that night where the king's guards were sleeping. They laid out blankets in the snow, layers and layers of them, and they covered themselves with even more. When the deep night rolled in and the snow was cast in the sapphire blue light of Tun-Sen, they held each other close, looking up at the stars. "I try to imagine that there has never been any distance between us," Gendorn said, "but it seems to me that we have spent a lifetime apart."

"We're not the same people we were at the beginning of last Sen," Kamira answered, "and we never will be. There is a lot of distance. It's hard to move beyond it."

"It will be hard, I believe," Gendorn said, "for a long time." *Time, and that's all there is to it.*

"When the warm winds come again and the earth is soft," Kamira said sweetly, "we should come out again and lay beneath the stars, and find a nice patch of dirt, and draw pictures of our future."

"Yes," Gendorn said noncommittally. "We should."

"You don't sound excited."

"The future is more grim than it once was."

"It is," Kamira said, "and our dreams cannot be as large, not any longer. As you said."

"Perhaps they can," Gendorn said, with a renewed note of energy. "I am a king now, after all. Maybe I am the king that this world has been waiting for."

Kamira smiled at him. "Well, I think you are."

For a time they just lay in silence, gazing at the stars or into each other's eyes. Gendorn almost fell asleep like that, entangled with Kamira as if they were a single body, but the girl poked him hard in the stomach as he began to drift away and Gendorn's eye opened wide. "What?" he asked.

Kamira pointed to the sky. "You were as tiny as that star when I met you. You were in a tiny little rag for your tiny little body." Gendorn smiled, and Kamira looked at him cutely. "And your face was covered in mud. You were a prisoner who only dreamed of ever knowing freedom— and now you're a free man. Nevermind that you're a king. I really think that's a mistake." Gendorn nudged her, and Kamira shoved him over on his side.

"We are both free, Kamira. And you were smaller than I was." Kamira looked at him slyly. "I wish I had someone who could teach me like Menuld taught Joel. I wasn't raised to be a king."

"You'll make a better king than half of those who were raised to be them," Kamira said sincerely, "so have some faith."

They took all of next morning to wake up, rolling around and dozing in and out of wakefulness, always in each other's arms. Gendorn saw Kamira's eyes as they opened slowly, then closed again, and then opened again. He fixed his eye on her and watched her chest expand and contrast as she breathed in and out so gently. He watched that little smile on her face, the one that was always there whether she was sleeping or waking, sure as her own breathing, and saw her as a tiny little thing in a single smock of a rag whose smile was larger than her face— *that smile, it's all I'll ever need*, he thought to himself, and his face broke into an uncontrollable grin. *I think she'll make a good queen.*

"Go to sleep. Stop staring at me."

"Kamira!" Gendorn laughed, "it's almost noon! We've been keeping the guards waiting— "

"Don't pretend that they haven't gone back to bed already, they're just as tired as we are."

Gendorn sighed reluctantly. "How you can manage to stay asleep all day…"

"I haven't a lot of obligations these days," Kamira said happily. "All we've got to do is visit Iuna. I'm so glad Komu and Iuna agreed to take Bendoraun in— I think Pas will really love

having him around, someone to look up to— another Gaolnian!"
Gendorn started to rise, but Kamira threw her arms around one
of his legs and pulled him down. Gendorn could only smile. "I'm
not letting you leave again."

Well, that was the best thing he had ever heard.

It was well past noon when they finally did get up. Kamira
had been silent for some time, so Gendorn allowed her thoughts
to be her own, and only took her hand to urge her to her feet.

Unprompted, she explained to him, "I had nightmares all the
time in Laeolin. Some of us went mad. We could never tell when
we were dreaming or awake— it was all just one endless,
torturous episode, until we were slaughtered."

"You said 'we'— you still feel like you should have died in
the tower?"

She nodded gravely. "I always will. I knew we would die,
Gendorn, I knew it. It was on the very first night that I arrived
when I knew as much. There was a bird that had poked its head
above the clouds, to see what was out there I suppose. I prayed
to the bird, to the wind it rode upon, and to whatever guides the
wind— that they would carry our message out to the world, that
something would save us. You know what?"

"What?"

"The bird dipped right back below the clouds, and it never
came back up."

"I don't think the bird could have saved you, Kamira."

"But something, someone, could have— and should have.
Someone who could have made a difference— there was no
shortage of them, Gendorn. You and your friends tried. A few
of the Lonins lost their lives to try and save us. The rest of them?
They did nothing. They just waited."

Gendorn gave her a kiss and took her hand. "You belong
with me, Kamira, not in that tower, and you know it."

"I know," she said very softly, "it's just not something that I
can move beyond. I can never do anything but hate Laeolin. And

as much as I hate it, I belong there. I belong there dead, and not alive."

"I don't think anyone could ever expect you to move beyond it," he said sincerely, "but you're wrong. You do not belong in Laeolin, and you are meant to be alive."

Kamira paused for a second, then she said "You're right, love. I know. But you know, you said in your speech that two thousand of us had come out from the shadows of Laeolin." She was looking at the tower now, not at Gendorn. "But I won't ever come back from the shadows of Laeolin. Night will never end for me. Do you understand that?"

"I do," Gendorn whispered. "No one will ask of you what you cannot give, or to do what can't be done."

Kamira let her gaze fall away from the tower. She nodded, and they walked on in silence.

When she spoke again, it was in her usual cheery voice, with no hint of what they had been discussing. "Did you ever find a home for Promise?"

"Bendoraun planted the seed when he thought I was dying, thirty days before Seun Bastion."

"Good then. A part of Gaoln will always have a home in Skaen."

"There is no Gaoln, Kamira. We are Freepeople of the Kingdom of the Free."

Kamira saw before her one hundred and fifty thousand corpses who had gone lifeless before ever knowing their freedom, and answered stiffly: "I will never be anything but Gaolnian, Gendorn."

The silence returned.

The sunlight was running like rivers through breaks in a mostly cloudy sky as Gendorn and Kamira walked out of the meadow and into the forest toward their camp. Gendorn's thoughts drifted back to Skaen. He imagined chancing upon a town of veterans who were only wanting to live the rest of their days in peace, or upon a village recently burned whose residents knew that many of their neighbors would not survive to see the snows melt. He could see a man impaled on a branch, his eyes looking heavenward, as if Fate might come down to finish the job he'd left undone. He imagined five thousand men hanging their heads to cry as a messenger from Gonaka told them that all their families were dead. And though he might have been the sort of man to smile in the most grim of situations, there was nothing happy in his eyes, nothing smiling on his face, as he saw such memories before him.

Kamira was just as quiet. She'd stare down at the ground and watch footprint after footprint come into view before her as Gendorn walked on just ahead of her. She'd imagine so many footprints there, pounding the earth down, jaunting and hateful cheers cast her way as she followed the footprints and kept her head down. Sometimes the footprints would disappear, and other shapes would form, and other voices would come— and Laeolin would come alive with the fire and the arrows and the cold red snow and the heartless men. Curileyn would hold a baby in her arms, and then an adult Kamira would cry for a slightly aged Curileyn who could not bear to leave her child behind. Her mother would disappear behind the line of soldiers, and then the soldiers would fade into the dust, and in an instant there was nothing but the footprint in the snow immediately before her.

Then she found her thoughts escaping to more abstract realms, and she would ponder, on occasion, the feeling of wind dying into stillness, or the reflection of light on the snow, or the sound of a bird calling out to the open world.

- Chapter Three -

The sound of music was something apart from him. Something distant, strange, and awkward. It should not be here. The sun in its sky should not shine on a city and a people so wicked. The birds should not sing here in celebration. But they did. The people sang here.

Gendorn remained with such grim thoughts through the remainder of that Sen, and into the beginnings of Trest, until it occurred to him what this song was all about.

All throughout Laeolin and for miles beyond its walls, through the rivers and to the coasts, to Benin and to Aois, across the Cold Ocean in a free land and across the dust in Gonaka, people sang with one voice. They were rebuilding their lives.

It was the sound of people building homes and wounded fighters returning to their peacetime trades as they came into good health. And what Gendorn had first snarled at, he came to love and to cherish; this was not the sound of people who had forgotten war, or who ignored it, or who encouraged it— it was only the sound of people moving on with their lives with all they had left. The sound of people walking out from the shadows and into the daylight of the open world.

There were a great many things that had kept the King of the Free in Laeolin for so long, and he was only now getting around to preparing for his return to Freetown.

Since the day of his speech, the Freepeople had been conducting a thorough search in Laeolin and in the towns outside of the city, and they found that nearly four thousand of the hostages had survived in hiding. A number tragic all the same, it was heartening on every occasion when the Freepeople could gather and watch a family being reunited. Those who had provided harbor made themselves public and were received as heroes by the people of Laeolin. Those who had been loyal to Seagraul had been scared or shunned or shamed into silence, and now those who had supported the resistance had all day and all night of every day and every night to say anything they wanted to say. It had been long since Laeolin had known such freedom. Very long.

And these people, to everyone's delight, had a great deal to say. Every hour of daylight and into the twilight, and even into the night, men and women, elders and youths, resistance veterans and citizens who had kept quiet, all spoke out on podiums to crowds of excited fellows. The audience would cheer them or jeer them, but, most importantly of all, they spoke to one another. Those from the crowds reacted to every idea espoused by the speakers, and the speakers reacted accordingly. They spent every moment of every day of every week after Seagraul's death creating the new government, the new people, the new Laen— everything was to be new and promising and built for the people, and against the tyranny of kings, and everything these people decided went through votes before being submitted to the Council's Assembly that now governed Laeolin. The speakers, before writing to the Council's Assembly, would ask for the approval of everyone present before doing so, a process they called "A Centreal's vote". That pleased Gendorn to no end whatsoever.

The Council of Nations Assembly of Laeolin, the full name of the governing assembly, had taken eagerly to executing the mandate of the Council of Nations. All through the night men worked the forges, and hot fires burned. Piles of armor and axes and swords and shields, some with dents and some with seiln lining, all alike were thrown into these fires and remade into instruments of peace. Sweet as the music of people rebuilding their homes and lives was to Gendorn's ears, sweet though the sound of men and women building the future of a nation through speeches and arguments and consensus in public debating rooms, there was no sound like the sound of a sword and shield being destroyed, no smell like the fires of peace coming from the forges, to a man who had suffered such war. It was enough to bring tears to his one eye, when the king stopped and considered how important were these sights and sounds. Enough to break him completely with joy so that he could never stop crying.

When he stood out on the balcony on the top floor of the palace in Gruso, he could count thirty-six forges burning in different parts of Laeolin. Thirty-six factories of peace, where the means for war were being taken forever from the arms of man. They burned always and without end. *Let them always burn*, thought the king. *And burn bright, so that all the world can see.*

And schools! Schools being built everywhere, where the young of this nation and all nations besides could come and learn history and the humanities, where they could understand the tragic scope of their past and the unique chance they had for a new future. For every one of those thirty-six fires burning, one school had been zoned for construction nearby, with the understanding that those least educated lived near the forges and other businesses that were loud and dirty and unsanitary. *No child will grow up in Laeolin and not know what has happened here.* That had been Gendorn's direct order, and the Council of Nations listened well.

Gendorn smiled. He had ordered the same done in the Free Kingdom. And he had issued one additional order for his own kingdom. Well, one list of additional orders, anyway. He had ordered that every Skaelin village that had suffered and survived Gaolnian attacks be reimbursed and that the soldiers go to rebuild those villages and work the farms and trades until production was back to normal. No one would be building more of Freetown, or fortifying Gatsesilli, until these things were taken care of. All of those who had been displaced, or who had been torn from all family, and everyone else who no longer had any home, was to be placed in communities where they could live together and begin a new life. The men were to clear the roads to the major castles so that the villagers could resume their trade, and they were to open the border with the Skaelin Lands that remained sovereign in the east, and allow villagers to go there if they chose to. There was little else the king could think to do. What else would Behk and Synla have asked of him? These orders were nothing, compared to the crimes the Gaolnians had committed under orders from the king and Luncas. But was there anything else he could do?

He spent more time on this question than on any other one thing for all the long weeks, month after month, that he spent in Laeolin after the war. No answer was good enough to satisfy the king, but there was no answer he could find.

In the meantime, the Council was erecting a memorial by the Black Tower to commemorate those who had struggled against genocide and war. Gendorn refused the offer of one being built for himself.

The Council's men spent all the rest of the cold season and the first weeks of the warm season designing it, and when it came time to build the thing it did not take all that long.

Every survivor of Laeolin came to see it on the day of its completion, and as many Freepeople as had stayed in Laeolin for the Finding, that is, the mission to recover all of the survivors. It was a warm day when it was completed, with an air that promised things would be growing soon.

A ring of statues in pure white mourning gowns held each other's hands, their faces toward the Black Tower and away from the crowd of observers. They encircled the tower completely, so that a person would not be able to get to the tower without climbing over the ring of statues. There was no great inscription or dedication, no lengthy commemoration. There was only one phrase etched in red on the white stone: *Here where dreams died, may they grow again.*

The Black Tower was sealed off by the ring of statues in eternal mourning, no man or woman or king or emperor allowed to enter, with the final marks of those few words.

- Chapter Four -

It was something out of a dream. The sun was shining warm on their skins and on the waves crashing and rolling back and forth. The clouds were thin and did not threaten to block their light. Pas, having regained his childhood, was running next to Bendoraun, who had never lost his, on the beach. They had built something out of shells and sand and seagrass but Gendorn could not have said what it was if his life had depended on it.

Well, it was almost perfect. Bendoraun ran with a gimp and every now and then he slowed to a walk or hunched over. He was not supposed to be running. He was not even supposed to be walking. He could do those things, but it was both painful and dangerous to do so. Bendoraun didn't care. Likely he wouldn't care until he was dead for snapping his neck, and even then just because he wouldn't be able to run on the beach any longer or see the light on its shores. *Someday we won't*, Gendorn thought. Well, that was someday, and not today.

When he closed his one eye he could feel his senses linger. His back on the sand, the sound of the seabirds calling, the rush of the waves and the wind and the warmth and comfort of Kamira's hand in his own. He could feel Kamira's happiness. As happy as they could be, these days.

When he woke up, the sun was lower and was behind them in the west, toward Laeolin, toward Gaoln, and, if you went north across the Cold Ocean, toward the Kingdom of the Free. He and Kamira would return there in just two days, to Freetown. They had already heard the news there when the litha came in just after the war. Proclamations from the king: Your families are dead. Our elders, our children, our women, our pasts and futures and everything with them are dead. We have only our freedom and the chance to build again.

They had won a war, somewhere in that horrible mess of all things lost and gone forever. It was of little importance next to such news. No other news could make it through the numbness and the loss. Nothing else. The messenger could not find it in his heart to leave the men. He stayed with them a full two weeks.

Kamira's hand tightened, and he opened his eyes. A chill crept over him. What a beautiful sunset! Bendoraun was holding Pas with their feet in the water, pointing to the sky and probably making up some ridiculous story about where clouds came from and what sunlight is. Such a tragedy to know that Bendoraun would not walk again, that he could not afford to take such chances as this even a few times a year. He would have been such a wonderful father, active and eager to do the job. *Men are wasted in war*, the thought came to him quite suddenly. *Your friends are not excused from it.*

Kamira's hand tightened again. He had to stop trailing off. "What is it, Kamira?"

"What are we going to do now?"

Gendorn replied quite matter-of-factly: "Build the world again." It was solemn, not optimistic. It was a duty, a hard matter of fact.

Kamira smiled at him all the same. The smile took a while— longer than it ever had before— but she smiled, and when he turned to see her it almost looked the same as it did before their parting. Almost. *Some things are lost in war.*

"Will you help me build?" The young king asked, and he was smiling now too. It had taken him longer, he realized with a start. Longer than her.

"I will help you build, my king and husband," Kamira answered cutely.

"I said nothing about husbanding! I know you are only after the seat of the queen, anyway." Kamira slapped him. She actually slapped him!

"Let's get back to town for the night and I will show you why I should be your queen."

Gendorn's eye nearly popped out, and for a moment he was seven years old again standing on top of a dirt hill all blushing and befuddled. Where had *that* come from!? Was this Kamira? Gendorn's mouth was hanging and he didn't realize it until

Kamira shut it for him. "Don't be all surprised. We are getting married, aren't we?"

That was something he knew how to respond to. "Of course we are."

They helped Bendoraun back to the litter that would carry him into town. Bendoraun laid down straight on the cloth and they lifted him up and began to trek westward. Pas ran beside the litter talking to Bendoraun, excited and childish as if there was nothing out of the ordinary. Gendorn and Kamira walked behind them both, and they almost teared up. That was priceless, it was. What a thing to see.

Kamira's face in the light of the setting sun, now, that was a thing to see. That was really something out of a dream. It was something Gendorn was sure he had seen buried in the snows of Skaen, a haunting that had come to him in the caves by Gatsesilli, something out of the past and never-was that he would never see again or for the first time. Here it was before him, just a hand's touch away. It was not fair that he was so lucky. There was not a man luckier in the world, least of all among Freemen, whose loved ones' faces had not risen up once buried in Laeolin forever. Why was he, among them, the luckiest? He realized he was staring only when he saw Kamira's eyes looking into his in the very same way. Was his face as beautiful? *Doubtful.*

But the thing more beautiful was the child running circles around the litter, shouting and screeching and otherwise being an altogether obnoxious young boy, the whole scene bathed in orange and gold as the sun, before their own eyes, led them westward. Bendoraun was motionless on the litter, but Gendorn knew he was smiling. Bendoraun would never lose his smile. Not ever.

When Gendorn looked back he noticed that Kamira's eyes were still set upon him. He stopped, turned her toward him, and kissed her on the lips, and wondered if she remembered that time long ago in the dust of a prison colony lost now to history forevermore, when a kiss had rendered him mute and motionless. When they had dreamed of freedom and the open world. She laughed. So she did remember.

They gave their hands to one another, their hearts and whole lives too, heavy as they were, and when the sun rose in the east they began to dream again.

ABOUT THE AUTHOR:

Photo by Arianna Fischer, rendered in black and white by Elizabeth Linares

Matthew R. Bishop is a traveling storyteller and adventurer. When not in his home library, he enjoys hiking, climbing, swimming, and exploring the open world. Check out Matt's author website at MatthewRBishop.com to find more books and embark on new adventures.

Matt's first series, *The Kingdom of the Free*, is a humanist low-fantasy adventure set in Fengorian. His most recent series, *Legends of Elyria*, is a mythological high-fantasy epic set in Elyria. These two projects take very different approaches to the fantasy genre, and challenge its traditional boundaries in different ways. Explore both of Matt's original worlds to complete your journey and find your own story.

Matt also has two degrees in history and political science. Outside of his fiction and fantasy work, Matt writes non-fiction news articles and opinion pieces on current political issues and global affairs. To view his recent work in non-fiction journalism, visit his blog at https://matthewrbishop.medium.com.